**I heard crashing behind me as Trap cried out.
"No humans backstage!"**

The Magi ignored the spider wraiths, his footsteps closing in behind me. But he hadn't Called yet, and I used my Fire to propel me forward, pushing me toward Purgatory's stage entrance and the street. There, I could hopefully put enough distance between me and the Magi for Pittsburgh's steel-stained environment to help me hide.

The cool spring air hit all my bare skin like a slap as I plunged into the night, cutting right down the alley. It was a wide, empty East Liberty alley, giving me plenty of room to run. But the guy chasing me was fast, and his hand managed to catch my elbow, twirling me around to face his glowing eyes. He stared at me in wonder for a split second and I thought I might just have time to kick him in the balls before he could speak.

But it was too late.

ALSO BY NICOLE PEELER

Jinn and Juice

Jane True

Tempest Rising

Tracking the Tempest

Tempest's Legacy

Tempest's Fury

Tempest Reborn

Jane True Short Fiction

Something Wikkid This Way Comes

JINN AND JUICE

NICOLE PEELER

www.orbitbooks.net

Orbit
Hachette Book Group
1290 Avenue of the Americas, New York, NY 10104
HachetteBookGroup.com

Originally published as an e-book by Orbit Books
First print edition: April 2015

Orbit is an imprint of Hachette Book Group, Inc. The Orbit name and logo are
trademarks of Little, Brown Book Group Limited.

The Hachette Speakers Bureau provides a wide range of authors for speaking
events. To find out more, go to www.hachettespeakersbureau.com or call (866)
376-6591.

The publisher is not responsible for websites (or their content) that are not owned
by the publisher.

The characters and events in this book are fictitious. Any similarity to real persons,
living or dead, is coincidental and not intended by the author.

Library of Congress Cataloging-in-Publication Data

Peeler, Nicole, 1978-
    Jinn and juice / Nicole Peeler.—First edition.
        pages; cm
    Summary: "Born in ancient Persia, Lyla turned to her house Jinni, Kouros,
for help escaping an arranged marriage. Kouros did make it impossible for her to
marry—by cursing Lyla to live a thousand years as a Jinni herself. Unfortunately,
becoming Bound may risk more than just her chance to be human once more—it
could risk her very soul."—Provided by publisher.
    ISBN 978-0-316-40735-9 (softcover)
    1. Jinn—Fiction.   2. Pittsburgh (Pa.)—Fiction.   3. Urban fiction.   I. Title.
PS3616.E326J56 2014
813'.6—dc23
                                                                        2014031327

10 9 8 7 6 5 4 3 2 1

RRD-C

Printed in the United States of America

For my mom and dad. The biggest fans a girl could have, minus the sledgehammer.

Chapter One

The chubby little human was doing his damndest to hump my leg, but the palm I'd placed on his forehead kept him at arm's length.

"You're so beautiful," he said, panting up at me as he air-humped, his eyes glazed.

I sighed, feeling bad for the guy. He was wearing full nerd garb, including a pocket protector and an extremely unfortunate, thin, brunet comb-over. One leg of his corduroys was pegged for biking, and I thought I could see a fanny pack peeking at me from over his rounded hips.

He was hardly Purgatory's average customer, since our clientele was more apt to sport fangs, gills, or claws than this guy's sad clip-on tie. This dude was all human and also, considering his dilated pupils and complete lack of reserve, very obviously glamoured out of his mind. He wasn't here by choice.

"Mister, you've got so much mojo in your system you'd hit on a grizzly. Who brought you here?"

The man jerked his head toward the bar, where a blonde wearing a pornographically tight silver dress flirted with Trey, tonight's werewolf bartender. I'd seen her around a few times—the daughter of a succubus and a human, she'd sought refuge in steel-stained Pittsburgh after being rejected by her mother's Tribe.

But a sad childhood was no excuse for a messy feed.

"Let's get you home safe," I said, putting an arm around the human to lead him to the door. He acquiesced willingly, his arm fumbling around my waist, one hand moving to my ass. I gave a warning shimmy, the coins on my scarf-belt jingling like a rattler. He jerked his hand back, only to sweep it up my bare back.

"Lyla, what the fuck?" The voice came from behind me, pitched to a petulant whine. I turned to find the silver-clad hoochie eyeing me reproachfully.

"He's my catch," she said. "You don't even eat people."

My lips pursed as I sought her name. I never forgot a face, but after a thousand-something years on this earth, names weren't my strong suit.

"Crystal?" I hazarded. I knew it was something strippery.

"Diamond," she said, hissing like a cat and taking a step toward her prey.

"Right. Sorry, Diamond. I wasn't poaching, just helping this gentleman outside. You know the rules."

Diamond's wide red mouth bowed in a frown. "This place has rules?" A long, graceful arm swept open, indicating the pool table, where a pooka was currently snorting a line of faux-brosia off the bared tits of a weredeer.

"Granted, not many," I acknowledged. "But there are a few. One of which is no luring humans on premises. If they wander in on their own steam, they're fair game. But something tells me that's not the case here, is it?"

As if to prove my point, the human stared fixedly at my

cleavage, one glassy pupil dilated, the other a pinpoint. He looked like the CPA version of Marilyn Manson.

Narrowing her eyes, Diamond took a step forward. "I'm sure we can work something out. I just want a little of his vitality. You can have his wallet."

I moved between her and the little man. Annoyingly, he took his opportunity to grind up on my behind like a corpulent schnauzer.

"That's generous," I said, swatting him away. "But no. What we *are* going to do is put this guy in a taxi and send him home to his wife." I grabbed for the pudgy hand groping for a boob, raising it so Diamond could see the gold wedding ring glinting on the human's finger. "As for you, feel free to stay for the show. I'll buy you a drink. But you'll have to find your next meal elsewhere."

"Fuck you, Lyla," Diamond said, her red lips receding alarmingly, succubus-style, to reveal her hitherto-hidden fangs. "You're not the boss of this place."

"No," I said quietly. "I'm not."

And with that I let my Fire flare as much as my unBound state would allow. Unnatural black flames licked along my pale skin, blending upward to ignite my long tresses till they lifted like raven wings framing my face.

Behind me I heard the human groan. I hoped he hadn't soiled his pegged corduroys.

"But I can easily be the boss of you, dear Diamond."

She crouched, hissing at me again, but my flames were already licking at her skin like thirsty tongues. Not burning, though. Not yet.

Her head drooped and she dropped to one knee, submissive.

"Bertha, call this gentleman a cab," I said to the bouncer lurking at the corner of my vision. Big Bertha nodded, her massive frame lumbering over to where the human stood, quivering in genuine fear and glamoured lust. Bertha's fuzzy monobrow twitched at me, waiting for my next move. This was why we all loved her: despite her size, she let us fight our own battles, unless we needed her.

"Diamond, release him," I said, keeping my voice pleasant.

Resting on the carpet, Diamond's hands clenched into fists, but I felt a small *pop* as her magic fizzled.

"Wha'?" said the human, Bertha already leading him up Purgatory's stairs, toward the entrance guarding the outside world from the freaks that found shelter behind our doors.

I approached the figure hunched on the carpet. "Thank you, Diamond. Like I said, your next drink is on me. But please remember not to bring your own dinner into the bar next time."

She didn't look at me. I felt the resentful shift of her power, but she didn't attempt another challenge. An Immunda, Diamond was no real opponent. She could glamour using the magic she took feeding from humans, but other than that she may as well have been one.

Her vulnerability made me sad. I'd been powerless once, after all.

Pushing thoughts of my curse aside, I stepped over Diamond and headed backstage to our dressing room.

The show must go on.

I could hear Rachel's bass voice crooning even before I opened the door.

The not-so-eensy willy
Went up between my legs
Up go my berries,
So pretty like Old Gregg's...

"It's tucking song time!" I called as I entered the dressing room I shared with my best friend, Yulia, our resident will-o'-the-wisp, and Rachel Divide. Rachel was a human, but a powerful psychic. She was also a drag queen and the lover of my oldest friend and current boss.

"You bet yo' white ass it's tucking time." Rachel's syrupy Southern accent wrapped around me almost as tight as the gaff she was hauling up between her legs. She reached for her Spanx as I sat down at my dressing station.

"Are you doing 'Old Man River'?" I asked, noting the sequined gown hanging off the corner of Rachel's trifold mirror. It was extra glamorous, which usually meant we were in store for some *Showboat*.

" 'Old Man River' is my favorite," Yulia said, peering down her nose at herself as she layered on her signature silver eye shadow. Her Slavic accent was thick, proof she was concentrating.

"Mine, too," I said, reaching for my liquid eyeliner.

Rachel was shoehorning herself into her Spanx, sweating with the effort. Not for the first time I was grateful that belly dancing precluded support garments.

"Jesus H. Christ, I swear to God that one day Imma burn these damned drawers." Rachel hauled the Spanx the last of the way up, then did a few deep squats to get them situated. Her tucked-away junk didn't move an inch, and I wondered how the hell that could be comfortable.

When she was done, Rachel smoothed her hands over her round belly, then pivoted on her heel to check herself out from the back. Obviously satisfied, she reached for her sparkly tights.

"You doing the snake dance again?" Yulia asked me.

"Yep. That head took forever to make. I'm getting my time's worth."

"Whatever, girl. You just like getting your hands on my man," said Rachel, leering at me mischievously in the mirror.

I grinned back, finishing the thick lines of eyeliner with expert precision. "He's certainly not bad eye candy, for an antique."

Rachel grunted obscenely, fanning herself. "He's not old, he's wise. Lawd have mercy, the things he can teach a girl!"

"Age does have its benefits," I acknowledged, reaching for the glittery bronzer I used all over my body.

"And you should know, old lady." Yulia was belting herself into her own costume—a sort of dominatrix-meets-ice-queen-meets-showgirl hybrid.

At over a millennium old, I didn't take offense at that comment. However... "You're hardly a spring chicken," I said, dryly. Yulia had been leading unwary strangers off the path for a few centuries herself.

"I was never a chicken anything," she said, letting her wisps glow faintly, individual strands of light floating around her like celestial tentacles.

"She's more of a peacock," Rachel clarified, hitching up her tights and reaching for her gown.

Yulia's graceful white arm extended along with one of her wisps to pluck the gown off of Rachel's mirror and hand it to her. Rachel nodded her thanks, the heavily eye-shadowed skin around her rich mahogany eyes crinkling in amusement.

"Hey, you heard from Aki?" Rachel asked.

"The kitsune?" asked Yulia.

"Yeah, he didn't show up for work yesterday, or today. That ain't like him."

I frowned, thinking. "No," I said. "I haven't. And come to mention it, he was supposed to borrow that costume for me, from the Heinz Museum."

Aki was technically Purgatory's dishwasher, but like any kitsune worth his fox fur, he was also a fabulous thief, spy, sneak, and general ne'er-do-well. Needless to say, he was a great friend to have in your corner. Able to get virtually anything, he also knew everyone and everything that was happening in our fair city of Pittsburgh.

"I'll text him," said Yulia, reaching for her phone.

"Please do," said Rachel. "But I already did, like nine times."

"He's probably on a job. Or lying low," I said, since lying low was the natural consequence of the majority of Aki's jobs outside of Purgatory.

Yulia tapped away at her phone, while her wisps delicately placed feathers in her hair, much to my jealousy. My own Fire was nowhere near as compliant as her wisps, even if it was worth a hell of a lot more in a fight.

"Maybe he finally quit after being spurned by Lyla too many times," Yulia said, arcing a brow at me in her mirror as she tapped one last time and put down her phone.

I rolled my eyes. "Ohmigod. You're not bringing that up again. Aki is like a zygote compared to me."

"Girl, everybody is a zygote compared to you," Rachel said, tutting at me in her own mirror. "You are like a gabillion years old. If you use age as an excuse not to get any, you will have to go down on Methuselah."

"I am not going down on Methuselah. That shit's gotta be bitter by now."

"Well, then, you will never get some." Rachel slipped her ball gown up her generous frame, a frame that needed very little extra in the way of padding to look utterly feminine. "'Cuz Methuselah," she added helpfully, "is the only motherfucker on this planet older than you."

"Mmmhmm," purred Yulia.

I glared at both of them. "Ladies, I have bigger fish to fry than dudes."

"Like what?" Yulia asked, turning around to face me.

"Like my curse, for one," I said.

"Whatever, Lyla," she said, rolling her eyes dramatically. "The point of your curse is you don't have to do anything. Just not get Bound again. And there haven't been any Magi in Pittsburgh since... well, probably since forever."

"I know, but still," I said, sounding prim even to my own ears.

"But still what?" asked Rachel, motioning toward Yulia, who sent a wisp snaking out to pull up Rachel's zipper. "The fact is you've been alone for longer than I've been alive. And that's fucked up, girl."

"I haven't been alone! What about that siren? And that werewolf. And those two trolls... they were brothers!"

"And yeah, you fucked the hell out of them," said Yulia. "I had to leave the apartment you were so loud. But those were all one-night stands, Lyla."

"Hey," I started, but Yulia cut me off.

"Fine, one-week stands. But they were stands, *angel moy*."

"So what?"

"So, there's more to life than your curse," Rachel said, gently.

It was my turn to roll my eyes. "How can I do anything when I'm not even free?"

"But you *are* free," said Yulia. "You haven't been Bound in centuries."

"As long as I'm living as a jinni, I'm not really free," I said, my jaw clenching involuntarily.

"I know you think your situation is different, sugar," Rachel said, her voice gentle. "And it is certainly unique. But when it comes down to it, we're all bound to different things. And one of the only bindings worth anything is what you make with other people."

"And I do have those ties," I said, my exasperation coming out in my voice. "Look at you assholes, grilling me an hour before I have to go on stage. If I'm not bound to *you* bitches, whom am I bound to?"

Rachel laughed her big, booming laugh and Yulia smiled, but it was sad. "And we'd do anything for you, *zaychick*. But just as there is more to your life than your curse, there is more to any life than freedom. I worry about you."

I stood up, opening my arms to my friend. "Don't worry, you two. Seriously. I'm so close to being human again. When I am, I can start over. I'll be different. I promise."

Yulia came and gave me a hug, her always-cool skin making my own flesh goose-pimple reflexively.

"Not too different, please," she whispered, and I hugged her hard.

"If you two hookers make me cry off my makeup, I'll shave your eyebrows," said Rachel, her voice quivering slightly. We broke off our hug immediately, knowing she was completely serious.

Nothing, not even friendship, could get between a drag queen and her makeup. Not without feeling the wrath of fabulous scorned.

Chapter Two

The air whispered cool over my arms as I stood on stage, ready to be announced. The room was dark, the wisp-lights glowing on our small café tables the room's only illumination.

Suddenly Charlie's smoky voice oozed over the audience like KY at a porn shoot, getting all up in the audience's aural cavities.

"Ladies and gentlemen, I know you've been waiting for this. Straight from the sultan's bedchamber, a woman of fire too hot for the harem—put your hands together for our very own... Lyla La More!"

Applause, wolf whistles, and a few ululations echoed from the crowd, but the lights stayed off and I remained still. The crowd quieted, growing totally silent as it heard the first low strike of the bass drum. A deep, dark sound, it echoed through my bones as it thumped again, and again, speeding up by infinitesimal degrees. Stock-still, I moved only when the low sweet strain of a cello cut across the drum, and my left hip lifted and dropped. The cello sounded again as my right hip lifted and dropped. And then my hips erupted in a chaos of shimmies with the entrance of more drums and a violin. Beats Antique rocketed out of the speakers, taking the audience out of its seats and my limbs into hyperdrive.

The dance was a serpentine one, my costume signaling the theme with tight, sheer green fabric sheathing my legs from where it hung off the heavy, crazily Bedazzled belt slung low on my hips. The smooth, soft skin of my belly was bare, of course, and above my ribs metallic serpents cupped my breasts, holding more green fabric to protect my modesty.

It was the headdress that stole the show: a great papier-mâché serpent reared above me, its fangs glittering with rubies and its eyes with emeralds. Or the craft store versions of precious gems. It was heavy and awkward, but it looked marvelous in the low light, winking malevolently at the crowd as I danced for their entertainment.

My hips slowed as my chest took up the dance, lifting and shifting, my spine arching as I raised my hands in snake arms. I did a slow circle, alternating movements between hips and chest. As the music swelled into a crescendo I faced the audience again, letting my hands fall to frame my hips. My belly bowed and swooped, muscles pulling in and then relaxing. The beat increasing, I moved as much as my tight costume would allow, darting my hands at the audience like another pair of striking snakes doing the bidding of the great snake that loomed above. The audience went wild, thumping the tables and calling for more. But the music slowed, and I let my shifting carry me downward, my hands above my head. I knelt before them, my snake's head weaving and my arms undulating as the violin cut out, then the cello, leaving only that slow thrum of the bass drum once again. The lights lowered, and for a split second I could hear only the thudding of my heart and the rough pant of my breath through my toothy smile, until the first clap sounded in the room, sending everyone into another round of applause. The lights went up again and I stood, Charlie coming to take my hand.

Charlie was wearing all of his clothes, since it was relatively early in the evening. Soon enough he'd be stripped of his red velvet ringmaster's coat, underneath which he wore only lovely white skin and black suspenders holding up tight black jodhpurs. His mustache was twirled into two rakish whiskers flaring over thin lips, black guyliner smudged around his eerily colorless eyes.

He gave me his sexy ringmaster's leer as he approached, those pale eyes sweeping over my body. His interest was all part of the show, though—Charlie was both gay and taken.

The clapping slowed as Charlie grabbed my arm, jerking me around and toward him. For a split second we were nose-to-nose, me on my tiptoes and him bending over me. Then his arm wrapped around my waist, pulling my hips against his and arching my back. I melted against him, my hands slipping inside the lapels of his coat to lie against his chilly skin. We stayed in that classic pose for a second, Charlie's lean frame looming above me—the alpha male subduing his exotic female. I let my Fire flare just enough to swirl my hair, its sinuous weight mimicking the natural movements of the snake I still wore on my head.

On cue, Charlie whipped me around so I faced the audience. He stepped behind me, his hands moving to my headdress. He undid the strap beneath my chin, lifting the heavy snake's head off me. He set it by my feet, reaching for the belt at my waist.

The audience, having fallen silent when Charlie first grabbed me, began to clap with Trey, who'd initiated a slow beat from behind the bar.

The clapping sped up as Charlie's hand reached for the knot of the belt, undoing it with theatrical slowness. On cue, my next song began. "Hey, Miss Kiss, let us dance," echoed out of the speakers as Charlie whipped my skirt off, leaving me clad in a coin-covered G-string. The audience was on its feet, clapping as Purgatory's ringmaster grabbed my serpent head and, wielding my skirt like a bullfighter's cape, plunged offstage.

It stayed on its feet for the second half of my act, a traditional burlesque number to which I gave only the slightest belly dance flair. I was already pretty nude, but that didn't mean I couldn't tease. And tease I did.

In fact, I got so deep into the dance I went ahead and let my Fire flare again, its dark shadow swooping around me like a doppelgänger, its preternatural heat caressing my skin like a familiar lover.

I would miss my Fire when my curse was lifted.

As the song ended I let the black flames fall around me like a cloak. My hands went behind my back, finding the knot that held on my bra. Then I let the dark swath of my Fire peel away, letting the coin bra fall with it and leaving me clad only in my coin G-string and a pair of pasties in the shape of genie lamps. The audience hooted as my Fire dissipated and my arms fell to my sides, leaving my mostly bare flesh sweating in the hot lights of the stage. Charlie came out again, leading me stage left, where I made a deep curtsy, peeping up at the audience provocatively through my lashes. I repeated the movement stage right, and then finally center.

Straightening from my final bow, I caught a glimpse of a man sitting toward the back, his silver eyes opened wide.

And glowing like fucking headlamps in the dark.

Magi, chimed my brain, unhelpfully.

I pulled sharply away, startling Charlie, who dropped my hand. A smart move on his part, because I was already running.

Panties a-jangling.

*   *   *

Trip hissed at me as I leaped over her and Trap. The twin spider wraiths were currently conjoined at the waist, their legs splaying around them as they prepared for their act.

I didn't respond, since I was in fully panicked fleeing mode. Trip and Trap, after all, couldn't help me. Neither could Trey, or Big Bertha, or Charlie, or any of my other friends. Not unless they ripped that fucking Magi's tongue out before he could speak. For Magi he certainly was, his eyes Flaring to my Fire.

I heard crashing behind me as Trap cried out, "No humans backstage!"

The Magi ignored the spider wraiths, his footsteps closing in behind me. But he hadn't Called yet, and I used my Fire to propel me forward, pushing me toward Purgatory's stage entrance and the street. There I could hopefully put enough distance between me and the Magi for Pittsburgh's steel-stained environment to help me hide.

The cool spring air hit all my bare skin like a slap as I plunged into the night, cutting right down the alley. It was a wide, empty East Liberty alley, giving me plenty of room to run. But the guy chasing me was fast, and his hand managed to catch my elbow, twirling me around to face his glowing eyes. He stared at me in wonder for a split second and I thought I might just have time to kick him in the balls before he could speak.

But it was too late.

"Hatenach farat a si." I See you, he said, in a language older than humanity. Older than time. A language of smoke and fire; a language of magic. The language of the being that made me what I am today, which had the power to make me a slave.

Fuck if I was ever going to be a slave again.

With a harsh cry I launched myself at the man, skimming off the surface of the magical Node beneath the city to shift my nails into long, wicked talons. A look of surprise twisted his features, but he had good reflexes. He threw himself out of my way with a neat somersault that had him back on his feet, his fists raised as he balanced on the balls of his feet—the stance of an experienced boxer.

I lunged at him again, calling my Fire to flame around me. I hoped to intimidate him even if a jinni's black flames wouldn't burn a Magi. His eyes grew even wider at the sight, but he didn't budge. So I slashed at him again with my talons, but he got under my guard and I overextended badly, cursing my inability to use my strongest weapon even as I fell.

I landed hard on the ground, my breath knocked out of my lungs. He kicked away my hands and jumped on top of me. Concentrating on the words, he opened his mouth to speak. Before he could get out the rest of the spell, I struck upward with both my hands bent, the heels of my palms striking him in the chin.

His eyes, already glowing in reaction to my presence, Flared brighter in the darkness, causing my anger to blaze with them.

"Magi," I hissed, and I hit him again. This time he caught my wrists, his hands like vises. Now that he had me on the ground, his bigger size gave him the advantage.

At least for those few seconds.

It was his turn to hiss as suddenly, instead of being a tiny Jasmine-stripper look-alike, I blossomed into obesity. My fat hips knocked his thighs open, pushing him off balance. I heaved myself over, morphing into a taller, more muscular version of me as I did so. Unable to tap the Deep Magic unless Bound, I couldn't get that much bigger, but it made the fight a little more fair.

"Why don't you take on someone your own size?" I growled as I dove for him.

In retrospect, I should have taken the fight slower. I was just so pissed and so panicked. I hadn't heard anyone with those eyes speak that language in a century—not since I'd escaped Europe for the New World, and found refuge in steel-soaked Pittsburgh, where only Immunda could survive. Recognizing a true, Initiated Magi, my crazy inner she-bear emerged, gibbering about never being taken alive. If I had any thought at all it was that my sense of self-preservation would give me an edge. I was fighting for my life, after all, while this guy was just a jerk trying to Bind a jinni.

Unfortunately he didn't fight like a jerk; he fought like a cornered wolverine. He fought as if he were the one who'd be enslaved if he lost this match. He fought like his life depended on it. Which, considering I was intent on killing him, I guess it did.

He fought better than me.

I was hitting him, hard, but I'd lost my talons shifting to a bigger size. Being unBound meant I was far less powerful, even with my unusual access to all of Pittsburgh's corrupted magic swirling at my feet. And now that I was unarmed, he wasn't hitting back, just using his big body to deflect the majority of my blows. Until I overextended a kick.

His own booted foot lashed out, knocking my leg out from under me. I was on the ground again and this time he didn't underestimate my abilities.

He pinned me down with all his weight, his knees pressing painfully into my thighs and his chest blanketing mine, his hands holding down my wrists. His face was inches from mine, but his features were entirely obscured by the bright glow of his Flaring eyes.

Not me, my brain howled. *Not when I'm so close to being free.* I started to shift again in a last, desperate attempt. But before I could change, he'd spoken.

It was the second part of the spell that was the real bitch. And I was too late to stop him.

"Te vash anuk a si," he chanted over and over. *I Call you.* His pronunciation grew more confident with every repetition. The harsh sibilance of the language of the jinn reached toward me, wrapping around my soul. I cried out, but the spell blanketed me, muting my powers. I stopped mid-shift, my power whoomping out, leaving me beneath him in my own small form.

My wide brown eyes stared up at him, begging him silently to stop, not to say the last bit. The bit that made me his; that made me do his bidding; that made me a slave until he either let me go or died.

He spoke the words.

"Hatenoi faroush a mi." *I Bind you.*

And just like that, I was caught. Bound to a human. Again.

There were no lights or sounds or other magical occurrences, but we both felt it. I was his. He stared at me with eyes gone wide with shock, his Flare fading as his magic accepted my acquiescence.

He was my Master.

"Göt," I muttered. Then I switched to English, so he'd understand.

"Asshole."

Chapter Three

Charlie's dagger ground to a halt inches from the Magi's face, caught in a black tendril of my Fire.

"It's too late," I told my friend, but he didn't listen. He pulled another knife from inside his ringmaster's jacket and let it fly.

I caught it, too, letting it drop to the ground with a clatter. But he just reached into his pocket of Sideways and grabbed another. I caught that one before it found my new Master's throat.

We could play this game forever, as Charlie had an infinite number of knives stashed Sideways.

The rest of my friends piled out onto the brick alleyway and, loyally, they all attacked. A deadly wisp shot at the Magi, courtesy of Yulia, which my Fire snared.

It also caught the twin nets that Trip and Trap shot out of the spinnerets located near the bases of their spines. The spider wraiths had turned as one, their midsections still joined by a thin veil of skin that was separating to let them run free. Trip kept spinning, leaping up onto the neighboring building and shimmying toward the sky. Trap did the same on Purgatory's rough brick. When they had enough height, they turned as if on cue to drop out of the sky like creepy missiles trained on their target.

Both bounced off the dome of black Fire with which I automatically shielded the Magi.

It was Big Bertha who intervened, although she didn't look happy about it. Half human and half troll, she towered above all of us, her enormously muscled frame clad in her usual dark suit, huge breasts straining at the buttons of her blouse. Like all troll women, she wore her beard long, framing her surprisingly delicate features.

"Stop it!" she roared.

Everyone stopped. Bertha rarely had to roar, given her size. So when she did, people listened.

"You're too late. She's Bound," the troll explained, using her Patient Bouncer voice.

Yulia, being Yulia, acted like she hadn't heard and shot a series of wisps at the Magi that my jinni caught. Charlie reached for another knife.

With a sigh Bertha snagged her boss around the midsection, pinning his arms to his sides. "She has to protect him, sir. You're just wearing her out."

Trip and Trap looked at each other and skittered into the shadows, undoubtedly planning a new form of attack.

Bertha looked at me. "Get him out of here," she said. "They're not going to listen."

I nodded gratefully to her, turning to collect my new Master. The Magi who'd Bound me was standing there, staring ahead of him, eyes round as a tarsier's. In the dim light of the street-lamp, I could see he was a large man—tall and well muscled, dressed in raw denim jeans, wide cuffs light against his solid black boots. He wore a T-shirt under a thick flannel shirt cut in that slim-fitting hipster interpretation of Western gear. In the hollow of his throat I could see a tattoo—an anchor.

"Nice ink," I told him. "Now run."

When he only blinked at me, I grabbed his arm and dragged him toward my scruffy black El Camino, throwing up a huge wall of my Fire to protect our progress.

As I threw my new Master into the passenger seat I used a spark of magic to start the car, since the keys were still in my purse in the dressing room, and another spout of black Fire carried me up and over the car to my own side. As I dove in to drive away I heard my friends shouting and Bertha, above the din, using her outside voice to remind them, over and over, that it was too late. They couldn't do anything.

I was Bound.

Pittsburgh is made up of a series of tiny neighborhoods, and Purgatory, right on the main strip of East Liberty, was only a few minutes away from where I lived in Highland Park. But it felt like the drive took forever.

Not least because we didn't say a word to each other. Knowing Magi, he wouldn't deign to speak to me except to command me to do something. Why he hadn't commanded anything yet was confusing, but my jinni was determined to get him to safety. And my jinni didn't take no for an answer.

While I drove, I kept one eye on my new Master. He peered out the windows with large, unseeing eyes as the buildings went from glass-and-concrete shop fronts to the small row houses at the edge of East Liberty, and then to the much larger houses of once-affluent Highland Park.

The pack of werewolves that lived on the corner of Highland and Stanton gave me the bird or howled as I drove by, but I didn't stop for my usual bourbon and chitchat. Not least because they'd probably try to snack on the Magi.

My jinni breathed a sigh of relief when we pulled up to the former carriage house I shared with Yulia, but I still had to get us inside. Black flames cloaked us as we hustled out of my old El Camino.

"Where are we?" the Magi asked as I unlocked the bright-purple door that led up to our apartment. He stood on my stoop, peering about, until I grabbed his wrist to pull him inside.

"My house," I said, shutting the door firmly behind him. "Unless you have somewhere you need to be?"

He shook his head, and I realized I knew absolutely nothing about my new Master. But that didn't matter; we were still far from safe. I knew my friends wouldn't listen to Bertha, even if they knew she was right. They'd bust down the door in about two minutes if I didn't work fast.

I led him up the stairs and through the interior door that led into our actual apartment. I pushed him through, slamming the door behind us, and immediately put my hands on its frame in order to reset the wards that protected our home. Unsure of exactly what would happen when I reached for Pittsburgh's Deep Magic, since I'd not been Bound here before and had no idea how the Node would react to my intrusion, I homed in on Yulia's magical signature and reached for the ley line beneath us.

I gasped as my newly Bound power surged with Pittsburgh's potent, steel-stained magic. My knees buckled and strong hands caught my elbow, keeping me standing. Apparently I would have no more trouble using the Deep stuff while Bound than I had had skimming off it while unBound.

A point in favor of my mostly human, if cursed, genetic makeup, I guessed.

"What's wrong?" My Master sounded genuinely worried, despite the fact that he'd just Bound me. I also had to answer his question, even though I'd rather have punched him in the goolies.

"The magic's a lot stronger now that I'm Bound...," I managed to get out between panting breaths.

The Magi's grip on my elbow tightened, his other hand clamping around my waist. I went ahead and leaned against him as I shut my eyes and followed the rabbit down its hole, trying desperately to adjust to the amount of juice flowing through me even as I reached for what I'd need for the wards.

"Lyla?" From a distance I heard the Magi's voice. For a second I wondered how he knew my name, then I remembered he'd seen me dance.

"Talk to me," he said. "You're scaring me."

Forced by the magic of his request, I heard myself respond. Despite the fact that I was locked in a desperate battle, my voice was calm, matter-of-fact.

"It's being Bound," I explained, wondering who was in charge at moments like this. A corner of my brain reserved for jinni duties? The magic of all jinn, itself, that flowed through us? Whatever it was, it talked real nice, although I wished it would shut up.

"When jinn are unBound, our powers are limited. When we are Bound, we have access to the Deep Magic."

"But what are you doing?" he asked. "I don't understand."

"I'm changing the wards on our door. They're magical locks. I don't want Yulia trying to kill you in your sleep." In truth, I'd love it if Yulia killed my new Master in his sleep. But the jinni in me wouldn't let that happen and I didn't want to have her up all night guarding him when we could both be sleeping.

"And it's difficult?" he asked. I wished I could tell him to shut up, but that wasn't how our relationship worked.

"It's just that I haven't had this much power in a while. It's like having something really big suddenly thrust inside of me…" The Magi's grip on my hip tightened and I suddenly remembered I was wearing only my burlesque costume. I'd stopped having much body shame after about the fifth century of my existence on this planet, and the supernaturals I now lived with were all equally louche, so that didn't bother me at all. But Magi, despite their abilities with jinn, were still human, with human mores.

So maybe I shouldn't talk about thrusting.

"It's also Pittsburgh," I said, changing subjects. "This city's magic is…funky…" My voice trailed off as I finally wrestled back control of my magical channels. I kept them open just enough to suck in a strong draught of steel-tainted magic, which I knew I'd regret later even as I funneled it at the wards.

The rest was easy. First a quick reset, which erased Yulia's magical signature. I hoped somebody could lend her a toothbrush over at the big house, because my roomie wasn't getting in here tonight.

Then I locked everything up tight, sealing the place against any form of intrusion, before adding a Silence ward on top of everything else. They could pound on the doors or windows all they wanted and we wouldn't hear a thing. My cell phone was with my car keys, in my purse in the dressing room. We'd be undisturbed until I could figure out who this guy was and what he wanted.

Taking a deep breath, I opened my eyes, detaching myself from the powerful ley lines that lurked beneath our land. I stepped neatly away from my Master, who let me go without a word.

"I'm going to go change," I said. "Make yourself comfortable. The kitchen is that way." I pointed straight ahead, before walking left toward the hallway that led to our bedrooms.

To my annoyance, however, the Magi followed me. I figured it was for the obvious reasons a man followed a woman wearing pasties and a thong, and I got ready to work some of my tricksy jinni magic in defense of my honor. But he just followed me into my bedroom, not touching or speaking.

I pulled open the door to my closet, giving him a pointed look. He didn't notice, however, being too busy staring around at my bedroom.

In all fairness, it did kinda look like a bevy of belly dancers had exploded. My antique four-poster stood in the center of my room, heavily curtained with colorful fabrics. Tons of pillows covered the bed, and there were quite a few on the floor. The walls were painted turquoise, except for the yellow accent wall. And the trim, which was scarlet.

I'd been told it was a bit much, but anyone who said so could go fuck themselves.

"Um," I said, choosing my words carefully. "I would like to change. Would you mind?"

My Master shook his head, crossing his arms over his chest so he suddenly resembled a shaggy Highland bull. "No. I need your help. I'm not letting you out of my sight."

I couldn't help it. I laughed. "Listen…" Only then did I realize I didn't know his name.

"Oz," he said. "You can call me Oz."

It wasn't a name I'd expected, but I figured it was short for something. "Okay, Oz. You've Bound me. I'm not going anywhere."

"Really?" He shifted from foot to foot, as if uncomfortable.

I raised an eyebrow. Who was this guy?

"That's what being Bound means."

He gave me a long side-eye. "How do I know you're not lying to me?"

I took a deep breath. "You've *Bound* me. As all Magi know, I can't tell you a direct lie."

Which was true. Although, as all jinn quickly realized, not telling a *direct* lie left a lot of wiggle room. And I'd been born a wiggler.

Oz's brow furrowed and I resisted the urge to roll my eyes. "Please. A little privacy?"

He nodded, stepping outside. I immediately shut the door in his face, leaning back and letting my head loll against the cool wood.

I considered crying, till I heard shuffling outside the door. Oz obviously didn't believe me and was lurking.

What the hell kind of Magi are you? I wondered, for about the hundredth time. He'd Bound me—known the spells passed down since ancient times through the Magi tribes. And yet he seemed to know very little about jinn, or being a Master.

I pushed away from the door, filled with sudden hope. Nowadays magic was something for Dungeons and Dragons. In books, vampires sparkled and really wanted to marry teen-agers who tripped a lot. Hollywood only dreamed about jinn. And none of these creatures or powers *really* existed in the same universe as chaos theory, or particle accelerators, or atomic bombs . . . except they did.

Was my Master one of the misfits? Cut off from their heritage only to stumble upon it in an ancestor's diary or have it, perhaps literally, bite them in the butt one night?

In other words, I had to find out how much my new Master knew.

And, more importantly, just how much he didn't.

Chapter Four

"My full name's Ozan," he said, to my surprise. He looked pure Irish to me, but that was a Turkish name. "Ozan Sawyer."

I cocked my head at my new Master, pouring him a large dram of Balvenie. I did the same for myself.

Ozan reached for his glass, and his Adam's apple bobbed as he swallowed. His silver Magi eyes met my own dark gaze as he set the glass down, empty, on my battered kitchen table. "And you're Lyla?"

I nodded.

"That's your real name?"

"Yes." Then I remembered he'd seen the show and heard my stage name. "Not the La More part. But Lyla is real."

His eyes swept over me, his head cocking as if he were confused. "And you're a jinni?"

I looked different to his Magi Sight from other jinn; I knew that. But I couldn't explain—conditions of the curse—so I just rolled my eyes and bluffed. "Long story, but yes, I'm a jinni. Who the hell are you?"

My new Master poured himself another snort of whiskey,

his Irish features crumpled in a rueful expression. "Not much of a Magi, to tell you the truth. I'm new to this whole thing. But I need your help."

Watching Ozan fiddle with his glass, I studied his features. He wore his sandy hair just long enough to give him the look of a little rockabilly boy lost, hair that might have been just this side of ginger under the right light. His nose was straight, his chin puckish. High cheekbones arched under eyes that were Magi-silver, when they weren't glowing like headlamps in the presence of a jinni.

Under normal circumstances I might have been tempted to play a little hide-the-shamrock with this guy. But these weren't normal circumstances. And he couldn't be *that* ignorant. After all, his eyes *were* silver. Someone had Initiated him, or he wouldn't have been able to Bind me.

"Start at the beginning," I said. "Who are your people?"

Ozan fiddled with his glass, looking down. For the first time I noticed the shadows under the silver eyes, the way his wide shoulders drooped with fatigue. He was exhausted. "My mom was Turkish. My dad met her in the service. But he's Irish-American, first generation. A soldier and a boxer. When she died..." He took a deep breath. "When she died he did his best. He loved me. Taught me to box. Supported me when I wanted to study something he didn't even understand. But he didn't know any of this. He was a freaking Catholic."

Leaning back, I crossed my legs. I was dressed comfortably, in yoga pants and an ex-lover's massive sweatshirt. I'd put my hair back in a ponytail and scrubbed off all my makeup. I wanted to look as unsexy and non-jinni as possible.

"Okay," I said. "So who Initiated you?"

He scrubbed his hands over his face. "Can I get something nonalcoholic to drink?"

"Of course," I said, fetching us each a glass. "Feel free to start talking," I said, doling out ice and water.

Oz obligingly did as he was told. I could get used to being the one in command.

"I was Initiated in Afghanistan," he said, my surprise evident as I nearly dropped the water I'd intended to place in front of him. His hand reached out, steadying the glass to keep it from spilling. "I'm a social scientist. A cultural anthropologist, to be exact. I study the effects of forced migration on vulnerable groups." He took a long draught of his drink, nearly emptying it.

It was my turn to blink. "Erm…"

"Basically, I study violence in refugee camps, especially sexual violence against women and children. We're trying to figure out how to make times of crisis safer for the vulnerable, which means proving there's a problem to start with."

"Wow," I said, trying to absorb this fact into the identity of the man who'd just attacked and Bound me against my will.

"My mother worked for the Red Crescent," he explained. "That's how she met my father. She was a do-gooder—his words. He was a soldier."

"And she was a Magi," I said. "You didn't inherit those eyes from your father. Ireland has its own magic, but not involving jinn."

"But she *didn't* have my eyes. *I* didn't have my eyes, until Afghanistan. Before I went, my eyes were like my mom's had been—sort of multicolored. My eyes changed colors in Afghanistan after my, um…my…"

"Initiation." I supplied the word for him. I leaned back in my chair, eyeing him speculatively. "An immature Magi has to be Initiated in the presence of another Magi, by a jinni. The mature Magi Calls the jinni, but does not Bind it. The jinni is given an offer: Initiate the immature Magi in exchange for its freedom. Once Initiated, the Magi's eyes turn silver. But before, Magi have the sort of multicolored eyes you describe."

"So my mother didn't know what she was?"

"Maybe not. Not if she was unInitiated and she never mentioned anything to you…" My voice trailed off when he shook his head.

"She wouldn't necessarily have had time to tell me. She died when I was five, in a car accident. If she knew what she was, she never left me any indication. And she was a doctor…a real one. Her family back in Turkey were all doctors, engineers…"

"So not likely to believe in myths like jinn?" I questioned, letting my dark Fire flare around me in ironic counterpoint to my talk of myths. Ozan swallowed, taking a nervous drink from his empty glass. I rose to fetch him another. "What exactly happened to you in Afghanistan?"

Oz thanked me as I handed him his refreshed water glass. "I lived there for three years, doing research for NATO. We were in refugee camps on the border, interviewing current and former refugees who'd returned to Afghanistan."

I raised an eyebrow. I could only imagine what the locals must have thought seeing an unInitiated ginger Magi running around. Oz didn't notice my expression and kept talking.

"When I first arrived, I was sort of…adopted by this family. My first day at the camp this little boy came straight up to me, pointing at my eyes and talking in Pashtu. He led me back to his parents, who introduced me to their whole tribe…they were so kind to me."

"Let me guess," I said, "they all had silver eyes."

He nodded, looking rueful again. "The adults did, yes. They were fascinated by me, asking all sorts of questions about my background. I didn't speak much Pashtu then, but there was a granddaughter who spoke English fluently. Tamina. She translated for me." At the mention of the girl, Oz's eyes squeezed shut.

"So she Initiated you and taught you to be a big bad Magi?" I asked, assuming a few things from the way Oz had said Tamina's name. First, that by "translated for me" he meant "slept with me," and second, that he'd lost her somehow, and was probably going to use me to get her back.

Which was why I was also starting to wonder why he was still humoring me by answering my questions. Normally a Magi blew in, Bound a gal, and then started telling her what to do. There was no chitchat, no "getting to know you" stage or pre-magic interview. There was a Master, giving commands, and a jinni, following them.

But I wasn't about to interrupt and remind Oz of this. The more I could figure him out, the more I could manipulate him. And I wasn't in any hurry to be commanded about, anyway.

"Tamina?" Oz asked, as if the idea of her Initiating him was ridiculous. "No, she was just a kid. She still had the greenish eyes, too." And with that he leaned forward in his chair to pull the wallet out of his back pocket. Flipping it open, he pulled out a creased Polaroid and handed it to me.

It looked almost exactly like the famous *National Geographic* photo of the Afghan girl with the unusual eyes. They were the multicolored eyes of an immature Magi, of course, but that had remained unreported.

And she wasn't that child, although the resemblance was striking. This girl was a tiny bit rounder and a little older. She was also considerably cleaner than that refugee child, and her lips curled in a tiny smile rather than bending in a sober frown.

"She's cute," I said, my voice carefully neutral. Oz picked up on the implication.

"She was thirteen when that was taken. That was when I met her. She was a child," he repeated, glaring at me. "A smart, precocious, awesome child, but just a child."

"And how many years ago was that?"

His eyes narrowed and his voice was like flint. "Three. She just turned seventeen, but she'll always be that little girl to me."

"Okay," I said, still carefully neutral. He looked annoyed, but didn't pursue my implications.

"Anyway," he said instead, "Tamina ended up translating for us a lot, with the other children and sometimes the women. She wasn't officially doing it, of course, but our official translators were all men and the women and children wouldn't always talk to them, so Tamina would help out. She did it for years and she seemed to love it. She was really ambitious."

"Oh?" I asked, cocking an eyebrow. I'd been an ambitious girl living in a patriarchal society once, too. That hadn't ended well.

"Like I said," he went on, ignoring me. At this point he was telling the story as much to himself as to me, as if prodding some trauma he couldn't stop touching. "I was there for three years. Then, like ten months ago, Tamina's parents suddenly immigrated to the States. It happened virtually overnight. One day Tamina was working for us; the next her father and mother had packed her up and taken her overseas."

"Really?" I said, surprised. Magi weren't huge fans of the States for a lot of reasons. What lurked Sideways off of the US wasn't jinni territory, so they had trouble Calling us.

"Yeah. It was odd...everyone was really weird about it. It was like they were unhappy about Tamina and her parents leaving, but they'd also pushed them to go..."

"Well, I imagine that's how it always is, when people move.

On the one hand, you want what's best for them. On the other, you're sad they're leaving."

Oz shrugged. "Maybe that was it. I don't know. But why, if it was so easy, didn't they all leave and come here?"

"Well," I said, delicately, "not everyone wants to live the American dream, no matter what their circumstances. Something must have happened to make them want to leave."

Oz grimaced. "I know Tamina's family were very well respected and lived well, even in the camps. I guess because they were Magi, right?"

"Yes," I said. Magi were a huge help to have around, for other humans at least. Not so much for jinn. "So Tamina and her family up and went to the U.S. Then what?"

"Everything went on as normal. We were finishing up our research, so we were traveling more than usual. We were gone for about three months, working in camps across the border in Pakistan, and when we got back to our base camp Tamina's grandparents immediately sought me out.

"Tamina's parents were dead, murdered here in the States, and Tamina was missing."

"Murdered?" I perked up. I do love a mystery. "How?"

"Their house was set on fire. The police believed it was arson. And there was no trace of Tamina."

"And that's why you're here? Searching for Tamina?"

Oz nodded. "Yes. They knew I was coming back to the States. I think they'd tried to find Tamina using jinn, but had failed for whatever reason. They're...they're family to me. And they didn't have anyone else here and they couldn't get anyone to America fast enough. So I guess I was their best option. They finally told me the truth about themselves, and about me. Then they Initiated me. I only had a few weeks to learn what I could. And I'm still learning, obviously..."

He looked down, lost in his own thoughts. "How long ago was that?" I asked, gently.

"The Initiation was a month ago. I was in that region another two weeks, wrapping stuff up, then I came home."

"And you started looking for the girl."

"Yes. First I tried looking for the jinn Tamina's parents had brought with them, even though I knew it was probably pointless. Tamina's grandmother told me they were probably dead."

"She tried to Call them?"

"Yes. There was no answer. And Tamina's grandmother is supposed to be really strong."

I pursed my lips. A powerful Magi who knew an unBound jinni's true name should have been able to Call it, even from that distance. And if Tamina's parents were dead, their jinn were automatically unBound.

"So then what?"

"I figured maybe we just needed a closer look, so first I tried to find other jinn. That was tough."

I bet it was. There were only a handful of jinn living in America—weirdos who liked the company of humans, but wanted to avoid Magi, for obvious reasons. For them America was great. But most jinn preferred the magical comforts of living Sideways.

"I found one in Boston, and Bound him. That jinni could trace Tamina's family's remaining jinn to somewhere around Pittsburgh, then they disappeared off the jinni radar. But they were definitely dead, and they had definitely not left Pittsburgh, so they must have died in Pittsburgh. I let the jinni in Boston go and came here."

I didn't have to ask how Oz had found the jinni he'd questioned...Magi were drawn to us like moths to a candle. And jinn had the same ability to sense each other—and to sense when one of their own had its Fire snuffed out.

What was more interesting to me was that Oz hadn't brought that Boston jinni to Pittsburgh. He'd let him go. While I wanted to ask him why that was, I didn't want to call attention to the idea that Magi letting jinni go was weird, so I held my tongue.

"You were in for a shock here in Pittsburgh," I said instead.

"Yes. I couldn't sense anything. It was like the jinni in Boston had described—my radar went fuzzy like an hour outside of the city. Luckily, I got hungry and decided to go to Primanti's, because I'd heard about their sandwiches..."

Damn Pittsburgh and its French-fry-laden sandwiches. The only Magi to bother coming to Pittsburgh *would* have to go to the tourist trap a stone's throw from Purgatory.

"I was eating and I felt something. It was faint, but I felt it. So I followed it to the bar."

I waved at him to skip this part. I knew what happened next.

He ignored me. "I saw you, and at first you seemed human, but then you did that dance, and you definitely used their Fire. I wasn't sure what you really were, though, until you ran. Then I knew you had to be a jinni, and I Bound you." He looked away from me, as if feeling guilty, at the same time that his jaw set, as if he was making a decision.

"You have to help me find Tamina," he said in a firm, determined voice. "I know it's unfair to you, but I need your help. *She* needs your help. Tamina's young, and vulnerable, and something terrible has happened to her."

"Are you asking me or telling me?" I said, genuinely curious. A lot depended on his answer.

He cocked his head at me. "What do you mean?"

When I saw his confusion, my mind went into overdrive. I knew only one thing: I should *not* answer that question, if he couldn't answer it himself.

"How are you feeling?" I said instead. "You look tired."

It was an old jinni trick, used on only the greenest Masters. And this one was so green I could have worn him in Pittsburgh's annual St. Patrick's Day parade.

"I am," he admitted.

"Trouble sleeping?"

He scrubbed a big hand over his face, a rough scraping of calluses over beard stubble. "Yeah," he admitted. "A lot on my mind."

I set the trap. "I bet. I always wish mine had an off switch."

He gave me a rueful smile before nibbling at my bait. "I know. I do, too."

"Do what?"

"Wish my brain had an off switch, so I could finally get some rest," he supplied, obligingly.

He watched as I reached my hand out to touch his forehead, obviously wondering what the hell I was doing. My fingers brushed his warm skin and I told him, "Sleep." He slumped forward onto the table, deep in dreamland.

I stood up and made my way over to the big house, my idiotic inner jinni happy to have done her duty while my outer woman was glad to be free, at least for now.

And eager to make that freedom permanent.

Chapter Five

So he's here to rescue someone, and he's enslaved you to do it. He does recognize that's bullshit, right?" Rachel's voice was pitched so low it was like thunder, and she resettled her lacy peignoir around herself to punctuate her sentence.

Yulia, Charlie, Rachel, and I were sitting in the gothic splendor of the big house's parlor, sipping champagne. Rachel met everything in life—be it tragedy or triumph—with bubbly. She had crowded her soft bulk next to me on one of the huge room's many sofas, which I appreciated. I was cold and Rachel was always so warm. Yulia sat in a chair to my left, and Charlie was sitting, leaning forward, on the sofa across from ours.

"That's my whole point," I said. "I don't think he really knows what he's done."

"He doesn't know what *Bound* means?" Rachel asked, her drawn-on eyebrows rocketing upward toward her hairline.

"The word defines itself, after all," said Yulia, equally skeptical.

"Not fully," I said. "I mean, yeah, he knows I'm *bound*, but I don't think he realizes the full implications of *Bound*."

Rachel waggled a beringed finger at me. "But that doesn't

make any sense! How could he not have known he was different? He has to See totally crazy shit, all the time—shit other humans can't see."

"Nope," I said. "He was unInitiated until like a minute ago. As an unInitiated Magi, he would have been able to See jinn from birth, even if he couldn't Call or Bind them. But his chances of randomly running across a jinni in the States were slim to none and, as for other supernaturals, he would have been as totally susceptible to their glamour as a normal human."

"So can he See us now, as we truly are?" asked Yulia.

I shrugged. "Maybe. I don't know. He lived so long unInitiated that his brain might be as hardwired to see what he expects to see as any normal human. He can certainly See jinn, though," I concluded, dryly.

Charlie interrupted. "None of this matters. Whatever his understanding of or excuse for Binding you might be, he needs to rescind that spell. How long do you have?"

I didn't need to ask Charlie what he meant—the only thing he could be referring to was the day my curse would be lifted, conditional on my being unBound.

"One week from now. On the day before Halloween."

"So he's got to release you. We'll make him." Yulia's already narrow eyes narrowed further when I shook my head.

"You can't," I said. "I mean I can't let you do that. I have to protect my Master. If you use violence or any other form of coercion, I'll *have* to defend him."

Charlie sighed. "At least tell us more about him."

"Well, the biggest thing is his background. Like I told you, he's not a typical Magi."

"What's a 'typical' Magi?" asked Rachel.

"They're taught to see jinn as property, not as sentient beings with their own wills and desires."

"Like in the slave days?" Rachel asked.

I nodded. "Yeah. The mentality is similar. I knew a few slave owners, when Charlie and I lived in New Orleans back in the day. They were jerks."

Charlie's nose wrinkled fastidiously. "The absolute worst. All rich men, big plantation owners. We had to be polite, as they were important clients. But they were crazy. Lived for honor, except that their version of 'honor' quite handily made them superior to everyone."

"Just like chivalry, back in the day," I said, and Charlie and I shared a look of mutual commiseration. We'd hated chivalry.

"Jesus, y'all are old," Rachel said, taking a deep breath. We didn't talk about the past much, as it *was* the past and it tended to freak out the younger people in our lives, especially Rachel.

"So he's not a typical Master," I said.

"Yes, but that's just because he hasn't had time to understand what being a Master means," Charlie said, frowning.

"What does he want from you, exactly?" Yulia asked, changing the subject.

"He wants help finding the missing girl I told you about. That's it."

"And he knows she's in Pittsburgh?"

I shrugged. "He's got some circumstantial evidence that says she might be. Personally, I think the whole thing is a wild-goose chase and she's dead. But maybe he does know more. We didn't get very far tonight—he gave me a window to use my power to make him sleep and I took it. He'll get a good night's rest and we can talk again tomorrow."

Rachel frowned at me. "Do you need to stay here tonight? I'm worried about you."

I patted Rachel's plump hand. "You're pretty awesome," I told my friend. "For a human..."

Rachel's long-nailed fingers found my hip to pinch me, hard. "I'll give you a human..."

I giggled hysterically: Rachel always knew exactly where to find my ticklish spots. "Stop!" I shrieked, squirming away from her questing, pinching fingers. "How do you do that?"

Rachel tapped her noggin with a long nail. "It's my super-power, remember?"

Besides being the sassiest drag queen since Ru first sashay-shantayed, Rachel was also a powerful psychic. It's how she'd met Charlie. Once a human psychic, too, Charlie had been chosen to serve as an Oracle. Like *the* Oracle, of Delphi, way back in ancient Greece. It was a huge honor, mostly because it was a death sentence. Charlie had lasted way longer than any other human had, though—sitting on top of that much mojo and letting the gods speak through you tended to scramble your brains.

Charlie was different, however. Very different. After about thirty years of his sitting there, Oracle-izing and yet not dying, someone had pointed out that he had barely aged. Freaked out by this realization, an attendant guard had skewered him. The sword had gone in, and Charlie had died. But as soon as it was removed, the wound healed and Charlie's eyes popped open, colorless as they were now.

He hadn't died again since.

Anyway, he'd recognized Rachel for what she was seconds after her blundering into Purgatory. She shouldn't even have been able to see the place—it had all sorts of wards on it to push away curious humans, plus it was just a tad bit Sideways, meaning pushed just a bit into the fey world. But one day Charlie had looked up from balancing the books to see a big, beautiful black woman had wandered in. She'd asked to speak to the manager in a voice so deep and dark it would have made James Earl Jones envious, and Charlie had hired Rachel Divide—his first human drag act—on the spot.

She'd moved into the big house with Charlie just three months later, and that had been over ten years ago.

"Lyla, honey," Rachel continued, "I'm serious. He can take *advantage* of you. I don't want that man poking his thingy into you just because he's your Master. Although he is pretty luscious." She narrowed her eyes at me. "You don't *want* him to poke his thingy in you, do you?"

I blinked at her. "His thingy? Poke his *thingy*?"

Rachel went ahead and poked me to demonstrate, but with her finger into my side. I squirmed and mewled again.

"What Rachel is trying to say in her nonsensical human way," Yulia said, putting her cool hand on my arm, "is that if he tries to use his position as your Master to force you into sex, we will kill him. And nothing you can do will stop us."

I looked at her long white face, bent toward me, a study in both earnestness and bloodthirstiness.

I burst out laughing.

"I'm so sorry," I said, seeing her frown. "You've only known me unBound. It's not funny." Choking back my giggles, I took both Rachel's and Yulia's hands in mine.

"You don't have to worry about me, guys. Seriously."

"But Charlie told us you have to do anything your Master says. Anything." To illustrate her point, Rachel unclasped my hand in order to make an *O* with two fingers, through which she plunged in and out the pointer finger of her other hand.

Subtlety was not one of Rachel's strengths.

41

"Yulia's right. When we're Bound, jinn have to serve their Masters—we have to do everything they tell us. But that's the great thing about human speech...it's not very accurate."

Charlie twirled one of his long mustachios, his lips curled in amusement.

"Lyla should have been a lawyer, not a dancer," he said, "for how fluid she finds language."

I grinned at him. We'd known each other for well over eight hundred years, and he'd seen me through a few Masters before we'd found refuge together in Pittsburgh.

"I don't get it," Yulia interrupted. "How can 'Lyla, I want to fuck you' be fluid?"

Rachel turned to the wisp. "Come on, girl. I know you've heard of water sports..."

Yulia glared as if she were going to murder our human friend.

"Think about it," I said hastily, to save Rachel the few mortal years she had left. "If you tell me you want to fuck me, you've articulated a desire to fuck me, yes. But I can fulfill that in any number of ways."

"How?" Yulia asked. "How can my wanting to fuck you be fulfilled any other way than by my fucking you?"

"Well, I could make you *think* you're fucking me. But you're really fucking a watermelon. Or a pillow. Or a succubus who pays me to make you think you're fucking me, when you're really feeding her."

Yulia raised an elegant eyebrow and I shrugged. "What, a girl's gotta pay her bills. Jinni isn't a salaried position."

Rachel shook her head. "So you can for real take a wish that specific and twist it around? Why do you ever do anything they say, if that's the case?"

I shrugged. "We don't, often. At least not the big stuff. You've probably heard at least some of the old legends. Did rubbing a genie's lamp ever work out well for a human?"

"Girl, I'm from Memphis. We don't know shit about genies. Except Aladdin."

I couldn't help but laugh. "Well, in most of the legends genies are like any fey, mostly because, like the fey, we can't lie when we're Bound—at least to our Masters. But we're generally pretty pissed at being Bound, so we don't really want to do our Masters any favors. The magic compels us, but we've got at least a little freedom in how we interpret the wishes we grant. So we become sorta...tricksters. Which is why my Master is currently snoring, facedown, and will be for the next eight hours as I figure out what to do with him. And," I added, bitterness making my voice brittle, "how I ended up cursed to be a jinni. I didn't ask for the exactly right thing."

My friends nodded, having heard the story before. I tended to trot it out if enough tequila was involved.

"So he can't make you do what you don't want to do?" Rachel asked, still concerned. I started to say no, then reconsidered. But Charlie answered her for me.

"I've known Lyla for centuries, for a few of which she's been Bound. She is very clever and she knows how to manipulate a Master as well as any jinni. However..."

He paused and I shivered. I knew all too well what his *however* entailed.

Charlie continued. "...there remains the fact that not even a jinni as clever as Lyla can get out of everything. A direct command is a direct command: she must obey. And if the Master understands language as well as Lyla does...there is always the potential for trouble."

We were all silent at that. I noticed my shoes were badly

scuffed, and they were my favorite flats. When this was over, and I was free, and human again, I'd order new ones. They'd be my treat to myself.

"So what can we do?" Yulia asked in a low voice. She was a wisp of action and she was visibly chafing at not being able to do anything.

Charlie stood, pacing toward the white marble fireplace dominating the room's far wall. "First of all, this Oz character needs to free Lyla as soon as possible, before he realizes his true power over her."

"Why doesn't Lyla just tell him about her curse?" asked the ever-practical Rachel.

Only my closest friends knew how I'd become a jinni, and most of those people were in this room. I kept it a secret mostly because I hated talking about it, but since moving to Pittsburgh I'd had other reasons to stay mum.

I'd never been Bound while living here, so I hadn't been sure about my ability to use the Deep Magic of the Node. But because I could skim off of it pretty easily, I'd wondered if more would be possible, should a Magi come along. The chances of that had been slim, but I'd still kept my trap shut.

Now, however, I'd love for my social anthropologist Master to know my secret. There was just one problem...

I shook my head. "That won't work. I can't talk about my curse to my own Master."

Yulia cocked her head, immediately seeing the big picture. "You can't tell him. But can *we*?"

I nodded. She grinned.

"So we *will* tell him," Yulia said, smiling as if she were a tiger being presented with a juicy bit of steak.

"What's your impression of him? Do you think he'll listen?" Charlie asked me.

I shrugged. "I have no idea. Oz seems like...well, like a good man, to be honest. He's obviously educated and he's chosen a career that faces social issues head on. He's also very obviously uncomfortable with the whole Master thing. He visibly cringes when he hears or says the word."

"So we talk to him," Rachel said, pouring us all another tot from the champagne bottle. "Appeal to his reason, to his goodness. Explain to him your curse and maybe he'll let you go."

"There's still the matter of the missing girl," I reminded them.

"Screw her," said Yulia, bluntly. "Like you said, she's probably dead."

"And if she is alive, you can find her without being Bound," Rachel said, more optimistically.

"Or we can leave it up to the Exterminators," Charlie said.

"Exterminators aren't going to help with a missing human, Magi or no," I pointed out. "They keep our kind in control and off the human radar, period. They're not going to deviate from the mission."

"So how do we play this? What should we say when we sit down with this guy?" Rachel asked, sitting forward on the sofa as if ready to go wake Oz immediately and have at him.

Charlie rolled his eyes at his love, a pointless gesture considering they were colorless. Anyone else would have just thought he was staring at Rachel while twitching his eyelids, but we knew the signs.

"We can't just hurl this at him," he said, turning to me. "You need to spend some time with him tomorrow. Get him on side; get him to like you. Then bring him here, so that we can talk to him. If those people told him that he needs a jinni, we'll tell him he has a jinni. That he has *all* of us. That we're more than willing to help him find this Tamina, *if* he sets you free."

"You'd do that?" I asked, feeling my eyes prickle.

"Of course. And I bet we can figure out a way to get the Exterminators involved. It should be a cinch to find this girl, with all of us looking."

Involuntarily I knocked on my own skull, just as Rachel and Yulia rapped the wooden table.

I didn't comment on our mutual bout of superstition, instead thanking them for being so willing to help me.

"Of course," my oldest friend said, his snow-white eyes paradoxically warm. "You're not alone, Lyla. Never alone."

I ducked my head, gratitude making my eyes sting with tears.

"Again, thanks. Now do y'all have a watermelon?"

Rachel grinned at me. "No, but we do have a cantaloupe. Would you like me to drill a hole in it?"

I leaned over to kiss her heavily rouged cheek with its five o'clock shadow.

"Yes, thank you. And be generous. He may be a few videos short of Netflix, but I'm pretty sure my new Master has a copy of *Shaft*."

Rachel shook her head. "That was terrible. I'm glad your hips don't lie, 'cuz your comedy sucks."

I shrugged. "Just go drill your hole."

She tutted, getting up to head into the kitchen while Yulia watched the both of us as she gave the slow headshake of shame.

Chapter Six

I was back in the harem where I'd been born. Soft light from outdoor lamps filtered through the filigree on the windows. Inside, fragrant beeswax candles set in sconces against the wall smoked gently, giving off their familiar, delicious scent of jasmine and sandalwood. It was hot, of course—all of my fully human memories were glazed with the desert heat of which my jinni Fire was a pale imitation.

Walking on quiet feet, I approached the door to the harem. In my real memories, I would have been tiptoeing through a mass of sleeping bodies, all the women and children of my family strewn about on thin mattresses. But here all was quiet, the floors empty and the air void of the quiet snores and mumblings of so many people sleeping in one place.

There was just me and the massive set of double doors that represented my freedom.

I knew I had to get outside. Although I wasn't sure what waited for me past those doors, I knew it was freedom. No more living in fear of my father or of the suitors I saw through the screens of our harem's balcony. At fourteen I was a woman, the daughter of a wealthy, powerful man, and purported to be a beauty—making me nothing but a pawn to the men who surrounded me and the lineage they sought to keep in power.

Expecting that at any minute one of our harem eunuchs would make himself known, appearing out of the shadows as was their wont to turn me away from my goal, to my surprise I was allowed to approach the doors. No one stopped me.

Reaching them, I tried to grasp a handle, but my hand fell to my side a second after it was raised. *What am I doing?* I thought. *What can I do on my own in the world? I have nothing...no one. Not even my name if I'm known to have run away.* A night away from the harem and my virginity would be in question, stripping me of my single intrinsic value. Until it was sold out from under me by my father, of course.

You own yourself in this moment, I told myself. *Take this chance...maybe you can finally be free, if you take this one chance...*

Grasping at this frail straw of hope, I raised both hands to grab the huge handle of either door. But as my fingers wrapped around the bronze I realized it was hot. Fiery hot, burning hot—instantly my flesh fused to it, the skin melting to the door handles. I screamed in agony, the smell of my burning skin obscuring that of the candles.

I pulled, trying desperately to free my hands, but neither they nor the door moved. Until, ripping the skin from my palms, my fingers, the doors suddenly flew outward. Dropping to my knees in agony, I clutched my ruined hands to my belly, sobbing in terror as the smoke from the candles thickened, becoming a roiling mass of eerie black flames that drifted over the white marble floor. Before me, on the lintel of the doorway, the smoke solidified. A flame-eyed being stood above me, leering down.

"You'll never be free, little Lyla," Kouros said, his mouth opening on a pit of red fire even more terrifying than the dark flames of his body. "I never let go of my treasures. Never..."

A hand of black flames reached toward, then through me, passing through the center of my chest. I could feel his Fire in my heart, burning a thousand times hotter than the flames that had mutilated my hands. I smelled the acrid scent of my own heart cooking as I screamed, and screamed, and screamed...

"Lyla!" said a voice. "Lyla, wake up!"

Hands on my shoulders shook me and I reached for the black flames of my own jinni Fire, prepared to strike. But it didn't answer me and my eyes opened in shock.

"Master," I murmured, seeing Ozan's silver eyes staring into mine. Of course my power hadn't responded; I wasn't allowed to hurt the Master.

"I hate that word," he said, but his voice was distracted, his slightly crooked boxer's features rumpled with concern. "Are you all right?"

"Yes. I'm fine, just a bad dream." Leaning back on my pillows I shut my eyes to gather my bearings. When I opened them again Ozan was still there, perched awkwardly on the edge of my bed, staring down at me.

Was now the time on *Sprockets* when I'd have to make him fuck a cantaloupe?

But instead of making a move, he ran his hands through his own sleep-mussed hair. "You scared the hell out of me," he admitted. "You were screaming like someone was murdering you."

"Yeah, well, I have bad dreams sometimes." Which was not strictly true. In reality I had lots of bad dreams. And they'd been increasing in intensity and frequency—an effect, no doubt, of my being so close to the end of my curse. But I couldn't share that last fact with my Master. "What time is it?"

"It's almost eleven," he said. "But I only just got up. I haven't slept that well in weeks. I feel amazing."

Those silver eyes peeked at me through thick lashes and I cursed his father for those Irish puppy-dog features. Not that I hadn't had handsome Masters in my day, and having someone enslave you tended to overshadow the appeal of high cheekbones or a finely muscled neck.

A muscular, tattooed neck that, in Ozan's case, I would have happily throttled if I had been allowed, to get back my freedom before this week was up.

"Well," I said, pulling the blankets with me to protect my modesty as I sat up. Oz glanced away quickly when he saw my bared shoulders, obviously only then realizing I slept à la Eve. "We might as well get started. First of all, we should pick up your stuff so you can move in here. Where have you been staying?"

"A motel. But I planned to stay there."

"Don't be silly," I said, keeping my voice neutral but warm. *Get him on side*, I thought, reminding myself of today's mission. "We have tons of room."

"What about your roommate?"

Oh yeah, I remembered. I had told him she would try to kill him.

"Don't worry about Yulia," I said. "You're welcome to stay in our guest room. Unless you'd prefer the motel?"

He narrowed his eyes, nobody's fool. "Why would you want me to stay here?"

"Because we have the space and having you here will make working together easier. We can find Tamina faster," I said, keeping my tone casual and friendly, my eyes round and innocent. Charlie would be proud.

Eventually, of course, Ozan agreed.

My face may only launch a few dozen ships, but my tongue can easily launch a few hundred. And that doesn't even take into account what I can do with it when I'm not talking.

Ozan had managed to find the floppiest flophouse in Wilkinsburg, which was saying something.

"Dude, were you cruising for bedbugs, or do you just like your sheets extra semen-encrusted?" I asked him, peering over the dash of my El Camino skeptically.

He gave me an imperious glare. "I'm a research scientist," he said. "I'm not exactly on a boutique hotel budget."

I pushed open my door, shaking my head. "I get that money's tight, but you would have been better off with a shopping cart and a piece of cardboard."

We got out of the car and headed toward the rickety-looking staircase that led to his second-story room. The motel was of the cheapest sort, built with the offices at the very front and a long line of rooms extending back like a scabby tail. A tail full of prostitutes, drug deals, and gang murders that the hotel manager never had to see, thus allowing him to claim full irresponsibility.

We got to the top of the stairs. There was a maid leaning against the doorjamb of an empty room, smoking. Dirty gray linens lay twisted into a ball next to her feet, the water in the bucket next to the linens an even sludgier color.

She was human, aged anywhere from thirty-five to fifty-five, with the hard, lined face of someone who'd not had a lot of chances or choices during her lifetime. Her flat, red-rimmed eyes flicked to mine and I gave her a little nudge with my magic as I said, "Why don't you take your cigarette downstairs?"

The human nodded amicably and walked to the stairs, Oz watching our exchange with arced brows.

"Was that magic?" he asked, when the maid was gone.

I nodded. "Just a smidge."

"Are we that easy to manipulate?"

"Most of you, yes."

He shook his head, either at what I'd said or my abrupt tone. "You must not have a lot of respect for humans."

I opened my mouth, but I couldn't tell him it wasn't precisely a lack of respect, since I'd once been human. My curse kept me from doing so. So I shrugged my shoulders, frustrated with the whole situation.

"She needed to be out of the way," I said.

"Why, expecting danger?"

I shook my head. "No. We're just picking up your stuff. But you never know." His silver eyes stayed on mine, radiating skepticism. "Look, supernaturals and humans should be kept separate. Usually for the humans' survival, or at least their virtue," I said, thinking of the poor humans Diamond was always dragging into Purgatory. "It becomes habit, after a while. See a human, get him or her away, so nobody gets eaten. Or boffed."

"So you're taking care of them?" he asked.

"I'm trying to. And before you get all uppity about personal choice and not manipulating people, keep in mind they have no idea what they're dealing with. They can't make responsible choices when they don't even know we exist. And that something trying to eat them is probably in the cards if they make the wrong decision."

Oz's brows knitted together, making him look pensive. And adorable. I reminded myself I was an idiot.

"I have so many questions," my Master said, digging in his pocket for his key. He unlocked the door and it opened onto a room that was as grim as I'd expected.

"Ask away," I said, checking out the room.

He walked toward a black duffel bag set on a cheap bureau upon which sat a TV that hadn't been state-of-the-art since the mid-eighties. He opened the bag, then paused, his brow furrowed in thought. "First of all, what's up with Pittsburgh? You mentioned a few things last night, when you were, um, resetting the wards." He spoke carefully, as if pronouncing words in a different language. I also cursed his obviously excellent memory. "Something about Pittsburgh's magic, you said...also the fact that I couldn't sense normally here, and neither could the jinni in Boston..." Ozan cocked his head. "So what is it with Pittsburgh, exactly? I just thought it was Steelers. And French fries on salads."

"While French fries on salads is pretty magical, that's not what makes Pittsburgh special," I said, as I took a prim seat on the edge of the bed. One that I reconsidered after seeing the brownish stain on the comforter, next to my right hand. I moved to lean up against the open doorway. "Do you know our geography at all?"

"Lots of hills?" he said, as he started gathering the few bits of clothes and other odds and ends—mostly books—strewn around the room.

"Yes. But in this case it's more the rivers that are important. There're three above ground and one underground. Rivers, running water, usually indicate magical ley lines—conduits for power," I explained to Ozan's rapidly elevating eyebrows.

"When you get a bunch of ley lines converging like that it's a sacred confluence—or what we call a Node. Nodes have a lot of power, and Pittsburgh's Node is crazy powerful."

"So Pittsburgh is extra magical?" Ozan looked skeptical. I couldn't blame him. While I loved my adopted home, *magical* was not Pittsburgh's most obvious descriptor.

"It used to be the most powerful Node on the planet. But then the humans and their steel industry came. Cold iron corrupts magic, so we're sitting on a lot of really polluted power; power so polluted that pureblood magical creatures can't access it. It's basically poisonous."

"Oh," said Ozan, clearly not actually understanding anything.

I waited patiently while he shoved the little pile of stuff he'd made into the duffel, frowning in concentration as he stood to put the bag on the bed.

My own lips curved in an answering smile. He had a very open face, and right now he was obviously thinking. "Ask whatever you like," I prompted.

"I don't understand how *you* live here, if you say all magical creatures can't live here. And then there's your friends..."

I shook my head. "I never said *all* magical creatures can't live here. I said all *pureblood* magical creatures can't live here."

What I said obviously hadn't clarified anything. "Huh?"

I nearly made a snarky comment about Tamina's tribe not having taught him anything useful, then I remembered I should be grateful for their negligence. I could tell him what he needed to know...and nothing more.

"Basically," I said cheerfully, "there are two categories of supernaturals. I mean, there are tons of species, but we break ourselves down into two categories: purebloods and Immunda. Purebloods are purely magical beings, things like jinn or the sidhe Lords, that use what we call the Deep Magic. That's the magic that runs deep in the ley lines and the Nodes. Because they can use the Deep Magic, purebloods are extremely powerful beings."

"And...Immunda?" Again, Oz carefully and precisely articulated the new word.

"Immunda are...everything else, really. Including creatures like sirens, vampires, gaki, succubi...anything that gathers its magic parasitically off humans; those are all Immunda. Also things with mixed human-and-magical blood, including shapeshifters. Those kinda creatures can skim off the surface of the Node and ley lines, but they can't use the Deep Magic. It's like they're permanently stuck using the kiddy pool and so the purebloods don't consider them equals. Which they're not—a pureblood could blow them away in seconds."

His frown deepened as he went into the room's little bathroom, returning after a minute with a small toiletry case.

"I had no idea it was all this complicated," he said, shoving it into the bag and zipping everything up.

I scanned the room, looking for anything he might have forgotten. "It's not, really. Think of it this way: there are only two types of magical creatures, when it comes right down to it: those who can use the Deep Magic and those who can't. Those who can use the Deep Magic cannot live in Pittsburgh. They need the Deep Magic to survive, like they need air or water, and the Deep Magic here is poisoned. So Pittsburgh's sort of a haven for the Immunda.

"We sometimes call it the City of Misfit Toys. The big guns don't come here, because the magic here is deadly to them. So Pittsburgh houses a lot of magical beings who like living without the risk of becoming the bitch of something a lot stronger."

Oz was standing, holding his duffel bag's handle in one big hand. He was giving me an odd look.

"So what are you?"

"What?" I asked, sounding sharp even to my own ears.

"You said only purebloods can access the Deep Magic. But you used it to reset the wards last night. And you said jinn are purebloods, not Immunda. So how do you live here?"

I hemmed and hawed at him, mentally cursing my babbling jinni in fifteen languages. *You're out of practice*, I told myself. *And he's a lot smarter than you're giving him credit for.*

Luckily, my curse wouldn't let me clarify what was going on, so I could only babble inanities as I shook my head. He was beginning to look distinctly suspicious when I was saved by the bell. Or a Call, as the case may be.

The burst of magic rang through my head like a shot and I felt my eyes cross.

"Lyla, what's wrong?" Oz asked, as I fell heavily against the door.

I took a deep breath, then another, letting the Call's message clarify itself.

"There's a problem," I said, utterly grateful for the distraction even though I normally hated being Called. "We've got to go."

I nipped out the door, darting to the stairs and freedom from Oz's questions. He kept up with me, taking just a second to drop the keys off with the meth-head smoking outside the manager's office. I was already in the driver's seat, pulling on my seat belt, as he jumped in. I'd put her into drive before he'd finished shutting his door.

"I'm taking it this is an emergency?" he said, hastily buckling his seat belt.

"It is. But you're in luck. You're going to get to see exactly how this new world fits into your old, live and in the flesh, rather than my having to describe it to you."

"Um, okay," he said. "This sounds . . . instructional."

"Oh, it will be," I said, grimly.

My Master gave me a long side-eye. "Good. I think."

"I'm delighted you approve, Master."

Oz frowned at that word. I smiled. He really was too easy.

Chapter Seven

W hat the hell is that?" Oz asked, peering out the window as I drove my El Camino up onto the sidewalk bordering Frick Park, right near Regent's Square.

This wasn't the time to think about traffic tickets.

"That is something that's not supposed to be here," I said. "C'mon."

Frick was Pittsburgh's answer to New York's Central Park. And, as in Central Park, there were parts that were wild and overgrown and parts that were absolutely not. The part that sat in Regent's Square, a little neighborhood near Wilkinsburg, was one of the absolutely-not-wild parts. It consisted of a few baseball diamonds, a playground, a nice running track...all the nice family stuff you didn't want attacked by a slobbering insect monster.

And it was currently under attack by a slobbering insect monster. In the middle of the park, some ways ahead, something many-limbed and hulking tossed around playground equipment like paper dolls.

Unfortunately, it was also a pretty October day, with just the slightest chill in the air. The kind of end-of-summer day humans wanted to savor out in the open, before it got too cold to do so.

People were everywhere.

"Shit," I said, watching a plastic kiddy slide arc through the air to hit the sidewalk near my car. "This is going to be fun."

Oz glanced at me. "I can't tell if you're being serious or sarcastic."

I grinned at him. "C'mon, Master. This is your chance to see how we all get along. Or don't, as the case may be."

"Ma'am, I can't let you in there," said one of the policemen standing in a huge circle, keeping the humans out of the way. His voice had the robotically repetitive tone of the heavily glamoured.

I used my own power on him, knowing the Exterminators' standard shtick. "We're with the special squad."

He nodded, pupils dilated, letting me and Oz pass.

"Why are the cops here if this is a supernatural problem?" he asked, as we hurried toward the flurry of activity at the far end of the park.

"In this case, they probably got here first," I said.

"How do you know?"

I pointed to the torso of the human policeman that lay, wrong way around, next to his own legs, so he could have sucked on his own toes had he been alive.

"Oh God," Oz said, turning green.

"We keep an eye on the police scanners. We have people who take care of this sort of thing, but when they need backup, they put out a Call. I was close and strong enough, so I could receive it."

"That poor guy," Oz said.

I nodded, flashing him an "I told you so" look. "Like I was saying, humans and supernaturals are best kept separate."

He looked troubled at that, but I didn't have time to pick his brain and he wasn't asking me to, so I ignored him.

We were nearly to the source of the problem. It looked kinda like the Tick, from that old cartoon about a guy dressed up as a giant superhero tick. Only this Tick was more actual tick: greenish-black and while the body was distinctly buff and humanoid, the head was all mandibles and antennae and weird bug eyes.

"Bugbear. Goddammit."

"A what?" Oz asked me, so I repeated myself, and then we were accosted by the Exterminator in charge of the whole shebang.

She was an old dancing buddy of mine, Loretta. A siren, she was all bouncing blonde curls, big blue eyes, and buxom figure. Also gills, third eyelids, and webbed fingers and toes, but from the way Oz was goggling at her, that didn't distract from her beauty. Like all sirens, she was great at glamouring the human witnesses but not the best offense.

"Lyla?" Loretta said, clearly surprised to see me. Calls were magically calibrated to seek out beings with an appropriate level of power for the problem. I was normally only Called for far lesser issues—crowd control, things like that. But now that I was Bound, I could handle a whole lot more, and the Exterminator's special Call knew that, even if Loretta didn't.

Just then a small plastic Pegasus—one of those park toys on a spring that kids ride on—nearly beaned me, and I decided now was not the time for explanations.

"Who are you with?" I asked, cutting to the chase.

"Suki and Punyabrata," she said in dulcet tones, naming two of Pittsburgh's big-gun Exterminators. Suki was a gaki and Puny a naga. Like sirens, both were Immunda races. Gakis, though rare and very strong for Immunda, were really just spirit vampires. Meanwhile Puny, a snake-shapeshifter, could skim just enough from the Node to fuel his transformations. And once he was transformed...

A snake the size of a big rig could do enough damage without resorting to any other magic than its own ability to slither over you like a steamroller.

"Suki's down," Loretta continued. "Puny's..."

Something darkened the sky above us and then landed with a resounding thud at our backs. Loretta swore and when we turned it was to see Puny, still in snake form, embedded a few feet into the grass like a hissing, disgruntled comet.

"Puny's having problems," I finished for her.

"Do you really think you can help?" Loretta asked, looking at me with doubt in her oceanic eyes.

I nodded. "I'm Bound now," I said, and she gaped from me to Oz and then back at me before her eyes narrowed in calculation.

"Oh."

Any more small talk was precluded by a horrible chittering cry, as the bugbear launched itself toward the line of humans huddled behind the police officers.

"Tell me to fight the bugbear," I told Oz, already reaching for the Node.

Oz did as I asked, without question. "Take that thing out, Lyla, before it hurts anyone else."

And just like that, Pittsburgh's steel-stained juice poured through my system. I launched myself on a wave of black Fire, forcing my shape to shift and grow huge even as I did so, into a size far more massive than I could have achieved unBound, fighting Oz the night before.

We met in midair, the bugbear and me, my Fire wrapping around both of us as I pushed it away from the humans and toward the ground. We landed, me on top, knocking the breath out of the bugbear as I was enveloped by the smell of rotten eggs.

From underneath me the bugbear blinked, obviously surprised at my aerial assault. I grinned at it, my lips feeling large and unwieldy, as I pulled back a fist and hit it square in the mandible.

The solid blow only pissed it off. It growled, mandibles opening wide to reveal jagged bug teeth covered in stinking saliva—the old-egg smell came from inside the creature, a charming discovery.

It blew its stinking breath right in my face, the reek so powerful I pulled back, then yelped as the beast yanked my arm hard, flinging me off. It bounded to its feet, lunging at Oz, who had gamely trotted over and assumed his boxer's stance. Just as the creature's meaty, armored fist hit my Master's nose with a crunch, I crashed into the beast from the side. We landed squarely in the center of a picnic table, spread with what looked like a lovely lunch. The table buckled under our combined weight, listing to the right. Rolling onto the ground, we scrabbled at each other with clawed hands, Oz, his nose streaming blood, shouting unhelpful exhortations of encouragement like an overzealous hockey mom as the creature breathed its reek all over me.

I managed to get on top of the beast, beefing up the thighs I wrapped around its neck with an extra layer or five of muscle, using my massive calves to restrain its arms. "Hit it with the bench!" shouted Ozan, and I had to obey. I reached for what had been one of the picnic table's benches, hefting it with ease in one of my hamlike hands. Raising it above my head, I brought it down with all my strength on the bugbear's head.

"Hulk smash!" I shouted, just for the fun of it.

It grunted, but didn't appear particularly fazed. So I brought the bench down again and again, although still to no effect. "What the hell?" I shouted at it. "Die already!"

It snarled, bucking like a bronco, ignoring my suggestion.

"Try the balls!" shouted Oz, and I did as he said, partly because it was a good idea and partly because I had to follow his commands. I raised the bench again, but twisted as I brought it down, landing it solidly in the creature's crotch.

I'm not sure bugbears have a gender—not all fey monsters do—but it definitely had something sensitive between its legs. The creature sat bolt upright, shock and pain giving it a surge of strength. The good news was that I seemed to have done some damage, as the creature stopped trying either to kill me or get to the humans ringing the park. The bad news was that it sat up so swiftly it flung me off, leaving it free to flee. Which it did, rolling like a massive, stinky tumbleweed away from me. Bounding to its feet, it leaped up and away from the main street of Regent's Square toward the wilder portions of Frick Park.

I was on my own feet, flinging a wave of black Fire at the creature, but I was too late. Bugbears could jump like fleas, and this one used its superpower to great effect.

"Shit!" I shot a few more waves of black Fire at the beast, but it was way out of my range.

Muttering Turkish imprecations under my breath, I turned to Oz. My Master's nose was still bleeding heavily, which I pointed out to him with a finger poked in his direction. His hand went to his face and he blanched when it came away wet and red. He stripped off his button-up, then his T-shirt, showing off an awful lot of muscled, lightly haired chest, all covered in vintage tattoos.

Pressing his T-shirt to his face, he looked me over with a

combination of shock and curiosity. I knew he'd have a thousand questions as, ever the scientist, he scanned down with clinical precision over my now hugely muscled shape. Only he suddenly blushed red and looked back up at my eyes, clearly forgetting his clinical detachment.

I looked down to discover what I'd expected. Only in superhero comics do clothes tear in such a way as to protect one's modesty. And so I'd burst out of my jeans and thin black sweater leaving one boob hanging out and my cooter exposed, a look that would have gotten me summarily stoned where and when I was from.

I shrugged ruefully at him as I reclaimed my true form, shifting down into my own comfortable shape. He watched with fascinated curiosity until the few wisps of clothing that had managed to cling to me in the first shift gave up the ghost and fell off entirely.

Not making me regret I'd left the cantaloupe at home, Ozan did the gentlemanly thing and whirled around, keeping his back turned as he tossed me the button-up he held in one hand.

I donned the shirt, staring at his broad, tattooed shoulders. My new Master kept surprising me, much to my own consternation.

"You decent?" he asked, using a phrase I hadn't heard for years outside of period drama.

"Yes," I said. "As decent as I get, at least." Then I walked toward him, hand outstretched. A small burst of magic fixed his busted nose.

When he lowered his T-shirt his mouth was quirked in a smile. Even bloody, he was handsome, and I regretted the day he learned what being a Magi really meant and did something to make me hate him.

Loretta pounded up next to him, squawking into her mobile phone. She lowered it from her ear to yell at me.

"That was insane, Lyla! Were you using the Node?"

Shit, I thought. "Uh, the Node? Hell no." *When it doubt, brazen it out.* "That was, um, jinni magic. From being Bound. Jinni magic."

Maybe not my best lie. Loretta did not look convinced but she didn't push. Oz looked between the two of us, his brow wrinkled in thoughts I probably didn't want him to be thinking.

"Well, whatever it was, that was a great job," Loretta said. "We've got a team tracking the thing."

"You need me to help?"

She shook her head. "Negative. We were just taken unawares. We haven't seen a bugbear this side of Sideways in a very long time."

"Yeah, what the hell was it doing here?"

"We have no idea," she said, grimly. "Something must have brought it over, but why?"

Bugbears lived Sideways, they were dumb and mean, and they tended to eat anything that moved that they came across. They couldn't be bought, or bribed, or blackmailed, so they didn't make good employees. Why anyone would bring such a thing to the human plane was completely mystifying.

And not my problem.

"I got ninety-nine problems and a bugbear ain't one, Loretta. Can we go?"

Loretta nodded. "You did a great job. We may need you again, if we find the thing." Her eyes narrowed further at me, a look that made my palms sweat. "I'll be seeing you.

"And thank you for your help, too," she said, turning to Oz.

He nodded, gesturing awkwardly with his bloody T-shirt as he told her it was no problem.

She smiled at him, openly admiring his chest as he talked. "Here," she said, reaching for the shirt. "I can take get rid of that for you. Least I can do." He handed it to her and she turned back to all the watching humans as I felt the powerful swell of her magic begin changing their perception of everything they'd just seen . . .

"She's gonna have to eat a lot of hearts tonight to refuel," I said, hoping the hospital morgues were stocked. Otherwise there'd be a few less homeless people wandering around tomorrow.

"What about hearts?" Oz asked, looking horrified.

"You don't want to know," I replied, truthfully. He gave me a long look but he took my answer at face value, for once.

"So, that was pretty amazing," he said, as we walked back to my El Camino.

"Having a bugbear in the park?"

"The bugbear *was* amazing, actually. In a stinky way. But no, I meant your . . . changing like that."

"We call it shifting," I said primly, scratching my belly. The bugbear must have gotten in a swipe I hadn't felt with all the adrenaline in my system. Wetness met my fingers and I knew I was bleeding. It was just a scratch, though, so I didn't bother shifting to heal it, having burned through enough mojo as it was. Speaking of which . . . I took a shallow draught of Pittsburgh's steel-corrupted power, careful to pull just a little this time. I'd woken up this morning with a queasy stomach and a bit of a headache as it was, having taken so much from the Node last night to change the wards. Tomorrow I was gonna feel like I'd gotten run over by Puny in his snake form.

"Can you shift into anything?"

"You mean like turn into a fly and spy on people?"

"What?" Oz asked, clearly amazed. "You can do that?"

I grinned, pushing through the humans on the sidewalk, feeling Loretta's magic swirling around me as they stared at her small shape, fixated. "No. I can only change in my human form, and I'm limited to what I can sculpt in my head. Like I can't look at a picture of Marilyn Monroe and become her. But I can make myself taller, or stronger, or fatter. I can make my limbs longer or shorter. That sort of stuff. I've gotten pretty good over the years." Modesty had long ceased to be a strong suit of mine.

He cocked his head at me, skirting an elderly woman who didn't notice he was trying to get around her. "How old are you?"

"I've been a jinni for nine hundred and ninety-nine years," I said, mostly answering his question. I didn't count my human years, not after the vastness of the curse.

He shook his head, marveling. "Wow."

"Yeah."

"And what do you look like normally?"

I waved my hand, Vanna White style, down my body. "What you see is what you get."

"But you look human."

I nodded. We were at the car. I realized I was hungry. I also needed pants and Oz needed his shirt back, so I reached into the little space behind my car seat and pulled out my emergency Romper Stash.

"Wanna get a hot dog?" I asked, hoping to change the subject. I bent over to pull up my old blue romper. Oz's shirt was so big I could get the sleeveless garment pulled up over my boobs without giving him another show.

"Yes, I'm starving. But how can you look human? The

creature Tamina's grandmother showed me was made of smoke and fire. You're . . . fleshy."

His eyes flicked to where I was bent over, undoubtedly exposing a little skin, and he blushed, pulling his eyes back up immediately like some kind of Boy Scout.

I unbuttoned his shirt and threw it to him, then grabbed a pair of flip-flops from my spare clothes bag. When he had his shirt back on, I locked up the car and indicated he should follow me down the street. "Sorry, buddy, that's the one question I can't answer."

"Why not?"

I glared at him. "I can't answer."

"That makes no sense." His mouth puckered, lines forming in his brow as he scrunched up his face. We walked past the little shops and restaurants that lined Braddock Street, till we hit D's Dawgs.

Like a lot of the reviving Rust Belt towns straddling the Midwest, Pittsburgh was getting a lot better, especially food-wise. But it still did crappy food beautifully, taking things like hot dogs very seriously. After a fight like that, I was definitely getting something with French fries on top of it.

"My poor scientist Master," I said as he opened the door of the restaurant for me. "You're going to have to realize one thing really quickly or you'll drive us both nuts."

"What?" he asked.

I waited till a waitress had sat us down with menus and I'd ordered a Coke. Oz ordered a water, but he was looking at me, clearly waiting for my answer.

I waited till she walked away. "None of this makes any sense," I explained patiently, leaning over the table toward him. "You've taken the red pill, Neo. You've followed the White Rabbit down its hole. You've made your choice.

"And nothing is going to make any sense for a while. At least, not until you relearn what *sense* means here, in your new world."

My Master's Adam's apple bobbed as he absorbed what I'd said.

The waitress came to take our order. We sat in silence throughout the meal, his brow furrowed in thought.

Then I took him to formally meet my friends, who would hopefully convince him to release me.

That or try to kill him a few more times, as only the best friends would.

Chapter Eight

On cue, I had to stop two daggers and a wisp garrote from maiming Ozan as soon as my friends caught a glimpse of me wearing his shirt.

"We gave you a cantaloupe!" Rachel shrieked, much to Ozan's bemusement. I shot her a dirty look, shaking my head to warn her from giving away my secrets.

"I had to shapeshift," I said, holding up my hands palm-forward in a placating gesture. "I ruined my clothes."

Charlie's eyebrow rose. A consummate professional, I almost never ruined clothes anymore, except under dire circumstances.

"Bugbear," I explained. His eyebrows rose farther.

"Where?" he asked.

"Frick Park. Right in Regent's Square. The Exterminators on the scene were in over their heads and they Called. We answered. Oz here got a crash course in supernatural-human relations." I pointed at my Master, who was wandering around Purgatory like he was at an art gallery. Or a zoo. Charlie and Yulia moved closer to me as Rachel kept an eye on Oz.

"A bugbear? In Regent's Square?" asked Charlie, white eyes wide.

"Believe me, we were all surprised."

"And it was on its own?" asked Yulia.

I nodded, shrugging as I did so to indicate I thought it was weird, too. There was always someone stupid enough to bring something like a bugbear Sideways, but such morons were incredibly rare and they usually at least *tried* to control whatever they brought.

"Whoever Called it probably got eaten." Yulia's fatalism never waned.

Charlie's brow furrowed. "Well, I'll check with Sid. The bugbear had to come from Sideways, so he may know who brought it over."

"Let me know what he says." Sid, Bertha's uncle, lived under a Bridge that went directly Sideways, the usual portal used by anyone trying to Call something as big as a bugbear.

"Will do," said Charlie, his gaze turning inward as he stroked his pointed Puck chin.

"How is he?" Yulia asked, sidling closer as she pointed to my new Master.

I knew she didn't mean how he was coping, but how he was behaving. "He's easy. Hasn't tried any funny business. But I was right, he *really* doesn't understand our relationship." What I meant was that he didn't know how much he could make me do, but she could translate.

"Good." Her always-grim Slavic voice was extra grim. She knew as well as I that Oz's wonderful ignorance wouldn't last.

Ozan was standing in front of our intricate Victorian bar, long since stained black. Red accents were lacquered into its intricately worked surface. The back-bar was from the same old-fashioned set, but it had been embellished by Charlie's favorite pastime...taxidermy.

Crows wearing top hats brandished tiny canes, while squirrels in tuxes played eternal hands of poker. A deer's open mouth also functioned as a bottle opener, and a set of rhesus monkeys held liquor bottles upside down, serving as the creepiest rack and pour system ever seen.

There was a ton of other taxidermy around the place, all blending with the overall theme of Purgatory, which was "early gothic circus from hell." A giant red-and-black striped circus tent hung from the ceiling and down the walls of the whole club, allowing Charlie to decorate with other examples of his work, such as a sloth wearing a sequined leotard and hanging from a trapeze.

Besides all the stuffed stuff, Purgatory was mostly dominated by the sort of stage normally found in a strip joint, with a runway that led to another circular platform in the center of the room. There we could set up a mic, or a portable pole, or a jinni-size glass lamp for bathing in champagne, depending on the act.

"This place is... interesting," Ozan said, staring with trepidation at the looming figure of a polar bear wearing a tutu and a monocle.

Charlie gave him a chilly grin, made chillier by his pale stare. "Thank you. I do the animals myself. Now, why don't you tell us about yourself?" He indicated the barstools and we all took a seat, Charlie taking his place behind the bar to serve.

"Well," Ozan said, warily eyeing the people who kept trying to kill him. "Like I told Lyla, I'm a cultural anthropologist. I was part of a research team working for the government on a study of violence against displaced people."

Rachel rolled her eyes, white against her dark skin. Today she was wearing a black caftan done all in sequins, her wig a sleek golden bob and her makeup smoky and shimmering.

"Boring," she yawned. "Lyla told us this bit."

Luckily Ozan didn't bother to wonder when I'd told them, but I shot Rach another warning look.

"Oh, okay," he said. "So what do you want to know?"

"Where are you from, boy?" Rachel said, leaning forward. "Who are your people?"

"I grew up all over," Ozan said. "My dad was in the service. But as an adult I've mostly lived in Chicago. That's where I went to school..."

I sat back, sipping an old-fashioned Charlie had made for me. He listened as Ozan shared with my friends the same story he'd told me last night about his background and how he'd learned of his Magi inheritance. Charlie also mixed Yulia's and Rachel's favorite drinks, pointedly ignoring Ozan till I gave him a look. With a sigh Charlie pulled out a can of PBR and placed it in front of my new Master, not even bothering to open it. Then he poured himself a generous dram of whiskey.

"So you want to find this girl?" Yulia asked.

Ozan nodded. "Her people were family to me. And she's just turned seventeen."

Charlie and I exchanged looks. He'd been ten when priests had plucked him from his parents to be entered by the gods. I'd been fourteen, and engaged to be married, when I'd made my devil's bargain and wound up a jinni.

Seventeen was practically ancient for bad shit to happen to you, in our books.

"Tell us what happened," Charlie said to Oz, who did. The story was identical to the one he'd told me, and he pulled out Tamina's picture as he'd done before. My friends passed it around, studying it, and it was his turn to watch them.

"Can I ask something?" he asked, as Charlie passed the photo to Rachel, who gave a soft *tsk* at the sight of the girl.

"Of course," said Charlie, although Yulia looked distinctly less benevolent.

"What are you all? I mean...you all look human. Like that woman we just met...Loretta? But Lyla said she was a siren, so I'm assuming you all are something..."

I blinked at Oz. Loretta had looked hot but she had also definitely looked like a siren—complete with gills and nictitating membranes. And Yulia's wisps were quivering around her like giant irritated ferrets, so I really couldn't understand why he thought she looked human...

Then it clicked. For one of us, at least. "Ask her to make you See, son," Rachel said, quietly. I groaned. Duh.

"But I thought Magi *can* See?" he said, brow furrowing.

"You can See jinn," I said. We'd discussed whether Oz could See, but I'd forgotten. Now I had my answer. "So while you're not entirely blind—your Magi blood gives you enough Sight to See through light glamours, like we have on Purgatory—you were raised totally human so you don't have *full* Sight."

"I could See the bugbear," he said.

I sighed. "Yeah, bugbears don't really bother trying to glamour themselves. They're dumb. And they eat everything."

"Just ask her to make you See," Yulia growled at Oz, cutting his constant questioning short with her usual impatience. She wasn't a big fan of humans at the best of times, and especially not of humans who Bound her bestie.

"Um, can you make me See?"

"Yes," I said. "But you have to tell me to do it, not ask if I can. I need big magic for this."

Nonplussed, Ozan rephrased his question as a command. "Make me See," he said.

I passed a small hand over his face, pulling on the Deep Magic. He blinked once...twice...we waited...

"What the fuck?" he yelled, jumping up from his bar seat. He stared around the room in horror, his eyes flicking around as if unsure where to settle. He yelped when they moved to Yulia, his eyes wide.

Then they sparked. Like, for real.

"Shit!" I shouted, lunging for him, but I was too late.

Ozan hit the ground hard, passed out cold.

Yulia sauntered over to him, nudging him with her booted foot and grinning up at us. "I do have that effect on men."

After raising her glass at the prostrate form before her, she drained it in one gulp.

I felt like we were reenacting the final scene in *The Wizard of Oz*, with all her friends surrounding Dorothy while she says, "And you were there, and you were there, and you were there..."

Only none of us were Oz's friends and he hadn't woken up from a nightmare.

He was living it.

"Will he be okay?" Rachel asked, as Oz started to stir.

"Who gives a shit?" Yulia said. "Hopefully he dies."

"Shush," said Rachel. "You don't mean that."

"Yes, she does," Charlie said. "And she's right. He Bound Lyla, and with only a week left of her curse."

"And he doesn't even know what that means." Rachel rounded on the rest of us crowded into my dressing room, where we'd carried Ozan after he collapsed, a victim of what we affectionately knew as over-Sight. Suddenly gifted with true Sight of the world that existed Sideways from theirs, most humans had a little trouble accommodating their new vision and their little brains shorted out. "He's just doing what he thinks he has to, to save a *child*. And y'all have been so busy trying to kill him you haven't even told him what he really *has* done. I bet if he knew..."

"Knew what?" Oz croaked from the head of my chaise longue. He opened his eyes and sat up, only to take one look at Yulia and collapse back onto the chaise.

"What the hell happened?" he asked, eyes tightly shut.

Rachel took his hand, her dark skin very dark against his normally pale flesh, which had gone almost albino with shock.

"Lyla gave you the Sight," she said. "Until now you've been seeing our natural glamours. But now you're Seeing everyone as they really are."

He cracked open one eye. "You look the same," he said to the drag queen.

"I'm human," she said. "A psychic, but human. Mostly."

"Mostly?" he asked. I could tell he was focusing on Rachel while he got his bearings.

"Psychics are usually humans with a little fey in their background. I probably have a fairy grandfather, or something."

"Oh." Ozan accepted this tidbit of information, opening both eyes and shifting them slowly to Yulia.

"What are you?"

I knew that Yulia no longer looked like the tall, androgynous blonde he'd first met. He was Seeing her in her true form, that of a wisp. Just as long and slender, but with a bright, enticing glow, the lines of her body faded so that she appeared made of light.

As he grew used to her, she'd glow less brightly, as she did for us. He'd see Yulia within the light. But until he adjusted, she'd blind him.

"I'm a will o' the wisp," she said. "I lead men into the swamps and drown them, feeding off their vital energy to fuel my magic."

His pale face managed to whiten further. "Do you really?"

She grinned at him, showing off her long, thin fangs. "Not so much anymore. But I'd make an exception for you."

I kicked her in the shin, and his eyes shifted to me.

"You look the same, too," he said. "Like a human, but with black fire for hair and eyes that glow red sometimes."

I nodded. "You Saw me from the beginning. That's your gift, as a Magi: the power to See jinn as they truly are."

"But the other jinn are made of fire and smoke. Why do you look different?"

Unable to speak of my curse, I looked helplessly at Charlie.

"That's what you need to know," said my oldest friend. "Lyla wasn't born jinni."

Oz looked at me. "What? How?"

Unable even to acknowledge my curse in front of my Master, I sat, mute.

"She can't talk about it," Rachel explained. "Well, not to you. Not to her Master."

"You're part of her curse," Yulia growled, flashing him those fangs again. He gulped.

"How can I be part of her curse?" Oz said. "I just met her and she said she's been alive for nine hundred and ninety-nine years…"

"She's been a *jinni* for nine hundred and ninety-nine years," Charlie explained. "Before that she was human."

"Human?" Oz's eyes met mine, his gaze racing over me as if trying to strip me of the Fire surrounding me at all times.

"Yes. That's why her natural shape isn't pure Fire, as were the born jinn shown to you by Tamina's tribe. You See her as she is, a human being cursed to be a jinni."

77

"Cursed? How was she cursed?"

I hated this. Hated having my story told by another. Hated the curse that bound my tongue as thoroughly as it bound my body. This was my story—the agony I'd lived through. It should be mine to tell.

Charlie took my hand, sensing my consternation. "Lyla was born to a wealthy merchant family, at around the time the Mongol hordes were making a nuisance of themselves. Her father, wanting to keep his business interests safe, promised her in marriage to a famously brutal Mongol warlord. She was fourteen."

I lowered my head, not wanting to see the pity in Ozan's eyes.

"Her father employed a Magi, as did all men of wealth in that place at that time. He was powerful, and had Bound an incredibly old jinni named Kouros to serve the family."

I shivered, hearing that name. Unbidden, I saw those red eyes before me, that taloned hand reaching for my heart...

"Desperate, Lyla approached Kouros, asking him to help her. She told the jinni she didn't want to be married. She asked that she no longer be a woman, to be bought and sold like an animal. But she didn't specify what she *did* want to be.

"So Kouros made her a jinni, like him. No longer a woman, not technically. And he cursed to her to live a thousand years like that."

"Why a curse? And why a thousand years?"

Charlie took a sip of his Scotch before replying. "Magic has its own laws, and one of them is that curses cost less power than more permanent solutions. The gods only know what it took for Kouros just to curse Lyla, but we know he hasn't been seen on the human plane since shortly after he made her a jinni. We figure he didn't have enough mojo to turn her into a jinni permanently or fully, just enough for a curse."

"Why did he do it, then? That seems like a pretty extreme thing to do, just to mess with someone."

Charlie and I exchanged glances. That was one question neither of us had ever figured out. And at this point in the game, we hoped we never would.

"We don't know why," was all Charlie said in response.

"But she's almost free, you said?"

"No. She's not almost free," Charlie said. "Not as long as you have her Bound."

"What?"

"That's the condition of the curse," Charlie explained, keeping his voice neutral. "She has to be unBound at the thousand-year anniversary of its being cast. Otherwise she'll be a jinni for another thousand years."

"Oh," Ozan said, his voice small.

"Yes, 'oh,'" said Yulia, her tone harsh, mocking. "Now you see what you have done?"

Ozan sat quietly for a full minute, looking between me and his big hands resting on his lap. I could see tattoos peeking out at his wrist, and another vintage anchor decorated the fleshy space between the thumb and pointer finger of his right hand.

"I do see," he said, looking up at me. "But I can't do this alone. And I *have* to do this, I *have* to repay my debt. They were my family."

Ozan's voice vibrated with passion and we all shifted uncomfortably. We understood debt, and what it was like to live with a true debt, a debt of the soul, gone unpaid.

As if he'd come to some sort of agreement with himself, Ozan looked at me, his face set. "I'm sorry. I don't want to hurt you and I don't want to keep you cursed. But I want my life back, like none of this ever happened. I need to find Tamina, send her back to her family, so I can forget. And to do that, I need help. I know nothing of this world..." His eyes crept to Yulia, darting back to me before she could blind him.

"I hate myself for using you like this, but I don't know what else to do," he said, his voice quiet. For me, only. "Please, give me another option."

"A bargain," I croaked. It was about all I could get out before my curse clamped my lips shut again.

He looked up, hopeful. "A bargain?"

"Yes," Charlie said. "An offer from all of us. If you unBind Lyla, we'll help you. All of us. Lyla, me, Rachel, Yulia, Bertha... I'm sure other people at Purgatory will help, too. Trip and Trap, Trey... we'll all help you. We just want Lyla back."

"You're making this sound like a ransom," said Oz, obviously uncomfortable.

"Well, son, it is," said Charlie. Physically, he appeared younger than Oz, but something about how he said "son" had all of his hundreds of years of experience laced through it. "If you don't let our friend go, she's going to be cursed again. That's not fair."

"Of course it's not," Oz said, but he didn't look like a man who'd seen a clear injustice and was ready to act to fix it. He looked confused. And guilty.

"Are you Immunda?" he asked me suddenly, and my heart thudded in my chest.

"I...," my jinni started to say, as I struggled with her to keep control of my tongue. But I couldn't refuse a direct question.

"No." My voice was clipped. I had to answer, but I didn't have to supply a critical exegesis on the subject.

"But you're not pureblood." Oz's eyes were narrowed in

thought, undoubtedly putting two and two together to make slavery.

"No," I said.

"I'm not sure what this has to do with anything," Charlie began, but Oz interrupted.

"That's what you did when you reset the wards. And why you were stronger even than that snake thing. You're neither Immunda nor pureblood, so you can use the Node you said was so powerful."

Charlie swore, Yulia sneakily tried to garrote Oz (my jinni caught the wisp without even trying), and Rachel looked confused. But I understood what was happening. My Master had grown teeth.

"I don't want to do this, but sometimes things are bigger than we are," he said. "And I swear to God I'll let you go the *second* we find Tamina. But I *will* find her. She's just a child and she's alone and I can't do this by myself. You said yourself you're stronger Bound to me. We'll find her faster this way and *then* I can let you go. But until she's found…"

"Until then, you belong to me."

His words dropped like a bomb in the otherwise silent room. Charlie paled, Yulia bared her teeth in a snarl, Rachel fanned herself, and Oz sat, looking determined and guilty at the same time.

I felt about six thousand emotions, most of them located on the rage continuum, but my jinni wouldn't let me castrate him or peel off his tattooed skin to wear as a raincoat. I tried to find purchase among all that anger, to reclaim myself, but all I could feel was my rage and my jinni and my bondage.

"Who died?" came a new voice, from the door to Purgatory.

It was Loretta. Her blonde curls were ratted, her face pale, and her siren's third eyelids were blinking overtime, a nervous habit she'd had to work on suppressing when I taught her to dance. Charlie's already glum expression turned even dourer. Exterminators were never the bearers of good news, and, despite our long friendship, Loretta was no exception.

I obviously hadn't rapped hard enough at that wooden skull of mine, because this situation wasn't turning out to be any kind of cinch.

Chapter Nine

So who are we looking for?" Ozan asked skeptically, eyeing the copper-roofed cairn upon which was etched "Frick Park." It'd taken some convincing to get Oz to believe that *this* Frick Park, which looked like a wild nature reserve, was the same Frick Park that had just played temporary home to a bugbear.

I kept telling him it was a big park. But he was apparently deaf as well as an enslaver of (not-so-) young ladies.

"His name's Sid," I grumbled, checking the lacings on the hiking boots I'd put on after we'd gone back to my place for a much-needed quick change. "He's a troll."

"I'm assuming you mean like Big Bertha, and not a jerk on the Internet."

I stood, huffing at his lame attempt at a joke. "He's actually Bertha's great-uncle."

"And why are we visiting Sid the troll?"

Zipping up my jacket, I frowned at him. "We're trying to kill two birds with one stone. Loretta wants me to find out who brought that bugbear over *and* find out where it went, since they somehow managed to lose it. But Sid also knows everything that comes over *and* everything that's happening in Pittsburgh. So we can ask him about Loretta's problem and if he's heard rumors of Tamina's whereabouts, at the same time. I just wish he would answer his stupid phone."

"Trolls have phones?"

I glowered at my Master. "Here's Random Supernatural Rule Number Forty-Nine: If it's got thumbs it's got a phone."

Oz gave me a long look. "I'm sorry I have to keep you Bound. But I swear it's only till we find Tamina. Then I'll free you."

I took a deep breath, reminding myself that antagonizing him wouldn't help. Angry Masters were nasty Masters.

"Okay," I said shortly.

"Even Loretta said it was for the best."

I would have given anything to throttle him. But he was right. In the fight with the bugbear, Loretta had obviously noticed I could do the impossible: use the Deep Magic of our steel-stained Node now that I was Bound. And the Exterminators wanted that bugbear taken care of pronto. With their two best fighters out of commission after the Frick Park incident, I was the strongest thing in Pittsburgh.

Loretta had been happy to agree Oz shouldn't unBind me until I found his missing girl . . . if I took care of their Exterminator problems first.

Oz had been very evidently thrilled to have another voice backing up his Master plan, and he'd promised her and everyone else in the room it was just for now. Charlie had taken me aside and reminded me that (a) I had no choice in the matter and (b) it was smarter to play nice with Oz, hoping he'd stick to his word, than piss him off. I'd already known both of those things, so we'd formally "agreed" to Oz's terms.

Although it wasn't really agreement if, technically, I didn't have any real choice.

"Yes," I said, through gritted teeth. "Loretta was keen on your plan. So let's get going and find Tamina quickly . . . for the girl's sake," I amended, managing a faint smile at him.

And before you realize how cool it is to be a Magi. I kept that thought to myself.

Oz managed to keep his trap shut as we started down the park's steep paths. I knew my science-minded Master wouldn't be able to maintain such quiet for long, however, and soon enough he was pestering me again.

"Why don't you tell me more about Purgatory? Why it's so hard to find. It's a nice bar and the dancers are pretty good."

"Pretty good?" I said, feigning outrage. He winked at me, an act of flirtation that I chose to ignore. "Well, we don't make it easy for humans."

"And how do you do that? I know it's magic, but . . ."

The bright fall day was just crisp enough for my breath to hang in the air as I answered. "Warding, mostly. Wards make humans not want to approach, unless they have a bit of the Sight, like Rachel, or they're pulled towards something, like you were to me. Purgatory is also a bit Sideways, mostly for space purposes, although just a bit."

Oz frowned at me. " 'Sideways'? What the hell is that?"

"You're Irish," I said. "You've probably heard of Faerie."

He nodded. "Yeah, my dad's mom was from Cork. She talked about the Little People."

"That's right, although I'm talking about the place more than the people."

"Oh, right," he said, his brow furrowing as he thought back. "I remember them telling me stories about the fey living underground, sort of? But not?"

I nodded. "Yeah. Well, that's Sideways. All purely magical beings have the ability to go Sideways. It's called different things in your mythologies...the demonic plane, Faerie, Olympus, whatever. A place that's here, but not."

"And Purgatory is Sideways?"

"Only a little bit. If you were a human who bumbled upon Purgatory's door without any Sight whatever, you'd walk down the stairs and into a very small basement. Unless you were led by the hand, of course, by a pure supernatural or someone like me or you—a human who is a bit extra."

We walked in silence for a while. This densely wooded part of the park gave the illusion of real wilderness as long as one ignored the nice wide dirt tracks and the occasional park benches. When Ozan finally spoke again, his voice was soft. Hesitant.

"Is that what I am, then?" he asked. I cast him a confused glance.

"Huh?"

"Human. Am I human?"

I laughed. "Is that what you're worried about? Well, have no fear. You're totally human. Just with a bit extra, like I said."

"But how? Why?"

Thinking through the best way to answer, I finally opened my arms wide, gesturing to our surroundings. "It's the natural law," I said. "Take what you know of life, and add magic to it. Magic is part of the world, but I guess it's like the God particle, or dark matter, or whatever they're calling it these days. It's all around humans, even if they can't see it.

"But magic is like anything else in nature. It has its own laws. And for every action there has to be a reaction. For every sheep there's a wolf. And for every wolf there's a lion."

Oz frowned at me. "You sound like a fortune cookie."

I grinned. "Yeah, well, I'm a belly dancer. You're lucky I'm not full hippie."

"I dunno about that. I've seen your room."

"That's Bohemian chic, you Philistine."

"Whatever, I still don't have a clue what you're saying. Where did jinn come from, first of all? Are they all like you? Cursed?"

I shook my head. "No. I'm the only one like me."

Oz blinked at that. He was a smart guy and I could see the wheels of his brain churning over the implications of my experience.

"Wow," he said, after a bit. "That must be lonely."

"It is," I said, sounding curt even to my own ears. I moderated my tone. "Or it was. Now it's not so bad. But to answer your question, jinn are normally born, not made, as I was."

We were walking steadily downward, away from cultivated grass. The path was still wide and clean, but other signs of man like signs and benches were becoming fewer and farther between.

"But where did jinn come from?"

"I don't know. They have their own origination myth and it accords with the one I was taught as a child, which was that Allah made the jinn out of smoke and fire, while he made humans out of earth. They leave Allah out of it, of course, but they also trace their lineage back to a single being, who forged himself out of the heat of the universe."

"Did this jinni-Adam have an Eve?" Oz asked.

"Yes. According to their legends, that first jinni created his own mate—Called her into being and Bound her to him. It was the first Binding, and the spell you spoke is supposed to be the same one he shouted into the darkness to find her."

"Wow," Oz said. He looked sorta like he might explode.

"I think your nose is twitching, you're thinking so hard," I observed.

"This is just so cool," he replied, in the excited voice of a child with a new toy. "I mean, I'm an anthropologist. To hear there's an entirely new world out there, one that I can study..."

"First of all," I said, "It's not new. We've existed alongside humanity forever, Oz. Literally forever. Which leads me to number two..." My voice trailed off as I stepped onto and then over a huge tree that had fallen across the path. Oz hopped nimbly over, and I envied him his height. At five-four, I'd been tallish for a woman of my time and place. Now I was definitively short, especially next to my new Master, who stood well over six feet.

"There's a reason you only just found out about us," I said. "We keep ourselves secret, on purpose. A lot of us prey on humanity, in some capacity or other. And most of us are too vulnerable to your steel, your iron. If humanity knew about us, we'd be destroyed.

"So," I said, choosing my next words carefully so he understood the importance of what I was saying, "we guard our secrets zealously. And by zealously, I mean we greet threats to our secrets with death. If you try to publish a paper or something about us, they will come after you. And I will have to protect you. Which means they'll destroy us both."

Oz raised his eyebrows. "By 'they,' do you mean the Exterminators? So they're like some kind of secret police for you people?"

"We're not people, Oz. Never expect human mercy or logic or reasonable behavior from one of us. If there's any hint that you'd betray your heritage, not only would everything Other that knew your intent come after you, but so would other Magi."

"But I thought you said Magi were human..."

"Magi are Magi," I said, cutting him off. "Yes, you're human. But every time, Magi trumps humanity."

Oz fell silent, processing that last bit of info until he spoke again. More questions, of course. Having a scientist for a Master obviously entailed a lot of talking.

"So if jinn were created out of smoke and fire, what created Magi?"

I shrugged. "Evolution, I guess. Jinn are powerful. Some born jinn are as powerful unBound as I am Bound. Nature abhors such unfair advantages. So voilà...Magi emerged to keep jinn under control."

"Is that the official story?"

I grinned. "No. The official jinni mythology is that humanity, seeing the glory of the jinn, were jealous. They raged at their own gods until their gods took pity on human weakness and made some of them Magi. But that's like my theory, only the jinn stripped out the word *evolution* and put in the word *god*."

He laughed. "Isn't that what all religion does? Try to explain what science either hasn't or can't?"

I shrugged. "I'm no philosopher."

The look he gave me was sharp. "Stop being so self-deprecating," he said, probably not realizing I would literally have to stop being self-deprecating now. "And tell me...what are you, then?"

I cocked my head at him. "What do you mean?"

"You say you're a human made into a jinni. So which are you? Human or jinni?"

I shrugged. "I dunno. Neither, I guess. Not anymore. But we're almost there."

I turned onto a narrow path that led sharply downward off the trail we'd been using.

"Watch your step. It gets a bit treacherous from here on out."

*   *   *

We half-hiked, half-slid down a steep hill toward the wide, marshy plain that led toward our destination. Oz struggled gamely behind me, his upturned nose wrinkling as cold water undoubtedly rushed into his boots. He wasn't exactly dressed for the wilderness, but he didn't complain.

When he realized our destination, he groaned. I couldn't help but smile.

"They really do live under bridges?"

"Yep. Humans get most things mostly right about us," I said, casting him a sideways glance. He shook his head.

"Amazing."

We were slogging our way toward the Parkway bridge that loomed over Frick Park. The sounds of traffic and occasional huge piles of slag, signs of Pittsburgh's industrial past, marred the otherwise beautiful landscape. But I couldn't complain too much about such things. After all, it was all that cold steel that made Pittsburgh a haven for one with my unique heritage.

"So what do trolls do?"

"They eat humans who ask too many questions," I replied.

"Very funny. I'm serious."

"So am I. I can't lie to you, remember? They do prefer to eat people."

Ozan stopped short. "Um..."

"Don't worry. They rarely do it anymore. And you're safe with me."

Ozan caught up with me with a few strides of his long legs. "So what do they spend their time doing now that they can't eat people?"

I didn't comment on the specificity of his question, although I certainly noticed it. He was learning, damn it.

"They still live under bridges. But they feed on deer nowa-

days, mostly. Of which there is no shortage, around here."
If there weren't trolls, all of Pennsylvania would probably be
drowning in whitetails.

"And why are we visiting one?"

"Living under bridges, they get a lot of supernatural foot
traffic, so they hear a lot. I'm hoping Sid knows who brought
over the bugbear, since using the Bridge is the only way to
bring something that big over. Sid also loves to gossip, and living under our main Bridge he gets a lot of opportunity to do
so. He may know where we can start looking for your Tamina."

"That's all great, but what's the significance of a bridge that
crosses a park?"

"It may just cross a park for humans, but not for supernaturals. Bridges have their own magic," I explained. "And don't
ask why. I have no idea. I guess magic likes a metaphor. But
oftentimes bridges serve as a conduit to Sideways—the place
your ancestors might have called Faerie."

"So Sideways is an actual place?"

"It can be, yes. If you go all the way Sideways, you're basically in a world parallel to our own, that only magicals can
find—purely supernatural creatures or humans with magic,
like you. That's where the majority of pure supernatural creatures live nowadays, because humans and their steel are everywhere. Supernaturals don't like steel. So yes, Sideways is a
place.

"But Sideways is also…I dunno how to explain it. The
route, as well as the place. So you move Sideways to get Sideways, and you can have pockets of Sideways. Big pockets, like
where Purgatory's located, or little pockets that you can use
like they're actual pockets—little magical closets where you
store stuff. I keep my swords Sideways, for example."

"This makes no sense," Oz said. "You realize that, right?"

I grimaced, remembering my own steep learning curve when I'd been cursed to live as a jinni. "No, it doesn't. But I already warned you: magic has its own rules. You'll learn."

"So can anyone go all the way Sideways, like to a parallel world?" he asked.

"Yes, but only with the help of a Bridge," I said. "Something pure and powerful, like a sidhe Lord or a really powerful jinni, can propel themselves directly Sideways. But something with that much power is rare. And they don't usually enter the human plane at all; they prefer to stay Sideways permanently."

"And bridges always lead Sideways?"

"Not always, but often."

Ozan shook his head as if trying to clear it. "There's so much to learn."

I jumped over a big puddle, landing lithely on the other side. Oz tried to follow my lead, but landed short, his big booted feet splashing my gray skinny jeans with mud. I gave him a dirty look and he winced.

"Sorry," he said.

I flicked something globular and gross off of my thigh. "It is a lot," I said. "But you'll absorb it all. You're part of this world now, whether you like it or not."

Oz fell silent for a moment and only then did I notice how quiet everything had gotten. Too quiet.

"Maybe when we're done here," he continued, "we can sit down and talk. I could buy you dinner. You can tell me more about all this. I don't understand how your power's different, for example..."

I lifted my hand to shush him.

"Something's wrong. Stay here..."

"Huh?" he said, ignoring me and keeping to my heels.

"Quiet," I said. I crouched down and he followed suit. Lifting my nose, I breathed deeply.

"No birds calling. And no fires," I explained in a whisper. "Trolls always keep a fire burning..."

"Stay here," I repeated, creeping forward. I knew it was useless, however. Sure enough, Ozan stuck to me like a burr.

We were getting close to one of the concrete struts holding up the Bridge, but everything was wrong. No smell of fire, or roasting meat. Not even a whiff of troll droppings or the musky scent of their border markings.

And no deep rumble from Sid, an old friend. There was no sneaking up on a troll in his own territory, and I'd been expecting a greeting for the last few minutes.

We crept all the way up to the concrete strut, but still there was no sign of my friend or his brothers.

"Something was here," Oz whispered, pointing at the old oil drums standing at odd intervals, their interiors darkened from fire.

Sid's tribal marks were also still there, graffitied in spray paint on the concrete of the Bridge and carved into the few trees that grew in this boggy patch of the park. But there was no sign of the trolls who had made them.

"Maybe they left?" Oz said.

I shook my head. "Trolls are territorial. Sid's family has been in this park since before it was America. There's no way they just up and left."

Oz inspected one of the markings, a complicated tribal rune that declared this property as troll territory. "Well, if they're not here and they wouldn't leave..."

"Either something made them go, or they're dead."

"Could they have just died out?"

I shook my head. "I was here a few weeks ago, with Bertha. Everything was fine. Whatever happened was recent."

"Well," he said, using a Very Reasonable Voice. "What could move or kill a troll?"

I frowned. "Not a lot. They're pretty tough. It would have to be something pretty badass..."

"Lyla," Oz said sharply. "Over there."

I looked to where he was pointing, feeling my face break out into a wide smile.

"Well, that takes care of that." The head of the bugbear was sitting on top of a little mound, one of its mandibles torn off and its antennae in disarray. Considering there was no body attached to the head, I felt confident we could report back to Loretta that the bugbear was dead.

"Yeah, but what killed it?" Oz asked.

That wiped the smile off my face. I looked around, the hair on my arms prickling.

"Maybe Sid?" I said, doubt making my voice lilt into a question. Trolls were tough, but bugbears were too. And there was still no sign of Sid.

"Sid!" I shouted, not wanting to walk any farther into that wide, empty field until I could see my friend. "Sid!"

The ground beneath my feet rumbled ominously, shutting me up.

"What the...," Oz began, but I cut him off with a sharp look.

The earth rumbled again, definitely shifting under my feet. From the way Oz swayed, he was getting the same treatment. But I noticed the trees around us didn't move at all.

"Oz," I whispered, reaching out to him with my left hand. "You need to take my hand. But don't move otherwise."

For once, undoubtedly seeing my expression, he had no

questions. He reached for me silently, and I grasped his fingers tight in mine. At the same time, I reached into my very own pocket of Sideways, calling to me the Turkish saber I kept there for just such emergencies.

Also for sexy dances, as I was that sort of girl.

Appearing as it did out of thin air, the deadly curve of my beloved kilij made Ozan gasp.

"Don't move," I repeated, but he already had—just the slight shift of his weight away from me.

The rumble beneath our feet increased, causing us both to shuffle to keep our footing.

"Fodden!" I shouted, as the first skeletal black-clawed hand broached the surface of the dirt, slashing at our legs.

Chapter Ten

The hand that had grabbed hold of my ankle was already flying through the air, cut off neatly at the wrist. More hands were quickly clawing their way out of the earth, however, reaching for Oz and me.

I swept a strong arc with my armed right hand, pulling Oz closer to me with my left. He let me take the lead, since I had the sword, stumbling toward me on the still-shifting ground.

Jerking him hard, I pulled us both backward when the earth crumbled ominously under his boot to reveal a gaping, many-toothed maw. The teeth closed on nothing, but I nearly fell as Ozan's weight crashed into me.

I felt a hand grab my calf and then another wrap around my foot. I swept low and hard with the kilij, its razor-sharp edge cutting off both offending limbs, then a third that was groping up Ozan's leg.

"What the hell?" he shouted, over the din of shifting earth and the noisy squawk of the mouths appearing in the dirt around us.

"Fodden!" I repeated, kicking one hand away from his shin as I cut off another, jerking us back another step or two as I felt the telltale shifting of the ground underneath my feet. A gaping maw appeared where we'd been standing a few seconds earlier, snapping on empty air. It opened again and a long black tongue snaked out of its depths, reaching toward us.

"Rude!" I shouted at it, slicing off the tongue and a few more grasping claws for good measure. I inhaled sharply as one long-limbed hand got past my sword, scoring my ribs with a merciless slash that cut to the bone.

Ozan came to my rescue then, grabbing my sword from me and chopping the offending fodden arm off at the elbow, before it could get in another strike. I nodded my thanks, letting go of my bleeding side to reach Sideways for my other sword, thankful that the finale of the belly dance act I used them for required me to have two.

More hands were popping out of the ground all around us. This wasn't just a rogue fodden crossed over from the Other Realm by accident; this was an infestation. Keeping Ozan's free hand tight in my grip, I slashed at the hands reaching for us, shuffling us around to stay out of the way of the incredible appearing mouths, as I pulled, hard, on Pittsburgh's raw magic.

"Hold on!" I shouted, even as I sighted up the path, away from the sodden terrain near the Bridge and the fodden who'd made it their home. Focusing on a patch of dry land, I took a deep breath, cutting away the hands that had managed to wrap themselves around my nether regions and Oz's. As I exhaled I pulled again on the steel-stained power pulsing through the ground at my feet and I reached . . .

My magic found root in the dry patch just as the ground shifted at my feet, beginning to crumble as the mouth of the fodden underneath us opened. But before we toppled into its gaping maw, we were hurtling through the air as if on an invisible reel, pulled from where we stood to the patch of dry ground where I'd embedded my magic. Ozan cried out as I jerked him behind me, clutching tighter to my hand as I pulled us out of harm's way.

We came to a sudden, painful halt at the very spot I'd sighted on, Ozan crashing into me from behind, sending us both flying. I landed hard on the ground, the nasty wound in my side sliding painfully through the mud and dirt, opening it still further. But knowing the fodden would quickly feel our reverberating landing, I woozily climbed to my feet a split second later, looking around for Oz. He, too, was already standing, rubbing his shoulder with a pained expression. I'd probably jerked it nearly out of its socket when I'd pulled him behind me, but it couldn't be helped.

"Come on!" I yelled, grabbing for him. I noticed there was a fodden arm still clenched around a handful of his jeans, stringy ligaments hanging from where it had been ripped off when I reached. I plucked it off of him before we raced up the hill toward my car. I loved my hideous old El Camino, but I'd never been happier to see the ugly bulk of its steel chassis.

I hurled open its long door, pushing Ozan in and through to the passenger side, sliding in not a second too soon behind him. Hundreds of hands of various sizes popped up around the car, reaching for the El Camino but jerking away, smoking, when they came in contact with its steel. I turned the key, throwing us into reverse to pivot around, peeling out onto the paved asphalt of the main road. There I idled just long enough to see the hands waving in the breeze, like the worst flowers ever created, before eventually pulling back down into the ground.

Only then did I pull out of Frick Park and onto the main road, pain starting to seep through my system as my adrenaline faded, letting my hurts make themselves known.

"You're bleeding," Oz said, his face white but his voice steady. I looked down to see the entire front and side of my hoodie was dark red, and the stain was spreading quickly.

"Thank you, Captain Obvious," I said, the jinni in me allowing the slur because it was technically a thank-you and because he *was* being obvious.

He ignored me. "What the hell are fodden?"

"Not supposed to be here," I said, wincing and hissing in pain as I reached to shift down to first.

"You need a hospital," he said. But I shook my head.

"No hospitals. Computers suck," I said, realizing I felt a bit light-headed. I only just managed to pull to the side of the road, putting the car into park as I looked over at him.

"I think maybe you'll have to drive," I said, marveling at how concerned my Master looked as everything went dark.

"No hospitals," I mumbled, feeling pain as a strong arm went under my knees and another under my shoulders. My head lolled on something warm and my eyes shot open as another jolt of pain racked my body. I was staring at the corded muscles of my Master's neck, the tips of various tattoos peeking out from the neckline of his shirt.

"You're home," he said. "But I need your keys."

I shook my head—a mistake. I nearly passed out again but I managed to hang grimly on to consciousness. When I could speak again, I raised my eyes to his strong jaw, clenched with the effort of carrying my weight.

While very much in shape and very much a dancer, I was a belly dancer. Which meant I was built for comfort, not for speed.

"Just take me to the door," I said. He climbed the few steps up to the carriage house and I reached out a hand to touch the brass knocker. The door swung open, recognizing me, and he led me the rest of the way upstairs, stopping so I could do the same thing to our inner door.

I concentrated on bringing my hand back to my chest, rather than just letting it fall. But before cradling it to me, I allowed my traitorous fingers to touch the little anchor in Oz's clavicle, as they'd wanted to do since I'd first seen the damned man.

He took me into the big living room to the right of the entryway, setting me down on the low couch against the wall in that room. I let myself go ahead and flop to the side, making sure it was the one without the enormous bloody cut.

"Do you have a first aid kit?" he asked.

"Kitchen," I replied, woozily. "Under the sink."

I shut my eyes as he left the room, only for a second but it must have been longer as when they jerked open again it was because something horrible and stinging was being pressed against the wound.

"Motherfucker," I hissed, momentarily blinded by the light and pain. Then my eyes focused on Oz's concerned face.

"You really need a doctor," he said, his mouth bowed in a frown. "I can clean this out, but I can't stitch it..."

"Just get it clean," I said, through gritted teeth. "I can do the rest."

Oz shrugged as if to say it was my funeral, swabbing away at the wound. I went ahead and closed my eyes again, clenching them against the pain.

"It's still bleeding like crazy," he said, after what felt like hours of torture but couldn't have been more than ten minutes. "But it's clean. Now what?"

"Now I work my mojo," I said. "Tell me to heal myself."

"Heal yourself, Lyla," he said without hesitation, for once not asking a thousand questions.

At his command my Fire rose inside me, focused on my wound. Taking a deep breath, I steadied myself. If cleaning the wound had hurt, this was going to feel like pure torture. Then I reached deep...

The Node's powerful magic responded beautifully. But it was Pittsburgh magic, which meant it was dirty as sin. I was going to feel this in the morning.

But one extreme magical hangover was better than bleeding out, so I went ahead and pulled, filtering the power even as I shifted...

Concentrating on my wound, I imagined the skin and muscle, the blood vessels and arteries, all knitting together and becoming whole—severed ends reaching for severed ends. My power bloomed, Bound-strong magical channels absorbing the shock of my magic even as they set it to work fixing me.

Ozan's breath rasped in and out a few times as I healed, the hand he'd left resting on my hip from when he'd held me still to clean the wound squeezing me occasionally as something slithered into place, but otherwise he was quiet.

"How's it look?" I gasped, unable to sit up and see it myself while trying to keep the magic on its short leash.

"Good," he said, keeping his voice neutral. "It's almost healed. Just a little way to go."

With one more push I took the wound as close to closing as I could before it was all too much. Feeling the once-familiar buzzing in the base of my neck and my spine that forewarned of imminent systems failure, I shut down my mojo, drawing back from the magic of the ley line beneath us.

I took a few deep breaths before opening my eyes, feeling the oily tang of Pittsburgh's magic settle into my bones. Tomorrow was going to be a bear.

When I finally did open my eyes, I reached a small hand out to my Master. He took it immediately, concern etched across his handsome features.

"Can you please call Charlie," I asked, "and tell him I won't be in tonight?"

"Of course," he said. He brushed the hair from my eyes with gentle fingers. I trembled involuntarily.

"Can I do anything else?" His voice was soft. As if he was genuinely worried; as if I were something other than property.

"You can get me some water," I said. "And some Advil. Advil's in the bathroom cupboard."

He nodded, and I watched him stand, walking toward the door.

"Thank you," I muttered to the sofa, as I laid my cheek down on the rough fabric of the cushion and closed my eyes.

"Now aren't you glad you were Bound, and had that much extra power?" I heard Oz say, from the doorframe.

I tried to give him the finger but I was too tired, and sleep soon swallowed me whole.

Chapter Eleven

Kouros and I were sitting at my dining room table, sharing a plate of cookies and milk as if we were old friends.

"What do you want?" I asked him, but my tone was light. Conversational.

Red eyes peered at me from the black flames of his face. "What do you think I want?"

I picked up a cookie, at the last second remembering to examine it before biting. I set the cookie back when I realized that what had appeared to be chocolate chips had antennae that were waving.

"Why would I know that?" My voice held none of the bitterness I felt toward the creature that had cursed me, a trick of the dream.

The roiling black flames of Kouros's lips split in a smile, revealing the red fire that was his insides. "Because we're a part of each other, little Lyla. You came to me willingly enough once, didn't you?"

I nodded. What he said was true. "But you tricked me."

His Fire flared even darker, making him appear larger. "I gave you a gift. A taste of immortality. Of power. You would be a pile of bones in a dank hole somewhere were it not for me; instead, still you glow."

"You made me a slave," I replied, simply.

Those red eyes flared brighter and I felt that old, remembered pain in my chest. My fingers touched the space between my breasts to find it hot and I knew my heart was on fire beneath my ribs.

"I made you appreciate freedom," Kouros said, standing up from the table to tower above me, his body swirling black smoke from the waist down.

"And I'm not done with you yet, child. You're mine..."

The fire in my chest grew till my whole body was in flames and, finally, I screamed.

I woke up covered in sweat in my own bed, blinking in confusion. I'd gone to sleep on the couch. What the hell?

Sitting up, I swiftly regretted that decision as pain shot through my head. Groaning, I flopped back, shutting my eyes against the weak light peering around my well-lined curtains.

Three deep breaths later I was able to crack my eyes enough to see the glass of water and bottle of Advil on my nightstand. Oz had remembered.

I swallowed a handful, not bothering to count, and drank the entire glass of water.

Ten minutes later I felt less like the victim of a thousand hangovers and much more...well, *human* isn't entirely accurate.

Peeling back my duvet, I assessed the damage. The wound was almost entirely closed, a fat red scar the only sign that I'd had to interfere with myself. It would fade.

I was also very clean. I peered down at my side, reaching my fingers to stroke my skin.

Yes, very clean. And much more naked. I thought I'd still been wearing the scraps of my shirt when I'd passed out on the sofa. I had definitely been wearing yoga pants and hiking boots. Now I was clad only in panties and a bra.

Since Yulia and everyone else was still warded out of the carriage house, that meant only one person could have stripped me down and cleaned me up.

My Master, Ozan.

Heat flamed my face and for a second I remembered the smooth skin of his tattooed throat under my fingertips. Had he seen that as an invitation to get frisky?

I shut my eyes against that thought and stayed in bed for another half hour, letting the Advil soak up into the crevices. But I was fighting a losing battle. It was already five thirty on the following day; I'd lost almost twenty-four hours to the strain of healing myself, and I really had to pee.

I got up and used my en suite facilities, pulling on my favorite black-and-red silk geisha robe after a little quick clean-up. I don't know why I was bothering, since Oz had already seen most of me yesterday—and all of me must have looked like death warmed over with some cream of hot mess soup for flavor.

Squaring my shoulders, I left my room, walking down the hallway to the kitchen. Oz sat with his back to me, reading one of my belly dancing magazines and eating something.

"Good evening," I said, striding toward the refrigerator.

He shot up like he'd been fired from a gun, looking worried. "How are you? You slept so long...I was worried..."

I fluttered my fingers at him as I reached into the fridge for a Coke. I needed caffeine, stat, and wasn't willing to wait for coffee to brew. "I'm fine. I just used a lot of energy on the healing." I opened the Coke and tipped it back, nearly doing a spit take as I caught a glimpse of what Ozan was eating.

It was the cantaloupe, neatly sliced into long segments and displayed on a plate.

Choking the cola down, I watched my Master pull out a chair for me. To my surprise he helped me into it, as if I were an invalid.

"Are you sure you are okay? That cut was horrible. I know you're strong, but..."

"I'm fine," I said, cutting him off. I knew I sounded rude, but there were bigger fish to fry.

Oz's silver eyes met mine, big and guileless and shockingly, irritatingly kind. "I put you to bed. I hope you don't mind. It's just..."

Feeling my heart stutter, I raised an eyebrow at him.

"It's just I used to do that for my dad, after a fight. He hated waking up all bloody, and there was so much blood...I figured I could get it out if I got your clothes into cold water fast enough. They're soaking in your washing machine. Well, the jeans are. The shirt and the hoodie were pretty destroyed."

I reached for a slice of cantaloupe, unsure of what to say. He'd stripped me, cleaned me up, and put my clothes to soak...because it was the right thing to do?

Sure.

"Well, thank you," I said, trying to keep my voice neutral. "That was...kind."

Oz ducked his head, his thick hair looking very red in the soft light of my kitchen. "I hope I wasn't too forward...I just figured I'd already seen you in your costume. And you were getting blood everywhere. I had to Resolve the shit out of your sofa."

When I realized I was shaking my head at him in obvious disbelief, I only just managed to stop.

"It's fine," I said, faintly. Because it was. He could have done pretty much anything he'd wanted to me last night, and I wouldn't have been able to do anything about it. Not only had I been dead to the world, but I was Bound to him by every magical law in existence.

My new Master must play a mean long game, because his short game was already confusing the hell out of me.

"I'm going to have to go to work tonight," I said. "And I need to talk to Charlie. And to Bertha."

She wasn't going to be happy her great-uncle was missing, but maybe she knew something we didn't. Did trolls take vacations, for example?

"Hopefully her uncle wasn't eaten. Maybe he just moved?" Ozan said, as if reading my thoughts.

"Hopefully," I replied, with about as much confidence as I felt for that rosy scenario.

I went to get another Coke from the fridge, grabbing a plastic container of Giant Eagle chocolate chip cookies while I was at it. Ozan watched me skeptically as I gobbled a cookie, swigging it down with the Coke.

Unsure why I felt the need to defend myself, I still heard my own voice explaining. "Headache. Sugar helps."

He raised an eyebrow, but I pointedly ignored him, reaching instead for my cell phone. Ozan, helpful Master that he was, must've put it on the little speaker I used as its charger.

I scrolled through my messages—a few from Charlie and Yulia, asking if I was okay, one from Bertha asking me to call her. I texted them all, telling everyone I was fine and I'd see them at Purgatory tonight. What had happened in the fodden-littered field, and the probable demise of Bertha's great-uncle, wasn't appropriate for a text.

But I did send a quick text to Loretta, to let her know the bugbear had been taken care of . . . by the field of fodden they'd now need to clear out. Luckily, fodden and slugs share a similar reaction to salt, so they are easy to kill if you knew they're there. And if they don't eat you before you can grab the Morton's.

"What's wrong?" Oz asked, and I realized I was frowning.

"Nothing. I just haven't heard from my friend Aki. But he's like that...I shouldn't worry."

"But you are worried," Oz said. "Is it because of what happened at the park?"

I put my phone down, determined not to let my kitsune friend's lack of a text bother me. "Aki wouldn't be caught dead hiking, so he's safe from those fodden. And he's like this—he disappears all the time. It's no biggie. He'll pop back up."

Oz raised an eyebrow at me, but my new Master didn't say anything else till I'd polished off the rest of my cookie and another to boot.

"Your friends are very important to you," he said, as I closed the package of cookies.

"Of course they are. They're my friends."

"They seem more like family."

I smiled. "Talk about dysfunction junction. But yeah, you could say we're family."

"It's weird, though, because you seem really alone. Like you think you're alone, even though you're obviously not."

It was my turn to raise an eyebrow. "What the hell does that mean?"

"I just mean that there's something about you. Like you don't let things touch you."

I raised the hem of my T-shirt just enough to show off the pink scar from last night. "I let plenty of things touch me."

He grimaced. "That's not what I mean."

"Look," I said, leaning forward. "The thing is, I know you think you're a nice guy. You probably want to be a nice guy. But in this scenario, you're my Master. We're not buddies. We're never going to be friends. You *own* me."

His eyes widened a bit, and the creamy Irish skin he'd inherited from his daddy somehow managed to pale a few shades more.

"I already said I'd release you, the second we find Tamina. And I mean it."

I took a deep breath, trying to keep my anger in check. Blowing up at him and making him mad, too, wouldn't help my situation any.

"Besides," he said, "yesterday proves I'm not just being a dick. We would have been fodden snacks if you hadn't had your magic yesterday."

My eyes narrowed, my temper boiling. The part of me that wasn't completely immature knew that part of my anger stemmed from the fact that he was right, damn him. But there's nothing like a "told you so" to make me Stabby McStabberson.

"If you hadn't Bound me, then I wouldn't have come on Loretta's radar," I said, mulishly.

Oz squared his wide shoulders, clearly not accepting my logic. "And if you hadn't been Bound, that bugbear would still be running around eating people."

That took me a second. "The Exterminators would have figured something out," I said, eventually.

Oz knew he had me. "Bullshit. Or they wouldn't have Called you, right? You were the only thing standing between that bugbear and all of those people, and you couldn't have helped if you weren't Bound."

"But what about my curse?" I shouted, my voice admittedly petulant.

"I will free you," he said, his eyes locking on mine. "I swear on my mother's grave that I will free you the minute we find

Tamina. And in the meantime, stop blaming me for keeping you Bound. It has saved our lives twice now."

We both fell silent, him staring at me in challenge and me keeping my head ducked.

"It's not that simple," I said eventually, peering up through my bangs at him. "It's just…"

"I get it," Oz said. "At least as much as I can. I get that anywhere you are, everything you have can be taken from you. I get that you've lived like that for longer than I can imagine, and that you've probably had it happen to you—over, and over, and over. So I get why you feel like you're alone and why you're scared and why you don't want to believe me."

Tears prickled my eyes and I furiously blinked them away.

When he spoke again, his voice was gentle. He leaned forward, staring at me intently. "But that's life, Lyla. Any life can be turned upside down, just like that." He snapped his fingers. "Mine was, too. I went from living in one world that I knew and thought I could make better, to living in an entirely different one, overnight. Everything I took for granted is gone. And *that* is why I'm going to free you as soon as I can, and certainly before your curse is up."

I blinked at him, feeling hollow. I hadn't thought of it like that; hadn't thought about *him* at all. Oz was just a Master to be outsmarted, not a man who'd gone through his own ordeal and might be different than I'd assumed.

"How are you so calm about everything?" I asked, giving him that.

He gave me a grim smile. "Because I came to terms with the fact life is unfair a long time ago, when my mom died. Then I made it my job to study the fact that life was even more unfair to millions of other people. In my studies, then in my career, I chose to rub my nose in the fact that nothing's static, that there are no guarantees. And so I couldn't be all that surprised when it happened to me.

"Life is what it is. A crapshoot."

I shook my head. I was being lectured by a man who was a veritable infant compared to me.

And who was infinitely more wise, it seemed.

"So that's it? You just accept that life sucks?" I wanted to deflate him a little bit; poke some holes in his Yoda mask.

"Nope. I wish I was that strong, but acceptance is hard. Instead I focus on the good stuff. Yeah, I've lost my old world. But this new one seems pretty cool. It's definitely full of interesting people."

I felt my cheeks heat, to my horror. Was I blushing?

"Yeah, well, we're all interesting until we try to eat you."

All I received from Oz was a raised eyebrow and I felt my face grow even hotter. Damn.

"Look, we've gotta go," I said. "If you're done Dear Abby-ing me?"

He smiled. "I'm done. If you're done threatening to eat me."

"I was not threatening to eat you," I said, using my prim voice again. "And I thought you were just doing all of this so you could find Tamina, discharge your debt, and go back to normal?"

His silver eyes gazed into my brown. "I do. I think. But I'm beginning to realize that may not be feasible."

"Another thing you're okay with?"

He nodded, but the smile was gone. His eyes never wavered from mine. "Yes and no. I'm scared. But there are aspects of this world that I find more and more appealing."

I had nothing to say to that.

"What should we do next?" he asked, breaking the silence for me.

I cleared my throat. "I need to tell everyone at Purgatory what happened. Talk to Bertha. I'm scheduled to perform tonight. Then we need to knuckle down. Start looking for your Tamina."

"She's not mine," he said, gently. "But I would like to find her, when you're finished doing what you need to do."

He still wasn't commanding me, damn him. He was the worst Master ever.

Chapter Twelve

Bertha's big face, normally placid, was lined with grief. She was sitting bolt upright across from me at one of Purgatory's small café tables. Charlie sat next to her, a hand on the shoulder of her black suit, and Oz sat next to me.

"Fodden?" she repeated, for about the tenth time.

"I know. I can't believe it either," I said.

"And not just one?"

"An infestation." I looked at Charlie. "One that I hope the Exterminators take care of, before they realize humans are food, too."

Normally creatures that only lived Sideways, fodden weren't aware people were just as tasty a treat as the supernaturals upon which they normally feasted. But occasionally a rogue fodden somehow found itself on the human plane, and it never took it long to discover that the strange-smelling creatures in its new habitat made for yummy snacks.

"Are they aware of the situation?" asked Charlie.

"I texted Loretta earlier."

My attention turned to Bertha when I heard her sniffle.

"Do you think Sid could have made it out?" I asked her, gently.

She shook her head. "Where would he go?"

I bowed my head, sharing in Bertha's grief. I'd been hoping for a different answer, but I'd known the truth. A troll's territory was everything to him; Sid would never have willingly left the place he'd been born.

"How could that many fodden have crossed the Bridge?" Bertha looked at Charlie, her long mustaches quivering along with the hand beneath mine. I'm not sure whether it was suppressed rage or grief or fear, or a combination of all three.

"They couldn't have. At least, not on their own steam," Charlie said. "They had to have been brought over."

"Who the hell would do that?" I asked. "They're useless."

"Useless?" Oz asked. "One sliced you up pretty good."

Charlie gave me a concerned look. "Are you all right now?"

"Yeah, all healed. Well, mostly healed." I turned to Oz. "And what I meant by 'useless' is that fodden aren't good for anything. They attack whatever they think is food, and they eat virtually anything. So you can't use them for either defense *or* offense. And they're super-invasive, so they can't be contained. Most of Sideways is uninhabitable because of fodden, and the great Lords are said to have to go culling every few years or all of it would fall to the brutes.

"So nothing in its right mind would bring fodden over. It'd be like unleashing velociraptors to guard the house you have to live in, if velociraptors bred like rabbits."

"And yet we've got an infestation in Frick Park," Charlie said, his voice musing. "The bugbear and the fodden may be connected."

"How? Fodden eat bugbears," I said, thinking about the head with broken mandibles lying in Frick Park.

"Can I ask a question?" asked Oz. I'd known it was coming, had seen that now-familiar look of consternation creasing his forehead.

"Of course," I said, while Charlie looked down his nose at my Master.

"How do you Call a bugbear? I mean, I know I can Call jinn, as a Magi..." He actually looked guilty when he said that, bless him. "But how can someone Call a bugbear?"

"Anything can be Called, son," said Bertha, visibly pulling herself together. "You can be even Called, if someone has your blood and your true name."

"My true name?" Oz's face showed that unique combination of eager curiosity and trepidation with which he met everything we told him. Part of him very obviously loved this steep learning curve, even while the rest of him was continually braced for something terrifying.

"Yes. We all have a true name. But 'name' isn't really accurate...it's like a..." I looked at Charlie for help.

"Like a tone. A resonance. A vibration."

I nodded. "Yes. Those. Remember when you first Saw me?"

"Of course," he said, his eyes turning inward. "You glowed. You were beautiful, of course, and you had all that black Fire around you. But there was something else...it pulled at me."

I ignored the "beautiful" bit just as I ignored Charlie's twitching brows. "The pull you felt, that was the connection between a jinni and a Magi. You can See me, See my true name. And you can use that connection to Call me."

"But you were standing in front of me."

"You still Called," I reminded him. "The second part of the spell you spoke. In this case, it didn't pull me Sideways, but it did stopper my magic. And you'd do the same thing to Call a jinni from Sideways...you'd use your magic to seek for that magical resonance. Once you hooked into a jinni's true name, you'd Call, pulling the jinni Sideways."

"And that same thing can be done to anyone," Charlie said, to Oz's obvious horror.

"Anyone and anything. *If,*" I clarified, "you have the power. All Magi have innate, varying degrees of power over jinn. But something with a lot of power can Call virtually anything if they have what they need—usually a spell that homes in on a certain kind of creature's magical signature and the Will to work it."

"So something used a lot of power to Call over a bugbear and some fodden, assuming it was the same person, but from what you said they're not very useful?" Oz asked, bringing our conversation back into focus.

I nodded. "That's what makes no sense. Although whoever called it didn't have to be that strong; if you know what you're doing, bugbears are pretty quick to Call. And yet *why*?"

Charlie interrupted. "Maybe we should start with other questions. Like when?"

"I talked to my uncle a few days ago. Maybe Monday?" Bertha said, her eyes glistening with suppressed tears but her voice remaining steady. "And we've not heard anything about humans disappearing, so the fodden couldn't have been in that field for much more than twenty-four hours."

"Which means enough of them had to come over all at once to infest that field that quickly," Charlie said.

I met his colorless gaze. "Let's go over the possibilities. Somebody could have Called the bugbear and the fodden specifically, although it makes no sense for anyone to want *any* fodden, let alone a metric fuck-ton of fodden. Or a bugbear, for that matter."

"Sometimes bugbears are Called by creatures arrogant

enough to think they will be able to control them. Maybe someone Called the bugbear, and the fodden were an accident," Bertha said.

Hearing that inspired a third option, one that made me grimace. But Charlie beat me to it.

"Or someone was trying to Call something very, very big from Sideways, and *both* the fodden and the bugbear were accidents." Charlie's voice was deep and low, but his words were anything but comforting.

We three magical folks all peered at each other as goose bumps rose on my skin. Oz looked more confused than ever.

"But who would do that, and why?" he asked, his gaze shifting among our worried faces.

"We have no idea who, or why. That's not the kind of thing that happens in Pittsburgh," I said.

"Nobody here has that much power," Bertha explained to Oz. "No pure supernaturals with any real magical capacity can touch the poisoned Node."

"Except for Lyla, now that she's Bound," came Loretta's voice from behind me.

I clutched my hand to my chest, my heart beating like it was imitating a death metal drum solo.

"We should tie a bell on her," Oz said to me, making me snort.

"Loretta," said Charlie, rising to his feet to greet our guest. "To what do we owe this honor?"

"We sent a team to take care of the fodden," said the Exterminator. She turned to Bertha. "I'm very sorry about Sid. He was a good troll."

Bertha sniffled. "Did you find anything?"

Loretta shook her head. "Once the fodden were cleared, the Bridge was accessible. But there was no sign of Sid."

Loretta didn't have to clarify what that meant. The fodden must have gotten him.

"Excuse me," Bertha said. She stood and made her way to the storage room.

"What are you doing here, Loretta?" I asked, turning to the Exterminator. We'd been sorta-friends for a long time, but I knew she wasn't here to ask me to lunch.

"We recognize you're on a time budget," Loretta said, her nictitating membranes working overtime. After a pregnant pause, I realized she was talking about my curse. "But new circumstances have arisen. We're going to need more help."

Charlie's mouth tightened into a thin line, but, to my surprise, it was Oz who spoke up in my defense. I was too busy trying to figure out how Loretta knew about my curse.

"Lyla has already helped you," he said. "When we spoke the other night, you didn't mention anything about her help being ongoing. She already did what you asked."

That's it, I thought, relieved. I remembered Oz's "put a bell" comment about Loretta. Who knew how long she'd been listening to our conversation the other night at Purgatory regarding my curse? One mystery solved. And as for the other...

"What do you need?" I asked. "The bugbear's taken care of. So are the fodden."

Loretta took the seat Bertha had vacated, crossing her long legs primly. The gills at her neck flared, causing Oz to startle.

Not so hot now, is she? I thought, feeling smug.

"Yes," Loretta replied. "But we have a bigger problem."

"Bigger than a bugbear?" I quipped, feeling punchy.

"Yes." Loretta obviously wasn't in the mood for jokes. "Creatures have been disappearing."

My eyes flew to Charlie's. Loretta didn't miss his reaction.

"You know something," she said. It wasn't a question.

I nodded, thinking of Aki. Loretta leaned over the table toward us.

"Tell me everything."

"What's a kitsune again?" Oz asked, peering up at the facade of Aki's condo building.

"A kitsune is a fox spirit," I replied, hitting the buzzer one last time. Loretta had charged us with checking out the apartment while she continued her own investigation. She'd have more for me to do after we checked on Aki, I was sure.

"What's a fox spirit?"

"Aki's a shapeshifter. He has two natural forms, a fox or a human. He's also super-quiet, super-fast, and super-good at all things thieving or spying." As I talked, I rooted around in my too-large purse for Aki's extra set of keys.

"Are you going to break in?" Oz asked, just as my hand closed on his rabbit's-paw key ring.

"Nope," I said, pulling the keys out and holding them up for him to see. "We're using the old-fashioned method. Keys."

"Oh," Oz said, looking disappointed.

"What's up?" I asked, as I unlocked the big front door. Aki lived in a recently refurbished loft complex in Lawrenceville, the coolest neighborhood in Pittsburgh at the moment. It had been a dump until a few years ago, but now the properties were flying into the hands of developers like homing pigeons to their mark. Hipsters had set up residence, and Butler Street, Lawrenceville's main thoroughfare, was full of craft beer joints and cafés where the bartenders and baristas sported more facial hair and tats than the crew of a pirate ship.

Personally I preferred living in much quieter, more sedate Highland Park, but Aki had drifted from cool spot to cool spot in our city ever since he'd first come to Pittsburgh seeking shelter.

"It's just weird, how you all live so normally," Oz said, inspecting the neat rows of mail slots as I unlocked the inner door of Aki's building.

"What do you mean?" I pulled open the heavy inner door and led Oz into the well-lit hallway, painted a very au courant shade of gunmetal gray with clean white trim.

"I mean, you guys are magic. But this guy lives in a condo."

I snorted. "Where are we supposed to live?"

"I dunno," he said, grinning ruefully at me. "Maybe under toadstools?"

"That'd be a bit of a squeeze," I said, waving a hand in front of my substantial hips.

To my amusement, he stammered. "I just meant it's weird you guys live like humans. It makes sense you do, since you were human. But a fox spirit paying condo fees? Seems odd."

Avoiding the elevators, I led Oz toward the stairs, marked Fire Escape, that no one ever used. "Well, I already told you most of us in Pittsburgh are misfit toys. We can't depend on our magic for day-to-day stuff. And we *do* live in the same world as humans, so why not take advantage of human conveniences?"

I stopped in front of the door leading to the fourth-floor hallway and pulled it open. Like the entry hall, the walls here were painted gray, with expensive-looking dark wood floors covered in the center by a thick dark carpet runner.

"I get it," Oz said. "But it still strikes me as odd. Especially someone like you working at a place like Purgatory."

I raised an eyebrow at him, leading him down the hall toward Aki's apartment. "And why does that strike you as odd?"

He cast me a long side-eye, probably knowing he was on

thin ice. "It's just that you've lived for so long. You must have so much to tell…so much knowledge to share. And you dance in a bar."

I couldn't help but laugh. "I'm sorry to disappoint you," I said. "But I love dancing. And I gave up crashing against human ignorance about three centuries ago, which is why I don't participate in coffee klatches anymore. I don't have anything to tell anyone that's not already on Wikipedia. It's not that the stories aren't out there, it's that humans don't listen."

"But still…"

"Oz. I dance in a bar because I like dancing in a bar. I like being with my friends; I like performing. It pays the bills at the same time that it gives me room to express myself. Not to mention, I don't have to have a human birth certificate or a piece of paper from a university. The only real job I've had in years is Exterminator lackey, and I'm not sure how to put that on a résumé without an explanation.

"But the real answer is I like dancing. So drop it." By that point we were at Aki's door, painted the same gray as the rest of the doors. Only Aki's sported about fifteen locks. I sighed and began tracking down the appropriate keys on the key ring.

Oz pursed his lips, obviously not happy with my response but willing to move the conversation on to other questions on what was probably an interminable mental list.

"Are Exterminators just in Pittsburgh?" he asked.

"No, there are Exterminators everywhere."

"Who controls them?"

I unlocked another few locks as I talked. "Nobody, really. They keep their own counsel. But we all know the rules. Don't end up in the papers. Don't go on killing sprees. Don't attract attention. They're pretty simple."

"Common sense," Oz said, dryly, as I finally opened the last of the locks.

I pushed open Aki's door, and I heard Ozan's indrawn breath. Moving my eyes from him to the sight of Aki's living room, I sighed.

It had been destroyed. There'd obviously been a massive fight, upturning just about every piece of furniture in the open-plan studio apartment.

"What the hell did that?" Oz asked, pointing at the granite work surface of the kitchen island, which had been smashed neatly in half.

"Someone Aki managed to piss off with his shenanigans," I repeated. "But that's pretty normal for Aki."

Even now I was only a little worried about our ne'er-do-well kitsune. He got in this kind of trouble all the time and he always got out of it.

We picked our way into the apartment, avoiding broken furniture and crockery. It wasn't till we'd rounded the corner and saw the bedroom area that my heart grew heavy.

There was blood everywhere.

"Aki's?" Ozan asked.

I gave him a sharp look. "What do I look like, *CSI: Miami*? I've got no idea whose blood it is."

But if Aki had gotten in a bad-enough fight that someone had ended up hurt—and seriously hurt, judging by the amount of blood on the walls—his second port of call would almost definitely have been Purgatory. We were good at hiding people, and he'd have needed hiding if he'd gotten in a fight this bad.

Oz was picking his way toward the bathroom next to the destroyed bed frame, but the mattress—shredded in half—lay in the way. He bent down to move it and I heard a sharp hiss when he did so. He dropped the mattress back to the floor and sprang away, eyes wide.

"What?" I said, hurrying toward him.

"I'm sorry," he said, as he helped me lift the mattress away from what he'd found.

I'd been expecting a body, even though the space was really too small. But what lay underneath it was almost as bad.

On the floor, in a small puddle of blood, lay the thick, luxuriant tail of a fox. I'd know that tail anywhere.

It was Aki's.

Chapter Thirteen

I lifted and dropped each of my hips once, twice, and then shimmied, the coins of my costume rattling ominously. Raising my arms to the heavens, I looked up as if in supplication as the last beats of the song pulsed from Purgatory's speakers.

The crowd hooted and clapped as I forced my lips into a smile. I took my bows, sidling offstage into Rachel's waiting arms.

"I'm sorry, baby doll," she whispered into my ear. Tucking my long, dark hair behind my ears, she met my eyes. "You doing okay?"

"I will be," I said, sniffling despite my words. "It's not like any of us expected Aki to die of old age."

"That don't matter," she said, her big dark eyes sad underneath their wings of purple makeup. "It still hurts. You go back to the dressing room and get cleaned up. We'll get good and drunk tonight, for Aki's sake. How's that sound?"

I nodded, letting the tears fall. "Like a plan." I gave Rachel a hug and watched as she drew herself up, putting on her own game face for the audience.

The show must go on.

The dressing room was empty when I got there, and for that I was glad. I lay back on the chaise we kept tucked by the door, shutting my eyes against the wave of grief that threatened to overwhelm me.

The fact was, Aki and I hadn't even been that close. We'd always liked each other, but he was the sort who kept all but a very few at arm's length. I'd known him for almost two centuries, however, and I'd been relying on him as a disruption of the steady rhythm of my life for a long time. We never knew when Aki was going to pop up with a crisis biting at his heels, or in need of shelter or for us to hide something for him. And he always knew what was going on, everywhere. He'd been my eyes and ears since I'd met him, telling me about the wider world in which I was afraid to walk for fear of being Bound.

And I'd liked him, despite the fact that his profession was being untrustworthy. I'd liked his humor and his sly fox face that somehow looked the same in either his human or his animal shape. Between losing Sid and now Aki, I felt like my life had gone significantly darker.

Someone knocked gently on the door and I called for whoever it was to enter. It was Bertha, looking as miserable as I felt.

"Hey," I said, patting the chaise next to me. "You shouldn't be working, babe. Take some time off, whatever you need."

Bertha moved into the room, carefully squeezing herself next to me. "No, I'd rather be here. Being home just makes me sad."

I patted her on the back, understanding what she meant. Oz had been surprised when I'd told him I had to dance tonight, but I did have to. Not least because it was my job, and I'd already missed one night chasing shadows. But also because I needed to feel normal again, even if it was just for the space of a few songs.

"I can't believe Aki's gone," Bertha said.

"I know. He's...Aki."

"That fox had more lives than ten cats."

I laughed, but it sounded as bitter as it felt. "No shit."

"I went out to the Bridge today," she said. "The fodden are cleared out, Exterminators did a good job."

"And no sign of Sid?"

"No. He's gotta be gone. Dead, I mean. He wouldn't leave his home."

I turned my patting into a one-armed hug, leaning my head against hers. "I'm so sorry, Bertha. We all loved him."

She made a sound like a jet engine roaring, and I realized it was the troll version of a sniffle. "I know. Do you think their deaths are related?"

I shrugged. "It's impossible to say. Aki was...Aki. He could have pissed off any number of people."

"Yeah. Still, seems weird."

"There's a lot going on that's weird," I said, my voice grim. "Speaking of which, I've gotta go find my darling Master. I left him back here, but he must have gone out front."

Bertha shook her head. "He's not out front. I thought he was back here waiting for you?"

We stared at each for a second and then I swore and we both took off running for the front of the house.

Oz wasn't anywhere—not at the bar, not at any of the low tables. I did notice Diamond glowering at me from one corner, but no Oz.

"Trey, you seen Oz?"

Our bartender nodded at my question, pointing at one of our fire escapes. "He went up the side stairs, with some kid."

"Kid?" I asked, confused. We didn't have any age requirements at Purgatory, since it was pretty common to have practically ageless beings who looked like children running around wanting a few drinks and a show. But we also wouldn't refer to such creatures as "kids."

"Yeah," Trey said. "Never seen 'im here before. He wasn't human; he came down here like he owned the place. But I don't know what he was."

"Shit," I said, moving toward the side exit just as the magic struck.

Oz was Calling, loud and clear, and the jinni in me was frantic to get to him. She reached out to the Node, opening my channels wide before I could even think, and next thing I knew I was standing in the alley behind Purgatory.

I stumbled, almost crashing into the brick wall of our neighbor as I regained my sea legs. Apparating was something only the most powerful jinn could do, and I'd never done it before—Oz had some Will behind his Calls, that was for sure.

As I was shaking my head to clear the cobwebs, the sound came on all of a sudden, only then making me aware I'd apparently pressed the mute button.

I heard the sound of fighting behind me, and Oz chanting my name.

He was doing a good job, my Master was. For a confused couple of seconds I watched him fight, dishing out a fast upper-cut to the jaw that sent one young man reeling while his next punch fended off the second. But I'd gotten there just in time. The kids weren't human, however human they looked. They were too fast and immediately came back at Oz despite receiving blows that would have felled a normal teenager.

My jinni kicked in right then and next thing I knew I was pulling one of my swords from my little pocket of Sideways, yelling as I charged the boys attacking Oz. Before I could get there, however, the cavalry arrived in the form of one large shape that descended from an upper window of Purgatory, separating into two shapes as it hurtled toward us.

Trip and Trap.

The spider wraiths fell on their targets like bombs. Trip's hands went around one boy's skull, breaking his neck. Never one to miss an opportunity, she also pulled, separating his head neatly from his body with a sickly ripping sound.

Trap took the tougher target, who dodged before the wraith could land upon him. The teen ducked the sticky web that Trap shot out of his butt, and managed to pivot neatly on his heel to climb up the wall next to him. Trap went to follow but Oz shouted for him to stop. When I looked over at my Master he was staring in horror at the head of the boy on the ground, his eyes trailing up to where Trip greedily drank the blood spurting from the neck stump.

When Trap joined her in feeding, Oz vomited copiously and loudly into the drain near his feet.

"Welcome to our world," I mumbled, walking toward the head on the ground, then bending to pick it up by the hair. The kid had had vampire blood, all right, but also human. His fangs were more like seriously vicious canines than the double row of shark teeth a full vamp sported, and his skin wasn't their eerie pinkish-gray but that of an abnormally pale human.

"What the hell?" Trey's normally languid southern drawl sounded sharp from behind me. I turned to see him and Charlie gaping at us from the entrance to Purgatory.

"Trey, go get a tarp," I called. The bartender looked at where Trip and Trap were huddled, sucking noisily, and turned without a backward glance.

"What happened?" Charlie demanded of Oz.

"I was in the dressing room, and I got thirsty. So I went to the bar. I was just about to order a drink when this kid came in. He looked right at me and indicated I should follow. So I did."

"You followed an unknown dude into an alley?" I asked, my voice adequately expressing my feelings on the wisdom of such a move.

"He was a kid!" Oz said. "I figured you'd sent him to give me a message or something. Why would anyone else even know I'm here?"

Why indeed? I thought. Today was getting curiouser and curiouser.

"When you got to the alley the boy attacked?" asked Charlie.

Oz shook his head. "Yes, but not to hurt me. The other boy was here, waiting for us. They wanted to take me somewhere. I wanted to know what the hell was going on."

"They were trying to abduct you? Why?" Charlie asked.

"How the hell should I know?" Oz asked, his voice rising slightly. His eyes shot to Trip and Trap, and he turned decidedly green. "And we can't ask, because your buddies murdered the poor kid before he could talk."

Charlie's colorless eyes narrowed at Oz. "Be careful what you say, boy. Trip and Trap saved your life. And that 'kid,' as you called him, has probably murdered scores of humans."

Oz took a step toward Charlie and I marveled at his bravery even as I put a restraining hand on his shoulder. "How can a kid be a murderer?"

"He's not a kid, Master," I said, my voice low and soothing. "He may have been relatively young, but he was born a predator. Half-vampires are usually not allowed to live. They're born with all of the hunger of a normal vamp and none of the conscience or control. He's probably killed a lot of people in his short life."

Oz shook his head. "I can't believe that. He's a teenager."

"And I bet he has quite a history of family killed, neighbors murdered, classmates gone missing." Oz opened his mouth to protest but I wouldn't let him. "All of this is beside the point. The real question is what they were doing here. What they wanted with you."

"Who sent them," added Charlie.

"And how they hell they found you," I finished.

It was quite a laundry list of problems. I pinched the bridge of my nose, feeling a headache coming on. What had Charlie said about this being a cinch, again?

Trey had returned with a tarp, and he and Big Bertha managed to pull Trip and Trap off their dinner. They'd reverted to full spider wraith form, their midsections merged, leaving their four legs sprouting beneath them. They clung to each other like drunkards, swaying slightly. They hadn't had that much fresh blood in one go for almost a hundred years, I bet.

Our bartender and bouncer were done wrapping the body when I made my request.

"Bertha, go get Diamond," I said. "I saw her in the corner near the polar bear."

Bertha nodded and headed back inside.

"Diamond's Blood Sect," I said to Charlie.

"I thought she was a Crypt?"

I shook my head. "She changed allegiance after Bernard was killed. Mostly because I'm pretty sure she helped kill him, and joining the Sects was her reward."

"Diamond sucks," he said.

"Yep. And speak of the devil…"

"What the hell?" said a petulant voice from our side stairs. "You can't just kick me out, Purgatory is a public…"

"You're not in trouble," I said to the succubus. She was wearing as pornographically startling a dress as she had been last week—this one a violent highlighter yellow. Her heels were clear Lucite.

Considering I was only wearing a skimpy black robe I shouldn't have been judgy, but I was anyway.

"We need you to ID this guy," I said. "Is he one of yours?"

Seeing the plastic-wrapped figure, Diamond perked up. "You kill somebody?"

"Not me. But you know this guy?" I raised the head to her eyeline, causing Oz to grunt and turn away.

My Master wasn't very good with heads, apparently.

Diamond studied the head with open curiosity. "Nope. He's not Sect. And not Crypt, either."

"And not unaffiliated?"

She studied the head for another few seconds. "No, I don't think so. We did another purge last year that got most of them, and none of them were half-vamps. Those're always complete bastards; we kill them at birth."

Oz made a strangled sound.

"Your guy can't be from Pittsburgh," Diamond said. "No way he'd live past infancy, let alone get this big. He must have been feeding like crazy to grow to this age."

"Thanks, Diamond. Trey will have a free drink for you whenever you want it."

Diamond pouted. "Is that it?"

I ignored the succubus. "Bertha, take her back inside."

"So he's not a local," I said, popping the head in with the half-vamp's body as Bertha led a complaining Diamond away from the scene.

"Well, there's some good news," Charlie said, running a hand through his thickly curled hair. "But why is some unaffiliated half-vampire trying to abduct your new Master?"

Big Bertha returned from escorting Diamond to the door

and picked up the body as if it were a feather duster, swinging it over her shoulder with ease. I hadn't tied the bundle tight enough, however, and the head popped out to land in a puddle with a sickly splat. Oz looked like he might pass out.

"He wasn't human," I reminded my Master. "I know that's hard for you to understand, but it's true: his nature *was* to kill. I don't know what he wanted with you but it wasn't to play patty-cake."

"As of now, we have quite a list of mysteries," Charlie said, tapping his forefinger on his jaw in thought. "We've got this attempted abduction and a missing troll along with a dead kitsune, not to mention a random bugbear attack and the fodden infestation. But we don't know what's connected to what, or even if they are connected."

I raised my arms helplessly. "I've got no fucking clue what's going on."

Charlie looked at me. "We've gotta find out, Lyla."

"No, Charlie," I said. "Absolutely not."

Oz was looking between the two of us, nonplussed.

Charlie, for his part, ignored my protestations entirely. "We'll go tonight after the show."

"What part of 'no' did you not understand?" I demanded, stepping up to peer into his face.

"I've got to, honey." His voice was soft and worry lines etched his forehead. "There's something going on here we don't get and we need to figure it out as soon as possible. You don't have much time."

"But I'll take care of it," I said, sharply. "It's not your call."

"You're my friend," he said. "So it is my call, if I can help."

Then he turned and walked back toward the club, his shoulders set in a line I knew all too well.

"I said no, Charlie!" I called, knowing I was way too late. "Damn it!"

"What just happened?" Oz asked, a few seconds later, during which I'd managed to cuss about a thousand times.

"Charlie's a shitball goatfucker," I said, unhelpfully. Oz raised an eyebrow.

I took a calming breath. "Charlie's going to try to use a vision to See what's happening."

"Oh. OK. But isn't that what he does?"

I shook my head. "You don't understand. I mean, yes, it's what he does. But he has to do it using the Pittsburgh Node, which isn't the pure source that Delphi was."

"Oh. So...what? It'll hurt him, like it does you?"

"Yes. Very badly, and worse every time. But that's not the worst part." I shuddered, remembering the last time Charlie had used his powers. He'd Seen his own death, although he refused to talk about it, even now.

"What's the worst part?" Oz prompted.

I rounded on my Master. "The worst part is he Sees everything. So not just what he wants to See, but everything he doesn't want. And none of it is ever good."

We walked toward the stairs that led to Purgatory, as I wondered what Charlie would See that night.

And how long it'd take him to recover from those visions this time.

Chapter Fourteen

The fountain at Point State Park is one of Pittsburgh's major landmarks. Sitting smack between two rivers and giving birth to a third, it's always been an important site, and not only to humans.

"I feel...funny," Oz said.

I looked at my Master, whose eyes were lit up like torches. All the magic underfoot, plus my jinni Fire standing next to him, meant Oz had the magical equivalent of a boner.

"It's the confluence," I said, "the nodal point. There's a metric shit-ton of magic running underneath your feet right now."

He grunted, swaying slightly. "It feels good."

I felt my brow creep up my forehead. "I bet it does. But put your game face on, Master; we've got a job to do."

His Flaring silver eyes met mine, calling my Fire to kindle in response.

"You're really beautiful, you know," he said, his voice dreamy, distant.

Despite me, my face went hot. "And you're high on mojo," I said, brusquely pulling him toward the fountain.

"I don't like this at all," Rachel was saying, tottering behind us on enormous platform heels. Luckily there was nothing even vaguely park-like about Point State Park, or our favorite drag queen—whose definition of *sensible shoes* was a pair of kitten-heeled, ostrich-feather slippers—would never have made it. Instead the "park" was almost entirely concrete, with beautifully paved sidewalks leading straight to the enormous fountain, the jewel in the crown made up of many bridges that was Pittsburgh's skyline.

Like the rest of the city, the fountain and its surrounding monuments fell into disrepair after the steel industry collapsed. The park had even been closed for a few years, until it was finally renovated and only recently reopened. For many, the fountain's refurbishment symbolized how Pittsburgh itself was rising, Phoenix-like, from its own ashes.

That metaphor would have been avoided, however, if normal humans knew that Phoenixes are complete assholes.

"I don't like this either," I said, stopping to tug on Charlie's sleeve. "Why don't we just head over to Butcher and the Rye for something butchered. And something rye."

Charlie gave me an incredibly dark look for someone with colorless eyes. "We need some answers, and not the kind that come at the bottom of a bottle."

"Nothing good ever comes of your visions," I reminded him.

Charlie laid a hand over mine, resting still on his forearm. "I'm an Oracle. And I've had a bad feeling all week. A vision itch. I can't fight it any longer. I *shouldn't* fight it any longer. Something obviously wants me to know...something."

"Fine." I knew he couldn't fight his own cursed existence any more than I could fight mine. "But I'm pulling you out if something goes funky."

His head bowed in a grave nod. "I'm counting on it. Are you prepared to do what we talked about?"

After a moment's silent protest, I eventually nodded. In the past, when Charlie had done a reading, I'd skimmed off whatever power from the Node I could and sent it over to him, to give his visions extra oomph.

He wanted me to do the same thing tonight, but with the Deep Magic to which I now had access. I'd put up a good fight, but he'd won in the end, as he normally did in our friendship.

"Good," he said, taking my hand and giving it a squeeze. "I want to find this girl; get you free." I gave his hand its own squeeze and thanked him before letting him go.

We walked the rest of the way to the fountain, all lit up for the night. Oz stood peering up at it, swaying like a drunk. I put a hand on his shoulder and felt the heat coming off him.

"You okay, Master?"

"Don't call me that," he repeated. His tone was still harsh but he paired the words with a sweet smile. I hated myself for liking him at that moment.

"Master," I repeated, forcing myself to say the word coldly, clinically. I didn't have to obey that command, after all, because it would be a lie. He *was* my Master. "We need your help."

His silver eyes closed for a second, as if my words had hurt him, and when he opened them again he took a step away from me, giving me space.

"Of course. Whatever you need."

"We need you to command a few things from me. Rachel will instruct you. I've told her what you should ask me," I said.

We watched as Charlie prepared himself: Rachel and I resigned, Oz openly fascinated. First Charlie used chalk to draw a huge sigil, an ancient Greek declaration of Will and invocation. It looked a bit like a pentagram, covered in squiggles.

Then he took off his clothes, all of them, and lay down in the middle of the circle. His pale flesh goose-pimpled like crazy when it made contact with the cold pavement, and my own flesh crawled in sympathy. As if to make us all more miserable, the wind shifted direction then, casting a fine spray of water from the fountain.

Charlie's chalk symbol was safe, however, as it instantly flared into a cold white fire around his thin frame.

"I'm ready," my friend called, peering over at me.

Rachel looked at me, and I nodded. "Tell Lyla to bind him, and bind him fast," she said to Oz.

My Master's eyes Flared again as he looked at me, causing my Fire to fan out around me.

"Bind him," he commanded me, "and bind him fast."

I swallowed at the sound of his voice, even as my jinni began her work. This close to the Node, I didn't even have to reach for Pittsburgh's stained magic for it to come boiling up inside me, filtering through the channels made wide by Oz's command. My Fire surged forward, wrapping around my friend's body like dozens of black snakes, dark against his white skin.

"Now tell her to help focus him, so he can See," Rachel said, once her man was firmly rooted to the ground.

Oz did as she commanded, and once again my power reached out...only this time it went into Charlie, bowing his back as every muscle in his body tightened like he'd been electrocuted.

Rachel made a choking noise beside me. We all hated this part.

I did my best to filter as much of the gunk as I could out of the mojo I speared into our Oracle, knowing I'd have a hell of a headache tomorrow. But I knew it still hurt my friend, even as I pushed more and more power into him. "He's taking it," I told Rachel. "It's opening up."

"What's going on?" Oz asked. My little scholar hated to be left in the dark.

"As an Oracle," I said, "Charlie has a conduit, straight to... something. His people thought it was the gods, and maybe it is. Maybe it's the universe. Maybe it's just something that likes to meddle. Anyway, Charlie was born with the conduit, but it has to be forced open by magic to be big enough for the power to speak through him. That's what he used to sit on at Delphi: a great big magic-channel-opener."

Oz's wide shoulder brushed against me in the dark. I nearly took his hand, before I realized that was inappropriate on about five thousand levels.

"He's almost there," I said, feeling the exodus of my own power meet what I knew was Charlie's saturation point. "He should start talking soon..."

I began to switch it off, knowing Charlie had enough. But it didn't work. The power rushed out of me even faster.

Pulled into Charlie.

"Charlie, stop!" I shrieked, but he didn't appear to hear me. His face was constricted in a terrible grimace, his eyes squeezed shut. I didn't think he was any more in charge of his own power than I was of mine.

Suddenly my knees buckled. Charlie sucked another huge wave of power out of me. Only my grip on Rachel's hand, and Oz's immediately grabbing my elbow, kept me on my feet. I swayed backward, my eyes rolling in my head.

As if in sync, Charlie's prostrate form heaved again, bucking against my bindings. Rachel, torn between her love and me, pulled me toward Charlie, trying to get to him. But before she could get too near, Charlie's mouth opened, a stream of white fire geysering out of his mouth in imitation of the fountain behind him.

"What's happening, Lyla!" she shrieked, turning to me and shaking me roughly. "What are you doing to him?"

"Not me," I managed to choke out between panting breaths. I'd watched Charlie See a dozen times, feeding him the small amounts of power I could handle unBound. But I'd never felt anything like this. It was like the suction end of a gigantic Dyson had attached itself to the Node, through me, and turned itself on.

"Tell her to stop," Rachel said to Oz. "Tell her now!"

"Lyla, stop what you're doing," Oz said, his voice calm despite the pale terror of his face. "Whatever it is you're doing, I command you to stop."

But I couldn't. The jinni in me screamed in protest, but something else had a hold on me. Something more powerful than my own Master. More powerful than my own nature. As powerful as anything in creation...and it had me tight, by the scruff of the neck, wringing the power out of me and into my friend...

Charlie's sigil flared up, suddenly, and the fire pouring from his mouth shot even higher. His poor body bucked one last time in a paroxysm so complete every muscle stood out as if it were being pulled from his bones.

His eyes, clamped shut until this point, suddenly opened.

And then, just like that, the fires died, the Dyson was shut off, and I saw Charlie's head slump to the side, lax in either sleep or death, just as my own consciousness hit the deck and everything went black.

"Lyla? Lyla?" Something was shaking my shoulders. I groaned feebly, squinching my eyes shut.

"Lyla? Are you there?" This time a big, rough hand wrapped around my jaw, another against my cheek, squeezing very gently. Something soft pressed against my forehead. "Lyla, please," the voice murmured, and the softness pressed against my cheek again.

I opened my eyes to find Oz's, scant inches from my own. The silver in them Flared with my consciousness, and my Fire wrapped around us like a cloak…

A cloak I pulled right the fuck back off of him as I sat up, pushing him roughly away.

And then I was on my feet, stumbling toward my oldest friend.

"Charlie!" I croaked, letting my stumble carry me to my knees next to him.

Rachel was clutching his hand, tears and makeup running down her face.

"Help him, Lyla," she gasped. Then she turned to Oz. "Tell her to help him."

"Help him," he commanded automatically, his own face pale as he peered down at Charlie's slack features.

I let my jinni go, and my Fire coursed out of me and into Charlie, this time seeking out his hurts. "He's breathing," I said. "But it's really weak. He's in shock. Physical and magical."

I let my Fire heat up, bringing up his core body temperature. A tendril of my Fire wrapped around his heart, pumping it for him as I leaned forward to breathe air into his lungs. After a few terrifying minutes, his heart picked up its own rhythm and my Fire withdrew, although I left it lying on him, like a giant magical heating pad.

"Charlie," I said, straining to keep my voice calm. "We're here, honey. It's okay. You're safe. The magic's gone."

His chest rose and fell, but he didn't respond.

I kept murmuring to him, as did Rachel. But when Charlie didn't answer for a few minutes, Oz looked between Rachel and me. "Should we try to wake him up?"

The jinni inside me said no. He was better off resting.

"Just let him sleep," I said. "He'll wake up when he's..."

A huge gasp of air left Charlie's lungs and he sat bolt upright, blinking and shaking.

"...ready," I finished, pushing back gently on Charlie's shoulders to get him prostrate again.

"Charlie, baby, you okay?" Rachel murmured, stroking a dark hand along Charlie's stubbled jaw. "Charlie?"

His eyes were still open, but I wasn't sure what he was seeing. Something told me it wasn't the night sky above us.

"Red," he said, quite calmly, at nothing, before shutting his eyes again.

I swore. "Let's get him home. Put him to bed. Hope he remembers something in the morning and didn't just risk his life for nothing."

Oz and I bent to lift Charlie, but when I touched him he jolted, grabbing my hand.

"You," he said. "He's coming for you." And then he passed out, his head lolling back on his shoulders.

"Fucking hell, Charlie," I said. "Way to give me a heart attack."

It took all three of us to get Charlie back into Rachel's SUV. He was dead weight, although his quiet snores kept us content that he was sleeping, and not actively dying on us.

We drove straight back to Highland Park, where Yulia used her wisps to help us carry our lifeless burden. We laid him on the chaise, and before we could lift a finger to stop her, Yulia smacked Charlie hard across the mouth.

"Wake up!" she yelled, causing us all to jump back, and then rush toward her.

"What are you doing, you lunatic!" Rachel yelled back at Yulia, grabbing her long-fingered hands. But Rachel couldn't then stop the wisp Yulia sent to smack Charlie again, and then a third time.

"He needs to wake up!"

"Yulia, stop," I said, but a moan from Charlie cut me off. He was stirring, rustling weakly under the throw rug we'd draped around him before putting him in the car.

"See, he wants to wake up," the will-o'-the-wisp murmured, her Slavic accent making her voice sound extra smug.

Rachel shot Yulia a dirty look before turning to Charlie. "Baby, you coming back to me?"

He moaned, a low, dry sound, raising a hand to his lover.

Without being asked, Oz headed into the kitchen we'd passed. I heard cupboards opening and closing, then the sound of running water. Oz returned a few seconds later with a glass he passed silently to Rachel. She accepted it with a low murmur, not looking at him, and helped Charlie drink.

After a few gulps, he'd drained the whole glass.

"Another?" Rachel asked, holding out the glass, but Charlie opened his eyes at that.

"Something stronger?" he asked, his voice breathless and weak.

Rachel gave the glass back to Oz, nodding at the little bar cupboard that stood in one corner of the room. Oz opened it up, then looked inquiringly at me when greeted with its shelves of bottles.

"The Glenfarclas," I said, after glancing at the contents. It was the most expensive Scotch on hand, and I figured Charlie would rather live than see it go to waste.

Oz filled the glass with what was probably a thousand dollars' worth of whiskey, and handed it to me. I held it up for Charlie.

"Here you go, brother. If you die on us, we'll guzzle this as if it's swill, like the Philistines we are," I reminded him. He gave me a sour look, but drank deeply when I held the glass to his lips.

When he was finished, he leaned back with a sigh. "Nectar of the gods."

"And you should know," I murmured, running a knuckle over his cheekbone.

"Those were the days." He gave a dry cough, then looked expectantly at the glass in my hand. I gave him another long draft.

"Do you remember what you Saw, Charlie?" Yulia asked. Rachel gave her a chilly look.

Charlie looked at the wisp, then at me.

"I do," he said. "But I think I need to finish my drink first."

He was strong enough now to take it himself, and drink he did. The entire glass, in long gulps that made me feel a bit nauseous. I would have been under the table with all that booze in me, but it only seemed to steady Charlie. He set the glass on the table next to him, then scooched up into a sitting position on the chaise.

"What I Saw wasn't good," he said.

"It never is. I'm sorry." I just hoped he hadn't Seen his own death again.

The look he gave me was pained. "It wasn't about me, this time," he said, taking my hand. "It was about you."

I blinked at him.

"What did you See?" Oz asked. I felt his hand, heavy and strong on my shoulder, gently kneading my muscles. It felt comforting. I should have twitched it off, but seeing the worried look on Charlie's face made me leave it be.

"Red eyes," he said. "Red eyes that were waiting for me."

I shivered, remembering seeing red eyes waiting for me, in another time, another room.

"Okay," I said. "What else?"

"I Saw a cage. With something inside it. Something that wants out. And it wants you, Lyla."

Oz's hand on my shoulder tightened almost painfully, but I welcomed the distraction.

"What do you mean, it wants Lyla?" asked my Master, but Charlie's eyes stayed on mine.

"I Saw you," he said. "You were pregnant."

My whole system screeched to a halt at that, like someone dragging the needle of a gramophone over a record.

"What?" I asked. "That's impossible."

And I should know. They don't make birth control for jinn, let alone jinn-who-were-once-human. But despite a millennium of sexual escapades, I'd never gotten pregnant. And after a few hundred years of not getting pregnant, I'd decided that, like all the best genetic crossbreeds, my hybrid jinni-human nature had left me like a jackass: infertile.

"I Saw it," Charlie said. "You were pregnant. Giving birth."

My hands went to my stomach. Charlie pulled them away, holding them in his.

"What you gave birth to. It was...it was strong."

"What was it?" I asked. I had to. I didn't know what I was, ferchrissakes. What would I give birth to? But I guess that would depend on the father...

"It wasn't anything I've ever Seen before," Charlie said. "It was just...power." He took a deep breath, squeezing my hands. It was like we were the only two people in the room. Just me and my oldest friend, about to tell me something he knew might break me.

"It ate the world."

"It what the what?" I said, my voice remarkably calm considering how I was feeling inside.

"It ate the world," he said. "I Saw it. It ate the world."

"But how? What can do that? Nothing can do that."

"There have been things," Charlie said. "Old things. But there have been things."

"How can I give birth to an old thing? This makes no sense. What was it?"

"I don't know," he said. "But its eyes...they were red."

"Red eyes," I murmured, remembering red eyes blinking back at me, the hot talons around my heart, the Fire that consumed me...

Suddenly it was like no time at all had passed between the moment of my curse and now. I was back in that overheated room near the harem, feeling my own heart burn in my chest and every atom in my body scream in pain as it turned... Other.

My voice choked on a silent scream as my lungs refused to expand, to give my body the oxygen it needed. My vision blurred.

And for the second time that evening, I passed out. But I did so quite decorously, drooping across Charlie's lap like a puppet whose strings had been cut.

My last thought was relief we'd wrapped him in a blanket, or I would have nuzzled his junk.

Chapter Fifteen

My eyes felt gummy, hard to open. But when I did manage to pry them apart, I slammed my lids back down, gritting my teeth against the pain.

Some animal was making a low whine and it took me a second to realize it was me.

"Here," said my Master softly, his deep voice pitched even lower. A strong hand slid under my head, lifting it gently. I felt the nudge of a capsule against my lips and I opened my mouth obediently. Oz popped four of something—hopefully ibuprofen, but at that point I didn't care if it was rat poison—into my mouth, then held a water glass to my lips so I could drink.

"Thank you," I said, after I'd swallowed the pills. I kept my eyes shut, but the hand on the back of my neck gave me a gentle caress in response.

"Keep drinking," was all he said. "You've got to be dehydrated."

I did as he commanded. As I drained the glass I finally risked opening my eyes again against the dim sunlight coming through the curtains I recognized as those in one of the big house's guest rooms.

"What happened?" I asked, when I'd finished my water and

he'd moved the glass away. He lowered my head back to the pillow.

"Charlie said something about red eyes and you giving birth, and you went purple and collapsed. You've been out all night. Everyone said you were just sleeping off using all that power, but I was worried."

I felt my skin grow cold when he reminded me about the red eyes, and I was glad I was still lying down. Oz's face hovered over mine.

"You look like you're going to pass out again. Lyla?"

"I'm okay," I said, after a breathless few moments. "I'm sorry. I don't know what's happening to me."

"If I tell you, do you promise not to punch me?"

"I'm not allowed to punch you," I reminded him, giving him a rude side-eye but staying still, trying to calm my breathing.

"Well, I can tell you what's wrong with you, but you're not going to like it. You're having panic attacks."

I snorted. "Bullshit."

"Red eyes," said Oz.

I hyperventilated, turning away from him onto my side in a fetal position. I crushed my eyes shut.

A big hand stroked gently over my hair, calming me. He made gentle, nonsensical noises until I had myself back under control.

"Like I said...," he began. I opened my eyes to give him a baleful glare. "Panic attacks."

"That's so...Dr. Phil," I snarled, forcing myself to sit up.

The smile he gave me was sweet and sad. He stood to help me sit up, plumping the pillows so I could lean back comfortably.

I wanted to punch him. I also wanted to curl up in his lap and tell him to keep stroking my hair.

It had felt good.

When I was situated, he asked if I wanted more water. I shook my head. He got some for me from the en suite bathroom anyway, giving me a moment to collect my thoughts.

"So," I said, fiddling with the glass he handed me. "Panic attacks."

He nodded, sitting back down. "Yup."

"And you know this how?"

He cocked his head at me. "Because I had them, after Afghanistan. The work was really...intense. The people we met, they'd lived through some shit. Collecting their stories was harrowing. Then Tamina's disappearance tipped me over the edge. I just kept imagining her going through the same things as the women we'd talked to...my mind was a pretty bad place for a while."

"Oh." That was a new spin on his need to find Tamina. He'd told me he researched violence against women, but I hadn't hooked the two together. I also realized I hated the thought of him hurting that much. I shook my head, clearing away such rubbish.

"So why am I having stupid panic attacks?"

He sat back, folding his arms across his chest. He was wearing that same button-up he'd had on earlier, the sleeves rolled up to the elbows, showing an impressive array of tattooed muscular forearm. "You tell me, Lyla. It's obviously to do with red..."

"Don't say it," I interrupted, feeling my breathing hitch.

He frowned. "But don't all jinn have...the words I can't say, don't they? That was one of the first things Tamina's grandmother told me. Jinn are made of black smoke, with red you-know-whats and red mouths."

"They're fire inside," I said, in response.

He looked at me curiously. He'd seen my tummy split just a tiny bit open, and knew I was anything but fire inside.

"I'm a horrible example of a jinni," I said in explanation.

His lips twitched at that. "So why would red eyes be special for you?"

"They're not. I mean, they shouldn't be. All jinn have red eyes, except me. But it's still what…it's what I dream about. When I dream of…the thing that made me."

"The jinni that cursed you? Kouros?"

I nodded.

"Can you tell me about it?"

I shook my head.

He leaned forward, taking my hand. I resisted, then let him fold my little paw in his giant one. "Lyla, listen to me. I know the last thing you want to do is talk about what happened to you. I know, because I felt the same way about what happened to me. But the only way to start healing is to talk."

"You *are* Dr. Phil," I accused.

"You can call me that, if it helps. Because I'm serious. You need to talk about it."

"Oz," I said, sitting up again as if propelled. "I'm like a gajillion years old. I've talked about it. Roughly a gajillion times."

"I'm sure you have," he said, sounding eminently reasonable. "Charlie and your friends obviously know the details about your curse."

"Exactly. See?" I tried to pull my hand back.

He kept it. "But I bet," he said, "you haven't really *talked* about it. About what really happened. What it felt like."

That made me shut up. My hand went limp in his and his thumb caressed my wrist gently.

"You might be right," I admitted, eventually.

"And that's the kicker. You have to talk about that stuff— the stuff you don't want to talk about. I told roughly a gajillion people, as you put it, about my research. But it was just the facts. It wasn't until I confronted how I'd felt about what I'd heard that I started to come to terms with everything."

"And how *did* you feel?" I asked, knowing my voice sounded challenging.

It was a challenge Oz was happy to accept.

"I felt helpless. Useless. Everything my father had told me about being a man—about fighting your own battles, standing up for yourself, being strong... well, that all went out the window when I was confronted with these people who'd not had any choices. And I couldn't help them. All I could do was nod and write down what they told me. There wasn't going to be any justice for them, ever. And now the country's even more dangerous, so we can do very little to implement the changes we think would help..." He took a deep breath, letting me know that despite the blasé delivery, his words had cost him.

"I couldn't save anyone," he continued. "I couldn't help anybody. I couldn't fight. All I could do was scribble down ideas and hope those things weren't being done to Tamina."

I flinched. When I spoke again my voice was husky. "I'm sorry you experienced that."

He gave me a lopsided smile. "I experienced very little compared to the people I was talking with. But to get back to the panic attacks, it wasn't the facts I had to admit, it was the emotional truth of the situation. That I'd had my vision of the world and my place in it totally rocked. Which wasn't an entirely bad thing, by the way. But I had to acknowledge it and make adjustments."

He fell silent, letting his words soak in. My eyes fell to our still-clasped hands. I knew I should pull free, but his hand in mine felt good, like an anchor.

"You can tell me about what happened to you," he said. I sat, mute, staring at him with tears in my eyes.

"Is it your curse?" he asked. I nodded.

"What if I were to command you to tell me?" I shrugged. I didn't know what was more powerful, the curse or my Master's commands. I'd never had a Master care about my story enough to demand it, after all.

"Tell me your story, Lyla. As your Master, I command you."

I felt the clash of the magic inside of me, an odd feeling of disorientation that left me nauseous and sweating.

But able to talk.

"I was born in what later became Persia, then Iran. Then, it was the Sultanate of Rum. Like all of our region, we were conquered by the Mongols."

Oz's eyes bulged, but he kept any comments to himself.

"My father was a wealthy merchant and I, as his daughter, was one of his most prized possessions. So when he wanted to get the attention of the new Mongol administration, he offered me to the warlord in charge.

"This man had dozens of wives and a reputation for brutality. I was a girl who, up to that point, had been spoiled... treated like a beloved pet. I couldn't believe my father would do that to me."

Oz's fingers continued to grip mine, his eyes never leaving my face. My story kept coming, the words falling from my mouth as if eager to greet him.

"My father kept a Magi. He'd been one of the most powerful Magi of his day, but he was very old by then, and very addicted to opium. But he had Bound one of the most powerful jinn in history, Kouros.

"Our family knew the truth, of course...that the jinni was Bound only in theory. The old man hadn't been in control for years...if he ever was. But Kouros seemed pleased to serve us."

"Wait, what?" asked Oz. "How could that be?"

I shrugged. "I don't know. None of the normal rules applied to Kouros, ever. He could do things no other jinni could. And he loved meddling, which is why I thought he might be willing to help me.

"So, when I discovered the truth of my upcoming nuptials, I went to Kouros. I was furious. Terrified, but mostly furious. I was young, and dumb, and so angry...I didn't think. I didn't want to be a woman, if it meant I had to marry the warlord. Would he help me?

"And he helped me, all right. I'd meant for him to make me a man—a son, so that I could inherit my father's property, not be married off to ensure it. Instead he made me a jinni."

"What was that like?" Oz asked after a few moments, after I fell silent.

"It was horrible," I said, feeling a tremble start deep in my bones and work its way out. Only Oz's hand in mine kept me steady. "He told me that he'd been waiting for me to come to him. That my wish was his command. Then he reached into my chest..."

I took a long, shuddering breath. Oz squeezed my fingers in sympathy.

"He reached into my chest, wrapped his claws around my heart and...it ignited. I'd never felt a pain so terrible. I thought I would die, of course, but I didn't. It just went on, and on, and on, until I blacked out.

"And when I woke up, I was as I am now."

"What happened then?"

"Well, I was no longer an eligible bachelorette, as a jinni. So my marriage was off the books. But I learned that day just how much of a piece of property I really was. My dad went ahead and let our house Magi Bind me, so at least I could be of use to the family."

Oz winced. "Oh, Lyla. I'm so sorry."

I shrugged. "It was the time."

"But what happened to Kouros?" he asked.

"That's the weird thing. When I came to, he was gone. I was out for a few hours, until one of our eunuchs discovered me. The room Kouros had taken me to, after I asked for his help, was a big empty room in a part of our palace we never used. I was found buck naked but for my Fire, lying in a room that was totally empty but that reeked of sulfur and was covered in ash."

"Ash?"

"The kind jinn leave when they die."

"Oh. So Kouros died?"

I shook my head. "No. There were a lot of piles...way too many for a single dead jinni. And what he did to me was hugely, crazily powerful for a jinni...but Kouros would never have cursed me if it would have killed him."

"So why is hearing about red eyes making you react so powerfully now, do you think?"

I felt my heart skip at the mention of red eyes and I took a deep breath. "Who knows? Maybe because I'm so close to the curse being lifted? Or maybe that little thing Charlie said about me giving birth to a monster."

"Yeah, what was that about?"

"I have no idea. But I can't. Give birth, I mean."

"Oh," he said, as if that thought had never occurred to him. "I'm sorry."

"It's okay," I said, my voice dry. "It'd be hard to explain never aging to the other PTA mommies. And God knows what I'd give birth to, what with not really being human *or* jinni, and all."

Oz's forehead wrinkled in thought. "Do jinn give birth?"

"They don't pop up out of the ether, so yes. But it's obviously a different process. More like...kindling a new fire. But they do mate and gestate, and everything."

"They mate? Really? How?"

I couldn't help but smile at his curiosity. "Are you asking as a scientist, or a voyeur?"

"Admittedly, probably a little of both."

"From what I can tell, they sort of...merge. Jinn aren't strictly corporeal the way we are. So from what I've been told, it's more like they decide to blend, which feels good, and then they can decide to blend and procreate, although that takes a lot of Will and a lot of magic."

"From what you've been told?" Oz asked. "So you don't, um, mate like a jinni?"

I felt my cheeks grow hot but I tried to keep my voice normal. "Nope. My lady plumbing's human, even if it no longer works properly."

"Oh, well, that's good," he said, his pale skin flushing. "I mean, that's good for you. I mean, not the part about your plumbing, but...would you like more water?" He reached over to the nightstand and held up my glass.

"Sure," I said. We both needed a moment.

He went to the en suite bathroom and I heard the sound of water pouring from the tap, then a glass being filled. He returned and gave me the glass and I noticed his hairline and neck were damp, like he'd stuck his head in the sink.

"So what, exactly, did you make of Charlie's vision?" he asked, once I'd taken a long draft of water and he'd settled back in his chair.

I toyed with the glass in my hands, mulling it over. "To be honest, I have no idea. And visions are assholes. But we did ask about Tamina. And what we got in reply wasn't anything about you, or her, but about me and red eyes."

"So you think you're connected to all of this?"

"It seems ridiculous. But if Kouros is somehow involved..." My voice trailed off. I couldn't begin to finish that sentence.

Oz sat back. "So what's our next move?"

I put the water down on the bedside table, and then twisted around, curling up into a fetal position.

"You're gonna have to practice your Calling," I said, closing my eyes on the sudden wave of exhaustion swamping me. "'Cuz we need a jinni. A real one."

I heard Oz get to his feet, and then a swoosh of fabric as the blankets were pulled up under my chin.

"Why?" he asked, smoothing the hair around my face.

"So many reasons," I said, yawning. "Help finding Tamina. Ask about what happened to Kouros. How he's connected to Charlie's vision..."

"Okay," he said, as my voice trailed off. Then, a moment later, "Do you feel better?"

I opened my eyes again. "Yes," I said, surprise lacing my voice. "I do, actually."

"Good," was all he said, as he turned to leave.

"Hey, wait." I took a deep breath. "Thank you for listening. And thank you for waiting till I was ready. For not commanding me to talk about it until then."

Oz's head reared back, expressing his surprise. "I would

never make you do anything I knew you didn't want to, Lyla."
I could tell he was horrified I'd even thought that way. I didn't
argue with him, for a lot of reasons.

"I know you wouldn't," I said, very quietly, after he'd left the
room.

Chapter Sixteen

"Feeling better after your night's sleep?" Yulia asked, glaring at me critically.

I ignored her while I finished drawing the circle of oil on the tarp we'd laid in Charlie's basement, taking a few deep breaths as I called upon my patience. The floors and walls were concrete, as it was easy to scrub, with sconces set in the wall for torches. We didn't do much ritual work here in Pittsburgh, since most of the creatures one might Call couldn't do dick without a clean power source. But old habits died hard, and every once in a while we needed the space.

Luckily, concrete floors also lent themselves to Charlie's favorite pastime, and I also ignored the stuffed, half-stuffed, or not-yet-stuffed animals strewn about, not to mention the jars full of...substances.

"Lyla," Yulia said, proving once again that she was much harder to ignore than jars full of internal organs, "I asked you a question."

"Yes, I am feeling better," I said. "Why?"

"You had such attentive nursing, is all," she said, as sarcastically as a Slav could, which was pretty fucking sarcastically.

"What's that supposed to mean?"

"It means you're getting pretty cozy with that Master of yours."

"How was I getting cozy, exactly? Considering I was sleeping?"

She glared at me mulishly. I knew she was worried about me, but I kinda wanted to punch her. Instead I began coating the oil in a thick layer of coal-flecked salt.

"He was like your frigging nursemaid. We told him you just needed to sleep it off, but he wouldn't leave your side."

"So? I had nothing to do with that."

"He's your Master, Lyla. Not your bosom buddy. What are you doing?"

"I am not doing anything. I passed out. I have no control over what Oz does or does not do when I'm passed out."

I realized that sounded bad even as I said it.

"Not that he does anything when I'm passed out," I told her, hastily.

"He'd better not. Because I swear to the goddess if I find out he's touched you I will slit him from crotch to tongue."

"Wow," I said, sitting back on my heels. "That was vivid."

"Thank you."

"You know, he's not that bad."

Yulia looked at me like I'd just asked her to shop at Payless. "What?"

I fiddled with the bag of sea salt and coal dust, studiously peering at the curves of the circle and adding a little of the mixture here and there.

"He's not that bad," I repeated, finally, wondering why I was persisting in this madness. Yulia would never understand.

And what exactly is there to understand? screamed the part of my brain that was as uncomfortable as my friend with the direction in which my mouth was headed.

Ozan and Charlie came downstairs just then, keeping me from getting murdered by my bestie, which was sweet of them. She glared between me and Ozan, muttering and waving her wisps, causing him to blanch.

"You feeling okay?" I asked Charlie, in an overly loud voice. He looked curiously at me and Yulia, but nodded amiably.

"Yes. How are you?"

"Recovered. Mostly," I said.

We stared at each other, communing companionably in silence in the way of long friends. I knew he was worried about me, and I was acknowledging that I was worried about myself. Charlie sighed. "We should begin."

I nodded, indicating that Oz should sit next to the circle.

"Why?" he asked.

"If your Will is strong, the circle will hold the jinni you've Called in its confines, until you're ready to Bind it. It will also amplify your power," I replied, "which we need. This isn't a normal Call. There aren't many jinn in North America, and none anywhere near Pittsburgh. So we've not only got to call one from Sideways, but also from a distance."

Apparently satisfied with my response, Oz stepped close to the circle. I told him to go ahead and sit.

"We ready?" I asked everyone. I really only meant the question for Oz, as he was the only one who mattered. Yulia was here because she was nosy, and Charlie could help ask questions.

Oz nodded, and I began his instructions.

"Okay. First things first, you'll need to command me to help you Call. I can feed you power."

"Are you sure? You just recovered from the last bout." Ozan looked worried. Yulia nearly choked on her own tongue.

"This'll be nothing like that," I assured him. "This is pretty simple. But like I said, we want some juice. Go ahead and command me."

He did so, asking me to help him Call.

My jinni responded, causing me to wince as Pittsburgh's steel-stained magic washed over my admittedly raw channels.

"I'm fine," I said through gritted teeth, when Oz said my name, jinxing Yulia, who said it at the same time.

Ignoring their shenanigans, I focused the filtered power at Oz.

"Focus," I said. "Just as you were taught."

Oz closed his silver eyes, focusing his Will. All magic worked as much on Will, on intent, as on raw power. I felt the power I was feeding Oz being channeled immediately outward. My Master's Will was considerable, which surprised me. But it shouldn't have.

I needed to stop underestimating my Master, on a number of levels.

"Now Call," I whispered, feeding him even more power as I assessed how much he could take.

Oz opened his eyes, his Flare so bright even Yulia, a being made of light, flinched back. Charlie calmly pulled a pair of Dolce and Gabbana shades from his front pocket, as if he'd been expecting this to happen. Maybe he had. Despite having known him for centuries, I still wasn't sure how much my friend Saw every day.

"*Te vash anuk a si,*" Oz said, his accent atrocious, but effective. He repeated the ancient jinni words of Calling, "*Te vash anuk a si,*" over and over, rocking gently back and forth as his Will built.

"Let it collect," I instructed, gently. "Can you feel the circle binding the Call?"

Oz nodded almost imperceptibly, never ceasing his chant.

The power built and built till it was sparking around him, visible energy waiting to explode.

"Can you feel a target?" I murmured. Oz nodded, a faraway look in his glowing silver eyes.

"Then release. When you're ready, release the Call."

He nodded again and a few seconds later, it was done. With a whoosh of power that made the torches gutter in their sconces, my Master Called with a strength and clarity that gave me goose bumps.

Within seconds a swirl of dark smoke formed in the center of the circle. It was so dark and thick it resembled a trickle of sludge, but it quickly grew, the trickle turning into a man-size tornado of smoke that began to coalesce. I shuddered, catching the sight of red eyes in the dark smoke.

What if we Called Kouros himself? I thought, nearly bolting in panic at the idea.

The smoke continued to condense, until a masculine, humanoid figure crouched on the tarp. He opened his eyes, glaring around the room at all of us with a furious scarlet stare.

He wasn't Kouros, of course. He was a jinni of medium power, from the thickness and opacity of his smoke and the brightness of his internal fire, glowing from his red eyes.

"You Called?" he said, his voice full of barely contained wrath. The only reason he wasn't killing us all was that the words of Calling effectively dampened a jinni's powers, even if he wasn't fully Bound yet, and the strength of Oz's Will kept him contained in the circle we'd created.

"We seek answers," Charlie said, even as I fed more power to Oz. Just because the jinni was Called didn't mean he was happy, and my Master was feeling the strain.

The jinni's eyes flicked around the room, and I felt his dampened Will reaching toward the power he could feel pulsing under his feet. But his Will recoiled with an audible snap when he tasted the filth in that power.

"Pittsburgh," he said in a deep, smoky voice laced with disgust. "You Called me to *Pittsburgh*?"

I sighed. "Relax. We're not Binding you. We just need some answers."

The jinni looked at me as if he had only just seen me, although I knew he'd clocked me second only to Oz.

"Ah," he said. "I should have known this is where you'd end up, you abomination. A filthy city for a filthy little bottom-feeder."

I squared my shoulders, the sting of rejection having long since lost its real edge.

"My people," I said, faking a sweet tone. "I've forgotten just how hard you suck."

"And I'd forgotten what abomination smells like," the jinni replied, unfazed, taking a long sniff of the air. "Rotten meat and rejection. What a disgusting cologne."

I rolled my eyes. "That the best you can do?"

His eyes Flared, an intense red far darker and wilder than my own. My own Fire ripped up in response, standing above me in clear challenge.

"Put your hackles down," the jinni said, waving a limb lazily at me. "I wouldn't waste my power on a smear like you."

He watched as I struggled to bank my Fire. I hadn't been around another jinni since moving to Pittsburgh, and my natural defenses were freaking out.

I didn't have a very good history with my smokier relations.

"That was pathetic," he intoned, when I'd finally gotten myself under control. "How are you still alive?"

"As the lady says," Ozan interrupted, pulling me back by the elbow so he stood in front of me. "We have questions."

The jinni cocked its head at my Master, assessing him with burning eyes. "So this is what Called me? Another mongrel?" A slit of red cracked the black smoke of the jinni's face at mouth level: a smile. "You two are suited to one another."

Oz's big hand wrapped around my own, causing me to start.

"I've heard it all already," he said, calmly. "As I'm sure Lyla has too. So why don't we get down to business?"

"Why did you summon me?" asked our guest. "You can't do anything with me, not in this shit hole of a city." The jinni eyed me again. "Although this explains so much."

"Explains what?" I asked, despite myself.

"We were looking for you," he said. The smile widened, not a nice effect.

"Why were you looking for Lyla?" Oz asked, although I already knew.

"We don't like loose ends," he said. "Or the abominations they're attached to."

"My end is anything but loose. Now stop wasting our time. Where's Kouros?"

The creature blinked at me. "What?"

"Kouros. We need to know about Kouros. Where is he?"

The jinni shook its head. "Oh no, little mongrel. We're not talking about Kouros. Anything but that."

I'd been expecting general noncompliance. "Then we Bind you. And ask you Bound."

"I still won't answer."

That would be tough to do, Bound. But I didn't bother to argue, instead keeping with the threats. "Then we leave you in this cage until you get hungry. And the only power available is our Node."

That brought the jinni up short. I felt his magic reach, touch the steel-tainted juice beneath our feet, and withdraw like a burnt paw. The jinni would have a little fat reserve of magic, of course. But if he burned that off, he would need more, like a human needing food for energy. Unfortunately, like cakes in which the sugar had been replaced with rat poison, our magic was deadly.

"You bitch," hissed the jinni.

I shrugged. It was accurate enough. "First off, what happened to Kouros?"

I thought that was the best place to start. Maybe Kouros was dead and I was wrong about Charlie's vision.

Please tell me he's dead, I thought. The jinni didn't.

"Even if I tell you where he is," he said instead, "you'll never find him."

I sighed. "Believe me, I don't want to find him. We just need to know what happened to him."

The jinni paused, considering his response. Finally he answered. "Luckily for us, *you* happened to him."

"Less cryptic," Charlie demanded, from an armchair tucked in a corner. "That's my game."

The jinni's eyes flared in annoyance, but he answered Charlie. "When he cursed you, Kouros made his first real mistake. He used an enormous amount of power. We were finally able to take him."

"Take him?" I asked. "Where? Why?"

"Why? Because Kouros is a problem. But he's *our* problem. As for where we took him, we took him as far Sideways as we could—further than any being has ever gone. And then we caged him, and we left him, and he's never getting out. Ever."

"Ask about Tamina," said Oz. I glanced at him and noticed the sheen of sweat on his brow, so I threw him a little more juice. Holding a Called jinni took a lot of energy.

The jinni's gaze jerked toward me, the red Fire of his eyes widening. "You can use this magic?"

I didn't answer.

The jinni, not fooled by my silence, narrowed his eyes. "So you have access to the Node?"

"That's none of your business." I didn't like how the jinni was eyeing me.

The jinni's gaze narrowed to a slit of ominous red. "We should have killed you when we had the chance."

"You tried," I reminded him. "Luckily, I was fast."

"We'll let you go," Oz said, breaking up our pissing party. "After you answer one more question."

"It's a deal," the jinni said before I could interrupt.

I swore and our guest grinned broadly. Oz may have thought he was using a casual expression, but in reality he'd just made a promise next to a magical circle, which meant he couldn't renege without serious consequences.

"I'm looking for a girl named Tamina," Oz said, speaking slowly in order to word his question carefully. "Tell me whatever you can about her current whereabouts."

I felt a small swell of magic as the jinni pulled on his own reserves, careful not to touch any of Pittsburgh's tainted juice. Those red eyes shut, the dense smoke of his body became even more opaque, until the magic was released with a faint pop.

"I can't see anything in this miasma of a city," the jinni said, with a frown. "But I did see a place where you can find answers. A house, with a Man Hole."

"A house with a manhole?" Oz repeated, confused. The jinni pointed a swirling finger at Charlie.

"The sparkly man connected to that one knows the place. That is all I can ascertain," he said. "Now release me."

And just like that, the circle gave up our jinni.

"Hey!" Oz cried, but he was already gone.

We stared at the empty circle for a few moments, until Yulia spoke. "Well, that was a waste of time," she said.

"Not necessarily," I said, trying to think through where my brain was leading. "We know that Kouros is alive, first of all."

"And trapped somewhere," said Charlie, musing.

"Which he would not be happy about," I said. Then it hit me.

"Someone tried to call something from Sideways," I said, remembering our earlier conversation. "Something big... something powerful. Something so big and powerful they opened the Bridge wide enough to bring over a ton of fodden and a bugbear."

Charlie nodded. "That is a possibility," he said.

"So what if it was Kouros?" I said. "If the jinni was telling the truth, and I don't see why he would lie, considering he didn't give anything away except that Kouros was trapped Sideways, what if someone were trying to free Kouros?"

"That would make sense," Charlie said, after a few moments' thought. "If the jinni is that deep Sideways, it would take a tremendous amount of power."

"That's it," breathed Oz, his head rocking back on his neck as if he'd been smacked in the forehead.

"What?" I asked.

"Why Tamina was taken," Oz said, looking at me like I was an idiot.

In fact, I thought, as realization flashed through me, *I* am *an idiot*.

"Of course," I said. It was obvious. But Charlie was confused.

"What's 'of course'?" he asked, snippily.

"If they were using the Bridge, someone's trying everything he or she can to get Kouros free of that cage, except the most obvious," started Oz, who looked at me expectantly.

"Use a Magi," I supplied.

Charlie's colorless eyes widened. "Tamina," he said.

Exactly. Tamina.

Chapter Seventeen

The Man Hole, it turned out, was a long-defunct gay bar in Greensburg, about an hour's drive from Pittsburgh.

We'd needed that hour drive to explain to everyone how Tamina would have seemed like a great choice if one was trying to Call a jinni...except for one small fact: as her picture attested, she was unInitiated.

So she couldn't Call squat. And we didn't know much more than squat, despite our theory that Tamina had been taken for her Magi potential.

"Oh, the mammaries," Rachel said, her voice thick as we ignored the stately front entrance of the house to drive around to the side, where lurked what looked like a hobbit door with a speakeasy grille. Oz and I gave each other a confused look but Charlie reached over from the driver's seat to pat Rachel's hand comfortingly.

"*This* is a gay bar?" I asked, eyeing the building doubtfully as I got out of the car.

Greensburg was dominated by a small university perched atop a large hill, looking down upon the town it fostered.

Luckily for Greensburg, the university was doing well and had started building "downtown," as the locals called the two smaller hills, traversed by two one-way streets, that held "downtown's" courthouse, and its handful of businesses, shops, and restaurants.

The Man Hole was actually the basement of a large Victorian house on the wrong end of one of those one-way streets. An absolute beauty of a dwelling, it had definitely seen better days. It was also the only house left on a thoroughfare that must once have been all residences and small shops, but had long since been converted into grim cement warehouses and auto-repair garages.

Against this squat gray background soared the graceful lines of the old house, a reminder of a bygone age in Greensburg's history—and the apparent home of an entirely random gay bar.

"It was a speakeasy gay bar," Rachel replied, taking Charlie's hand and stepping fastidiously out of the car among the pebbles and broken glass that was the tiny strip of parking lot lining the side of the house. "Back in the seventies and eighties, before gay bars existed outside of the major cities. In the nineties, when I was there, it was less of a secret, but still the only gay bar in the area."

"Wow," I said. "Who owned it?"

"Miss Rose," she said. "She bought the house for a song and fixed it up. Before her, the guy who ran it put in the bar for his cronies, when he retired. She made it pretty and played the songs she liked. Brought in local entertainers. The sort of stuff cronies hate, but gays dig. It evolved, quietly, into a gay bar. She ran a tight ship, though. It still wasn't a gay bar in a big city— no go-go dancers or cages or drugs in the bathroom. She was a lady who wore a hat and gloves to the store, and her bar was the same kinda place."

"I just fell in love with Miss Rose," I said, my mind creating a perfect version of her, gloves and all.

"We were all in love with Miss Rose," Rachel said. "She gave me my first job, as a teenager, when my parents moved here to work in the Westinghouse factory. I was a gay black drag queen living in Western Pennsylvania and she loved everything about me. Made me love myself."

"What happened to her?" Oz asked, also clearly mesmerized by Miss Rose.

"Oh, she got old and died. Kept the bar open till right before her death, though. Between the staff and the patrons, we did everything for her."

"And she really called it the Man Hole?" I asked, realizing something wasn't right.

"Nah, she called it the Golden Arrow. But we all called it the Man Hole—never where Miss Rose could hear, though."

"Wow," I said. "And it's still here."

"Yeah. The house was passed to a relative, who ran a real estate business out of the first floor for a while. But even that's been gone for ages. I'm wonder if they left the bar?" Rachel mused. "They may have torn it out."

"Only one way to find out," I said, approaching the hobbit door.

"Careful," Oz said, hovering beside me protectively. "We have no idea what's in there."

I nodded, surrounding us in a circle of black Fire that would turn to real fire if I needed it to. Then I used another wave of Fire to batter down the door.

We heard rushing feet inside the house. Rachel yelled "Front door!" and Oz was off. We followed, Charlie sprinting after my

Master, me running behind Charlie, and Rachel toddling after all of us in her heels. We rounded the corner of the house just as Oz tackled someone on the sidewalk in front of the hideous neighboring building. Whoever he'd snagged was fighting like a cornered cat, and Oz was barely managing to keep him down when Charlie and I pounded up. Charlie was there first and I heard him swear in both relief and anger.

"Aki?" I said, a second later.

Sure enough, tucked firmly in Oz's grip was our favorite dishwashing kitsune.

"We thought you were dead," I said, kicking him lightly in the ribs. Not enough to hurt, but enough that he knew letting us assume the worst was not okay.

Aki looked up at me, his enormous amber eyes unrepentant.

"I nearly was dead," he said. "They killed my *tail*."

I sighed as Charlie put a hand on Oz's shoulder. Oz moved, letting our kitsune friend right himself. Aki gave my Master a baleful look, rubbing gingerly at a scraped palm.

"Who's this knucklehead?" he asked.

"My new Master," I replied.

Aki raised an eyebrow. "Bummer," he said.

I resisted the urge to punch him for that bit of understatement. But he wasn't part of the inner circle that knew about my curse, so he had no reason to know my being Bound deserved more than a "bummer."

"What the hell are you doing out here?" Rachel demanded, puffing slightly from her little sprint.

"Let's not do this here," he countered. "Can I take you to my gay bar?"

A few minutes later we were all perched at the horseshoe-shaped bar in the Man Hole, Aki doling out snorts of whiskey in plastic cups. To Rachel's delight, nothing had changed. The bar was a seventies paean to the color brown: brown flock wall-paper on all the walls, and brown carpet on the floor that went up the sides of the bar. It was the first truly ugly gay bar I'd ever seen, but Rachel was in heaven, with a faraway look in her eye as she remembered her heyday.

"Long story short," Aki said, "I still don't know who attacked me, or why."

I resisted the urge to flail. "What? We were told you could help us."

Aki gave me a dirty look. "I'm glad to see I'm alive after you thought I was dead, too."

"I am glad you're alive," I amended. "But seriously, we need some answers, and you're the one we were told had them."

"What answers? Who told you?"

Charlie gave Aki the rundown, telling him about the jinni and how it had told Oz there were answers as to Tamina's whereabouts in the Man Hole.

"Maybe he meant an actual manhole?" Aki mused.

"No," I said. "It was clear about the Man Hole. But Man Holes aside..."

"You just like saying *Man Hole*," Aki said.

"Man Holes aside," I repeated, "you must know something. Even if you don't know you know it."

"This is like philosophy," Aki said. "I hate philosophy."

"Humor us," I said. "Maybe it has something to do with who attacked you?"

"Like I said, I still don't know who attacked me. It was a couple of half-vamps I'd never seen before. They weren't locals, not least because the blood gangs would never let a half-vamp live."

Charlie, Oz, and I exchanged looks. "Were they kids?" Oz asked.

"If by 'kids' you mean deadly kill machines with teenage acne, then yes."

"And you hadn't seen them before?" Oz asked.

Aki shook his head. "No. Never."

"Okay," I said, "This can't be too complicated. Aki, you're usually attacked because you've pissed someone off. Who have you pissed off lately?"

"No one," he said. "And I don't piss people off. I mean, it's not my fault if people are old-fashioned about things like personal property."

"Have you stolen anything from anyone?" Charlie asked. "Anything big?"

"No, and I don't 'steal.' I liberate."

We ignored him. "Then what were you up to?" I asked. "I know you, Aki. You weren't scrapbooking. What pie did you have your hand shoved into this time?"

Aki's stomach rumbled. "Please stop talking about pie."

"Aki," Charlie said, using his Patient Voice. "What exactly happened the day you were attacked?"

"Well, it started with that douchebag bartender at Slides telling me the Exterminators were asking about me. That blonde, the siren?"

"Loretta?" I said, surprised.

"Yeah. I figured she either wanted to conscript me or to find out for herself if what all the ladies say about my fox-style is true."

My eyes rolled in their sockets like bowling balls spinning in their ball return.

"What?" Aki said, catching the waves of scorn flowing from me. "I'm sexy and dangerous. Ladies love sexy and dangerous."

"So Loretta was looking for you," Charlie said, trying to move the conversation past Aki's enormous ego.

"Yes. And you know I'm not about to work for free for anybody, and Loretta's hot but I'm not a fan of her diet. So..."

"You're a fox, Aki. You eat garbage." Rachel said it before I could.

"Only delicious garbage," he said, clearly affronted.

"What does Loretta have to do with getting attacked?" Charlie asked, getting us back on topic.

"I'm trying to get to that, if you'd stopped interrupting me." Aki's slender hips twitched and I felt a wave of sympathy for him. He was trying to flick his missing tail in irritation, but all he could do was waggle his little booty.

"I was so upset about Loretta that I figured I should probably take a little vacation, till she forgot about everything and anything she wanted me for." He winked at me and my eyes once again auto-rolled. "So I went home. I was so busy looking out for blue eyes and blonde hair I didn't notice the two half-vamps till it was too late."

"Where did they jump you?" I asked.

"Right outside my loft, as I was opening the door. One minute I'm all alone, sniffing for siren, and the next minute I'm being set upon by hooligans reeking of Clearasil."

"We've been to your apartment. That was quite the brawl."

"No shit. Half-vamps are the *worst*. You saw what I had to do."

I nodded solemnly, remembering that brilliant brush of red and gold lying on the dark-stained wood of his loft. "You sacrificed your tail."

"I sacrificed my tail," he agreed, eyes filling with tears.

Rachel snuffled. "It was a beautiful tail."

Charlie, Rachel, and I bowed our heads for a moment of silence. Burlesque to the bone, we understood the loss of beauty, in whatever form.

Oz looked at all of us like we were nuts.

"So what happened after you got away?" Rachel said, after the moment was over.

"I ran like hell. Then I stopped running long enough to get mad. So I went back to my apartment, which was empty by then. And I followed their trail. They didn't even try to hide it."

"To where?" asked Oz, looking more than curious.

"It was weird. A squat across the river from Point State Park. Looked like the kind of place tweakers would set up shop. But there were a bunch of kids going in and out instead. And I didn't recognize any of them, but they were all Immunda, obviously."

Oz and I exchanged looks. Could Tamina have been one of those kids?

"Were they being held captive?" he asked.

Aki shrugged. "I don't think so. But maybe. Some looked happier to be there than others. And there was definitely a kid in charge, a human sorcerer. And a strong one, at that."

"A sorcerer?" I asked, alarmed.

Humans were sometimes gifted with the ability to manipulate the magic around them. Some could even go into the Deep Magic. But it was incredibly rare and usually did not end well, either for the human sorcerer or whomever he attacked before being put down.

There's a reason humans can't use magic. It scrambles their brains.

"Yes, a sorcerer," said the kitsune, meeting my eyes with a

dramatic tossing of his hair. "Can you believe it? And he wasn't even trying to hide it. He was casting spells right and left."

"Well, this should be exciting. We haven't seen a sorcerer here since…" I thought, hard.

"Nineteen fifty-four," Charlie supplied, his voice grim. "That one lasted all of three days before the Exterminators caught up with her."

I shuddered, remembering. "That's right. The evisceration."

Oz was staring between Charlie and me, his eyes round with his trademark look of horror and curiosity.

"What?" he squeaked.

I explained to Oz about sorcerers, adding, "Normally they're not that powerful compared to a truly magical being, however, and they're usually left alone until they fuck up. But not when they come to Pittsburgh."

"What happens if they come to Pittsburgh?"

"If they try to stay, things like evisceration," I said. "Because they're human, they can use the Node. And sorcerers never come to Pittsburgh for the pierogi."

"They come to rule over the misfit toys?" he asked.

"Exactly. Needless to say, the misfit toys don't like that very much."

"So it's a big deal that there's a new sorcerer in town," Aki said, nodding emphatically.

"What did you do after you found the squat?" asked Charlie.

"I got the hell out of there. I figured the sorcerer explained why Loretta was looking for me—so I could help get rid of him. But I'd already lost my tail to the cause; I did my part. I figured I'd lay low till they did their jobs and then I could come back."

"Way to be civic-minded," I said. He batted his long eyelashes at me.

"This is all fascinating," Charlie said, "But it doesn't explain why the half-vamps were after you. Did they say anything when they attacked you?"

"Are you crazy?" asked Aki. "They were *half-vampires*. The second I started bleeding, which was about a half-second after they pounced on me, they lost their damned minds."

"Think hard, Aki. They didn't say anything? Nothing at all?"

Aki pouted, but then his eyes widened as he remembered something. "They did keep raving about me being the person who could find things, which is true, of course. They wanted me to find the Cursed One... that's what they kept saying. The Cursed One. Before I could ask more, the smell of blood got to them and they went totally crazy..."

At hearing "the Cursed One," I'd frozen. Aki kept chatting about the fight, detailing the loss of his tail, but I was a million miles away.

I tuned in just long enough for Oz to ask about Tamina. Aki said he'd seen a few girls fitting her description, but hadn't paid enough attention to know for certain if one was an immature Magi.

Soon enough we were back in Charlie's car, headed toward the city.

Finally I spoke.

"When did this suddenly become all about me?" I asked. No one tried to persuade me that the half-vamps had meant someone else. Real curses are rare, powerful things, and I'd only met a handful of fellow cursed beings in my long life.

None of them were in Pittsburgh.

No one answered, but I heard Rachel rooting around in her purse. A second later she passed me back a very full flask.

"We'll figure it out," Oz told me as I took a long drink. "It'll be okay."

Then he took my hand, and I let him. Charlie raised an eyebrow at me in the rearview, but I ignored him.

I took another long, hard swallow of whisky, wondering when my world had gone Fresh Prince and flip-turned upside down.

Chapter Eighteen

From a hill above the house, Oz and I surveyed the abandoned bungalow tucked between two equally abandoned buildings. They were what you'd expect from a couple of long-abandoned houses: grotty, run-down, and distinctly dangerous-looking.

A great place to hide out, if you didn't care about getting fleas.

When we'd gotten back to Charlie's after finding Aki, we'd had a serious powwow and decided the first thing to be done was some reconnaissance—find out exactly who was living in that squat, and whether Tamina was among them. We also decided not to tell Loretta about the squat until we had something more concrete than "Aki found it," not least because we didn't want to tattle about Aki's whereabouts.

So it was just my Master and me, on a stakeout.

A very surprising stakeout, it turned out, for nearly all the magicals coming and going from the house were like the half-vamps who had attacked Aki and, later, Oz: teenagers.

"It's like the most dangerous boy band ever," Oz mused from beneath his binoculars, as we watched a pair of wyverns come out of the house and scuffle briefly, lighting each other on fire. They were reprimanded by an older ghoul who emerged a few minutes later, and the three walked down the sidewalk together.

We counted at least two dozen young people either leaving the building or entering it. The ones leaving carried empty backpacks; the ones entering carried full backpacks. Just as Aki had said, they were also all Immunda races, and all in their teens to maybe early twenties, at a stretch.

And each of the small groups contained at least one older magical, who was the clear leader.

Maybe more sinister than mere leaders? I mused, watching a scuffle between a much-older werewolf and a pubescent-looking incubus. The werewolf was clearly putting the incubus in his place, smacking the kid around until he visibly folded into himself in defeat.

"I can't tell what these kids are," I said, lowering my own binoculars. "Are they runaways or are they captives?"

Oz shrugged, sweeping his binoculars across the scene below us. "Hard to tell. Maybe both."

"Do you see Tamina?" I asked.

Oz shook his head. "No. Do you see the sorcerer? I don't know what one looks like."

"They look human. Until they blow something up with magic."

We watched in silence for a while, till Oz got bored.

"Tell me more about jinn," he said.

"What do you want to know?"

"Everything," he said. "Tamina's tribe told me some things... that you're made of God's fire. But I don't know much else."

"Well, first of all, I'm not really a jinni, so I'm not made of fire, as you know. And only humans think they're made from

Abrahamic God's fire; jinn think they were made in *their* god's image, just like humans."

"Who is older, jinn or man?"

"Jinn are much older."

"Where do they live?"

"Most live Sideways, like the sidhe. They have their own cities, the purebloods, and some of the greatest Sideways cities are creations of the jinn. But, like the sidhe, they also like to roam among mortals."

"So when I Call a jinni, where am I Calling them from?"

I moved my binoculars left, to where a bunch of children were walking out of a small outbuilding. But they were all boys...no Tamina.

"It depends on your power," I said. "Some Magi have more Will than others. Yours is very strong. That's why you could Call that jinni all the way from Sideways."

"I wish I could take credit, but your power helped a lot. How, exactly, does all of that work, anyway?"

"It's just what your magic does naturally. It automatically Calls to the most powerful jinni it can, that's closest. Then you pulled him into our world through your Will and your Call."

"That has to be awful," he said. "Knowing you can be Called like that."

I nodded. "Yeah, it is. But Magi are rare nowadays, while jinn are numerous. So your chances of being Bound are slim, at least in these times."

"How often have you been Bound?"

I lowered my binoculars to look at him. He was watching me, his Magi eyes wide, innocent.

"A lot," I said. "I can't go Sideways, so I've always been easy to Call."

"Why can't you go Sideways?"

181

"I can, but I have to take a Bridge, like the one we saw. And even if I did get there, where would I go? I'm loathed by the jinn."

"I'm sorry," he said. "But at least you're human, too."

"Oh, I'm loathed by humans as well," I said. "They sense I'm not right, just as easily as the jinn do. Humans can't usually put a finger on why I'm off, but they know I am."

"So how did you end up in Pittsburgh?"

I raised my binos again, recalling with a smile the move Charlie and I had made, so many years ago.

"Pittsburgh is legendary among us. There are a lot of cities that were as heavily industrialized by humans as Pittsburgh, obviously, but none that sat upon a Node this powerful. Before humanity, one of the greatest fey cities existed directly Sideways from here. But all that magic worked against itself, acting like a system of veins and arteries that pumped the steel everywhere—it spread so deep it went Sideways, destroying the city and totally corrupting the magic."

"So only Immunda can live here. Along with you and Charlie, who don't quite fit anywhere," Oz said.

I smiled at his analysis. "Charlie and I are certainly different. I think it's that we're not *half* of something, we're *extra* something. Charlie had gods inside of him—his magical channels are about as wide and well-worn as you can get. And I'm just...different. I'm decently strong for a jinni, which means I'm strong enough to at least skim the Node, even when I'm unBound. When I'm Bound, I'm a lot stronger. And when I'm Bound to a strong Magi, like you, I'm even stronger than that."

"So that's why you came to Pittsburgh? For the power?"

"Absolutely not," I said. "We came to the city because we're just as much misfit toys as everyone else here. Also, normal jinn can't come to Pittsburgh, at least not for anything but a *very* short visit, like the one you Called. They can't touch the Node and, as purebloods, they need magic all the time to live. So jinn avoid this place like the plague. And if jinn avoid it, so do Magi."

"Except for me," he said. "Sorry about that. But I know we'll find Tamina. And even if we don't... I would let you go before your curse was up."

I wanted desperately to believe him, but I couldn't be entirely confident he wouldn't get a taste for power and realize what he'd be giving up if he freed me.

"We will find her," I agreed, wanting to change the subject. "And then you can go back to 'normal,' whatever that is."

He smiled ruefully, his eyes warm on mine. "I don't think that's going to be possible. I've seen too much of your world... I'm too intrigued. I want to explore more. Plus I'd like to help you. I feel badly for Binding you, but I can make it up to you. And I can finally take you to that dinner..."

I opened my mouth, ready to tell him that wasn't necessary, that I could take care of myself, that he didn't owe me anything.

But help would be nice, whispered a traitorous voice in my mind. *You've never thought beyond breaking the curse. You have no idea what it means to be human, nowadays.*

And dinner would be nice...

"Oz, I..." I began, but before I could finish, his hand shot out and gripped my elbow.

"Tamina," he said. "Two o'clock. Getting out of the SUV."

Training my binoculars where he'd indicated, I saw a young woman wearing jeans, a long tunic, and a headscarf standing next to a battered old Highlander. Surrounding her were a group of young men and women. They stayed in a tight circle around the girl as the group headed toward the house.

"That's your Magi, all right," I said.

"Who are the people around her?"

"I dunno who they are, but I see another half-vamp...one young full vamp...a troll...all muscle."

"She looks okay, though," he said. "She doesn't look hurt."

"No," I said, "she looks healthy. I can't see her face..."

My voice cut off as a young man appeared out of the doorway, greeting Tamina and her cohort. He was a wiry young man with thickly curled, dirty-red hair. His arms went around Tamina, a greeting she did *not* reciprocate. Then the whole group walked toward the door, only to disappear entirely. One second they were about to walk in the house, the next second they were gone.

"What the hell happened?" Oz asked, sounding panicked. "Where'd they go?"

"Sideways," I said, sounding calm but feeling anything but. "They just went Sideways."

"How?" he demanded. "Why?"

"I don't know," I said. "They either found a portal, or they built one."

Oz looked at me, then his face went tight again as he registered my alarm.

"Is that not normal?" he asked.

I shook my head. "We need to get back to Purgatory. We're gonna need some advice."

Oz took a deep breath and began packing away his binoculars. "I'm just glad we found her, and that she's safe."

Again I made a noncommittal noise, packing away my own binoculars. She'd looked healthy and unhurt. But the sorcerer holding her was stronger than I'd feared.

So yes, she did appear to be safe. But everything else had suddenly gotten a lot more complicated.

*　　*　　*

I pulled up in front of Purgatory, parking the El Camino at a rakish angle. Normally I parked in back, but, still rattled by the memory of the sorcerer pulling Tamina Sideways, I wanted to talk to Charlie as quickly as possible.

Oz followed me in silence as I clattered down the steep staircase that led to the bar. I felt that cool whisper of magic at Purgatory's lintel, the one that let us pass slightly Sideways into the bar, rather than staying on the human plane.

As if reading my thoughts, Oz spoke. "Could that sorcerer have what you guys have here? What did you call it? A pocket of Sideways?"

"Yeah, he could," I said. "But Charlie and I built this, and it took years and a lot of luck. He had to use his Sight to find the right spot, and then I had to build it using power from the Node, and it took a long time."

Oz was about to reply when I held up my hand.

"Do you hear that?" I hissed. He glanced at me quizzically and was about to speak when Charlie came hurtling through the double doors that led to the stock room behind the bar. He leaped over the bar, landing in an ungainly sprawl, a café table breaking his fall. A second later three forms sprang after him, growling and spitting blood.

Before I could stop him, Oz had jumped past me, rushing to meet Charlie's assailants.

"Shit," I muttered, watching as Charlie rose, swinging one of the table legs at two of his attackers, just as the third adjusted his sights onto Oz.

My jinni kicked into high gear, and I felt myself swell with power as she reached through me into the Node, pulling hard. I sighted and pulled, popping up fist-first in front of my Master so that the nose of his would-be killer crunched wetly into my knuckles. My other fist was already in motion, smashing into the side of the thing's face with a blow that sent him flying. He was a full vamp, registered the tiny part of me that was still Lyla and not angry jinni, but I didn't have time right then to think through the implications of that fact.

My fist, which had swelled to the size of one of those Hulk-hand toys, deflated back to normal size even as it reached into my pocket of Sideways for a sword. A quick sight to where the vamp lay crumpled against the wall and I was there, slashing with a neat blow that decapitated the fanger in an instant.

Charlie was making equally short work of one of his attackers, staking the vamp quite neatly with the table leg. Which left the third…

…hurtling through the air toward Oz, who gamely took a fighter's stance, ready to face down what looked like the vampire version of Bruce Lee. If Bruce Lee had started taking a fuck-ton of steroids at some point in his career.

My Master, good boxer or not, was going to get creamed.

I sighted and popped up a few yards in front of Oz, but a full vampire in a blood rage is fast and ruthless, and he was happy to use my spine as a trampoline to facilitate his forward momentum toward my Master. I felt a terrific pain in my back as my knees buckled, but I kept my eyes fastened on the vamp.

My jinni was frantically healing me, trying to get me back up and into the running so I could do some rescuin', but I couldn't get my legs working fast enough. The vampire's long, black-clawed fingers brushed away Oz's punches like he was a toddler, reaching for his throat…

What happened next I only remember as pain. It made having a broken vertebra or two, along with some cracked ribs, feel like a gentle massage.

The claws found Oz's throat and I saw a bright bead of red blood mar the ink of his anchor tattoo and my jinni flipped the fuck out. She reached deep and hard into the Node, pulling out more juice in an instant than I'd probably used my entire time living in Pittsburgh, including the last few days. I felt the steel-stained mojo blast through me and a mushroom cloud of Fire rose and then fell, blasting outward in a burst of black Flame that picked the vampire up and incinerated him like he was a gasoline-soaked match.

"Well this is new," I said, my voice oddly conversational, still kneeling, as I watched my Fire dance around me. Oz was staring, a hand pressed against the small wound at his neck. Charlie, meanwhile, dropped his impromptu weapon and raised both his hands in supplication.

"Honey, put out your Fire," he said. "Your Master is safe. You hear me? Oz is safe."

My eyes flicked between my Master and my friend, the jinni in me registering his words. She backed down, taking my Fire with her as she did so.

Leaving me to crumple forward onto my face, every nerve in my body on fire.

Charlie and Oz were at my side a second later. Charlie went to lift me but Oz stopped him, tracing a hand down my spine and ribs. I cried out, thumping my fist against the concrete floor of our bar.

"Lyla," said my Master. "Talk to me. What hurts?"

I sobbed incoherently, tears streaming down my face. It wasn't my back—that hurt, but my jinni had taken care of most of the real damage in her effort to get to Oz.

"Magic," I managed to say, my voice cracking. "Too much..."

"She's blasted out her channels," Charlie said, grimly. "I've never seen her use that much power. She must like you, boyo."

I groaned and Oz ignored Charlie's comment. "What can I do?" he asked me.

Whimpering, I tried to move my eerily still legs. There was nothing he could do. I'd never done this before; I had no cure. The only magic I could access to heal myself was the same poison that had abraded me raw.

Oz, crouching next to me, lowered himself to the concrete. He stretched his long length next to me, wrapping a strong arm around my waist, cuddling me close.

"I need you, Lyla," he said. "I need your help. I can't do this without you. I command you to feel better. Do you hear me? I command you to heal yourself, because I can't do this without you…" He pulled me even closer, his breath hot against my ear. "Damn it, you fucking jinni. You did this to her. You can help her get out of it, or I swear to God I will send you so far Sideways you'll only have that bastard Kouros to play with…"

And like that, I felt my jinni uncurl inside me, and I felt her dark Fire cloak me, but this time in a soft wave of healing that soothed the fire of my magical channels. Then the comfort ended and the pain swelled, causing me to choke, as she reached for the Node… but then that power turned comforting again, clean and soft, like magical Neosporin smeared on my wounds.

I hiccupped once, twice, little shaky half-sobs, as I took deep breaths, pushing out the memory of that agony with each exhalation.

Finally I was able to crack open an eye, blurry with tears. Oz's bleary face was inches from mine, his Magi eyes glowing disconcertingly but his face expressing only concern.

He reached down and fumbled with something in his pocket, then I felt a soft cloth mop at the sticky mess of sweat, tears, and snot that was my face.

"You carry a handkerchief," I said, stupidly, as he mopped. "That's old-fashioned."

He continued swabbing gently. "Mm-hmm. But I'm wishing I carried two. You've got a two-handkerchief face happening at the moment."

I sniffed, trying to pull some of the snot up and away from his mopping. My finger rose, trembling like a pocket rocket, to touch the bloody nick that now marred his lovely anchor.

"You got hurt," I said. My jinni flared, unhappy with this fact, and I blamed her for the fear I still felt, like an oozing sore in my stomach, remembering the sight of that vampire hurtling through the air toward his throat.

"Not as hurt as you," he said. "You're going to give me a heart attack if you don't stop."

"Saving your life?" I said, feeling my snark muscles reengage in self-defense.

"Risking *your* life," he clarified. The hand he pressed to my cheek was empty of handkerchief, just his roughly calloused palm lying against my damp skin. "What did you do that for? I thought the vampire killed you with that kick. Then I thought you killed yourself with that magical stunt..."

"It was my jinni," I said, lowering my eyes from his gaze and rolling onto my back. "It's what a jinni does, for her Master. I had no control over it."

I blinked at the ceiling, happy to see Charlie's concerned face looming above me. "Are you two through?"

He took the hand I raised, pulling me up into a sitting position. I swayed like a drunken sailor, refusing to look at Oz.

"Who the fuck attacked us?" I asked. "They were vamps..."

Immediately my thoughts turned to Aki, and his attackers. But, as if reading my thoughts, Charlie spoke again.

"Full vamps, with tattoos. They're Blood Sect soldiers."

"Motherfucker," I groaned, wishing I could lie back down, but instead reaching for Charlie again. He pulled me to my feet, helping me to a chair. Oz stayed on the floor, watching me with inscrutable silver eyes.

"Why the hell would the Blood Sect attack us? We've never had any beef with them. What did you do, Charlie?"

Charlie gave me a sharp look as he stood and went to the bar. He grabbed a bottle of Balvenie and three highball glasses before returning to the table at which he'd sat me. Oz moved another chair to sit next to me, accepting a glass from Charlie but not looking at me.

"I didn't *do* anything. I came in early today, to check some inventory. I heard a sound from the stage and I came out to find those three heading toward the dressing rooms, bold as could be. They were surprised to see me. I asked if I could help them, and they just attacked. The storage room is a wreck," he said, indicating the double swinging doors out of which he'd been flung when we entered.

I drained my glass and then poured myself another.

"Great. We'll have to contact Lorenzo. Is he still head of the Sect?"

"Yeah. And he owes me. He'll tell me what those three were up to."

"If he's not the one who sent 'em," I added. Oz hadn't spoken, but he was drinking—a second helping of whiskey slid down his throat.

"He'll tell me if he was. Lorenzo likes you to know he wants to kill you; he likes the sport of your anticipation."

I shuddered. "Fucking fangers. Okay, I need to freshen up. Then we can go check on the vamps."

Standing, however, was a mistake. I swayed on my feet and felt Ozan's hand on my elbow. As soon as I regained my sea legs, I pulled my arm away, maybe a little too sharply. Again his eyes turned from me, fixing on the bottle as he poured himself another drink.

"Go," he said, his voice rough. "Go get cleaned up."

I gave him a mocking bow. "Yes, Master."

He flinched but we both needed the reminder. His pretty talk about dinner and helping me and everything else had muddled the facts.

He was my Master, not my friend.

And nothing would change that, no amount of anchor tattoos or pretty eyes or calloused hands that were so paradoxically gentle.

He was my Master.

And that was that.

Chapter Nineteen

My dressing room was blessedly cool and even more blessedly empty. With a sigh I lowered myself down onto my chaise, curling up into a ball.

I still ached everywhere, although I'd take this ache over my previous agony anytime. But it wasn't physical bruising that had me so upset; it was my emotional imbalance.

What the hell was that back there? I mused. I'd never used so much power for anything or anyone, ever. And that didn't make any sense.

I tried to logic it out. Oz was a powerful Magi. Maybe it was *his* strength that had made me pull so deep.

But that was bullshit. Oz was strong, but not anywhere near as powerful as some of my previous Masters.

So maybe it was Pittsburgh's juice? That could be it... the power had a mind of its own sometimes. Maybe opening myself up like that had allowed it free rein...

But that's where the "blame Pittsburgh" logic broke down. Even if the magic had taken control, that didn't explain how I'd opened myself so wide for it.

Or how I'd used it.

I sighed, shutting my eyes. The only other variable was Oz. I had been lying to him, and to myself, when I'd said my jinni had taken over entirely. Yeah, she had taken over. But she'd taken over many times throughout my life, and nothing like this had ever happened.

Because I'd been fighting her every other time, and this time I hadn't.

I'd wanted her to take over. I'd wanted her to save Oz, in a way I'd never wanted my jinni to take care of any of my other Masters. Even the ones who'd been pretty okay—if they died I was free, and I'd always been fine with that.

I just haven't been Bound in so long, I told myself. *I've lost perspective.*

So I tried to remind myself. I was dealing with Magi—a race of humans taught that another species of being existed simply to serve them, whether they liked it or not. Magi had no problem yanking jinn away from their smoky lives Sideways, from their jinni families and friends. And powerful Magi tribes would keep a jinni forever if they could, passing down a Binding from parent to child. I'd met some jinn who'd forgotten freedom; others who'd gone mad—like caged tigers—from centuries of captivity.

It was only luck, and Charlie's interference, that meant I wasn't one of those jinn, rattling against my cage with vacant, fiery eyes.

And Oz was one of them, I reminded myself. He was a Magi…

I felt fat tears in my eyes again, felt them hot on my cheek as they rolled down toward my parted lips.

He is a Magi, I repeated.

A Magi who flinched every time I called him Master. A Magi who never looked at me as if I were his toy. A Magi who hadn't tried any funny business with me. A Magi who kept asking me to fucking dinner.

I jumped to my feet and headed toward our small bathroom to wash my face. Bent over the sink, sudsing my salty cheeks, I heard the door to our dressing room open.

I lowered my head again to rinse off, bracing myself for anyone from Oz to Yulia to be standing behind me when I looked up, demanding answers to questions I didn't want asked.

But when I raised my head, it wasn't any of my friends standing there. It was the succubus, Diamond.

Reaching for a towel, I raised it to my face as I spoke. "Can I help you? You're really not supposed to be backstage..."

"Shut the fuck up, you cunt," Diamond said, her glamour-model features ruched in an ugly snarl.

I sighed, turning to face her. "Are we going to have to do this again, Diamond? Because I'm really not in the mood for a pissing con—"

Before I could articulate "test," Diamond was nose-to-nose with me, her hand wrapped around my throat.

"What the hell?" I managed to squeak, before her hand tightened. I tried to call my Fire, but to my horror, nothing happened. It was like flicking the switch to a broken bulb...I kept flicking, and flicking, but my powers weren't answering.

Diamond gave me an ugly grin. "I've been waiting for this. Ever since I came here you've thought you were better than me. But who's better now, bitch? Who's better now?" she repeated, squeezing my neck infinitesimally harder.

I wheezed, trying to shapeshift, trying anything to get away from her. I could feel the magic just at arm's length, but it was like Diamond had a buffer around her that encased me as well, the field dampening my own depleted reserves.

I was beginning to see stars when I heard a soft tread behind

Diamond and heard something solid thump against her blonde head, along with the crack of thick glass breaking. Diamond's eyes narrowed and she turned, her grip on my throat slackening even if she didn't release me. Oz stood behind her, clutching the broken champagne bottle with which he'd beaned the succubus.

"That hurt, Magi," she said. "When I'm done with your whore, I'm going to enjoy sucking you dry."

"Her heart," I wheezed, flicking my eyes between the bottle and Diamond's large breasts.

Without missing a beat, Oz struck a vicious uppercut with all his boxer's strength. Diamond's blue eyes widened and her mouth formed a perfect little moue as she looked down at the champagne bottle wedged underneath her ribs.

"Oh, my," she said, and then she died, sliding off the bottle to leave her heart, still shuddering faintly, wedged in the jagged circle of green glass.

Oz and I blinked at the horrific sight as I tried to get my breath back. "Lucky shot," I said, when I could talk again. Then he dropped the half bottle containing Diamond's heart to catch me as I toppled forward.

"We have to stop meeting like this," I wheezed, as he carried me back to my chaise.

Rachel gingerly picked the heart up in her gloved hand, her lush red lips pursed in disapproval.

"I know we like some goth decor up here in Purgatory, but this is a step too far," she said, awkwardly wedging Diamond's heart back into her body. Then she looked at her lover. "Don't you dare try to stuff this heart, Charlie. Or the succubus. We have enough clutter."

I was still leaning against Oz, his arm draped around my shoulder. Charlie was watching us with raised brows, but I didn't care. I was too tired to care about anything at that point.

And, to be honest, the heavy warmth of Oz's arm felt good. That was another thing I was too tired to care about.

"I knew Diamond hated me, but I didn't think she hated me that much," I said, staring at the still-blonde-and-beautiful, if now very bloody, corpse.

"This wasn't personal," Charlie said. "Well, not entirely. Remember, Diamond's now Blood Sect, too."

"Like the vampires that attacked you?" Oz asked. He was starting to get a handle on our supernatural world.

"Yes," said Charlie. "She either came with them or was their plan B."

"But why would the Blood Sect come after you?" Rachel asked Charlie. "All we've ever done is sling some booze their way and show them our tatas."

"They weren't coming after Charlie," I said, wearily. "They were coming after me, and Charlie got in the way."

Charlie nodded. "It seems that way. The vamps from earlier were headed toward the dressing room, and Diamond was obviously after Lyla. Although why she thought she could suddenly take you is beyond me..."

Only then did I remember the weird paralysis of my powers that I'd felt earlier, fighting Diamond.

"Wait," I said, before Rachel and Charlie could roll Diamond into the tarp they'd spread on the ground next to her.

I raised myself off the chaise slowly, painstakingly, feeling my thousand years in every joint, then plodded over to Diamond.

"She did something to me. I couldn't use my powers. I've kicked her ass a dozen times for bringing humans to Purgatory, but this time my mojo refused to work."

"Hmm," Charlie said, staring down at the dead succubus. "And she'd never had that effect on you before?"

"Nope. Hence all the prior ass-kickings."

Charlie crouched down next to the body, looking it over carefully. "There are a few creatures out there who can dampen another's power, but a succubus isn't one of them."

"Juju can stop mojo," Rachel said, from where she was mopping Diamond's blood toward her body and away from Rachel's shoe collection.

"Juju?" Oz asked, confused.

"She means a spell," Charlie said. "Or a charm."

"Like from a witch or a sorcerer?" I asked, thinking of the sorcerer we'd seen with Tamina. Oz shot me a dark look.

"Could be," Rachel said. "But I've seen charms made by supernaturals, too. Any creature with enough power can spell an object, if they know how."

"We'll have to search her," Charlie said, not making a move toward the body.

I swayed on my feet, catching the edge of my vanity, and Ozan rose to take my elbow.

"Goddammit," Rachel said, eyeing the lot of us as Oz steered me back toward the chaise. "Just because a lady is already wearing rubber gloves doesn't mean she has to search the corpse."

But even she was powerless to resist Charlie's eerily colorless version of puppy-dog eyes, either because she loved him that much or because his puppy-dog eyes were so fucking creepy.

She crouched awkwardly by the body, keeping her flowing skirts away from the blood. "I think we may have something," she said, patting around Diamond's breasts, avoiding the gaping hole underneath them.

"Um...," said Oz, clearly wondering why Rachel had immediately begun feeling up the cadaver.

"No pockets," I explained to him, suddenly realizing he'd tucked me against him again.

Rachel nodded. "She was her using her lady pockets. But luckily not her Lady Pocket."

With deft fingers Rachel reached down into Diamond's bra. She pulled out a bundle of sooty sticks wound around a charred bone and bound with something...either coarse hair or twine.

Wordlessly she passed it to Charlie, then she rolled Diamond onto the tarp, flicking the heavy material over to cover her.

"Hmmm," Charlie said, studying the little bundle. He was using both his sight and his Sight, creating a little swirl of magic in the room.

"Sticks," he said. "From a rowan tree? But one from Sideways, not a mortal rowan." *That makes sense*, I thought. Rowan often serves in charms as a binding agent, and even Sideways rowan is easy enough to come by on This Side. It would also be more powerful, saturated as it was with magic.

He placed two fingers on the bone, staring down at it with concentration. "The bone of a grundle, taken in violence."

"Grundle?" Oz queried.

"Not that kind of grundle," I said. "This kind looks like a tribble and is equally useless. Its only defense is to cancel out magical power if attacked."

"And this is its power source...," Charlie said, feeling the long strands of thick hair and staring hard at it using his Sight. "The hair of a sidhe Lord, also taken in violence."

I shivered. Charlie'd just described quite a powerful charm, binding a magic-canceling agent to a helluva battery.

Rachel made a face. "Not good," she said. "You pissed off someone strong, Lyla. A charm can only be made with materials gathered by the maker. So whoever made that was strong enough to take on a sidhe Lord, and live to rip out some of his hair."

I blanched. "Who made it? The human sorcerer?"

"No, not a human," Charlie said. "The signature's supernatural. But I've never seen anything like this before..."

He raised the eerie bundle to his nose, sniffing deeply. The pink tip of his tongue reached out for a taste, touching the charred tips of the sticks and the bone.

"Not fire," he said. "They *were* burned...but not with fire..."

Then his already pale skin went almost gray.

"Not fire," he repeated. "Fire..."

I froze against Oz, feeling myself growing cold. "What?" I asked, my voice sharp.

"Fire," Charlie said, looking up at me. "Jinni Fire..."

My hands were reaching without conscious thought, grabbing my phone from the little table next to the chaise. A few taps later and it was ringing. Lorenzo picked up on the sixth ring, his voice cold and inhuman as the rattle of a snake.

"So, I take it you survived," said the leader of the Blood Sect. "Good."

"What the fuck, Lorenzo," I said, only barely keeping my voice in check. "Why did you send your people after us?"

I wanted to hope beyond hope that it was the truth; that the charm was something they'd had in stock, maybe stolen or won in battle.

"It was a job, babe. One that didn't go through me, or I would have stopped it, obviously."

As he would have killed his own mother for a fifty, he was equally obviously lying, but I appreciated the gesture.

"Sure you would have. So who hired your boys? And girl," I amended, glancing at the wrapped-up form on my floor.

"I never reveal the names of my clients," Lorenzo said. I took a deep breath to begin screaming at him but he continued before I had the chance.

"But they weren't technically *my* clients, so I can tell you. We were contacted late yesterday by an emissary asking for someone they could hire. I punted the emissary to Sebastian. I take it he's dead?"

"If he was one of the assholes who attacked us, then yes. They're all dead. Including Diamond."

"Pity," said Lorenzo, as one might mourn a spilled well cocktail.

"Not really," I said. "But you haven't answered my question. Who was the emissary?"

"I didn't catch his name. Or her name. I can never tell with you people."

A chill went through me. "You people?"

"Jinn," he said. "You all look the same to me. Except for you, obviously, lovely Lyla. You're all woman..."

I hung up on Lorenzo when he started flirting, something extra hard to stomach from a man who'd just allowed a hit on me.

"It was a jinni," I said to Charlie, although I knew he knew already, from tasting our Fire on the bundle.

He nodded. Oz and Rachel watched us, undoubtedly wondering what was going on but realizing it was big.

"They've left me alone for centuries," I said. "Why this again? Why now?"

Charlie gave me a sad frown. "Because they just discovered you're alive and living in Pittsburgh," he said. "But they're not going to get you. We're not going to let them."

Oz's arm around me tightened and Rachel came to sit on my other side, her arm going around me, too.

Just then Yulia came into the dressing room, wearing oversize sunglasses and sipping from an equally oversize, whipped-cream-laden coffee drink. She paused when she saw the tarp-covered body on the floor.

"Are we redecorating?" she asked.

"The jinn are trying to kill Lyla again," Rachel said.

"I thought they'd gotten over that," she said, pushing up her sunglasses to sit on top of her head. Then she shrugged, an "it is what it is" gesture that was pure Slav, even if she was a supernatural Slav. "Should I put the body with the others?"

Charlie nodded. "I'll help."

Together they carried Diamond out of the room. Oz turned to me, eyes wide. "Others?"

"Never go into the basement," I said.

Then I let myself lean against him, Master or no, and shut my eyes against the world.

Chapter Twenty

I woke up the next day ready to take matters into my own hands. The jinn's assassination attempt had been the last straw and I wanted some progress on the Tamina front, pronto, so I could deal with all the other bullshit as it came.

Luckily, my friends all felt the same way.

Oz eyed the flat ground in front of us warily. "Are you sure it's safe?"

"Should be," I said. "The Exterminators are thorough. Besides, if they'd been around to breed this whole time we'd have been swallowed by a fodden back in the parking lot. They're like rabbits."

"Rabbits that can take down a troll," Bertha said sadly. I patted her shoulder.

"I'm sorry. You don't have to come, you know."

Bertha shook her head. "No, I want to. Whoever was using this crossing brought over the fodden. They killed my people. I want to know why."

One of Yulia's wisps brushed gently against Bertha's cheek and Yulia's entire long frame stretched, glowing eerily. "We'll find out who did this. And roast their bones."

Oz shuddered and Yulia grinned at him, showing off her needle-sharp fangs.

"Yulia, Bertha, we're after facts, not revenge. At least for now," I amended, seeing Bertha's face fall like I'd just taken away her favorite toy. "We have no idea who or what we're up against. All we know is someone has mobilized these kids—"

"Or kidnapped them," Oz interrupted me, and I nodded.

"Or kidnapped them, and is using them for an unknown purpose."

"And they're definitely Sideways?" Yulia asked, gazing at the Bridge with a combination of anticipation and fear. Yulia loved a fight, and she knew she'd get one in the ruins of the abandoned magical city that awaited us.

I nodded. "They have a human sorcerer who can use the Node to take them Sideways."

"How powerful is this sorcerer, exactly?" Bertha asked, raising her eyebrows.

"We're not sure," I said. "That's one of the things we have to ascertain. Now, are you ready?" Everyone replied in the affirmative, and I waved back to Charlie and Rachel, sitting in Rachel's SUV.

"Why aren't they coming?" Oz asked as we started toward the Bridge. "You and Charlie seem to do everything together."

"'Cuz he'd be useless Sideways," I said. "Rachel would be, too, but Charlie would be completely nonfunctioning. The visions would take over."

"Oh," Oz said.

"And Rachel wouldn't be able to wear heels," Yulia said, grinning wickedly, her smile slipping as her own booted foot squelched wetly. It was getting swampy.

We walked the rest of the way to the Bridge in silence, concentrating on our footing. While the fodden were gone, the wet field around the Bridge was riddled with piles of salt and massive, dangerous holes, as if a community of mutant ground squirrels had made the field their home.

When we finally got to the Bridge, Oz looked up. "Now what?" he asked. A good question, as the Parkway bridge loomed about three stories above our heads, with no visible means of getting up on top of it.

"Here's where it gets weird," I said, calling my Fire. It responded with a whoosh, sensing Sideways so near. Closing my eyes, I let it kindle inside me till it was ready to blaze, then I unleashed it with an audible flare of power.

"Whoa," Oz said, stumbling back, stepping into a fodden hole and sitting down hard. But he didn't bother to get up; he was too busy staring upward, slack-jawed with wonder. "Wow…"

I nodded, feeling a rush of pleasure at his reaction. Which was silly, as I hadn't really done anything, just touched on the magic that was already there. But it did look amazing.

Overlying the world we saw—the human Frick Park with the noisy Parkway bridge above it—was a very different one. In this world a set of intricately carved wooden stairs curled around and around up to a massive stone Bridge, free of traffic, that led to a round gate through which no light penetrated.

"Which one's real?" Oz asked, looking around in amazement from where he sat.

"Both," I replied, letting my gaze shift between the two, trying to see what he saw, trying to remember what it was like to see magic for the first time.

If I focused on our world, the human world, then the stairs and the substantial stone Bridge appeared like a foggy watercolor done on clear plastic laid over the oil painting of our real world. But if I shifted my gaze a bit, focusing instead on

Sideways, then the paintings switched places like the ghostly writing of a palimpsest. The stone Bridge became substantial, a gauzy steel-and-concrete monstrosity overlying it like a shadow, ghost cars and phantom trucks hurtling down it like see-through missiles.

"C'mon," I said, holding out a hand for Oz. He took it and I pulled him to his feet. He never stopped gazing up in wonder and I felt a surge of affection for him that I quickly squashed.

"This is incredible," he murmured.

"And full of good things to eat," Yulia said, grinning evilly. "Let's go."

We walked toward the set of stairs and I explained to Oz that he needed to see them first, backgrounding the world he knew for this new, magical world. It took him a bit, but he got it, mumbling something about Magic Eyes.

"Now keep that version on the top," I said, and started walking. I went in front of him, holding his hand for moral support, and he followed, if with trepidation. But when his foot fell on the first wooden step he laughed, a short bark of amazement.

"They're real!" Then he laughed again, reaching down to touch the wood. "This is amazing!"

"It is pretty cool," I said. But he couldn't go into this thinking it was all fun and games. "But Sideways is also incredibly dangerous. And Pittsburgh Sideways even more so. It's kinda like *Mad Max* in there, only less civilized. So stay on your toes."

Oz nodded, still staring at everything in awe, and I hoped he'd heard me.

We went up, Bertha and Yulia first, then Oz, then me guarding our rears. As we climbed upward, the wood under our feet became more substantial, the world of humanity fading. By the time we got to the top of the Bridge—now entirely stone—the Parkway bridge was gone, an occasional half-felt whoosh of air raising the hair on our arms the only indication of the traffic tumbling past us on that side of Sideways.

We walked toward the stone gate at the far end of the Bridge, shifting into a protective formation with Yulia and me walking next to Oz and Bertha behind us. I let my Fire flare and Yulia's wisps framed her body like deadly whips of light. Bertha pulled her favorite weapon—a nail-studded club—from her own pocket of Sideways and we were ready for just about anything.

"Wait, who the hell built this Bridge?" Oz asked, when we were almost to the opaque gate. "The Parkway can't be that old, and you said the supernatural Sideways city was abandoned a long time ago."

Yulia shrugged, her wisps echoing the gesture with a graceful motion. "It built itself."

Oz looked at her like she was crazy, so I stepped in.

"You don't build things Sideways, the way you do in the human world," I said. "Sideways builds itself. Magic-based stuff isn't like carbon-based stuff. It's a lot more...alive."

"As in sentient?" Oz asked, reaching out to touch the stone of the Bridge wall keeping us from falling off.

"Sort of," I said. "Not the way we understand sentience, but there's a kind of consciousness. It can be directed by the very powerful, which is how sidhe Lords and powerful jinn were able to create our cities. But it also creates what it thinks people will use. It likes to be manipulated...using magic creates more magic."

"So magical beings are really like helpful parasites, and Sideways evolves to attract magicians, like flowers evolve to attract bees?" Oz asked, ever the scientist.

I couldn't help but smile. "Yeah, I guess that would be one way to see it."

Once again his face took on that wide-eyed look of wonder, as if learning new things was the most pleasurable thing he could think of.

And once again I smiled at seeing that face, an echo of that pleasure sounding off in my own supposedly cynical bones.

Damn him.

I squished my face down into a frown and forced myself to look away, concentrating on the gates we were fast approaching.

"Be careful when we pass through," I said. "There's usually something nasty right on the other side of the gate, hoping to get across by accident, like those fodden did. Let us take care of whatever it is and try not to get yourself killed."

"Or do," Yulia said, smiling her toothy smile at my Master, who blanched.

"Yulia," I warned as we halted in front of the gate. If I shifted my gaze to the human side, I could see we were standing on a sidewalk in front of nothing, about two-thirds of the way across the concrete Parkway bridge. But Sideways, this was the Bridge's ending, and we stood at the lintel between the human world and the supernatural city magic had built around the Node marked on this side by Pittsburgh's three rivers.

"Everyone ready?" I asked.

In response Yulia cracked a wisp, Bertha flexed her powerful shoulders, and my Fire flared its own brief warm-up. Oz shrugged, knowing he was completely outside his own experience, a gesture of humility that I appreciated.

"On three," I said, pulling power and creating a sort of shield around us with my Fire.

"One," I said, and we shuffled right up to the gate. "Two . . ." We tensed, staring forward.

"And three," I said, and we all took a big step toward the black surface of the gate, our feet passing through it as Oz grabbed my hand and I squeezed an assurance. Then we shifted our weight forward, our faces plunging toward the black, and then we were through, our eyes blinking in the low light of the Sideways city as I built my Fire up fast around us and Yulia's wisps flared out, ready for an attack…

…that never came.

Instead we stood like Charlie's Angels around Ozan, prepared for, apparently, absolutely nothing but looking fierce.

"What the hell?" Yulia said, straightening.

"Hmmm," was Bertha's considered response, her eyes scanning around us.

"Wow," said Oz, and I knew that if I looked over he'd be smiling that contented puppy smile and I'd have to like him a little bit, so I didn't look.

That said—because the few times I'd crossed Sideways to this city I'd been immediately and viciously attacked, and had to fight for my life—I, too, was happy to look around.

And was not disappointed. When one wasn't pulling one's leg out of a fodden's gaping, many-toothed maw, the Sideways city built parallel to Pittsburgh was stunning. Frick Park wasn't a park, but a small square around which soaring, rounded buildings flowed. The architecture wasn't architecture—it was what magic did, left to its own devices, which made the buildings as quirky and fluid as you might imagine. And it stretched for miles, a beautiful skeleton of a once-great magical civilization.

One long abandoned, as became very apparent to the eye after that initial rush of awed wonder.

The stone was softly glowing, but the glow was dulled by an oily sheen—the visual evidence of all that steel's poison. And while the stone wasn't crumbling as might happen to abandoned buildings in the mortal world, it was obviously uncared for.

"It's like it's…dying," Oz said, after his initial stunned moments of silence.

I nodded at his apt description. "Yeah. That is what it's like…"

For the stone was faded and wearing thin in spots, with an air of defeat to it. It also held an air of menace, as if it contained some horrible cancer waiting to consume everything, including us.

"It's going feral," said Bertha, "with no one to feed it and cultivate it."

At her words I shivered, feeling as if all that white stone were watching us, wondering which of our little group to eat first.

"Let's move," Yulia said, her chilly voice even colder than usual. Clearly she felt the same.

Yulia led the way, toward the end of the little square that contained our gate. A statue to a long-gone sidhe Lady stood as if warning us, gazing down with somber eyes. I touched my fingers to my forehead in a supernatural gesture of respect as we passed, and the others did too, Ozan mimicking us with the trained accuracy of a student of culture.

We walked for about ten minutes through wide, long-abandoned streets, past beautiful empty buildings, before Yulia said what we were all thinking.

"Nothing is here. That's not right."

Oz looked at me. "Why not? I thought this place was abandoned."

"The original inhabitants are gone, yes. But other things have moved in, and we're not seeing any of them."

"What kinds of things?"

"Monsters," I said. "Things like fodden. Things that are hungry. Things that normally would have been at our throats from the second we came Sideways."

"Oh," Oz said. "And you're wondering where they went."

"Exactly. Not that I don't mind being left alone, but this isn't normal."

Bertha, who'd been suspiciously quiet since we crossed, finally spoke, her voice barely a whisper.

"You spoke too soon," she muttered. "We're being followed."

I tried not to react, but my eyes darted sideways. "Since when?"

"Since we got here. I wasn't sure at first. They're keeping their distance. But they're there."

A troll's ears were keen as a chef's blades, and I knew better than to question Bertha's call. So I told Yulia we were being followed, and we shifted around, keeping Oz central but putting Bertha in front and us at the back.

When the attack came, we were ready.

"They're coming," Bertha hissed, just as the first being rushed us.

The fight was short and relatively bloodless. Oz kept us from killing anyone with a shout of "They're just kids!" after which we changed tactics. Yulia's wisps went from bladelike to more like tentacles of light, and I used my Fire to catch, not to burn. Bertha put her club back into her pocket of Sideways, and Oz snagged two of the little buggers by their collars. When we were done we were left with eight whole struggling children, ranging from early to late teens and all some sort of Immunda.

We'd also all collected a fair number of cuts and bruises. The kids were young, but they weren't weaklings, and we might not have been so lucky if Bertha hadn't heard them coming.

"So what do we have here?" Yulia asked, pacing around the little cordon of Fire I'd made to pen the teens in.

There were two half-vamps, eyeing us hungrily. The rest were relatively innocuous races, except for the oldest boy, a disreputable-looking satyr with overdeveloped, bloodstained horns sprouting from his forehead. Sitting next to him was a girl with lush blonde ringlets, staring down at her feet.

Very familiar blonde ringlets.

"Hey," I said to her. "You. Look at me."

She refused and the satyr clamped a hand on her upper arm. "Don't do it, Marissa," he said.

Yulia, also looking suspicious, was sending a wisp creeping toward "Marissa" when the girl looked up, her gaze flicking between our eyes, her head giving an almost imperceptible shake. Yulia and I spoke at exactly the same time, in equally disbelieving tones.

"Loretta?"

The kids sitting around Loretta all turned to stare. One hissed. She rolled her eyes. "Nice work, morons," she said in adult tones. Then she balled up her fist and punched one of the half-vamps, who tried to bite her, and Yulia quickly lifted her out with a flick of her wisps, setting the Exterminator down in front of us while I flared up the Fire penning in the others, so they'd settle down.

We stared at Loretta in shock. Whatever was going on here, Loretta wasn't dressed as Loretta. The normally chic Exterminator was wearing dirty, camouflage-print leggings so cheap they were nearly see-through. She'd paired them with a very un-Loretta-like T-shirt featuring a current teenybopper band.

"I'm *undercover,*" she said. "And you've blown it."

"What the hell, Loretta?" Yulia spit. "You knew about all this and didn't tell us?"

Loretta's eyes narrowed and her gills flared. "I'm sorry. I didn't know the Exterminators were beholden to you, wisp.

And what, exactly, are all of you doing here? My cell phone wasn't ringing with news that you'd made this much progress, was it?"

"We were going to call you," I said, shifting awkwardly from foot to foot. "But we wanted to get you something more concrete. Connect some of the dots."

"Whatever," Loretta said, shortly. "I was getting something concrete, and then you four bumble in like the fucking Scoobies, ruining everything."

More awkward shifting. "Sorry, Loretta," I said, eventually.

She made a rude noise. "I have to think of how to salvage this."

"Have you seen Tamina?" asked Oz, obviously feeling no guilt of his own.

The siren looked up at him, her eyebrows flying up her forehead. They lowered, slowly, as she wrangled her temper.

"The Magi? Yeah. She's a nice kid. Doesn't deserve what she's landed herself in."

Oz's brow furrowed. "And what is that?"

"She was one of the first to run away with Dmitri…he's a human sorcerer with aspirations to take over the world, starting with Pittsburgh. A Russian," she added, glaring at Yulia.

"Great," said the wisp, in dripping Slavic tones. "Russian sorcerers are the *worst*."

Loretta nodded, as if this were common knowledge. Oz cast me a look and I shrugged.

"So what's different about this sorcerer?" Bertha asked. "He's not the first to come poking around our Node. Why isn't he dead already?"

"He's the first to bring an army with him, rather than assume he can waltz in here and take whatever he wants, for one."

"An army?" Then the other shoe dropped, right on my idiot head. "You mean the *kids*?"

"They're not kids," Loretta snapped. "They're killers. Killers who hate everyone and everything, except Dmitri. He's recreated himself as a savior to the poor, unwanted Immunda who were bullied and misunderstood for trying to eat their families."

"Sounds effective," said Oz, pinching the bridge of his nose.

"Yup," said Loretta.

"So they're all his followers? Even Tamina?" he asked, dread in his voice. If she didn't willingly go with him, I wasn't sure he was the type to rip her away from people she'd chosen to run with, even if they were dangerous.

"Your girl is different. Like I said, she was the first to run off with Dmitri. I think she thought they were doing just that... running off together. But he had other plans. Plans she's none too happy with.

"Actually, a lot of Dmitri's followers are like that. Most are with him willingly, but not all. Or they started out willing, but changed their minds when they realized his real intentions."

"How do you know all this?" Yulia asked, always suspicious.

"Tamina told me, obviously," snapped Loretta. "She and 'Marissa' were quite close. Before you blew my cover."

"We get it," I said. "We suck. But maybe we can salvage something from this. It sounds like Tamina is important to Dmitri?"

"Yes, very," Loretta said. "He is head over heels in love with her. She...well, it's hard to say what she feels about him. She's as much his prisoner as his girlfriend at this point, he's so afraid of losing her."

"Well, maybe we can multitask," I suggested. "We want to

get Tamina to safety. Back to her family. And it sounds like Dmitri would see losing Tamina as a real blow."

"Go on," Loretta said, her lips pursing in concentration.

"So help us get Tamina back. Our purpose is to get her back to her family, but Dmitri doesn't have to know that. We can use her to lure him out."

Loretta thought for a moment, chewing on her plump bottom lip, her third eyelids working overtime. Finally she nodded.

"That just might work. I know she's unhappy; she wants to go home. And I can't go back to being 'Marissa' for much longer, what with those bozos knowing my true identity." She pointed back to the penned-in gaggle of kids.

"We'll take care of them," Bertha said. Oz twitched.

"Not that kind of 'take care,'" the troll clarified. "We'll just get 'em back to the human plane, till you guys rescue Tamina."

Loretta nodded. "Fine. I can make contact with Tamina, see if she's willing to go, without letting her know I'm anything other than her ol' buddy Marissa. But if she's not, we'll have to rethink our plan, and you assholes will have to help me take out this sorcerer, Tamina or no."

"Done," I said, not needing to think about it. If we had Tamina in hand, and Oz had discharged his debt, I could help the Exterminators corral this Dmitri and be unBound by the time my curse was up. No matter what, I'd be free in just a few days.

Maybe it really was going to be a cinch, after all.

Chapter Twenty-One

Oz and I watched Bertha and Yulia herding the kids toward the gate out of Sideways, Yulia keeping a wisp harnessing the older kids and Bertha walking patiently behind the smaller children. They'd deliver the younger children to the human police, although—and I didn't tell Oz this—they'd probably take the older children to Loretta's coworkers. They'd question them and keep them safe till they could figure out what to do with them.

Loretta was all business.

"Here's how we'll play this," she said. "They're using the old palace as their clubhouse, it's got a direct portal to the human plane so it's convenient."

"And a palace," I murmured. Loretta ignored me.

"I'll go in as Marissa. Make contact with Tamina. Tell her there's someone who wants to see her. You can explain her family wants her back," she said to Oz.

"What about the rest of your patrol?" I asked.

"No problem. I'll say they went over to the human plane to forage after patrol. That's pretty common. Shall we start off?"

It wasn't a question, as Loretta turned on her heel and began marching off through the eerily empty, magic-laden city.

"Do you think she'll come with us?" Oz asked, as we followed quickly behind the Exterminator, allowing me to guard our rears.

Speaking of which, Oz's looked very nice in the high-quality hiking pants he was wearing today. I knew I shouldn't be looking, but I allowed it, since we were so close to victory.

"I dunno. She definitely cared for Dmitri at one point, but he's very different now from the boy she ran off with a year ago. And I know she misses her family."

Speaking of her family... "Did Dmitri kill them?" I asked.

Loretta paused, looking at me gravely. "I don't know. Tamina thinks the fire was an accident but we know better."

"Well, telling her the truth may help us convince her to leave. How easy will she be to get out of there?" I asked.

"Dmitri guards her pretty closely," Loretta said, jumping over a little puddle of pure power that lay, shimmering, on the wide white street. "He's very careful with her. That said, he won't be expecting anything like this. He doesn't know he's been discovered." She cast a baleful look over her shoulder, another reminder we'd blown her cover.

"What do you mean by 'careful' with her?" Oz asked, as we hopped across ourselves.

"He doesn't let her out without security. And he keeps her very close when they go to the human plane. But she does have the run of the palace."

"He hasn't hurt her?" asked my Master, concern lacing his voice.

"Oh, no. She's treated like his princess. He'd never harm her."

We passed under a series of intricately carved stone arches, the edges of which were starting to mutate in the way of magical architecture. The elaborate geometrical pattern was turning squirrely, and those patches of non-pattern were overlaid with a dark sheen.

"How does Dmitri support all these people?" I asked, keeping my eyes peeled as we went under the archways for anything trying to bomb us from above. We passed through unmolested.

"They steal," Loretta said. "Dmitri sends groups off to 'forage,' as he calls it. They either steal stuff from stores, or they steal money and buy stuff. Whatever's easier."

I remembered the empty backpacks leaving the squat, and the full backpacks returning.

"What happens if someone gets caught?" Oz asked, but I knew what the answer would be.

"They just have to sit tight and not ask any questions, and Dmitri comes to get them that night when they're alone."

"He just nips in, from Sideways," I said to Loretta, who nodded. As I'd thought, this Dmitri was far stronger than we'd originally assumed. And, apparently, the Fagin of Sideways.

"Shit," Oz said. "That'll make things difficult."

I knew he meant getting Tamina away from Dmitri, and keeping her away. "It doesn't sound like he's going to let us walk away with the girl," I said. "There's a good chance we'll have to take him out."

Loretta nodded gamely. Oz looked mutinous at this suggestion, but I could also tell he'd realized the same thing on his own. If we were attacked by someone as strong as Dmitri, neither of us could pull our punches, be they physical or magical. As a fighter he knew that, even if the justice-minded cultural anthropologist didn't want to admit it.

"We'll see what happens," he murmured noncommittally, and I didn't force the issue.

We walked for a few miles, Oz asking Loretta questions

about Tamina, then about Exterminators, then about being a siren. Loretta was exceptionally chatty with my Master. I'd known the siren for a century or two and considered her a friend—not as close a friend as my pals at Purgatory, but a friend. And even I'd never heard her talk this much.

Oz was good at getting people to open up, I thought wryly.

But Loretta never dropped her guard, helping us avoid at least two patrols we saw in the distance, steering us away from their route while keeping us from stumbling into other groups.

"We're just about there," I said suddenly, and Oz looked at me curiously.

"How can you tell?"

"We're close to the Node," I said, my voice soft, dreamy. I could feel all that power calling to me, wanting so badly to be used. And it knew I could use it. So it sang to me, in a voice even sweeter than Loretta's.

"It's crazy strong, isn't it?" Loretta said, her voice also husky.

"Can you use the power, Loretta?" Oz asked.

"I can feel it, but no, I can't use it," Loretta said, her eyes heavy-lidded, her lips bowed in a sweet smile. "We sirens don't get our magic that way."

"You eat...hearts?" Oz asked, remembering our early conversation.

"Oh, yes," she said, a sleepy, predatory smile arching her full lips. Oz blanched, but he looked curious as hell, so I explained.

"Sirens get their magic pre-filtered and concentrated through eating hearts. Preferably human. Magic's all around you guys, even if you can't use it, and it all has to go somewhere."

"So our hearts...filter it?"

"Yep. Which is why quite a few other magical beasties eat hearts, or drink blood, or whatever. They get their magic through human filters."

"And, um, who supplies these hearts?" Oz was being very open-minded.

"They don't have to be living hearts," I said, with a smile. "They strike deals with funeral homes, hospitals, stuff like that. But don't be fooled, it's not all aboveboard. Hunting still occurs, and more than is admitted."

Oz looked a little green as he contemplated that, and Loretta rolled her eyes.

"Don't be a baby; you eat living things," she told him. He was obviously about to protest, but words failed him as we turned a corner, and there it was.

As in Point State Park, which sat exactly Sideways from us in the human world, the Node was a fountain. This fountain, however, contained not water, but pure power, looping in a thick, shimmering, seemingly infinite wave. Meanwhile thick rivers of power fed the loop of magic, the ley lines that mimicked Pittsburgh's rivers.

It was beautiful, and the power called to me like a long-lost lover, just wanting me to touch it . . .

I awoke from my stupor to find myself directly in front of the Node, Oz's heavy hand on my shoulder, his arm about my waist.

"Lyla, I don't think you should climb in there," he was saying. I shook my head, trying to clear it of magic but apparently only making room for more. I swayed on my feet.

"Whoa, honey," he said, helping me sit down. "You all right?"

"Yeah," I panted, after a few minutes. "It's just really strong. Like nine thousand old-fashioneds."

"That's a lot of old-fashioneds," he said, sitting next to me companionably. "And that explains a lot."

I leaned against him, feeling like a woozy drunk, and apparently acting like one too, from his reaction to me. Closing my eyes, I took a few deep breaths against all the spinning the world was doing, and tried to ground myself against all that power.

A few minutes later I felt better...or at least less likely to keel over.

"We should go," I said, getting unsteadily to my feet. "It's not safe here..."

As if to prove my point, Loretta screamed a warning. Twirling toward her, I saw the first of the shadow wraiths detach from an actual shadow, gliding swiftly and inexorably toward the siren.

I used a coil of my Fire to pull her sharply back, pushing her and Oz behind me as an entire battalion of the shadows detached, advancing upon us like a wall of hazy gray in which just the faintest tracing of a face could be distinguished.

"What the hell?" Oz asked, putting Loretta protectively behind him and stepping up next to me.

"Shadow wraiths," I said, "although you'd call them ghosts. Those who used to live here, and were killed by the same steel that bound their magic to the place in the form of shadows of themselves."

"What do we do?"

"You do nothing. I kill them," I said, reaching even as I did so toward the Node.

I sank into all that juice like a fork into a meringue, and it flowed eagerly into me. Without my even consciously manipulating the power it streamed out of me in a single powerful beam of light that cut through the wall of wraiths, dispersing them in a shower of sparks that belied their superficially incorporeal appearance. They looked like shadows until they ripped your head off; then it was more than apparent they had some physical heft.

I had to wrestle with the Node to regain control of myself, and there were a few tense seconds during which I thought I might lose. But then the light streaming from me died with the last of the wraiths, and I collapsed to my knees, my channels burning and raw.

"Heal yourself," Oz's voice whispered in my ear. "I command you to make yourself feel better."

And just like before, my jinni did as my Master commanded, soothing the aching magical wounds inside me. They still felt stretched and sore, but I wasn't in agony.

I also realized that Oz was stroking my back with a big, gentle hand, comforting me immensely in a way I didn't want to examine.

Standing up, I nodded at him in thanks but didn't speak. Then I went to thank Loretta for the warning, but she was staring at me, open-mouthed with wonder.

"She said you'd be powerful now that you're Bound, but I've never seen anything like that," she said, then snapped her mouth shut as if realizing she'd made a boo-boo.

I narrowed my eyes at her. "What do you mean she said I'd be powerful?"

Loretta shook her head, as if she was confused. "Not *you* you, but anyone who could fully tap the Node. Tamina said that person would be very, very powerful. And she was right.

"Anyway, damn, girl," she said, acting like my old friend Loretta again. "I've never seen you do anything like that. That was some shit!" And with that, she turned on her heel, Oz following her after giving me a quizzical look.

After a moment I followed too, choosing to trust my old friend despite hearing that sweet little voice saying the same thing over and over, like a litany.

"She said you'd be powerful . . . she said you'd be powerful . . . she said you'd be powerful . . .

"And she was right."

"There's where they're kept," Loretta said, pointing at the palace nestled in the valley below us.

"The perks of Sideways," I muttered, mentally comparing the abandoned house in our world to its Sideways counterpart, before focusing on the task at hand. "OK, we need to get to Tamina and get out, preferably unseen. We can figure out what to do with the other kids later. Agreed?"

Before Oz could protest, I interrupted him.

"Look, it's not just my freedom I'm thinking about. We've got just a few days till my curse is up; we're good. But there are also two of us, and a shit-ton of those kids, not all of whom appear to resent their new existence. Our primary mission is Tamina. We get her out, get Loretta out, confab with both of them about the best way to get everyone else out if they want to leave."

"We need to get everyone out, get them back to their families," Oz said, but I shook my head. To my surprise, so did Loretta.

"Oh, no. Some of them wouldn't leave," said the Exterminator. "They'd rather die."

"They're not human," I reminded my Master. "They like it here."

Oz frowned, processing what we'd told him. "So just getting Tamina out, for now, is the plan?"

I nodded, then turned to our guide. "Loretta, it's your call on what we do next."

The Exterminator nodded, ringlets bouncing adorably but

blue eyes hard as ice. "As I said, I'll go down first. Tell Tamina I've found you, see what she wants to do."

"Tell her it's Oz," he said, his voice urgent. "From home."

Loretta nodded. "No prob."

"Okay," I said. "We'll stay here. For how long?"

"Probably a few hours," Loretta said. "Dmitri tends to keep Tamina close, so I'll have to wait till she's alone. That could take a while. But you should be okay here. Nobody ever comes this way; it's really boggy between here and the palace. Think you two can handle that?"

"We'll be fine," Oz said. "Stay safe. And thank you for helping us."

"Whatever," Loretta said. "At least I can do something good with the shambles you made of my hard work."

And then the Exterminator was gone, disappearing into the undergrowth and leaving me and my Master alone to keep each other company for the next few hours.

Chapter Twenty-Two

Oz and I stood staring at one another after Loretta left, like teenagers on a first date.

"There's a fallen log over there," Oz said, pointing behind me. "We can sit."

I turned to where he was pointing. "Okay."

We went, and sat side by side, about a foot between us. We passed about a half hour like that, sitting awkwardly, each thinking his or her own thoughts.

"We've found Tamina," he said, interrupting the silence. "If all goes well, you'll be free soon."

"And you'll have discharged your debt."

He nodded. "That will feel good."

"So will being free."

"I've been thinking...," he began, and I felt my stomach knot. I feared what would come next. He was going to tell me he'd changed his mind. That he'd realized what we could do together (meaning he'd realized what he could do with me). That he was my Master, and I was his to command.

"...you're going to need some help when your curse is lifted.

And I don't think any of your friends, as much as they love you, will be much use for this stuff. You need a human around, someone who can help you navigate. I took a year's leave when I got back from Afghanistan, so I have the time. I could stick around, help you adjust."

I stared at him like he'd grown another head. He coughed and looked at his feet.

"I mean, I don't have to. I could go back to Chicago. But if you think you do need help..."

"You really are going to let me go?" I said. Two things were finally dawning on me: that Ozan was legit and that part of me had always counted on my belief he'd welsh on his part of the deal. Once he came along, I'd believed I'd be a jinni forever.

"Of course," he said, looking confused. "I said I would."

"Yeah, but..." I wanted to say so many things that would be stupid, under the circumstances. Maybe he hadn't realized how much power he truly had over me?

"Look," he said, "I get it. I get that you're totally vulnerable. That you have this...condition, we'll call it, that makes you an easy target for someone like me. But I'm not like that."

He said that last line with such vehemence I was taken aback.

"Maybe I'd be different if I'd been raised as a Magi," he continued, his silver eyes locked on mine. "Maybe I'd think of you as my property, and see you as my natural servant, or whatever. But I was raised human. By a woman who loved me and a man who loved her so much that when she died his light went out till the day he followed her to the grave. Neither one of my parents were perfect, but they taught me to value others and to fight for the underdog.

"Now, you're not naturally an underdog," he said, his hand reaching up to brush my dark bangs from my face. "And I wouldn't want to get in a ring with you. Which is why I hate knowing that I've…caged you. I hate it. And I would never have done it if I hadn't been desperate for your help, or if I didn't know myself well enough to be confident I'd let you go when the time came."

I blinked at him, feeling overwhelmed. I was supposed to hate Ozan. And chances were good I'd hate him again before all this was over. But the problem with living so long was that I'd heard a lot of bullshit over the years, and I'd learned to *listen*. As he looked straight at me, talking from his heart, all I could see was his father's pugilistic Irish features, complete with battered nose and thin, wry lips, while his Turkish mother shone through his silver Magi eyes.

In that moment I *heard* him, and not just because of his ability to Call my Fire.

"You are really going to let me go," I said.

He nodded. "Of course. And I'll stay, if you'll let me. Just to help you adjust. Nothing more, unless you want it."

Today was apparently a day of revelations. Tamina's whereabouts, the fact Oz *really* wasn't a dick, that I would really be free of the curse that had bound me for centuries, and—much to my startlement—the fact I was pretty sure I did want "it," whatever form "it" would come in.

Also the fact that, as intent as I'd always been on my curse, I'd not really thought about what its being lifted would mean. I'd not considered the fact that I'd been a jinni for nearly a thousand years and that I had no idea how to be anything else anymore.

"I'll be human," I said. "Totally, absolutely human."

A wave of panic rose, making my stomach roil and my skin grow clammy. I felt sweat bead on my forehead. I wanted to not be a jinni so badly I'd never really thought through what it would mean to be human again.

Oz's eyes widened. "It'll be okay, Lyla. It'll be good. You'll be fine."

My breathing was ragged. He put his hand behind my head, pushing it toward my knees.

"Breathe, honey. Just breathe."

I tried to do as he said, realizing I was hyperventilating. His warm hand stroked down my back soothingly as I tried to wrestle control from my lungs, which were apparently determined to keep spasming on me.

"It'll be fine," he murmured. "I've made a list of things you'll need. And we'll get them. Starting with a Social Security number. Once you have that, we'll get you everything else…"

He had a list, I thought. While I was sitting around thinking of ways to escape his clutches, he had been making lists of ways to help me once I became human again.

I sat up abruptly, too quickly, and I almost fell backward off the tree trunk. His arm caught me, strong and warm, and on impulse I leaned forward and kissed him. I was still panting from panic, but his lips were firm and hot and they met mine like he was hungry for me. I pulled back almost immediately, drawing in a deep breath, but a second later he followed me, claiming my lips with his.

I'm not sure what would have happened if we hadn't heard an awkward throat-clearing from in front of us.

Loretta stood there, peering at us with a smirk draped languidly across her pink lips.

Oz shot up off the trunk and I looked down at my feet, a perfect tableau of teens caught necking, even though I was well over a millennium old and Oz was about as grown-up a man as I'd met in those thousand years.

"I found Tamina," Loretta said. "She's in her rooms. Are you ready?"

Oz held out his hand to me and I took it, letting him pull me to my feet. But he didn't let go, giving my hand a firm squeeze instead.

"We're ready," he said, speaking for both of us.

And just like that, I knew everything was going to be all right.

I was ready.

We followed, Oz first and me taking the rear. I was keeping an eye on Loretta as well as guarding our backs.

Then she raised her hand before pushing it down, indicating we should hide. We lowered ourselves behind the dense brush at the side of the path we were about to cross.

"Quiet," Loretta said, indicating with a little wave the path we waited near. "We have to take this all the way to a Bridge that crosses over a ley line—it's the only way over. And then we're almost at the palace. Ready?"

We nodded, and spent a tense fifteen minutes skittering toward and over a smooth stone bridge under which a river of magic flowed, its shining white power dulled by a dark stain on top, the steel polluting Pittsburgh's potent juice.

"Shhh," she whispered at one point, stopping us and pulling us off the road. Sure enough, a few minutes later a patrol passed by, consisting of a gaggle of what looked like seventh graders. One had a bloody mouth, however, and another was casually chewing on what I think must have been a fodden's clawed arm.

After the patrol passed, we were off again. A few minutes down the road, however, we veered off onto a small dirt path. A few twists and turns later, we could see, rising above the massive trees framing our heads, the spires of the palace warehousing Tamina and all the other taken children.

"There's a few entrances," Loretta said. "And a few extra places we can get in, that aren't exactly entrances." She gave us a vicious grin and was off, skittering through the trees like a squirrel with gills.

We followed her gleaming hair until it stopped in front of a round, dark hole in one of the stained white walls of the palace. It was huge, big enough that we could walk two abreast, and I could walk without even stooping, although Oz would have to duck.

"I think this used to be a poop hole, or something," she said. "But it's clean now. Mostly."

Loretta gave a laissez-faire shrug, then popped through the hole. I groaned inwardly, wondering what I'd done in a past life to deserve shimmying up a supernatural poop chute in this one, but followed gamely.

The tunnel was indeed mostly clean. We walked up a steep grade until we came to a fancy-looking grille big enough for us to fit through.

"This way," Loretta said, popping out the grille with practiced ease. She gestured us through into what had to be an abandoned hallway, thick with glowing flakes of magical dust.

She led us down a short corridor, then to another fancy grille. "We're almost there," she said, popping that one open as well. This tunnel was narrower and far lower, and we needed to crawl to get through. But after only a few minutes, Loretta came to a halt.

"Here," she said, scooching back so Oz and I could crawl forward, peering through the grille in front of us.

Below us, in a small if luxurious room, lay a girl. She was lying in the cool dark, a cloth over her eyes.

Her headscarf was gone, but she was wearing a modestly cut tunic over baggy jeans, and there was a pile of scarves draped over a side chair.

As if sensing someone was there, the girl removed the cloth from her eyes. When she opened them, they were still the multicolored eyes of an immature Magi, not the glowing silver eyes of a mature one. She hadn't yet been Initiated.

But she also wasn't the plump-cheeked thirteen-year-old in Oz's picture from when he'd first met her, at the beginning of his time overseas. At seventeen, she was a young woman, much prettier and older looking than we could see when we'd sighted her earlier, through our binoculars.

"Tamina," Oz said, sounding utterly grateful.

"Tamina," I repeated, surprised to find myself equally grateful to see my ticket out of jinnihood.

Maybe I was ready to be human again after all.

Chapter Twenty-Three

W ho's there?" Tamina whispered, sitting bolt upright in her luxuriant bed.

"It's Marissa," hissed Loretta, obviously sticking to her cover.

Tamina looked relieved. "Marissa, I was worried. What took you so long?" The girl's voice was soft, thickly accented but totally fluent.

"There were some patrols," Loretta said. "But I brought your friend."

"Oz?" Tamina sat bolt upright, looking toward the grille with avid eyes.

"Yeah," said Oz, his eyes glistening. "It's me, kid."

Fat tears rolled down Tamina's cheeks. "No. You lie. This cannot be true."

"It's no lie," Oz said, his voice gentle. "Your family sent me to look for you."

"And you found me." The girl was sobbing now and I felt my own eyes itching. When I sniffled, Oz took my hand. I gave his a squeeze.

"Yeah, I found you," Oz said. "And we'll take you home."

"Home," Tamina whispered, grinning through her tears.

Loretta hissed from behind us and I scootched back to let her crawl forward.

"Where should we go?" said the siren.

"Meet me in the blue bedroom," Tamina said. "I will be there in ten minutes."

"Be careful," Loretta replied.

We scuttled together back down to the abandoned hallway we'd walked down earlier, only this time we didn't take another tunnel, or vent, or whatever they were. Instead we walked, bold as could be, down the empty hallways.

"Quiet," Loretta said, sneaking us through a series of corridors, the smooth, magically formed stone of the palace walls winding around itself. It'd been almost a century since I was in such a building, and I'd forgotten how nonsensical magical architecture could be.

We wound up in a long, narrow corridor off of which many sealed doors stood—sealed by vines, or blocks of ice, or cold blue fire.

Who knows what they contained, if anything, or by whose whim? Perhaps that of the building itself.

"In here," Loretta said, holding open the normal, unblocked door to a room at the end of the hallway.

Inside stood Tamina, headscarved and rigid-backed. Oz beamed a smile when he saw her. She modestly dropped her gaze, glowing faintly at my own Bound presence.

Loretta approached the girl, pointing her webbed fingers at us.

"You know the dude," Loretta said. "And *that* is Lyla."

Tamina's eyes raked over me casually before she raised them shyly to Oz.

"It's so good to see you," she said softly, bowing her head to my Master.

Oz moved forward, but he didn't touch the girl. "You too, kid. It is *so* good to see you. You're a long way from home."

"You said my family sent you?" she asked, her voice quavering. My heart broke again for her.

"Yes, yes they did," said Oz. "They're very worried about you."

Her eyes flashed up to meet his, and for a second I saw rage and anguish in them, but they were gone as quickly as they had come. And then I doubted I'd ever seen them.

My mistake.

"I can't believe…" Her voice caught, and it took Tamina a second to recover. "I can't believe after everything that happened that they'll have me back."

"I know your culture has its own rules," Oz said, choosing his words carefully. "But they love you. And they know it wasn't your fault. They sent me here to find you."

Tamina's shining eyes met his. "This makes me very happy to hear," she said softly. "Thank you."

"Sorry to break this up," I said, because I was. I had a gajillion questions of my own to ask the girl, but time was not on our side. "We should get going."

Tamina cast me a dark look. "You haven't been spoken to."

Oz started, clearly taken aback by Tamina's tone. I rolled my eyes, suddenly feeling less empathetic toward the girl.

"As the humans say, you ain't the boss of me. And we really do have to get going."

Tamina looked even more pissed, and she glared at Oz. He misunderstood her request to shut me up as a request for help.

"Lyla's right," Oz said. "We need to go. I want to hear everything that happened to you, but now isn't the time. You guys are gonna have to lead us, sorry. We don't know our way around."

Tamina shot me a caustic look but Oz's words did seem to get her head in the game. She glanced at Loretta, who nodded. "This way," said the young woman we'd come all the way Sideways to find, before whisking out of the room.

Again, as we walked through the palace, the place was eerily empty. For all the kids we'd seen coming and going that day, none seemed to be in evidence at this moment.

Every once in a while we'd hear a faraway clatter, or Loretta or Tamina would claim to hear something and would pause. But we walked through the palace's winding corridors in virtual silence, with Tamina's captors apparently none the wiser.

Eventually we came to a wide, many-columned hallway leading to a large set of double doors. I was hoping that was an exit, but no such luck. "If we cut through the old throne room," Tamina explained, "we can use the permanent portal that Dmitri set up in the old armory. It'll spit us out right near the big fountain."

She meant Point State Park, where both the rivers and, in this world, the ley lines converged.

"Are you sure it's safe?" I asked Tamina, who pointedly ignored the question until Ozan, baffled by her behavior, repeated it.

"Everyone should be out foraging," Tamina explained. "And Dmitri will be waiting in the human world to collect them, but not at this portal. This is our emergency portal; he created a foraging portal that opens from a house on the human plane."

"That's cautious of him," I said, not telling her we already knew about the house across the river from the park. "This Dmitri is obviously good at self-preservation."

Tamina didn't respond, choosing instead to look at me like I'd pooped on her shoe. I sighed.

"Your jinni is talkative," she said, making a slow loop around me. "And not a normal jinni."

"Her name is Lyla." Oz repeated what Loretta had already told the girl, arching an eyebrow at Tamina. "And she's human, cursed to be a jinni."

Tamina didn't react with surprise at this last bit of information. An odd response, and I felt a bit disappointed—normally Magi discovered my true nature with the same shock a human might express wandering across a unicorn.

"And she can use Pittsburgh's magic," Oz said. At that Tamina raised an eyebrow. Maybe she didn't believe Oz?

"That's very good to hear," Tamina said, her eyes narrowing briefly at me.

Suddenly feeling like an animal at the zoo, I shuffled uncomfortably. "Yes, well, I'm just super-unique. Now can we get going? This place gives me the willies."

Tamina's brows arched again but this time she didn't protest my giving the orders. Instead she graciously inclined her head toward me, although her gaze was covetous.

Typical Magi, wanting all the jinn. Although she couldn't Bind me even if she wanted to, being unInitiated. Not to mention I already had a Master.

For the first time ever, I felt relief at that idea, on a number of levels. Relief Tamina couldn't have me, as, despite her youth, she obviously harbored a hardened Magi's prejudice against the jinn. But also genuine relief that my Master was Oz—the first time I'd ever felt such gratitude to one who'd Bound me.

I sneaked a glance at him, watching over all of us with concerned eyes. I'd always gone for the strong, silent types in the past, but there was something surprisingly sexy about a nurturing man. It was easy to be detached, after all—to be too cool to care; too selfish to do all the work it took to have real relationships, be they friendships or more.

It was a lot more difficult to be someone like Oz seemed to be—someone who worked at being good to those around him, someone who wanted to help the people he cared about, and even those he didn't.

"Yes, we should be going," Tamina said, giving me a predatory smile. "It is time."

As the girls led us down another spiraling corridor, Oz took my hand. It was a comforting gesture, as well as one of celebration. He looked happy, relieved, and optimistic. And his hand was strong, his grip firm.

Feeling bizarrely secure for someone traipsing through enemy territory, I allowed myself to wonder what it would be like to have someone take care of me for once. I'd always been owned—first by my family, as a commodity on the marriage market, and then as a jinni.

I had even less experience with being taken care of than I did with being human. And I was growing increasingly excited to experience both.

We were tiptoeing across some kind of great hall, dotted randomly by enormous smooth pillars. A large set of double doors lurked at the other end, clearly our destination.

"When we go through, it will probably be dark," Tamina said. "The throne room has a mind of its own. Just keep hold of our hands; we're used to it."

She took Oz's free hand in hers, and Loretta took mine, granting me a sweet smile.

As we approached the wide double doors, they opened smoothly. But despite that initial welcoming gesture, the throne room was filled with an inky darkness. And when we filed in, the darkness surrounded us like a cloak, muffling our vision. Oz's hand squeezed mine, and I squeezed back, beating back the panic that fluttered at the edges of my perception.

"We're fine," Tamina murmured. "Just keep moving forward…"

And we did, edging our way into the room. I knew I was feeling my way forward with each step, and I'm sure Oz was, too, but the floor in front of us was smooth and unbroken.

The exact moment I was starting to trust our guides, and had taken a few actual long strides, the lights suddenly switched on. My Fire flared protectively around us, reacting against my total blindness as my eyes adjusted. Loretta's hand never left mine, although her grip loosened.

"Shit," I heard Oz mutter, and then a second later I, too, could see enough to mutter my own expletive.

We were about halfway into the throne room. A raised dais stood before us, upon which sat a large white throne. It looked as if it was carved of ivory or porcelain, all curving, swooping lines like taffy being pulled and looped around itself.

It was a beautiful throne, marred only by the slender, red-haired, zit-faced young man who sat upon it, glowering at us. He had the soft, pale, badly nourished slenderness of a boy who'd grown up playing video games in a basement while subsisting on Doritos and Mountain Dew.

But he also had the upper hand, since he sat looking down upon not only us, but the battered, obviously enraged forms of Big Bertha and Yulia, who were being held by a gaggle of vicious-looking Immunda children, all bloody fangs and dirty, ragged claws.

I threw up a shield of protective Fire, stretching it to encompass Loretta and Tamina. They looked at me impassively, and

I wondered why Oz and I seemed like the only people scared in that room.

"Keep close," I told my cohort. "Stay within my Fire. I'll protect you."

"Once again, you haven't been spoken to," Tamina said to me, in the tone one uses to rebuke a naughty puppy. "I'm looking forward to teaching you some manners."

And with that she shook free of Oz's hand and walked calmly out of my protective circle. Loretta did the same, slipping free with an apologetic shrug.

"Tamina, stop!" yelled Oz, but I already knew it was too late. I gripped his hand tighter.

"It's a setup," I said to my Master, pulling him closer. I wasn't sure what type or why, yet, but it was obviously a setup.

"Why?" Oz asked, of either me or Tamina or Loretta. It didn't matter whom; I had no answers, and neither of them was ready to give us any.

We watched as Tamina approached the dais, Loretta trailing behind her. Dmitri stood from the throne to reach out a hand to the girl we'd just been intent on rescuing.

He helped her up with all the chivalry of a smitten lover, and I cursed myself for being nine times an idiot.

I thought she'd take her place beside him then. That he'd tell us what he was up to—that we'd learn what role they expected us to play in their little game.

But Tamina wasn't done with the surprises.

Instead of sitting back on the throne, Dmitri knelt in front of it. It was Tamina herself who sat primly on the edge of its immense whiteness, crossing her ankles and setting her hands on her knees.

It was to Tamina that the rest of the children bowed, after

they'd skittered from the darkness at the edge of the throne room to surround us and our bound friends.

It was Tamina they called their queen, in breathless chants of adulation.

"Worst rescue ever," I muttered to Oz, who squeezed my hand in either sympathy or shared regret.

So much for happy endings.

Chapter Twenty-Four

"Tamina?" Oz asked, looking at the girl with confusion.

"Loretta?" I demanded, looking at my former friend with rage snarling my features.

Loretta gave me one of her trademark insouciant shrugs, not bothering to fill me in on the motivation for her betrayal.

Tamina, however, rolled her eyes at us dramatically, leaning back in the throne. "Tamina," she repeated, mocking my Master. "Tamina, Tamina, Tamina."

I pulled my Fire in tight around Oz and me, looking around to assess our situation. Bertha and Yulia looked a bit gnawed-on, and more than a bit irritated at having been overpowered by a group of teenagers, albeit vicious teenagers. But they were still ambulatory and capable of fighting, which was what really mattered.

Yulia gave me a small nod, flexing her wisps just a tiny bit against her bindings. They were a mixture of real chains and some kind of magic, probably one of Dmitri's spells. I could see they were tight, but not tight enough. Dmitri might have been a strong sorcerer, but he was also young and human. He'd undoubtedly never seen a wisp, let alone tied one up before. Hopefully he'd soon learn that binding a wisp was one feat easier said than done.

"Time," I whispered to Oz, muffling my voice for anyone but my Master. "We need some time."

Oz didn't reply, but I knew he'd heard me. "Tamina," he said to the young girl on the throne. "What's going on? Your family sent me here to find you."

What Oz said worked. The girl's expression had gone from one of bored contempt at Oz's apology to one of scrunched, red-faced fury at his mention of "family."

"My family," she said, her knuckles going white where she clutched the arms of the throne. "My family! You think they want me home?"

She stood to pace in front of the throne, gesticulating like a madwoman. I banked my Fire, to make us appear more vulnerable and to keep her attention on Oz and me. Meanwhile Bertha and Yulia never moved, but a slight blurring of light around Yulia told me she was working at her bindings.

"They love you," Oz said to Tamina. He didn't hide his obvious confusion. "Of course they want you home."

She laughed, an ugly, brittle sound for one so young. "Why do you think we moved to this cursed country, Ozan? Do you think it was because they loved me? *They sent me away.*"

"Sent you away?" Oz said. "That's ridiculous. Why on earth would they do that?"

Tamina's face grew a shade redder and I thought she would reply. Instead she took a deep breath, reining in her temper. "There is no time for this. You will Initiate me."

Oz's face took on that stubborn cast I knew well, his jaw setting firmly, his lips thinning to nothing, his eyes narrowing.

"First of all, I don't know how to Initiate anything," he said. "And even if I did, I'm not helping you until I get some sort of an explanation. I need to know what's happening."

Tamina turned on her heel, glaring at Oz. "You have no

right to anything. I owe you nothing, no explanations. Besides, I have your friends—you will do as I say." She gestured at Dmitri, who gave her a sycophantic smile and raised a hand. Bertha and Yulia gasped as the bindings around them tightened.

"You're wasting your time," Oz said, his voice calm, almost bored. Only his clenched fists betrayed him to me. "First of all, they're not my friends. They're my jinni's." He let his voice take on that contemptuous cast he'd heard Tamina use. "She means nothing to me, and her friends mean even less. I don't care what you do to them."

I saw Loretta's mouth open and I flicked my Fire at her gills, sending a puff of pungent smoke into them. She bent over, struck by a sudden, inexplicable coughing fit.

Tamina cocked her head at Oz, then her eyes flicked back to her sorcerer. Obligingly he squeezed tighter. My Fire crept toward my friends but Oz stopped me with a quick reprimand, looking for all the world like a typically peeved Magi chastising a naughty jinni. After an excruciating minute listening to Bertha's and Yulia's pained pants and coughs, Tamina told Dmitri to stop.

"So you *are* a Magi," she said to Oz. "I figured that with your bleeding heart, you would actually care for that abomination you'd Bound."

Oz shrugged. "I'm new to this. But I'm catching on. And I'm enjoying the power." He put a hand around my waist and hauled me in close, his hand near my breast. I looked at Oz in horror, but when my eyes moved to Tamina she was watching avidly.

"You don't even know power yet, brother," said Tamina, casting on Oz that same predatory smile she'd reserved for me up until now. "But I can show you *true* power."

"Oh?" said Oz, arching an eyebrow at her coyly.

He released me, pushing me away to take a step closer to Tamina and partially obscure me with his muscular frame.

Clever boy.

"Before we go any further, I still want to know the truth," said my Master. "What happened to you?"

"That is simple," she said, her words vibrating with suppressed anger. "I was born with a spine. My people do not like that in a woman, and certainly not in a young girl. When I shared my plans with them, they sent me away. They moved me to keep me 'safe from myself,' they said. They thought to keep me somewhere where I would find it difficult to be Initiated. Where I could not pose a threat.

"Then, in Boston, I met Dmitri. We made our *own* plans." Here she looked at the young man, who returned her gaze with the lovesick adoration of a puppy.

"What happened to your parents?" Oz asked, although that was increasingly apparent.

Tamina gave Oz a look so cold and angry he took a step back.

"They were in the way," was all she said. It was enough.

She leaned back in her throne again, but her body wasn't relaxed. "Dmitri is powerful. I thought he would be able to find a...what do you call it? A work-around? Yes, a work-around for the Initiation spell. Then, when that proved impossible, we tried to Call a jinni directly, using the Bridge in the park."

Well, that explains the fodden, I thought.

"That also failed. But Dmitri *was* able to keep my parents' jinn caged, although he could not coerce them to help me."

"Which meant that they were in the way, too, right?" Oz asked, his shoulders squaring under the weight of the truth about Tamina.

243

The girl's full mouth thinned into a terrifying smile. "Being Magi is my birthright, and they refused to help me. I did what had to be done."

While Oz kept Tamina talking, I spared a quick glance at my friends. Bertha was containing her energy, obviously waiting for Yulia to get free. The wisp was glowing more brightly in tiny increments, her wisps undoubtedly busy behind her, working at their bonds.

"And that's where you come in," she said to Oz.

"How?" he asked, his voice carefully neutral.

"I know my family. I let them think I was taken and I knew they would send someone for me. I also assumed they would send you, at least at first, as you were an easy option."

"But why send anyone if they thought you were dangerous?" he began.

Tamina interrupted. "They don't think I'm dangerous. Little girls can't be *dangerous*," she said, blinking her large eyes at us in a terrible parody of innocence. "They can be misguided, or confused, but they can't be dangerous."

I was keeping an ear on Tamina while scanning her people. They were clustered in small groups, all watching the young woman rapturously. It wasn't too hard to see how they'd captured Bertha and Yulia. They were young, yes, but there were tons of them. And they *were* young. Even Yulia would hesitate before killing a half-vamp with the face of a twelve-year-old, despite its trying to rip her throat out. Which meant we'd have to be careful getting out... I wouldn't be any more comfortable hurting these little pains in the ass than my friends would have been...

All of my strategizing was brought to a halt, however, as Oz finally cut to the chase.

"But why did you do all of this, exactly?" he asked the girl.

"Oh," Tamina said, with a small wave of her little hand. "That's simple. I was chosen by Kouros."

"Kouros?" Oz and I both repeated, and I tried to get around Oz. He manhandled me back behind him before I could pounce on the girl.

"Yes, Kouros. You know him?" Again she feigned innocence, watching us squirm on her hook with obvious delight.

Oz nodded before shaking his head, his words mimicking his actions. "Yes, er, no. I don't know him, per se. He made Lyla...he cursed her."

"Yes he did," Tamina said. "And for his pains he was imprisoned by his own kind. Now he wants out."

"Out?" Oz said, keeping a hand on my forearm, his own arm bent behind him. His grip was comforting. I felt like all the heat had left my body.

"What part of 'out' don't you understand?" the girl asked, exasperated. "He wants free. And he needs me to do it."

I felt myself sway on my feet, but Oz's grip on my arm kept me upright.

"I don't understand. What does Kouros have to do with any of this?"

Tamina stood, walking off of the dais toward us. She moved around Oz to inspect me, as one would inspect a horse before taking it to the glue factory.

"It's because she's so 'super-unique,'" said Tamina, mocking my earlier words. "To free Kouros will take a tremendous amount of power."

"The Node," I breathed, feeling a chill.

"The Node," Tamina affirmed, smiling a reptile's grin. "The one who made you may be trapped, jinni, but he can See you.

He knows what you are capable of. He knows what you can do for him."

"What did he promise you?" I asked, in a small voice.

"He doesn't have to promise me anything," said Tamina. "I am a Magi. I will Call him across, pulling him from his cage using power you will give me from this corrupted Node. And then I will Bind him."

"And you'll be his Master," I said, but it wasn't a statement. It was a question.

"Of course," Tamina said blithely.

"You can't trust him," I told her, my tone desperate. "I'm telling you, he'll use you. He did it with my family, and every Magi who Bound him before us. He's not a normal jinni, he's too powerful..."

"Shut her up," Tamina said to Oz, her eyes sparking dangerously at me.

"Quiet, Lyla," Oz said. "Let Tamina talk."

My jaw snapped shut, and not only because he'd commanded me. He was right. She wouldn't listen to reason and the purpose of this whole exchange was to keep her talking and distracted.

"And what will you do when you Bind Kouros?" Oz asked.

Tamina cocked her head at Oz like she couldn't quite understand his question.

"What will I do?" she asked, in an incredulous voice. "What will I *do*?

"I'll have power, of course. All the power of the most powerful jinni in history, at my disposal. And me a mere girl." Her smile was vicious now. Predatory. Her small white teeth glittering like a fox's in the light of the throne room.

"I could go home. Show my family exactly what a girl is capable of."

She took a step toward Oz, raising a graceful white hand to his cheek. She touched him, very gently, before averting her eyes, so shy was our Tamina. "But I think I'll stay here," she said, peeping up at him. "There are so few Magi in this country, and no jinn as powerful as Kouros. The life we would lead..." Tamina trailed off, her eyes shining with greed.

Any sympathy I'd had for the girl began to melt when she touched my Master, and evaporated entirely at the avarice in her gaze.

Just then I saw a flutter of movement from my left. Yulia nodded to me. She was free. Then she glanced at Bertha, indicating our bouncer would be, too, in a few moments.

It was time to act. But how? We were strong, but hugely outnumbered. And I didn't want to use my power indiscriminately...from what Loretta had said, if she could be believed, some of these kids were here under duress. We had to treat everyone as a possible fellow hostage. We needed a distraction.

We have to give Tamina what she wants, I realized. Tamina's Initiation would be a perfect distraction. And once we were free, it wouldn't matter that Tamina was Initiated. She could Bind all the jinn she wanted, but they'd be powerless in Pittsburgh. And I'd still be Bound to Oz, meaning she couldn't get ahold of me. *We'll buy ourselves time to take care of her and her Exterminator sidekick*, I thought, glaring at Loretta, *before Tamina can get her hands on us again.*

"Do the ritual," I told Oz, magically sotto voce. "Now."

He didn't question me, bless him. "I've heard enough," said Oz, bowing to Tamina. "You are right about your birthright being that of a Magi. You were the smartest, the most interesting, of your tribe." He took her slim hand in his.

"So you'll Initiate me?" Tamina beamed at him.

"Of course," Oz said. "For a piece of the pie."

Tamina's eyes narrowed, but it was the perfect thing to say. Tamina understood ambition; she understood greed. She'd believe Oz would sell his soul for some of the power she offered, because she would have done the same thing.

Loretta tugged at the girl's sleeve, but Tamina flicked her away imperiously, too enthralled at the idea of being Initiated to listen to anything Loretta had to say.

I stepped back behind the cover of Oz's broad shoulders, quickly planning my next moves.

The game was afoot.

"I'm not exactly sure what I'm doing," Oz said as Tamina approached him. She'd come down from her dais, helped by Dmitri, who hovered over her with the lovesick air of a smitten eight-year-old. On closer inspection, the sorcerer wasn't that young—at least in his early twenties.

Tamina flicked her multicolored eyes at him coquettishly, but they never really warmed.

"I can guide you," she said. "And you must remember something from your own Initiation?"

Oz nodded. "A bit. But I didn't really believe what was happening. I thought your family had slipped me something and I was hallucinating."

Tamina shook her head, placing a small hand on Oz's large bicep. Dmitri shifted closer to Tamina, squaring his narrow, bony shoulders. She shot him a look and he backed off.

As she turned back to Oz, Tamina's eyes grew round and soft again. "It pains me you were cut off from your heritage. You have tremendous potential, I can feel it." Her voice lowered, as did her eyes. She peeped up at Oz with that patented expression of modesty. Such a look, coming from a woman raised in a culture that prized a woman's modesty above all else, was the equivalent of twerking against his groin.

Tamina was angling for my Master, in more ways than one. I found myself grinding my teeth. Dmitri cleared his throat.

"We should begin," Tamina said, withdrawing her hand. Until she had Kouros, she'd need Dmitri's power. But after that...

Something told me the kid would be back in whatever basement he'd come from, his Xbox and his right hand once again his only friends.

"Can you remember the stages?" Tamina asked Oz.

His brow furrowed. "I remember they drew a circle...salt mixed with coal dust?"

Tamina nodded. "Good. Loretta?"

The Exterminator, looking mulish but obeying, went behind the dais. We heard the opening of a door, some rustling, and then she came forward, hauling a large plastic jug that had once held road salt. Now it held a combination of salt and something powdery and gray. Coal dust.

Tamina put a hand on my former friend's cheek and the part of me that had wondered why Loretta would betray us the way she had vanished. If Dmitri looked at Tamina like a lovesick eight-year-old, Loretta looked at the girl like she was a perfectly cooked sirloin steak. She practically slavered under Tamina's hand.

Loretta'd always loved power. She'd stayed on as an Exterminator long after her required service was over. So no wonder she'd wanted the credit for our capture: Tamina offered power. Worse crimes had been committed for far less motivation.

Tamina made a shooing gesture at Loretta, but gave her a

small smile. The siren came forward, still hauling the large jug, then began to shakily pour out the salt to create a circle a few feet in radius.

"Now," Tamina said to Oz, when Loretta was finished. "What comes next?"

"After the circle," he replied, "they Called a jinni into it. An unBound one."

Tamina nodded. "Excellent. And then?"

"They asked the jinni to Initiate the new Magi, in exchange for its eternal freedom from that Magi's Binding. Then the jinni says something in its own language..."

Oz's voice trailed off. I'd been Called to a few Initiations myself, and I knew the process was painful for the Magi. Not that I'd had a lot of sympathy for them, before Oz.

"And then my blood learns its own power, and I can Call and Bind what before I could only See." Tamina's multicolored eyes sparked with suppressed power, and I normally would have pitied the jinni Bound by a Master such as she.

But, since she planned on Binding Kouros, I was pretty sure those eyes wouldn't be sparking for too much longer. If Tamina was a bad fruit, Kouros was a bad tree—one that could walk and talk, and whose only pleasure was sadistically torturing anyone who came near him.

He was also incredibly old—no one knew exactly how old, although I'd heard rumors from the few jinn who would talk to me that they thought him the oldest jinni still alive—and insanely powerful. That he'd been imprisoned by his own kind sorta said it all—he had the kind of personality not even his brethren could love.

"Shall we begin?" Tamina asked, her voice hoarse and dreamy. She was clearly excited to be Initiated, as in "excited."

Oz glanced at me uncomfortably and I gave him a nearly imperceptible nod.

"Okay, let's do this," Oz said, giving one loud clap like a dad rounding up his kids at a softball game. He walked toward the circle, Tamina by his side. I melted back a few steps, behind the various groups of children that all moved forward to watch the show. Even the ones ostensibly guarding Bertha and Yulia moved forward, forgetting their charges completely.

They were, after all, mostly children, without any discipline and easily distracted. Hence going through with Tamina's Initiation.

"First, Call," Tamina urged Oz. "Your power will automatically seek the most powerful jinni within the reach of your voice. And I can tell you have a very large…reach."

This time Tamina's look was less than modest. Oz's Adam's apple bobbed as he swallowed.

"Okay, but I'm not sure about the Calling part," he said. "I've never really done it. I found Lyla where your family said I would; I didn't really Call her."

"You know the words, correct?" Tamina asked. Oz nodded. "Then say them. Hear them. Lace them with your Will. You are not merely repeating the words, you are using them. They are your tool. They are a part of you…" And with that, she began to chant the ancient words of Calling, spoken in the language of the jinn.

"Te vash anuk a si. Te vash anuk a si. Te vash…"

Oz's bass rumble joined her lilting melody. *"…anuk a si. Te vash anuk a si…"*

For the first few lines, his Call was missing the call…he was merely repeating the words. But then he closed his eyes, and that little furrow of concentration I'd grown so used to seeing appeared, and when he opened them again his power bloomed forth, white and hot, from his silver Magi eyes.

I sighed. He really was a beautiful man.

Within the circle of salt and coal dust, dark smoke began to swirl. At first slowly, then pouring in thick black undulations that snaked around each other until something began to form out of the smoke. Arms, a torso, legs, finally a head...that opened glowing red eyes upon the two who stood before it.

I waited for the moment when it tried to ground itself in the power at its feet, watching as its eyes winced in pain, the smoke of its face curling in distaste.

Red fire formed its mouth as it spoke. "Pittsburgh?" it said, contempt lacing its words. "Really?"

Normally, as the Initiate, Tamina would be silent, letting the Magi who had Called the jinni say the words of the ancient ritual. But Oz didn't know them, and for all her faults involving megalomania, I did appreciate how Tamina was one young woman who got shit done. So she was the one who bargained with the jinni.

"We offer you a truce, Fire-born. You have been Called, but not yet Bound. In this moment, we promise you freedom, in exchange for your wisdom. Initiate me, and you go free."

The jinni looked at Tamina, cocking its head. "You are far from home," it said. "But I recognize you."

Its red eyes flicked around the girl till they lit on me. Shit. We really needed the distraction of Lyla's Initiation, but something told me the jig was up.

"You are rumored to seek Kouros," said the jinni. "And you have his creature."

It stood to full height, looking down at Tamina. "I think I will refuse your bargain, this time. I would rather be Bound than help you free he who is best kept prisoner."

Tamina rolled her eyes, a very American gesture, and I wondered if she'd been watching *30 Rock* when she wasn't planning to take over the world.

"Then my friend here will Bind you. And I will keep you here, in this room, in this circle, with only the Node at your feet to pull your power from. And I will ask you to perform services for me, until you are forced to tap into that power, and it poisons you. And then I will watch you die, slowly and painfully, and I will do the same thing to the next jinni we Call, until one of you Initiates me."

I blinked. It was basically the same thing with which we'd threatened the jinni we'd Called earlier, to get info on Kouros. But the difference between our threat and Tamina's? Tamina meant it. And she'd probably enjoy enforcing it.

The jinni's eyes narrowed even further, its smoky form lashing with anger. Then I saw its shoulders droop, the thin slit of its red eyes close for just a second, and I knew it had decided to play ball.

While I understood its reluctance, I rejoiced. We only had one shot at escape, and we needed Tamina out of the picture for it to work.

Not bothering with the formal exchange of words that normally accompanied the Initiation, the jinni glared at Tamina. "I do this and you free me?" She nodded.

"God help us," the jinni said, in its own language, beckoning Tamina forward.

She stepped toward the circle, just to within the reach of the jinni's outstretched finger. It touched her forehead, and I felt the rush of its power into the girl.

Tamina's eyes Flared painfully, too bright even to look at. Her body arched onto tiptoe, her spine bowed, her mouth open in a silent scream.

Then the light faded and her multicolored eyes were the pale silver of a full Magi's.

She let out a triumphant sigh, and then she collapsed to the floor.

I took the opportunity to raise my arms to my friends, who shook off the last of their bonds with gleeful expressions.

Showtime.

Chapter Twenty-Five

The jinni Oz had Called cast me a look of pure hatred and disappeared, automatically freed by the magic of the circle when it fulfilled its side of the deal.

Tamina's body was bucking like a rodeo bull, her eyes sparking as her power Flared uncontrollably. Dmitri rushed to her side, along with Loretta and a handful of kids. Everyone else moved just a little bit forward, as I'd planned on.

Everyone but my friends and me. Unnoticed, Oz slipped away from the press surrounding Tamina to join me.

I kept my hand raised, waiting for the perfect moment.

Our newly Initiated Magi screamed in agony, over and over again, victim of the inevitable rush of power that came with her new status. It happened to all Magi when Initiated, and it's what I'd been counting on.

My hand came down: our signal. Bright white light flared from behind me as Yulia went full wisp, slicing through the remaining bonds holding her and Bertha. Bertha shook herself like a giant Doberman, then pulled a club out of her own pocket of Sideways.

As a concession to the fact that our kidnappers were teen-agers, she left her studded club put away, choosing her regular club instead.

Everyone was so busy worrying about Tamina that no one noticed us creeping toward the throne room's wide double doors. It was that damned Loretta who, while bent solicitously over her new bestie, happened to glance up.

"They're escaping!" she shrieked. At least fifty small faces lifted toward us, and I swore.

"Run!" I shouted, but it was too late. Two half-vamps popped right in front of us, and I heard the footfalls of more behind us. The little monsters were intimidating, despite their youth. Sharp teeth decorated their slavering, snarling faces, their whole mien one of mindless hunger.

One of the bigger boys went after Bertha, who casually bopped him over the head with her club. He went down like a sack of rocks, unconscious. The other big ones went after Yulia, who grinned ferociously. Two long, pale tendrils of light lashed around the two kids, and her eyes closed infinitesimally as she fed deep of their life essence. Her wisp magic washed over them, and they went limp in her grasp until their heads lolled on their shoulders. They'd live, after sleeping for a week or two.

That left the last, littlest one to me.

With a flick of my Fire, I lit up the back of his T-shirt. The half-vamp squealed, running in a panic around the room.

Coast clear for the moment, we turned as one to the big dou-ble doors. We surged toward them but something arced over our heads to land in the doorway, exploding with a bang that made everything go white and soundless as pain pummeled my body and my vision went dark.

It came back only a few seconds later. I found myself sitting upright on the floor, like I was about to do leg stretches. Oz was beside me, curled away from me on his side, and Bertha was lying on top of Yulia.

Kids were heaped about the room in smoking puppy piles, and my eyes finally landed on Dmitri, standing beside Tamina, both of them looking at his hands in shock.

"Don't kill them, you idiot," snarled a still Flaring Tamina. "What is wrong with you?"

"Junior doesn't know his own strength," I muttered, giving my head a hard shake and turning toward Oz.

"Master?" I said. When he didn't respond, I grabbed his shoulder to shake him. "Master?"

"Okay," he muttered. "I'm all right..."

But when I got him to his feet I knew he wasn't. He kept one arm wrapped protectively around his ribs, making me think that was where he'd taken the brunt of the magic grenade that idiot sorcerer had lobbed.

That said, Oz was ambulatory if obviously in pain. Bertha was another matter.

The half-troll had taken most of the attack, shielding Yulia with her body. The wisp was kneeling over our friend, smacking her sharply while chanting, "Don't die, you bitch, don't die."

My magic automatically went in, sensing quite a bit of internal damage. "You've got to get her out of here," I said to Yulia, even as I did the same to Oz. As I thought, he had a few broken ribs, one of which was perilously close to a lung.

He wasn't going to be running anywhere. I needed to get him somewhere close by to heal that rib before he punctured something. But we didn't have time for the intense healing Bertha needed, although moving her wouldn't harm her any worse than she already had been. Luckily, Yulia was humming with energy from the force she'd taken out of the two young half-vamps.

257

"Take her home," I told Yulia. "Can you handle her?"

Yulia looked at me stubbornly. "We're not leaving you." But I shook my head.

"You have to," I said. "Bertha isn't going to make it, and you can move faster without us. I have to get him healed, then we can follow."

I figured our chances of getting away were pretty slim, actually, but Yulia didn't need to know that. Not least because Tamina didn't really want or need my friends; they'd just been insurance. We could give them time to escape, and they'd have time to regroup and bring the cavalry.

"You've gotta go now," I told Yulia. "We'll follow."

The kids around us were waking up, getting to their feet to reel around on uncertain legs.

Yulia gave me a desperate look. "But..."

"No buts. If you can take Bertha, go *now*. If you can't..."

"I can," Yulia said, her voice grim. Her wisps reached out to wrap around our friend, hefting her enormous bulk with apparent ease. "And you'll follow?"

I nodded, glancing at Oz, who was an unhealthy shade of green. "Of course. As soon as we can."

"Be careful," Yulia said. "We'll send help as soon as we can."

"Good plan. Now go," I said, urgency lacing my voice as a little knot of swaying children converged on us.

Yulia hauled Bertha out of the room, her wisps manhandling the half-troll as if she were the child. I turned to my Master.

"Can you run?" He shook his head.

"I don't think so. I can walk. If you help me..."

I slid under his armpit, letting his weight fall heavily on me. I set up a little wall of Fire behind us, keeping the kids at bay while we hustled out, much more slowly, in Yulia and Bertha's wake.

A bright silver light Flared again behind us, and I heard Tamina scream in pain. The few kids who'd pulled themselves together enough to head in our direction faltered, looking back at their leader. I banked my Fire even hotter and higher, so they wouldn't see in which direction we turned out of the throne room.

I went left, seeing a small door lurking off the long main hallway of the palace. I hoped this door wasn't a little ante-chamber or something, where we'd be trapped like idiots.

"Humph," Oz grunted as I jostled him pushing open the door.

"Sorry," I told him, feeling relief when I saw a hallway with more doors coming off of it. Good.

"I'm going to start healing you," I said. "I can't do much when we're moving like this, but I can start. It's going to hurt."

"It hurts now," he said, his face pale and sweating.

"I know, Master," I said, genuinely worried for him.

"Jesus, call me Oz," he snapped, the pain making him lose patience.

I rolled my eyes, but did as he said. "Bear down, Oz," I said. "I'm going to start..."

When I opened myself to the Node, its power almost over-whelmed me. It was right under our feet in Pittsburgh, but here the magic was all around us, saturating the air. I carefully grounded myself, keeping a tight grip on my magical channels so they didn't flood, and sent a tendril of magic out to Ozan.

"Shit," he hissed, as the magic hit him. I needed to concen-trate to do any real healing, but I could at least stabilize him as we moved, to keep that rib from puncturing his lung.

"None of this is going to feel good," I told him, grimly, as we ducked through a series of low doors leading through small stone rooms, the purpose of which was completely obscure.

"It's fine," he said, but his gritted teeth said otherwise.

Without thinking I gave him a squeeze with the arm I had wrapped around his waist. "I know it hurts," I said, then "Sorry," when he hissed. Not the best time for a motivational hug.

"No one seems to be following," I said, as we paused in another long hallway to catch our breath and listen. Oz nodded grimly, his eyes shut. I needed to get him healed, stat.

I knew we'd found the right place when we entered what looked like a medieval tennis court, although there were low stone walls instead of nets. But there was a gallery looming above the court, accessible from a winding staircase at either end. I could see a door in the center of the gallery, leading into a dark room behind.

"Let's go up there," I said. Oz nodded, although he eyed the staircase with more than a little dismay.

"You can do it. Just tell me you need help. Don't forget you're a Magi."

The look he gave me was dark, but he didn't argue. "I'll need help," he said shortly. It wasn't much of a command, but it would do.

Without my commanding it, my Fire blossomed, cocooning him in its swirling darkness. I carried him like that, up the stairs, my magic cushioning our ascent.

When we got to the top, I swore. The dark lintel off the gallery did not lead into the rest of the palace, as I'd assumed, but into a small, windowless room. I considered taking Oz back down, but listening to his rattling breath I knew we were running out of time.

"Tell me to heal you," I said as I laid him on the floor.

"Do I have to?"

I rolled my eyes. "My power works better that way. I'd do it myself, if that's what you're asking. But if you command me the jinni in me does it automatically, and better than I can by myself."

His concentration wrinkle formed and I knew he was filing away what I'd just told him, but before I could admonish him he said, "Heal me, please," and I thought the *please* was a nice touch.

My jinni went to work, seeking out his injuries. They were worse than I'd first assessed—stuff had been scraping around and there was some internal bleeding I quickly stanched. The soft tissue was easy, however, and quick to manipulate. It was the bones that would be a bitch.

I took Oz's hand as I started on his ribs, and he squeezed mine gratefully. His eyes were large, full of pain as he stared into mine. I smiled encouragingly at him as the bones were pulled into place.

My smile faltered, however, when we heard the shouts from down below. There were children in the court.

I ceased my healing as we listened. What had begun as a few quiet footfalls was now the sounds of quite a few feet, pattering around the court.

"I can smell them," said a snarling voice. One of the half-vamps. "They were here."

We were stock-still, our eyes still glued on each other's as we listened. We heard footsteps beneath us, then a voice saying, "Didn't go this way."

The footsteps came back into the room below. "What's up there?" a voice asked.

"Nuffin'," said a girl's voice. "Just a room."

"They don't know that," said the snarling voice.

And we knew we were fucked. Someone shouted and other kids responded, more voices and feet piling into the court. We heard shuffling at either end of our gallery—children waiting to ascend and find us, trapped.

"They can't get you," Oz said. I'd started healing him again, furiously, not wanting him to be vulnerable when they came up.

"They're about to get both of us," I said. "This is going to hurt, but we'll have you on your feet..."

"Lyla, stop," he commanded. My jinni did so, even as I squeaked a protest.

His voice was calm as he spoke, and his hand in mine was steady. "They can't get you," he said. "If they do, they're going to use you to bring your maker back to this world. Even I, with so little experience of jinn, can see that's a terrible idea. Plus I don't like Tamina very much anymore, and I don't want her to get her way."

"They're just kids," I lied. Dmitri was not just a kid, and enough kids could take us down as they had Bertha and Yulia. "I'll get us out."

"No, you won't. I know what I'm doing. You have to trust me. I'll be fine."

I cocked my head at him, about to ask what he meant, but he spoke first.

"Lyla, I command you to get yourself to safety. Now."

And with that, my jinni did as he said, even as I howled in protest. She drew heavily on the Node, more than I'd ever pulled. More than I'd thought I could pull. I shut my eyes against that schizoid feeling of my own power doing something against my will and suddenly I was opening them again standing outside the palace, my fingers closed around nothing.

And then Oz unBound me.

262

I gasped, feeling his power over me wink out of existence. I was free.

And I was pissed.

And then everything went dark...

I came to just a short while later, the shock of using and then losing all that magic having left my head buzzing painfully. I swore, remembering what Oz had done, and before Tamina could realize I was free I pulled, hard, on that last pocket of power being Bound to Oz had left me, feeling for him through the empty space his unBinding me had left, till my power found him, and I pulled...

He was sitting on a low stone bench in a small room off the throne room. I could hear Tamina yelling commands from somewhere nearby.

One of the two adult half-vamps guarding my erstwhile Master blinked at me in surprise. I walloped him, a smack with my Fire that sent him flying across the room to land against the wall with a thud. The other one turned just as I reached for one of my swords, only registering my presence a second before I whacked him in the base of the skull with my pommel. He, too, dropped like a sack.

"Find her!" I heard Tamina rage from the other room. "Find her now! She's all that matters! Find her!"

"I freed you," Oz said, staring at me mulishly. "Go away."

I rolled my eyes. "You're welcome. And you're an idiot."

Using my sword, I cut through the ropes binding his hands before I stored it Sideways again. I looked around the little room—no exits, except for a high window that overlooked empty sky.

Damn, I thought. Oh well...

"You have to Bind me again," I told him. "Quickly."

"No," he said. "I freed you. You're free. Go away."

"Stop being an idiot," I hissed, keeping one ear on Tamina still tantruming in the other room. "You have to Bind me. Otherwise *she* can Bind me."

"Oh," he said. "I forgot about that part. I just wanted you safe."

"It didn't work," I hissed. "Bind me!"

He scrubbed his hand through his hair. "Do I have to? I hate having you Bound. And I forced you to find that girl and she turns out to be evil, and intent on Calling back to earth the one creature that gives you nightmares every night."

I narrowed my eyes at him. "How did you..."

"I was your Master," he said, softly. "I know."

"So Bind me, otherwise that girl will," I said.

"I could just keep you Bound, and send you away again."

I took a deep breath. He didn't get it. "I'm rescuing you, you idiot. There's no way I'd leave you here and if you send me away again, I'll just come back. We can keep playing this stupid game over and over, or you can just stop being a fucking moron."

He blinked. "Maybe if you stop calling me a moron..."

We both shut up as we heard Tamina's voice getting closer.

"I will kill him," she screeched. "I will kill him slowly, and mail the pieces to that shit-hole nudie bar..."

I admired Tamina's grasp of English slang even as I raised an eyebrow at Oz.

"You were saying?"

He gulped. "Are you sure?"

"Yes, ohmigod, if you don't Bind me right now I'm going to..."

He Bound me, faster than I'd ever been Bound before, the words harsh but welcome in the air around us.

My jinni swelled within me, saturated with power once again as the door to the little stone room popped open.

"What the . . . ?" Tamina started.

"Tell me to get us the fuck out of here," I said to Oz. Until he'd told me to get myself out of there, I hadn't known apparating all the way Sideways would be an option. I'd never used that much power before.

Now I really hoped we could make it work a second time, for two people.

"Get us out of here, now," he commanded, his whole Will behind his words. My jinni answered him *tout suite*.

She pulled like I'd never felt her pull before, reaching so deep that, if the Node had been a person, I'd have been tickling its tonsils.

The last thing we saw was Tamina's face as I took us all the way out of Sideways and back to the mortal plane.

Chapter Twenty-Six

We popped out into my living room and I automatically added the last bit of magic coursing through my system to my wards, beefing them up to hide our presence from outsiders.

We'd be safe from Tamina's minions, at least for a while. Which was good, because I was going to be about as useful as balls on a lady-fish in about two seconds.

"Oh," I groaned, as the first wave of pain swept through me. If I thought I'd fried my channels before, now they were burnt to a crisp.

"Lyla!" said Oz, panic lacing his voice, as I swayed on my feet, my knees buckling.

He caught me, and then swore, his half-healed ribs flaring in a pain so sharp I felt it through our bond.

Together we stumbled to my couch, collapsing in a heap, our arms entwined around one another.

"Heal you," I mumbled, reaching out to the Node, then hissing as the magic washed over my raw magical wounds.

"Heal yourself," he said, taking my chin in his hand and looking at me with both pain and concern. "Now. I command you."

And like that I felt the magic transmute into something soothing, through the mysterious machinations of my jinni. I sighed, a rough sound of pleasure that made Oz's pupils dilate.

"Now you," I said, when I was healed enough to do the same for him. He didn't complain as I pushed my cold hands up his shirt, against his overly warm ribs, and began pummeling him with healing magics.

It was his turn to sigh, after a minute or two of pained grunts. I hated hurting him, but healing always hurt.

When I was finished, we were left lying against the back of the couch, sweating and sore, our eyes locked on each other's gaze.

I mustered up just enough strength to text Charlie, "we're safe. need to rest. Loretta turncoat. B&Y on way to u. shields up till am."

He'd know to circle his wagons till the morning, wherever he was at. I threw my phone somewhere near the coffee table and leaned back next to Oz again.

My Master raised a hand to my cheek, giving me a gentle, almost wondering caress.

"We need to talk," he said.

"We need to sleep," I said. "And then we can talk."

I pulled him with me as I listed sideways, grateful my sofa was wide, and soft, and accommodating. And even more grateful for the afghan that lived on the back of the couch, which I pulled over us.

My back was to Oz's chest, his knees tucked into mine. Humans called it spooning, and it felt perilously good.

"You came back for me," Oz mumbled sleepily into my ear.

"I did," I said, no less surprised than he was.

"Thank you," I heard him say.

I lay quietly, not knowing how to respond, but he wasn't expecting anything. His breath, hot against my scalp, grew longer, and then a gentle, whuffling snore told me he was asleep.

Healing took a lot of energy out of both parties, and he'd sleep till his body recovered.

But despite my exhaustion, I didn't join him and Morpheus as quickly as I'd thought I would. Instead I lay, listening to him breathe, wondering what I'd just done and what it meant.

"Two days," I told myself. Then I registered the soft light creeping into the room and realized it was dawn. "Less than two days."

I had less than forty-eight hours before my curse was lifted. After that, Tamina would have no use for me.

But until then?

I knew Oz would free me. All my skepticism about him was gone. He was exactly what he seemed—a genuinely good man. But that no longer mattered.

For Oz couldn't unBind me until the very last second, or I'd be vulnerable to Tamina's Call.

My Master's arm tightened around me and I tried not to think about what we'd do next. Instead I tried to imagine what it would be like to be human.

As I drifted off, scenes of human life drifted through my mind. They weren't much different from my daily routine as a cursed jinni: brunch at my favorite restaurant, dancing at the job I loved, spending time with my friends.

The only difference was that Oz was there and we were both human, and equal, and nothing stood between us.

He was what I dreamed about when I finally did sleep; my Master with his silver gaze and anchor tattoos, whose goodness I knew was more precious and rare than his magic.

*   *   *

I woke up when I hit the floor, my eyes snapping open in panic. I froze, recognizing my living room ceiling, but having no idea where I was or how I'd gotten there.

Registering that the shape next to me was my couch, I realized I must have fallen off it. A theory confirmed when Oz's bleary-eyed, whiskery face came into view above me.

"What're you doing down there?" he mumbled sleepily, extending a hand.

"Fell off," I said, taking it without thinking. He pulled me in his direction and I followed till I was back on the couch. Then he manhandled me down and against him, and I remembered falling asleep just like that, him holding me as we spooned.

It felt different, now that we were rested. Not to mention after the dreams I'd had.

His breathing was slow and even, and I wondered if he'd fallen asleep again. But then he spoke.

"Thank you for coming back for me," he said again. His arm around me tightened, pulling me closer.

It felt good. Too good. I pulled away, sitting up on the edge of the sofa and then getting to my feet.

"Coffee," I said, in both explanation and apology, and went to the kitchen. When I'd set the coffee maker percolating, I went to the bathroom to take a quick shower and brush my teeth. I came out wearing my bathrobe, to find Oz sitting at the kitchen table, sipping from one of my oversize mugs.

He smiled when he saw me. "You look okay," he said.

"Damning with faint praise?" I asked, raising an eyebrow.

He shook his head. "Not at all. But you looked pretty done in last night. I was worried about you."

"Yeah, well, you didn't look so hot yourself." I poured my own cup of coffee before digging into the fridge.

Oz stood, nodding ruefully. "And I bet I still don't look much better. If you'll excuse me..." With that he headed toward his bedroom. While I pulled bread from the freezer and eyeballed the "use by" date on a carton of eggs with trepidation, I heard the bathroom door shut and the water run.

I made us some breakfast, just scrambled eggs and toast. By the time it was ready, Oz had emerged, wearing a black T-shirt and soft gray-and-black pajama bottoms. He looked so clean and casual as he took his seat at the table, and as I served us breakfast, I had a flashback to my dreams last night. Us being normal, being human—a breakfast scene, dressed in our comfies, eating in companionable silence.

"We have to talk," I said, trying to bury those images. We were anything but normal: he was a Magi, I was cursed to be a jinni and Bound to him.

"I know," he said. "First of all...Tamina."

Her name dropped between us like a brick. We stared down at our plates.

"Well, she sucks," I said.

"Yep. What should we do?"

"No idea," I said. "We need to talk to Charlie. Get his advice."

Oz nodded. "Fine. But what about you? I hate having you Bound again."

My heart twinged.

"Thank you," I told him, meeting his silver eyes with mine. "But I have to be, for right now."

"Tamina?" he asked.

I nodded. "Yes. If I'm not Bound to you..."

"She can Call you," Oz finished.

"And Bind me to herself."

"Since she's a Magi now."

"We had to do it," I said. "Live to fight another day, and all of that. Incapacitating her was our only way out, and Initiating her was the only distraction I could think of. And it worked. Sort of."

He shrugged, but he dug into the breakfast I'd made. We ate in silence. When we were finished, he took our plates to the sink and rinsed them off before putting them in the dishwasher.

Then he came back to the table with the coffeepot and filled our mugs.

"I feel like this is all my fault," he said.

"What do you mean?" I added sugar and milk to my coffee; I drank mine as sweet as a child might like.

"Tamina, and you, and everything. If I hadn't been so stupid…"

"We were set up. And one of those people who set us up was *my* friend," I said bitterly, stirring my coffee with unnecessary aggression. "Truth be told," I said, putting down my spoon with care, "I'd rather this went down with you as my Master than anybody else."

His hand closed over mine, clutching my mug.

"I'm glad you feel that way and I'm also glad I met you, circumstances be damned. But I hate that I can't free you," he said.

I shrugged, meeting his eyes. "I appreciate that. But it's not possible…not with Tamina running around."

He sat back, his turn to frown down at his mug. "Well that sucks."

My head cocked. "Oh yeah? Are you that eager to be rid of me?"

Oz looked up, his eyes Flaring. He put down his coffee and turned to me, pulling my chair toward him. I squawked, putting my own mug down before I spilled on myself.

"No," he said, his voice very deep and low. "I'm not eager at all to get rid of you. But I *am* looking forward to setting you free."

"And why is that?" I asked, my voice sounding breathy even to me. I leaned back in my chair as he leaned forward, until I couldn't go any farther back and we were nose-to-nose.

"Because I want you to be mine by choice, not magic. I want you to choose me, Lyla. For your bed. For your life. For good."

My stomach clenched, a flash of heat shooting through me, lower down.

I almost made a joke, then. I thought of a thousand things to say that would be defensive, and snarky, and would rebuild that wall between us that his freeing me yesterday had torn down.

But I didn't. Instead I raised my hand to his rough cheek. His silver eyes Flared at my touch, their glow fractionally dimmed, however, by the dilation of his pupils.

He turned his face to nuzzle my wrist and his lips kissed my pulse point, so gently.

"Fuck it," I said, articulate and romantic as ever. My hand slipped farther back, getting a firm grip on his hair and pulling him toward me.

Our kiss wasn't gentle, our lips pressed against each other in a rough, wide-mouthed clash. My other found his hair and he pulled me forward, chair and all, till he could wrap his arms around my ribs and pull me closer still.

With a low moan that sounded suspiciously like a growl, I kissed across his jaw, toward his neck, sucking and biting at his smooth skin. He replied by clutching at my hips, sighing my name in a way that made both me and my jinni shudder.

I half-stood, still kissing his neck, moving up to suck and bite at his earlobe. His hands moved around to my ass but he murmured in surprise when I swung one leg, then another, over his thighs so that I straddled his lap.

"Lyla," he murmured, again, as I moved back to his mouth. I growled something inarticulate as I reached down to stroke that hard heat between us.

Then he grabbed my hand, pulling his mouth away from mine. He was breathing hard, lust suffusing his features, but he shook his head no.

"We can't," he gasped, his voice dark and rough. "Not like this."

"If you're not a kitchen fan, we can move to the bedroom," I said, going in to kiss him again.

"No, it's not that." He pulled his face away again, reaching up to cup my jaw in his palm. "I don't want it to be like this."

I felt heat rising in my face. Was I crazy? Was he leading me on? I went for the dismount, wondering how—at over a thousand years old—I'd been reduced to the discomfiture of a teenager by a boy.

But Oz wouldn't let me off his lap. His arms closed around my waist, his lips curling in a smile.

"I want you, Lyla," he whispered, moving underneath me just enough to remind me how much. "But not when you're Bound to me. I meant what I said about wanting to know I'm yours by your own choice."

I blinked at him. "You are, Oz. Believe me. Otherwise you'd be fucking a melon right now."

"Huh?"

"Never mind about the melon. But seriously, I have my ways. I'd never sleep with you if I didn't have to."

He smiled, stroking his hands through my hair, playing with it in the light.

"I'm happy to hear that," he said. "But it doesn't change how I feel. While I trust you, I can't trust your jinni. It would break my heart if, when all this is over, you regretted me. You regretted us. I'd rather wait."

I sat back in his lap, shaking my head. "Motherfucker," I said, before I burst out laughing. I leaned forward to muffle my giggles in his chest.

He stroked his big hands over my hair, down my back. "What's so funny?"

"You. Me. This whole thing…

"I finally meet a decent Master. One whom I'd sleep with. But you're so decent, you won't sleep with me."

His hands squeezed my hips. "That's not true, honey. I'll sleep with you all right. And I'm going to do a lot more than sleep with you, when you're free. You can count on that."

I looked regretfully down at his lap. "Are you sure? That looks super-uncomfortable…"

He caught my hand before I could touch. "Bad Lyla."

I blinked innocently up at him but he caught my other hand, too. He was quick.

"Let's get dressed and go talk to Charlie and the others," he said.

I sighed. "Fine." Then I clambered off his lap, helping him up. He stood, catching me in a hug that pulled me off my feet. His mouth found mine again, a gentle kiss, but one full of promise.

"And just so you know, I am a kitchen fan as well as a bedroom fan. And a fan of sofas, rugs in front of fireplaces, picnic blankets outdoors, and beach towels next to the ocean."

Whimpering, I tried to wiggle against him again. He put me down and pushed me toward my bedroom.

I went like a good soldier, feeling an entirely new resolve to lift my curse.

Chapter Twenty-Seven

So Tamina's the bad guy. As is Loretta," Rachel said from where she sat snuggled against Charlie. We'd met everyone at Purgatory to discuss the latest developments, hauling out various props to turn the stage into an impromptu conference room.

The nice thing about running a burlesque was we had a lot of things to sit on.

Rachel and Charlie had our stage chaise (we did a lot of lounging around at Purgatory, which explained all the chaises) and Yulia was perched on our swing. Trip and Trap were in attendance. I'm not sure the spider wraiths were friends, exactly—they were so wrapped up in each other (literally) that it was impossible to tell what they thought of anyone else. But they were always up for a fight, and were scary as shit, so they were more than welcome under the circumstances.

Bertha had also come, and she looked extra intimidating in her black suit. Under her suit jacket she was wearing a T-shirt instead of her usual button-up blouse, the half-troll's version of fightin' garb. She was standing, and everyone was clustered around where Oz and I sat in café chairs, looking like we were about to be interrogated.

"Did they kill Sid?" Bertha asked, giving all the explanation we needed for the outfit. Bertha was ready for some revenge.

I nodded at the troll. "Yes, I'm sorry. They were trying to free Kouros, but she couldn't Call him like a normal Magi because she was unInitiated. They tried using the Bridge and opened it too wide. The fodden slipped in that way, along with the bugbear."

Bertha's fists clenched at her sides, but she said nothing.

"Start from the beginning," Charlie said, his voice grim and his colorless eyes somehow managing to express concern.

"Turns out that I'm a patsy," Oz said, apologetically. One of Rachel's elegantly etched eyebrows lifted at him.

"Shush," I said, reaching over to give his hand a squeeze. "If you're a patsy, so am I."

Rachel's other eyebrow lifted to join the first, and Yulia made a Marge Simpson noise in the back of her throat.

Defiantly I kept my hand in my Master's. He ignored my friends' various glares and kept talking to Bertha, who watched him with nonjudgmental eyes.

Thank God for open-minded trolls.

"It seems Tamina has been behind everything," Oz said. "Half of her story was true. Her parents did die, and she did disappear. But that's because she killed them and ran away."

"With the human sorcerer," I clarified.

Yulia interrupted. "Like I said, Russian sorcerers are the worst."

"Well, this one is certainly strong as hell," I agreed.

"So Tamina ran off with this man," prompted Charlie.

"Yes. She thought he'd be strong enough to Initiate her and make her a full Magi. Then she would Call and Bind Kouros and together they'd run the world."

"As one does," Charlie said. Trip and Trap tittered, the only sign they'd been listening to anything we said, causing Oz to cast them a nervous glance. They both stared back at him, their laughter dying into silence.

"Anyway," he said, looking away from the spider wraiths. "Turns out he couldn't Initiate her."

"Duh," Yulia said, yawning. She extended a wisp toward her purse, which hung against the far wall, to pull out a nail file.

"So Tamina was stuck as an immature Magi, unable to use her power," I said, filling them in on everything Tamina had told us.

"But why latch on to Kouros?" Charlie asked. "That makes no sense; he hasn't been heard from since he cursed you. How does she even know about him?"

"Well, he's legendary among us. And...she claims he's communicated with her." I sounded very calm. I did not feel that way.

"What?" Charlie said. "That's impossible!"

"No," I said, my brain flashing to the truth in an instant of total clarity. Total, horrible clarity, that is. "Kouros *did* get in touch with her. He's been talking to me, too. Those weren't dreams," I said, looking to Oz. "He really has been talking to me in my sleep."

My lungs clutched at a broken breath and I leaned forward so my head was tucked between my knees. Oz's warm hand rubbed my back comfortingly.

"You never told me you were dreaming about him," Charlie said.

"I always dream about him," I said to my thighs, when I had my breath back. "But they've been different, recently. More... realistic. I just figured it was my curse almost being up, bringing everything back..."

"But really he wants out, as we saw in my vision." Charlie swore. "This isn't good."

I'd almost managed to forget Charlie's vision of me pregnant, and I shuddered.

"So Tamina wants to Call Kouros?"

"Yes. She wants to Bind him. But she doesn't have the power to Call him, even Initiated."

"Oh," said Charlie, using his "aha!" voice. He was piecing it all together. So was Rachel.

"The Node," she said. "And you."

I nodded. "Yeah, that's part two of the plan. They need access to the Node. It's one of the most powerful on the planet, and it's the only one that's not sitting under a magical city full of supernatural creatures that aren't fans of humans with magic, especially Magi."

"And you're the only jinni that can use Pittsburgh's magic." Yulia looked at me like I'd done that on purpose.

"What does she want out of all of this?" Bertha asked. "Not to mention Loretta. Are all the Exterminators in on this?"

Charlie shook his head. "No, I checked. Loretta's officially AWOL as far as they're concerned."

I deeply regretted the hours I'd spent teaching Loretta how to Ghawazee shimmy. "And as for why Loretta did it, that answer's easy: power. She's always wanted more power and she thinks Tamina will share Kouros's magic with her."

"What will Kouros do to them?" Bertha asked. The troll had a way of seeing to the point of an issue.

"Wring them out like a wet sponge," I said. "He's so strong. My family employed some of the most powerful Magi in our history, and they'd had him Bound for ages. But I listened; I knew the truth. They were really Kouros's puppets, acting like his Masters but really taking his orders. He couldn't hurt them overtly, but he wasn't like any jinn they'd encountered.

"Ironically, that's partially why I went to him. I knew he could act autonomously, unlike the rest of our house jinn."

Bertha interrupted. "We know what Tamina and her family want. They both want Kouros, and through Kouros they want power. But what does Kouros want?"

Crickets chirped as everyone looked at Charlie and I looked down at my knees, feeling panic swell again.

Charlie cleared his throat, uncomfortable. "He seems to want Lyla."

Oz's hand found my knee. I clutched at it, blindly.

"To free him," said my Master. "He knows she's the only one that can do it."

Charlie looked like he was going to speak, but shut his mouth. He didn't have to say it. Why had he seen me pregnant, and a jinni? And what did it have to do with why Kouros had obviously risked so much to curse me in the first place, and his desperate attempts to free himself now that my curse was coming to an end?

"None of that matters," said Trip, and then Trap took up the thought in an almost identically freaky voice. "What matters is what to do now."

We blinked at the spider wraiths and they grew together a little more in solidarity, their torsos melding until only a thin strip of skin separated their two heads. Oz's hand broke into a sweat in mine and I squeezed it sympathetically. I'd seen some shit in my life and Trip and Trap could still freak me out.

"Trip and Trap are right," Charlie said, his voice calm.

"Well, it's obvious we gotta keep Lyla safe till her curse is up," Rachel said. "But before that..."

"I can't be freed," I said. "Oz freed me when we were Sideways, and it looked like we might not get out of there." Yulia sat up in her chair and Rachel, Team Oz, cast her a "told you so" look. "I made him Bind me again, or we never would have gotten out of there." I had to raise my voice at that last bit to be heard over Yulia's protests.

"And now that Tamina's a full Magi, you have to stay Bound," Bertha said calmly. Yulia flopped back in the swing, kicking out her legs in protest. "Otherwise Tamina can Call her," the troll said.

"Whatever," Yulia muttered.

"So that's the plan?" Rachel asked. "Oz keeps Lyla Bound until just before her curse is up and then frees her?"

"She's no use to Tamina once she's human," Oz said, clearly in support of this non-confrontational route.

"But what's to stop Tamina Calling her the second she's unBound?" Yulia asked, her voice mulish. Trip and Trap nodded in agreement at her words. They weren't for non-confrontation, ever.

"We should take...the fight...to the enemy," said the spider wraiths, talking in synchronized succession. Oz shivered.

Rachel opened her mouth to argue but Charlie raised his hands, his colorless eyes focused inward.

"There's something pulling...," he said. "Can you feel it?" He turned to Oz and me, looking between the two of us. "They can't Call you, you're Bound. This makes no sense..."

His voice trailed off as his eyes shot to Oz. "Lyla, they have his blood!"

But before I could react, Oz's hand in mine vanished. My Master was pulled Sideways away from me so quickly that not even my jinni had time to react.

Until we both stood up and screamed.

*   *   *

"I can't find him," I babbled. "I can't even see him…" I was pulling like crazy on the Node, magical hangover be damned, trying to reach out to Oz.

One of Yulia's wisps smacked me smartly across the face. "Stop it! You're going to fry yourself!"

I stared at her in shock, then began to pull again. She slapped me again.

"What are you doing?" I shouted at her.

"Trying to get you to stop being an idiot!" she shouted back at me.

"I have to find him," I said, blocking her wisps with my Fire as I sought after my Master.

"Why?" she snarled. "What's wrong with you? Let them have him!"

I blinked at her, then looked at everyone else for help.

"That's not going to work, Yulia," Charlie said, standing up and walking toward me. "But Yulia's right, Lyla. You are going to burn yourself out."

I whimpered, but I pulled my magic back.

"How did they get him?" I asked my friend.

Charlie, now standing in front of me, smoothed back the hair from my sweating, red face.

"They had his blood and his true name. But how?"

"Tamina spent enough time with him to know his aura. As for the blood…" I wracked my memory trying to come up with something, anything, connecting Oz to Tamina…

…*Not Tamina, Loretta*, supplied my brain, helpfully.

"The bugbear." I swore. "It busted Oz's nose. There was blood everywhere. He used his T-shirt to mop it up…"

"And somehow Loretta got ahold of it," Charlie said.

"He gave it to her. We just handed it over." I felt sick to my stomach. "But I don't understand why I can't find him," I said.

"The sorcerer," Yulia answered. "As long as he has Oz's blood, he can keep him hidden."

"Fucking human magic," I said, kicking at the chair Oz had been sitting in, sending it flying.

"I don't understand why this is a big deal," Yulia said, her accent dangerously thick. "So they took the asshole that made you his slave. Who cares?"

"If they kill him, Tamina can Call Lyla," Bertha reminded Yulia, to Yulia's obvious horror.

And mine, because, quite honestly, I'd only been thinking about Oz. Now I was thinking about Oz being murdered.

"They're going to kill him?" I shrieked. "What?"

Charlie shook his head. "They're not going to kill him, at least not right away. Tamina is only newly Initiated; she doesn't know her own power yet. And our Lyla is tough to Call. It'll take Tamina's power at least twenty-four hours to settle. Until then they'll keep Oz alive and hidden, so Lyla has to come rescue him the old-fashioned way."

"Or we can just wait, Yulia said, with a snort. "In thirty-six hours Lyla can be free..."

"If Oz is in any condition to unBind her," Rachel pointed out. "All they have to do is knock him out, or cut out his tongue, and she's Bound another thousand years. The only answer is to get him back as soon as possible."

I swayed on my feet, glad I hadn't moved too far from my own chair as I sat down abruptly.

"We have to rescue him," I said, my voice pleading.

Yulia swore. "Shit. The fucker does need to be found, to keep you safe."

"No," I said, working hard to control my voice. "We have to rescue him. Not because of me, but because we have to rescue him."

Yulia frowned at me. "This is getting ridiculous, Lyla. He's not your friend; he's your Master. He can go to hell..."

"No," I said, sharply. "He freed me, Yulia. When he didn't have to and just because he thought I was in danger because of him."

"He Bound you," she said, stepping up into my face. I stared up at her mutinously.

"Yeah, he did. But that's not him. Not really. He's different..."

"What the hell, Lyla? What did this guy do to you, to make you lose your fucking mind? Is he that good in bed?"

"I wish I knew" fell out of my mouth, before I could stop it.

Totally awkward silence followed. Yulia looked at me in horror.

"I thought you used melons?" Rachel said, unhelpfully.

"He's not a normal Master," I said, trying to get my friend to understand. "I know what you're thinking. I've been thinking the same thing, up until super-recently. But he really is different."

"What if he's not?" Yulia asked urgently, taking my hands in her cool, long fingers. "What if he's not different? What if he keeps you Bound? Keeps you cursed?"

I squeezed her hands, my anger fading away as I saw the real issue here. My friend loved me, and was worried about me.

"Then I figure something out," I told her. "But I've realized something...I made a big mistake in the past, trusting Kouros. Since then, though, I've had pretty good people-dar. Like you guys. You're amazing friends. And I think Oz is like you guys."

"A snarky asshole who looks amazing in a wig?" Rachel asked, pulling both Yulia and me into a hug.

Yulia still didn't look happy. "You also trusted Loretta."

I sighed. "Yeah, well, she was never inner circle, no matter how hard she tried. I wasn't entirely off with her."

"None of this matters," Trip and Trap said, taking turns finishing the sentence. "Trust him or don't trust him, we have to kill the new Magi and save your Master, and then you can do what you like with him."

"We can kill him, too, if you like," Trap said, with a long yawn that showed off his fangs.

"He looks delicious," Trip added, a long, prehensile tongue snaking out to swipe the air in front of her.

"Not that delicious," Yulia said, shaking her head at me.

I tried to smile, but failed. I couldn't pinpoint Oz to pull him back to me, but I could feel his fear, tugging insistently at my jinni.

"I've gotta get him back," I told Yulia, letting her see all my cards.

She grimaced, but didn't argue this time. "If that's how it is, you know I'll help you."

"As will I," said Bertha, cracking her knuckles.

"Girl, we got you faded," added Rachel.

Trip and Trap grinned, a gruesome sight. "We only tolerate your various presences for the purpose of earning a wage. But we will help you kill," said Trip. "And eat," said Trap.

"That was beautiful," said Yulia, dabbing at imaginary tears. The spider wraiths shifted their eerily expressionless attention to her.

"Okay," I said, taking a deep breath. "Thank you, all of you. But what should we do?"

Charlie frowned. "I have a plan."

"Of course you do, boo," said Rachel.

"It's simple," said Charlie. "We just have to get everyone who wants to use and/or kill Lyla in the same room."

"Great," I said, frowning at my friend. "Nothing can go wrong there."

"Don't worry," Charlie said. "Lots can go wrong."

Trip and Trap giggled, then skittered up the wall, humming tunelessly as they went.

Chapter Twenty-Eight

The ransom call had come soon after we'd started prepping our counteroffensive. They'd give me Oz, if I came to them. We didn't talk about what they wanted me for. We didn't have to.

I agreed to come, but not until the next day. I told them I was hurt; that I had to heal myself. They told me, "No funny business, or the Magi gets it," and I made soothing, pathetic whimpers, assuring them I was in no condition to start trouble.

That was a lie.

"Are we ready?" Charlie asked, eyeballing our ragtag bunch with a worried expression. We didn't exactly look professional...in fact, we looked exactly as you'd imagine a gothic burlesque would look, if it decided to do a SWAT team number.

I was wearing tight jeans and this weird leather vest thing with a lot of pockets that I'd had for ages. I didn't actually have much in the pockets, but knowing I could put stuff in them made me feel organized and proactive. A pair of boots completed the ensemble. Charlie looked dangerous in a long duster over his undead-ringmaster attire, while Bertha had modified her usual black suit so that she looked a bit like a hedgehog, only instead of quills she had hafts and handles, pommels and grips, sticking out of her on all sides. Trip and Trap were extra nightmarish: buck naked, their white skin glittering as they skittered about on their hands and feet, their torsos combined into full spider mode.

For their part, Yulia and Rachel were wearing matching leather catsuits. I had no idea where they'd managed to get those, but I approved of the shotgun holster that Rachel had integrated into her costume.

"A lady is always prepared," Rachel purred, stroking the shotgun.

Charlie bit his tongue. He'd tried to leave his human lover home, but that hadn't worked. Not least because Charlie himself was still technically human, albeit slightly immortal.

"Should I go over the plan one more time?"

We all nodded. It was simple enough. And when Charlie was telling us what we were supposed to do it seemed completely logical and feasible.

When he stopped talking, it seemed batshit crazy.

"Okay, no problem. They want Oz and Lyla to rendezvous at Point State Park. But we're all going, and we're going our own route, back through the Frick Bridge, to give 'em a little surprise.

"We've got exactly four hours to pull this off, including an hour to get to Tamina. We couldn't get everything lined up before that, and we didn't want to. Time is both our enemy and our friend here, considering Lyla's curse is up tonight. We need to get in there, get them complacent, then wreck shop at the last minute. Our priority is to free Oz, but, again, only at that last minute. He unBinds Lyla, she turns human, they don't need her anymore, we have the upper hand."

"We still kick their asses because they suck, but the pressure's off," Yulia finished, shaking out her wisps menacingly.

"Concentrate on the plan first. Revenge is second," Charlie reminded the wisp. "You all know your roles?"

"*We're* supposed to hurt things," said Trip and Trap, in unison.

"I free Oz," Yulia said.

"I take care of the sorcerer," Bertha said.

"I help our special guests keep Tamina busy," I said.

"I look fabulous," said Rachel, running a hand over her smooth updo.

"And I See for trouble," Charlie said. "Good. I think that's it. Shall we?"

We nodded, psyched to get started. It was a totally sensible plan...if we didn't think too hard about it.

The trip to Frick, and then through the park, was surreal. We might as well have been off for a picnic after a long day of work. Yeah, we were subdued, but we gave no indication we were off on a dangerous mission to keep contained one of the world's great evils. For Kouros was that bad, I had no doubt. He had been bad when I was human, and after nearly a thousand years in a cage he must be an absolute nightmare.

When we crossed the Bridge, I saw Bertha's eyes linger on her family's fading tribal markings. Other trolls would move in soon. They never let a bridge go to waste, even one in such a magically blighted city. But in the meantime, I felt bad for anyone on the receiving end of one of Bertha's clubs. She was in no mood to pull her punches.

"You lead," Charlie said, once we were fully Sideways. I did as he asked. The walk to the abandoned palace felt shorter and yet also longer this time. I knew where I was going, making it seems shorter, and yet every minute Oz was with Tamina felt like an hour.

Finally we were in sight of the palace.

"Still impressive," Charlie grunted.

I nodded. "It's held up, although it's very confusing nowadays inside. It's losing whatever logic it had. But I can find the throne room."

"Good. That's all we need."

The wide gates through which we passed weren't guarded, but there were two younger half-vamps playing checkers in front of the double doors that were the main entrance. There was no point in sneaking around, as we just needed to get in, and get in position, and invite our own special guests, who weren't as expected.

The younger of the two hissed hungrily at us, lunging toward Yulia. She easily batted him down with a casual swat of her wisp. The other reined in his own attack, seeing his friend so easily dealt with.

"Tell your mistress we're here," Yulia said, her always chilly voice frozen.

They did as she asked, scurrying away like humanoid rats.

And then we waited.

"I told you not to bring anyone," drifted a voice from the dark doorway. It was Tamina, sounding as polite as ever.

"I decided to ignore that request," I said, with an insouciant shrug. "You already have enough of an upper hand, and I want to make it out of here alive with my Master intact."

Tamina stepped from the shadows to eyeball my compatriots. The girl's pale skin was white as a sheet, and dark smudges circled her now silver eyes. Initiation was hell on a body, and she wouldn't have full control of her powers for a little while yet.

"You pose no real threat," she said, after a moment. "And once I have what I want, you are free to go."

I had no doubt that what she really meant was that we didn't stand a chance against Kouros, once she'd pulled him from his cage. So she was fine with us hanging out until he could flame-broil us.

"So generous," I said to the girl. Tamina bowed her head in that beautiful tableau of modesty that she'd mastered. Charlie cast me a pointed look, stroking his watch fob as he did so.

"Can we get this started?" I asked, ever aware of the ticking clock standing between me and my freedom from jinnihood.

Tamina inclined her head, ushering us into her domain. We were flanked by her oldest half-vamps, all silent except for their obvious drooling as they stared at our necks. Charming.

"If you've hurt Oz," I said, conversationally, "I'm going to rip those new silver eyes out of your skull."

Tamina laughed, a rich, bell-like sound. "Oh, Lyla. You really are special. Your parents must have hated you."

"So we have a lot in common," I said, poking the bear. She shot me a less-than-pleased gaze.

"My family doesn't understand me," she said.

"And neither did mine. We're not all that different, you know."

For a second I imagined that was how we'd end this. That I'd share a heart-to-heart with Tamina, about where we'd come from and why it hadn't been enough. Because we *were* similar; that was the real kicker. I felt for the girl, even though I also wanted to knock her teeth out. But her need for more was something I'd felt, and just as desperately as she obviously had. Could I blame her for grasping at an opportunity when it plopped in her lap?

Tamina turned to me, ending my little fantasy of peaceful reconciliation. Her face was impassive but her left eye twitched with anger.

"We are entirely different," she said. "You are an abomination, to both humans and jinn. You were made so by your own weakness, a weakness I do not share. I will not make the mistakes you did. I will be my own Master."

And with that, Tamina turned with a flourish. Charlie raised his eyebrow at me, acknowledging both my attempt and what he'd seen in Tamina. While she put on a good show of bravado, she didn't believe her own words. She was scared.

Flanked by our salivating honor guard, we walked into the long-abandoned throne room. Charlie and Rachel looked around appreciatively, Rachel muttering something like "Now this is a living room." Trip and Trap—walking next to each other like the normal, if naked, humans they most certainly were not—also peered about, but they were probably deciding whom to eat first.

Tamina took her place on her throne, folding her ankles primly. "You know what I want."

I nodded. "Kouros."

"And I need you to free him."

I nodded again. "Apparently."

She looked down at me, her lips pursed in concentration. "I hate that I need you," she said, conversationally. "If I didn't, I'd have you destroyed. But I don't have that option."

"The Node," I said.

"The Node," she acknowledged. "You're the only being with enough power to actually do anything with it, without poisoning yourself." She sat back, her head cocked. "It's ironic, really. That Kouros inadvertently created the one being who could free him, so many centuries later."

"I would not assume his actions were inadvertent," said Charlie. "Kouros has powers beyond those of a normal jinni." He looked at me to emphasize his point.

"And this ain't no Alanis Morissette song," said Rachel, snapping her fingers.

"Be quiet!" Tamina growled. "None of this matters. You will do as I say, and help me free your creator."

I wasn't ready to call it quits on negotiating, however. "Tamina, please stop and think. You obviously have the same concerns we do. This whole thing, it feels like a setup. Why *did* Kouros create me? What does he really want? What's he going to do to you when he's free? Do you really think he's..."

"Shut up!" Tamina shouted, standing so fast her headscarf slipped back over her hair. She adjusted it with shaking hands, visibly getting a grip on herself.

"I am the Magi," she said. "He is a jinni. He will serve me. That is the way of things."

I felt my eyebrow creep up my forehead. Before I could comment on her charming ideology, Charlie interrupted.

"He's not serving anyone from his cage, and we're not doing anything to help you until we see Oz." Charlie's colorless eyes surveyed the room, and I felt him tap into the Node at our feet—just a small snort of power to sharpen his gaze without his falling into a full-on vision.

Tamina's eyes narrowed, but she lifted her hands and gave a sharp clap. "Bring our guest."

Motion from a far corner attracted my eye, and our friend Loretta pulled away from the group she'd been hidden among and waltzed from the room. A few minutes later Oz was led in. Ropes bound his wrists, and the young sorcerer Dmitri held Oz's elbow, the sorcerer's free hand holding a ball of power that he could use to blow off my Master's head. My Master looked mostly OK, although he had a fat lip and what would soon become an impressive shiner.

"Oz!" I shouted, suddenly recalling Charlie's earlier comment about cutting out his tongue. They hadn't, had they?

"I'm okay, Lyla," he said, relief flooding through me when I heard him speak.

"Shut up," said Dmitri, jerking Oz's elbow and letting his ball of power flare disturbingly close to Oz's ear.

"You're quite the sorcerer," Yulia purred, eyeing her countryman. Dmitri glanced at her, noticing she'd unzipped her catsuit perilously low. His cheeks went pink and his eyes turned to Tamina to ground him. "You pulled him all the way to you, and blocked him from his own jinni. Using his blood, I take it?"

Dmitri's Adam's apple bobbed, and his hand moved surreptitiously to his breast, as if feeling for something in his pocket. Tamina moved toward him and grabbed his hand in a smooth motion, but he'd given us what we needed—the location of the T-shirt they were using to hold Oz. Yulia's impassive face revealed nothing, but I knew from the telltale shiver of her wisps that she'd seen what she needed.

"Keep your pets silent," Tamina told Charlie, "including that jinni."

Charlie must have passed some sort of humanity paper bag test, and become our de facto leader in Tamina's eyes. I didn't argue with her—not only *was* he our leader, but he was also the least dangerous in a fight. The more attention people paid to him, the more damage could be done by the rest of us.

Charlie bowed graciously to Tamina, playing into the role she'd assigned him. "I'll do my best. What do you need from us to secure our friend's release?"

"It's simple," she said, straightening her shoulders. "Oz will command your jinni to feed me the power we need to Call Kouros, which will be done by both Oz and me. Once Kouros arrives, I will Bind him. Then you are free to go."

Sure, I thought, but Charlie didn't express any doubts. Instead he said, "Are you sure you have the strength for that?"

Tamina's silver eyes Flared dangerously. "You have no power here. Do not question me."

Charlie only watched her until Tamina shook her head angrily. "I do not need to be at full strength." Her voice was mulish. "Kouros wants me to Bind him. We have an agreement."

"An agreement?" Charlie said, his voice layered with skepticism.

"Yes. An agreement. One I do not have to discuss with you. I want to begin. Now."

Tamina moved toward Oz, pulling a slim dagger out of a sheath she had hidden in the folds of her long tunic. I hissed as she raised it to his neck, pressing its razor-sharp point against the pulse beating beneath the vulnerable skin of his neck.

"Do not assume that because I've been entertaining your questions, that I am distracted from my goal. I want Kouros. Tonight. And you're going to get him for me."

Charlie checked his watch and nodded. "Yes. It's time."

"Time?" Tamina asked, but we ignored her.

"Are you ready?" I asked, walking up to Oz. His eyes met mine, all questions. I gave him the slightest smile, hoping he'd understand we had a plan, but he still looked nervous.

"I'm going to need you to ground me," I said to him. "You have to command me to use the power of the Node."

"To free Kouros," said Tamina.

"To free Kouros," I echoed, using all the negative emotions I had in the hope that Oz would feel them and forget that part of the command. Oz's eyes widened and his nostrils flared.

"Ready?" I asked.

"Ready," he said.

"Ready?" I asked my friends. They all nodded, Trip and Trap drooling as copiously as the half-vamps surrounding us.

I turned to Oz. "Open me up," I said. His lips twitched, but he did as I said.

"Use the Node," he told me. "I command you."

And like that, the power was there. It flooded my widened channels, its poisonous taint leaching into me. My jinni pulled more and more into me.

"Tell her to send the power to us," hissed Tamina. "For Kouros."

"More," he commanded me instead. "More, Lyla. You can do this..."

And my channels opened even wider, pulling more power into me. When I was bursting with it, my jinni only just managing to keep it from exploding out of me, I turned beseeching eyes to Charlie.

"Tell her to do it!" Charlie shouted at Oz, who knew better than to ask what "it" was.

"Do it!" he shouted, just as Tamina's knife flicked toward his throat. But it was caught by one of Yulia's wisps, another wisp catching the sorcerer's wrist as he reached toward his breast pocket. A third wisp plucked a brown-stained hunk of cloth out of said pocket, disappearing it into Yulia's personal pocket of Sideways with practiced ease.

Meanwhile I reached, hard, pulling to the gate Dmitri had built in the room behind the throne, the one that led to the squat. But I didn't pull anyone from the human plane. Instead I reversed the gate, setting it even farther Sideways...

And in rushed the cavalry, through the gate and into the room. Roiling black smoke figures that fell on Tamina's minions. They tried to return the attack, but their claws and fangs slid through the red-eyed creatures, and then their hands found their own throats as the smoke slid into their mouths and noses, sliding down their gullets...

And now the eyes of Tamina's army burned red, possessed

by our allies, the jinn who hated Kouros even more than they hated me. They'd been willing to help us get Oz back, to end this madness.

Dmitri finally showed some sense, grabbing Tamina's hand and heading for the door. They were stopped by a swarm of their own half-vamps, now possessed by jinn, whose red eyes burned at them hungrily from teenage faces. Tamina was immediately gagged with the trailing ends of her headscarf to keep her from binding anything, and I caught a glimpse of Loretta among another knot of captives against a far wall.

"Lyla, no more!" said Oz, and my knees buckled as the magic left me in a whoosh. But I was giggling as I hit the ground, and I was still giggling when Oz turned me over, ever so gently, and wiped the tears of relief from my eyes.

"I can free you now?" he asked.

I nodded, unable to speak. I raised a trembling hand to his lips, and he kissed my fingers with a gentleness that broke my heart.

He opened his mouth to say the words of unBinding, but he stopped when the knife blade found his throat. It wasn't Tamina's knife, it was a curved length of supernaturally charged silver, similar to my own beloved swords.

And it was held by one of our rescuing jinn, a female not occupying a child's form.

"Not so fast," she said in paradoxically sultry voice, her red eyes burning into mine. "We're not done with you, abomination."

I glared over at Charlie, who shrugged.

So much for keeping our enemies closer.

Chapter Twenty-Nine

We'd expected to be betrayed, anticipating a dozen scenarios—most involving the jinn finally getting their long-awaited vengeance on me for the crime of existing. We'd created two dozen plans in response. We'd thought we were ready.

But nothing could have prepared us for what the jinn wanted.

"You will Call Kouros forth," the jinni explained, keeping her knife at Oz's throat. "And your Master will Bind him."

"Have you lost your damned minds?" Rachel asked, waving her shotgun for emphasis. She turned to Charlie. "Have they lost their damned minds?"

"Quiet the human," the jinni said to another of her smoky brethren who hadn't possessed one of Tamina's minions. Obligingly it whooshed through the air at Rachel's face. Yulia and I shouted as Charlie struggled against his bonds. Rachel got a shot off that caught in the jinni's smoke and fell to the ground like a handful of harmless bird feed. Then it was on her, entering through her nose and mouth till she, too, was possessed.

Rachel stood up straight, her mouth shut, but it wasn't her. When I looked at Rachel, I'd never before seen a man in a dress till right then, and I hated the jinn for that more than I'd ever hated them for anything.

"Release her!" I shouted, rounding on the jinni that held Oz.

"No," she said calmly. "We hold all of the cards, as you humans say. You will do as we say and maybe, just maybe, we will let you live."

"Step down, Lyla. Let's hear the jinni out," said Charlie, his voice cordial. If you didn't know my friend, you'd have thought he was calm. But I could see the vein throbbing in his temple that let me know he was feeling about as murderous as he'd ever felt. And yet he was right. We were outnumbered.

"Why do you want me to Call Kouros?" I asked the spokeswoman for our captors. "Because it really does sound like you've gone nuts."

The jinni raised herself to her full height, towering above us in her smoky glory. *My sort-of people can be beautiful*, I had to admit. But her red eyes were too malevolent to be anything but ugly.

"I owe you no explanation, abomination," she said. "You will Call Kouros."

"Actually, you do owe us an explanation," Oz interrupted. "Because if you don't give us one, I'm not doing shit. And if you kill me, Lyla won't have the power to access the Node. So..."

I knew that was only a little true, since they didn't have to kill Oz. If they hurt him, I'd cooperate.

I felt a tickle as Charlie accessed the Node again. His eyes were cast inward, but from the wrinkle in his forehead I knew he wasn't Seeing anything. He needed concentration and preparation to really See. Being held captive for the second time in one day, this time by our supposed allies, was hardly an ideal circumstance.

The leader of the jinn shrugged. "Fine. It is no matter to us what you do or do not know. Our elders wanted you dead; they sent an assassin after you."

Charlie and I exchanged glances. That explained the Blood Sect death squad.

"They wanted you off the field of play because they fear Kouros," she continued. "This fear has made them weak. They have compromised long-term security for a short-term solution. We will remedy their mistakes.

"You will Call Kouros, and free him, so that we may kill him."

"Why can't you just let him rot in his cage?" I asked, trying to buy us some time.

The jinni snorted, red tendrils of flame licking out of her nose. "Child, you have no idea who created you, do you?"

I raised my hands in a "not my fault" gesture. "You jinn never talked to me, except to warn me you were about to try to kill me. So all I know about Kouros is what my family told me. We knew he was powerful, so powerful that we used the term *Bound* loosely. He was more an ally..."

"Kouros is no one's ally," the jinni said, firmly, "as you should know."

I nodded, accepting the comment. I'd learned the hard way not to trust that particular jinni.

"So what makes him so powerful?" Oz asked, cutting to the chase. The jinni paced over to where her brethren held Tamina and Dmitri. They had pushed the trailing ends of the girl's headscarf into her mouth to keep her from Binding any of them, but her blazing eyes spoke eloquently of what she wanted to do to them.

"Your little friend here," said the jinni, very inaccurately cataloguing our relationship to Tamina, "not only wanted to Call and Bind one of the most powerful jinni in existence, but she wanted to Call the first ever to exist."

My eyes widened. I'd been expecting a lot of possibilities, but that was not one of them.

"What? The first? How?"

"Our legends say he Called himself into existence, before the dawn of time. Where there was nothing, suddenly there he was, seeking other life to entertain him. Eventually, after searching the cosmos, he found Man."

"That'd be news even to Neil deGrasse Tyson," Oz said. The jinni ignored him, turning to me instead.

"So your maker was the first jinni. He is our Adam."

I felt the blood drain from my face. "That does not make me his Eve."

The jinni's eyes blazed. "Not if we have anything to do with it."

"So why are you doing this?" I asked. "Why not just let Oz unBind me? I go back to being human in..." I looked at Charlie, who looked at his watch.

"In an hour and a half," said my friend.

"Then I'll be mortal, and I won't be able to touch the Node, let alone do anything with it. Kouros stays in his cage for eternity, out of our hair, easy peasy lemon squeezy."

"Not good enough," said the jinni, jerking her smoky chin at Tamina. "He's been able to contact this one, despite his imprisonment. His cage must be crumbling."

"So go shore it up. But leave us out of it."

"Impossible," the jinni said, impassively. "We don't know where the cage is hidden. We didn't capture him, and his location is kept secret."

"Convenient," Yulia muttered.

"But why risk freeing him totally, if all he's doing is chatting up strangers?" I asked.

"That's simple. We want him destroyed, once and for all. Our ancestors made a mistake in caging him; they should have killed him. He is more dangerous than you can ever know, with no sense of allegiance to anyone besides himself. And do not think he merely seeks his freedom. Kouros is plotting chaos—we are not sure exactly what that plot is, but we know it bodes as badly for us as it does for humanity.

"We should be united in this cause."

The jinni got down off her soapbox, looking as if she expected applause.

"What makes you think you can destroy him?" asked Charlie, who was always a fan of the obvious question.

"Because he's weak. He's been imprisoned as long as she's been cursed, with no access to any real power. And in this room are the strongest of at least twenty tribes; some of the greatest jinn currently in existence will fight this day." The jinni sounded proud, a pride answered by the straightening up of the various jinn around the room, whether they were currently possessing a body or not.

"We are many, and we are powerful, and we will destroy him, as our ancestors could not. We will no longer have to try to stay one step ahead of him, or root out his conspiracies. We will be free."

"I hear ya," I said, dryly. I looked at Oz, and then Charlie. Both looked as torn as I felt.

"Do we have any choice?" I asked the jinni.

She shook her head. "If you do not help us, we will kill all of your friends and your Master, but only after the deadline for your curse has passed with you Bound to him. You will remain a jinni, your friends will be dead, and we will put you in a cage

302

just like the one made for Kouros, and we will leave you as far Sideways as we can put you.

"I don't know if you'll die like that. Kouros didn't, but your essence is primarily human. Maybe you would starve, eventually. Or maybe your jinni would somehow sustain you, for another thousand years of torment before your curse finally lifted and your spark was snuffed."

I shuddered, but the jinni wasn't finished.

"The whole time you'll know that your stubbornness killed your friends. And we will kill them slowly, so that you remember every scream as you rot in that cage. And speaking of rot, maybe we'll put them in with you, to keep you company."

"And to think I was beginning to like you," I said, my voice soft. It was my dangerous voice. Every atom in my being said this was a terrible idea, that the arrogant young jinn standing before us had no idea what they were really up against. That Kouros would make mincemeat of them in seconds.

But did I really have any choice?

I looked around, and my friends looked back. Their eyes shone with worry and anger and a little fear, but they looked alive. I needed to keep them that way for as long as possible.

"Fine," I said. "We'll Call Kouros. But these are my conditions..."

At first the inky darkness dribbled from Rachel's lips slowly, but then it surged out like she'd been hit with a particularly bad bout of stomach flu. And had been eating smoke for the last twenty-four hours.

When the jinni possessing her was out and safely across the room, her hands immediately flew to her hair. No longer a puppet, she was Rachel again, a gorgeous dame who was all sass.

"Normally a man buys me a drink before he takes such liberties!" she yelled at her assailant, who actually hid a bit behind one of the jinni-possessed half-vamps.

I couldn't help but wince. These were the fierce warriors, the best of the best, who were going to take down Kouros?

But I'd made the deal: my friends' lives for my cooperation. Once they were out of the way, I could figure out how to free myself and Oz.

I'd tried to get them to allow my Master to command me from the human plane, but the jinn weren't having it, for about ninety-seven obvious reasons. They were desperate and, realistically, a little dumb, but not that dumb.

Oz and I watched as a few jinn herded our friends to the room behind the throne, where they were shoved unceremoniously through the gate there. We weren't allowed to talk to them, despite their various attempts. Only Trip and Trap had gone willingly, undoubtedly realizing they weren't going to get to kill anything they could actually eat on this mission. Surprisingly Charlie had also cooperated, his eyes so turned inward he looked actually blind. Rachel had to lead him out of the room.

Tamina and Dmitri were staying. I figured that whatever happened, they deserved to be a part of it. But that left their minions.

On the one hand, they looked young. But many of them were also creepy little killers who preyed on unsuspecting humans.

"Lock them up," Oz said. "There are enough rooms in this palace. Lock them up somewhere safe this side of Sideways, till everything's over. We can figure out what to do with them later."

The jinn, eager to be rid of their limiting skin suits, agreed without an argument. They marched Tamina's army into one of the many windowless rooms of the palace and we barred it from the outside. I'd lost track of Loretta by then, but I had bigger fish to fry than our turncoat Exterminator. After the room was sealed, a thick tidal wave of black smoke flowed underneath the lintel, separating into individual jinn once they were entirely present.

From within the room the children started howling, but we ignored them. They were safer where they were, and besides— they only wanted to eat us.

"And now you will Call Kouros," said the leader, after we'd been herded back into the throne room.

"Look, are you really sure about this?" I asked. "I know you think you can handle him, but you already told us he's not normal…"

"We are strong," the jinni said, calmly. "We will do what our ancestors could not."

And then I got it. This was less about addressing any threat Kouros might pose and more about a pissing contest with their ancestors.

These jinn were like the kids we'd just herded to safety. Powerful, supernatural teenagers, only these ones were made of fire and smoke. Teenagers who were probably all hundreds of years old, but shitty teenagers nonetheless—out to prove themselves through feats of strength, not caring how many they hurt in their attempt and not realizing their own smoky mortality.

This was going to be a disaster.

"We can't do this," Oz hissed at me as we were led toward the center of the throne room, where a lone jinni poured salt and coal dust onto the floor in a large, perfect circle.

"We have no choice," I said. "I can't let them hurt you. My jinni couldn't." I took a deep breath, preparing to admit the real truth. "But even if she could...I couldn't."

I looked down at my shoes, feeling like an idiot. I felt Oz's hand on my jaw as he raised my eyes to his.

"That feeling's mutual," he said, softly. Then he bent to graze his lips against mine, setting the beings around us to tittering.

Master/jinni fraternization was looked down upon by both species. Masters could use their jinni, but weren't supposed to feel the sort of care toward them that Oz had just demonstrated for me. And jinni were supposed to avoid any such use with the creative deployment of cantaloupes, pillows, or, in a pinch, something like a shoe.

We weren't supposed to fall in love; that was verboten.

"The circle is ready," said the jinni that had poured out the circle.

"Ready?" asked Oz.

"No," I said, "but go ahead."

"Give me your power," he said, and my jinni responded by tapping into the Node for the second time that day.

The power hurt even more this time as it flooded my already stretched channels. I was going to have to do the magical equivalent of Kegels when all this was over...if I was still alive, of course.

I focused the power toward Oz, who began his Call, this time using Kouros's name to Call him specifically.

"*Te vash anuk a Kouros. Te vash anuk a Kouros...,*" he began to chant, his silver eyes beginning to glow. "*Te vash anuk a Kouros. Te vash—*"

Then his eyes went into full Flare and his Call boomed out like a sonic blast, given legs by the power I was pumping him straight from the Node.

"Te vash anuk a Kouros! Te vash anuk a Kouros! Te vash anuk a Kouros!"

My jinni went even deeper into the Node, pushing more power through me into my Master, answering his need. I felt my knees give way but the power was literally propping me up, filling me like I was a sandbag.

It blasted out of my mouth, my eyes, as Oz's chant became a shout and the air around us began to swirl.

The swirling continued till there was a veritable mini-cyclone contained in the circle in front of us.

Oz's Call filled the room, but I could feel it reaching out even farther, through Sideways, echoing everywhere till it caught on...something.

That something caught back, pulling viciously at our connection. I gasped as my jinni reflexively reached for more power, throwing it at Oz, who pulled at what had grasped us, as if he were reeling in some terrible magical sturgeon.

One that threatened to pull us with it, far into a part of Sideways that I could only feel as utterly empty, where not even fodden roamed, where whatever pulled had lived, surrounded by silence, for centuries...

Kouros.

Up to that exact second, I'd truly believed this wasn't going to work. I imagined thousands of arrogant, powerful Magi had tried to Call Kouros over the centuries, and failed.

I figured we'd try, we'd fail, and then we'd have to fight a roomful of jinn to escape Sideways alive.

I'd been wrong. This damned Node was strong enough to reach Kouros, and Kouros was reaching back.

Through Oz, Kouros pulled again, a mighty effort that almost tore my channels asunder and made his eyes Flare like a nuclear blast. I thought we both might burn out with that last great effort, as whatever he was pulling suddenly came loose of its mooring, rocketing toward us so that we flew backward off of our feet.

I caught my Master as we tumbled ass over teakettle together, he still pulling and I still feeding him the raw, tainted power of Pittsburgh's Node. We struggled to our feet as the cyclone in the circle became darker, the swirling taking on form.

A form that stared at us with mad red eyes.

Until Kouros was there, just as I remembered him. Huge and imposing, far larger than any of the jinn in the room. And then he stood up, a giant among us, stretching his massive black-smoke limbs.

It was then that I looked down and saw, just as I'd expected, that all the swirling air had swept away the circle of salt, oil, and coal that was supposed to hold Kouros captive. The circle didn't do anything, after all, except focus your Will. And even Oz's powerful Will was nothing against that of Kouros.

"Shit," I said, just as Kouros's black-smoke foot took a step toward the jinni who'd threatened to kill my friends and stick them in a cage with me.

That jinni died about a second later, and I almost felt bad for her.

Until all hell broke loose.

Chapter Thirty

The jinn fought bravely, but their enemy wasn't less power-ful for his years in captivity. He was even stronger than when I'd last seen him, a millennium ago. His eyes glowed like he housed a nuclear reactor. Not being able to tap the Node wasn't going to be a problem for Kouros; he was like a Node unto himself.

"Lyla!" Ozan shouted, his arms wrapping around me, pull-ing me to a corner.

Kouros was everywhere. He grabbed the jinni leader around her smoky throat only to pull her apart, a sundering using both limb and magic that meant the jinni's smoke didn't reassemble, but drifted apart like that of a campfire rather than a living being.

The rest of the jinn swarmed Kouros, pulling magical weap-ons from their pockets of Sideways and screaming their various tribal battle cries.

Kouros swatted them away like they were children, then set upon them, ripping them apart one by one, his terrible red eyes glowing with pleasure.

"We have to get to the portal," Ozan shouted into my ear,

over the din of the jinn's dying cries. I nodded, and we tried to make our way to the tapestry covering that door.

Only to find it barred by a tail of Kouros's black Fire that swept us gently back to our corner. When I looked up at Kouros, he winked at me as he threw aside another black-smoke body that drifted into nothingness when he let it go.

"I think he wants us to stay," I said to Oz, unnecessarily.

He grimaced. "What are our options? If I command you to pull us out of here, could you do it?"

Black shapes were still flinging themselves at Kouros, their red eyes the only light in the smoke-filled room, but their numbers were decreasing. We had to get out, and fast.

"Maybe," I said. "Let's try."

"Lyla, I command you to—" Ozan choked suddenly as a black tendril of smoke wrapped around his neck, cutting off his air supply.

My jinni was roiling at the unfinished command, and I was roiling with her, but I couldn't pull that much magic without his helping me along. I tried, but it was like trying to suck on a straw with a hole in it.

So I grabbed ahold of Kouros's black Fire with my own, trying to get enough air to Oz that he could talk. And not die. But I got nowhere.

Kouros let Oz have just enough throat space to stay alive, but not enough to speak, and no matter how hard I pulled that was it.

When I finally gave up and turned around, it was to see my creator dispatching the last of the jinn. It died with a red flash of its internal fire before its smoke drifted up to join its brethren's at the ceiling.

They might have been the best of the best, but apparently no one had told Kouros that. Under the circumstances, however, I didn't feel up to saying, "I told you so."

Kouros stood up to his full height then, his glowing red eyes—all we could see in the miasma of thick smoke—almost at the ceiling of the great throne room. Then, to my horror, he took a huge, deep breath, sucking in all of that black smoke in the jinni version of a cannibalistic ritual.

After a few such long, deep breaths, there was no sign of our shortsighted former allies, except for the small piles of ash that were the only other physical markers of dead jinn.

Still ignoring Oz and me, Kouros turned to Tamina. The girl and her sorcerer had holed up in a far corner as we had, Dmitri shielding Tamina with his body. But Kouros plucked the young man away from her, squeezing like a child might a succulent grape. The sorcerer died with a pulpy squish that made my stomach heave.

"Tamina," Kouros purred, as the young Magi swayed on her feet. "Sweet little Tamina..."

Tamina might have been foolhardy, but she was brave. She stepped forward, beautiful silver eyes Flaring as she began the chant that would Bind Kouros.

The power wasn't there, however, her silver Flare stuttering along with her magic. Kouros laughed down at her, a tendril of his black Fire sneaking behind her. It wrapped around her forehead and a second later she was dead, her neck snapped efficiently, almost gracefully.

She looked very young and very frail when she fell, her head at an unnatural angle and the Flare of her eyes dying with her last breath.

"Thank you for your services," Kouros said to the bodies of Tamina and Dmitri, bowing low in mock salute.

That's when I decided we might as well get this over with.

"Still an asshole, I see!" I shouted, striding forward despite Oz's muffled protests. But Kouros still had my Master effectively gagged, so he couldn't force my sense of self-preservation any more than he could save us.

Kouros stood and turned, his red eyes smoldering extra hot as they found my tiny form.

I pointed at Tamina and her sorcerer. "Way to repay the help."

"Little Lyla," Kouros rumbled in his smoky bass, the voice I heard in my nightmares. "How good to see you."

I expected to die then. Speared through the heart by his Fire, or my head popped off like a Pez dispenser's. But instead he shrank himself down to big-human size, walking toward me, his Fire solidifying until he resembled a human carved from swirling ebony.

Oz came to stand beside me, taking my hand as Kouros approached us. I think he was manning up for a "We'll die together!" death scene, à la Titanic. But instead we received only a wide red smile from Kouros.

"Young love," he rumbled. "How sweet. You're making me a little jealous."

Kouros walked around us in a slow circle, inspecting us.

"He's handsome, Lyla. And young. A much more attractive suitor than that rapist Mongol your father wanted to sell you to." Kouros's circle ended with him almost nose-to-nose with Oz.

"Yes, very handsome. I can see his affection for you." Kouros sidled over to me, peering down into my own eyes. "And yours for him."

He glanced between the two of us. "I would kill him for that...eviscerate him right here, right in front of you, and

312

make you roll in his stinking intestines. But I need my sweet little protégée to be as strong as she can be." Kouros ran a black finger down my jaw, letting me feel the heat he contained, the power. Then he turned his eyes to Oz. "And so you live, human-excrement. At least for now."

"What do you want from us?" I asked, forcing my clenched jaw to work.

Kouros stepped away, pacing through the throne room, kicking up little piles of jinni-dust as he went.

"What if I told you I had a way to end all of this?" my creator asked me, kicking at one of the larger piles with his black foot.

"I wouldn't be all that surprised, since you started it," I replied.

"Always the comedian, Lyla. You laughed right up until I tore through your heart and replaced it with my Fire."

That shut me up. Kouros smiled at me in approval. "That's better. What I meant was, what if I told you I could end the servitude of our kind?"

I cocked my head at him. "I'd say you were crazy. The jinn have been trying for centuries. Even some renegade Magi have tried. We are as we are."

Kouros rounded on us, his eyes glowing bright. "All lies. I roamed this universe long before man even came into being. We were free, once, before these apes evolved to use us."

Oz looked at me, his eyes wide. I met his expression with equal concern. "You're not saying you want to wipe out man, do you?" I asked Kouros. "Because that would be..."

"That would be impossible," he interrupted.

"I was going to say it would be crazy, but impossible works, too."

"You are right," Kouros said. "While ending the human

race would be the ideal solution, it's an impossibility. At least for now."

"That's good?" I said, unsure what to make of the "for now." "So if you're not planning to destroy mankind, what are you intending?"

Kouros smiled at my Master and me the way you might smile at a pair of barking seals.

"If we can't deal with the problem that is man, we'll have to start with the problem that is the jinn. We need to be stronger, obviously."

"Oh, obviously," I said, wondering once again how the hell we were going to get out of this mess. Right now all I had in terms of a plan was to keep Kouros talking, mostly so that he wouldn't kill us. But that wasn't much to work with.

I looked to my Master for help, but he was looking at the ceiling. Oz's eyes suddenly flicked across to the far left corner and then shot back down, his face taking on that curious nonchalance I now recognized as his "I see nothing!" expression.

What the hell? I wanted to peer up at where he'd been looking, but I didn't want to give anything away.

"And how are you going to make the jinn stronger?" I asked.

Kouros grinned at me, a huge red smile, and began pacing energetically. I stole a look into the corner, but it was too dark to see anything. Still, I peered as Kouros talked.

"Isn't it obvious, darling Lyla? You're the answer, of course!"

That brought my attention back to him. "What?"

"Do you really think I would have weakened myself to the point of total vulnerability just to fuck with the little girl-child of my former Master? Did that ever make sense to you?"

I frowned. "I didn't realize what cursing me cost you, until very recently."

Kouros nodded. "Yes. The jinn kept that a secret. They

314

thought you might seek to free me... they didn't understand our relationship."

"You mean our lack of a relationship."

"Nonsense, child." Kouros was pacing again, and I risked another glance at that corner. Sure enough, I saw a glimmer of movement. Had one of the jinn survived?

"We most certainly do have a relationship. I am your creator. I gave you a new life—through the power of my Will and the force of my magic. I forged you anew."

I forced myself to look back at Kouros. "But what does that have to do with helping the jinn?"

"You were told I was the first, no?"

I nodded. Oz was looking at the corner again, but I didn't dare look, too. Instead I kept my eyes on Kouros.

"Yes. But what does that have to do with me?"

Kouros paced toward me, his eyes locked on mine. "I created you from a piece of myself, as Adam did Eve," crooned my creator, reaching a hand out as if to brush it through my hair. I shuddered, stepping away from him. He frowned. "You are my creation, Lyla. Mine. And I created you with a purpose."

I moved away from him, using the opportunity to look at the ceiling. There was definite movement there, a glimmering of something shiny. But it wasn't jinni Fire, and there was no smoke.

"I don't see how I can help you," I said, reminding myself to keep Kouros talking.

"Join with me in a ritual," Kouros said. "All I need is your power, your unique abilities. But that's it. You needn't do anything else."

"And then what?" I asked. "I have what... thirty minutes before midnight? I'd rather die than spend another thousand years like this."

"Of course," Kouros said. "You were never meant to be a jinni for this long. I was betrayed, so my plan couldn't happen the way I expected and you were left alone. But I can make it up to you now."

"How?" I asked, turning to Kouros but glancing up again as I did so.

Trip and Trap.

It was the spider wraiths in that corner, crouching low, keeping an eye on Kouros.

My friends had come back for me.

"All you have to do is join with me in a ritual I've created. Neither of you will come to harm, but the jinn will be free from the Magi forevermore. And then I'll let your Master unBind you. You'll be human again this night."

I glanced at Oz. His face still bore that nonchalant expression, but he glanced quickly to the throne and back and then to the door and back. It wasn't just Trip and Trap. The cavalry had arrived.

"What do you think?" I said to my Master. He looked at Kouros, then looked at me. He held out his hand and I took it. Together we took a step backward and together, as if showing our resolve.

Oz nodded. I smiled.

"I think we're ready," I said.

"To help me free our people?" Kouros asked.

"No," I said. "To get our asses out of here."

Chapter Thirty-One

ow!" I shouted, waiting to be rescued. For a split second nothing happened, and I managed to conjure up a whole scenario in which I'd imagined Trip and Trap, no one was there to rescue us, and I was shouting like a lunatic at empty air.

But I hadn't, and they were, and I wasn't. Trip and Trap had just needed a moment to spring.

They came out of nowhere, enveloping Kouros in a thick net of spider webbing. They were joined, moving faster than I'd ever seen them move, but they'd dart apart and then back together as the spinnerets at the bases of their spines created more silk that they threw around Kouros.

And then Yulia was beside us, her wisps forming paddles that kept batting Kouros back into the webbing. He was trying to escape by channeling his smoke through the fissures in the net holding him, but she kept whacking him back in like they were playing a manic game of squash.

Then Charlie was there, yanking us back toward the throne. "We have to get out of here. Move!"

I looked to my left and Bertha was behind Oz, using an iron crowbar to beat through the Fire Kouros had caused to spring up around Oz. It sizzled as it passed through Kouros's magic, but it was effective in freeing my Master. He took a huge gulp of air and reached for me.

"You're all right?" he asked.

I nodded. "You?"

"Yep."

And then he pulled me toward him and kissed me. It took a single second, just the briefest touch of his lips against mine, but it felt like I'd been walloped by a steel fist.

And then I was shoved by an angry half-troll. "What the hell are you doing?" Bertha said. "We're in a fight."

That was fair enough. Oz let me go and I laughed, a manic sound, but I had my shit together enough to grab his hand and we darted toward the throne.

We didn't get far before another wall of Kouros's Fire sprang up in front of us. He wasn't free of the webbing, and Trip and Trap were giving him a run for his money, but they wouldn't be able to hold him forever.

"Can you put that out?" Oz asked, pointing at the smoking wall. Kouros was letting it burn for real, and its heat flushed our faces.

"I can try. Just give me the command."

"Put that out," he told me.

"And hurry," Charlie said. "I've Seen what Kouros is really up to."

I glanced at him as I tapped into the Node and sent out a wave of my own Fire. "What did you See?"

"You pregnant, again," he said, dryly. "But this time I could See what you were pregnant with. Kouros."

"What?" I said, my Fire faltering for just a second until my jinni kicked in, fulfilling the command I'd forgotten. So I kept blasting even as I turned to Charlie.

"What the hell are you talking about? You Saw me pregnant with Kouros's baby?"

Charlie shook his head, but the relief was short-lived. "No, not with his baby. *With Kouros*."

"What the fuck? That's impossible! He's already born, for one. He's right there!" I pointed to where Kouros was struggling within Trip and Trap's bonds, Yulia and the spider wraiths still hard at work.

"Yes, but that's why he really created you. Not to mess with you or your family, as you assumed. He had an agenda."

"But he's right there!"

"He created himself once already. Don't you get it, Lyla? You know the mythology. He's *that* jinni. He Called himself into being, just like in the stories. And now he wants to recreate himself again...as Kouros version 2.0."

"But what does that have to do with Lyla being pregnant?" Oz asked.

"The ritual he's designed will bind his power and spirit to your flesh, in the form of a pregnancy. But what you'll give birth to will be Kouros—only he'll be even stronger. When he created you, he created a supernatural plus, right? Like we've talked about—you've got all the strengths of your human and jinni side, but all the weaknesses too.

"But what if you'd ended up with just the strengths? That would be Kouros. He'd have the jinni powers, but he'd have been born with a fully human body—so he'll be unBindable. No Magi could touch him. But he'd have all his original power."

"So he'd be kinda like Blade," Oz said, looking to me for affirmation.

"You are such a nerd," was all I could say to that, my mind boggling at the thought of an unstoppable Kouros. "What is his end game?" I asked Charlie.

Charlie gave me a pointed look. "He's a jinni Donald Trump, Lyla. You know that. What do you think he wants?"

"The world," Oz said, before I could form a conjecture.

Charlie nodded. "I Saw the whole thing. He'll be like a god."

"Criminy. What do we do?" I asked.

"We've got to get you to safety and think about how we destroy him," Charlie said. "But if we can get you home now, there's only like fifteen minutes before your curse is up."

I looked at the door behind the throne. It was so close. But then I looked back at Trip, Trap, and Yulia.

"What about them?" I asked, jerking my thumb back at my friends.

Charlie hesitated, then spoke. "We have to get you to safety. They'll follow."

I raised my eyebrows but Oz spoke first. "They won't get away. The moment they stop, or even slow down, Kouros will kill them."

Charlie's mouth thinned. "You didn't See what I Saw. Kouros's power will be unimaginable…"

"Then I have to stop him," I said. "I can't just walk away from this and let him kill my friends. I have the Node. I can take him."

"Lyla, it's not worth the risk. What if you fail?"

"Then Oz can free me. Keep his mouth free. Either I fight Kouros till my curse can be lifted or I die trying. Either way he doesn't get his way."

Oz didn't look happy, but he didn't argue. "Stay close to the door. Run for the portal if something happens to me," I told him.

"The hell I will," he said, coming with me. "Remember, I was a boxer's son. I grew up standing next to a ring, watching the fights. I can help you."

320

I ducked my head so he wouldn't see the expression on my face. "All right. You ready?"

He nodded and we turned as one, moving to face my ancient foe.

Trip and Trap were still darting around as fast as they had been, but Yulia's glow had faded and her face was pinched. I touched her shoulder.

"Let me," I said. "Go protect Charlie."

"You're supposed to be getting out of here," she barked instead. I shook my head.

"This is my fight, honey. Let me fight it."

She met my eyes, and whatever she saw there convinced her. She stepped back and I substituted my own Fire for her wisps. Then she went to stand next to Charlie, who watched with worried, colorless eyes.

"That's enough!" I called to Trip and Trap. "He's mine!"

The spider wraiths paused, glanced at each other, and then sprang apart, dusting Kouros with one last heavy spray of webbing before they skittered around the room only to rejoin, clinging to the ceiling over Yulia's and Charlie's heads. Bertha had joined Yulia and Charlie, and they all watched with concern as the bindings holding Kouros began to tremble.

And then they went up in flame, leaving my creator standing in front of me.

"I was willing to play nice," Kouros hissed at me, his form growing back up to giant size. I pretended to be unimpressed.

"Bullshit. You wanted to pull an *Alien* on me. Well, I'm no Sigourney Weaver…or I am, in that I'm going to kick your ass."

"You need a better writer. That was terrible," Oz quipped. I felt a surge of confidence then. I had my friends, a Master I was pretty sure I loved, and a fuck-ton of power at my fingertips.

"Tell me what to do," I told Oz, as I hunkered down into a fighting position.

"Use the Node," he told me. "And go for his midsection."

I opened my channels wide, feeling a rush of power that dwarfed anything I'd used till then, with the possible exception of freeing Kouros. That power propelled me forward as I rushed at my creator, wielding a battering ram of black Fire that caught Kouros off guard. It hit him square, and he wasn't able to absorb another jinni's Fire as he could the force of a human weapon, so it sent him flying off his feet. He landed with a soft plop in a pile of jinni ash, before climbing to his feet.

But I was on him a second later, hitting him with fists made of Fire. I pummeled his face, his chest, his midsection. He pummeled back, a blow that cut through the shield of Fire I'd built around myself, and sent me flying.

I landed with a much harder crash but Oz was shouting commands at me. He got me to my feet, and then I was flying at Kouros again, my Fire lashing out at him like dozens of cat-o'-nine-tails, whipping at the smoke of his flesh, revealing traces of red fire that closed as quickly as they opened.

I was pulling on the Node hard, trying to get ahold of Kouros, wanting to pull him apart like he had those other jinn. But he was huge, and strong, and I couldn't get a grip.

"Force him smaller!" Oz shouted, and my jinni responded with a wave of brutal energy that encapsulated Kouros's smoky figure. He had to shrink downward or come into contact with the steel-tainted energy, and that's when I realized what I had to do.

I kept shrinking him, till he was almost his real size. I pulled even harder at the Node, my channels fit to burst, trying to contain the tremendous energy he used against me.

"I need to be closer," I gasped, and Oz nodded.

"Walk up to him, Lyla. Get close."

My jinni rallied, pulling on the Node even as she forced me to stumble forward those critical few steps.

Then I reached Sideways, pulling out my belly dancing swords. Unlike the weapons I'd seen the jinn pull earlier, mine weren't magical.

They were old-fashioned American steel, and sharp as razors.

I had to drop the web of power I'd created around Kouros, but I did so only at the last second, stumbling a bit as the Node went silent inside me, its power no longer surging through my system. But I let the momentum carry me forward into a strike as I pushed more power through my arm, bringing it down in a vicious slash that sent my steel sword cutting across Kouros's smoky belly. A second strike of my left hand, slashing the other way, left a vicious red X across Kouros's midsection. He looked up at me in surprise, and then what looked like lava began to pour out of his belly. It was his power, draining onto the preternatural marble of the palace, which sucked it up hungrily as it fell.

I could feel Kouros trying to heal the cuts, but the steel was poisoning him. His power ebbing fast, he reached for the only other available power source...

The Node.

The poisoned power hit him like a punch. Kouros crumpled to the ground, his hand held out to me in appeal. I stepped back, my eyes as cold as my heart.

"Lyla," he said, his tone beseeching. "Help me..."

"Like you did me?" My words hung like bitter fruit in the air.

We watched Kouros die, his fiery innards pouring onto the stone of the abandoned palace, until we heard Charlie clear his throat.

"It's only a few minutes till," he said. "You may want to free Lyla."

"Holy shit," Oz said, turning to me. And then, without hesitation, he spoke the words of unBinding, his voice low but thrumming with power.

"Setenach, setenach, setenach." Be free, be free, be free.

I felt his hold over me die as his eyes Flared and then went dim. We were left staring at each other, my brown eyes melting into his silver. I took a step forward and he wrapped his arms around me.

"Lyla," he murmured in my ear, his breath making me shiver. "Are you ready to be human again?"

"I'm scared," I admitted. "I've been a jinni for a long time."

"I know," he said, pulling back to look into my eyes. His big hand cupped my jaw. "But I'm here to help. I have a list."

"You have a list," I said, my lips curling in a smile as I felt a sense of peace wash over me...

And then I screamed as the pain hit. It was midnight. My curse was lifting.

With a tremendous whooshing sound, my Fire left me. It flew toward the ceiling like a runaway cloak in a gust of wind, until it dissipated. It left a burning agony behind, as if it had been pulled from its roots deep inside me. I swayed on my feet as the rest of my power leached out, and I felt my body in a way I hadn't for a millennium.

I was only earth now. No Fire.

I swayed, and I fell.

But Oz was there to catch me.

"Lyla? Lyla?" Oz's voice was terrified, but he never let me go.

My eyelids felt like they weighed ninety pounds, but after a few false starts I managed to raise them. The bright light of the throne room made me close them again, hastily.

"I'm okay," I said, my throat hoarse.

"You scared the shit out of me," Oz said, pulling me into a bear hug. "Again."

"Mph," I said, all I could get out with the crush of his arms around me.

I felt other hands on my shoulder, my head, my hair. Yulia, and Charlie, and Bertha, asking if I was okay. Rachel was there, too, looking rumpled, her wig askew.

Oz finally let them pry me from his grasp, and they looked me over carefully. "How does it feel?"

And then I remembered. The curse.

I reached for my Fire, willing it to toss my hair as I liked to do on stage.

Nothing happened.

I did it again.

Still nothing.

"I think I'm human," I said, raising my forearms to stare at my hands, as if I might find confirmation there.

"Human," I repeated. Then I burst into tears.

Various hands patted my back and Oz's arm snaked around my waist.

"What's wrong, honey? Isn't this what you wanted?" asked Yulia.

I looked at her, then at Oz, who looked completely stricken. "Did I do the wrong thing?" he asked.

"No," I said, pulling him into a hug. "No."

I held him, gathering my scattering thoughts. Then I pulled away.

"It's just a lot. I've been living as a jinni for centuries. It'll take some time to adjust. But I'm happy. I wanted this."

"Good," he said. "I, for one, am glad you're human."

I couldn't resist touching that strong jaw, then the anchor at the heart of his clavicles.

"I'm glad, too," I said, quietly.

"Get a room!" called Rachel, adjusting her wig. "And give me a hug."

I hugged all my friends then, thanking them for coming back to me. Even Trip and Trap allowed an awkward embrace, but they said nothing to my whispered "Thank you."

Since they couldn't eat Kouros, though, and he'd been very dangerous, I could only assume they'd come back because they actually liked me. If only a little bit.

"Let's get out of here," I said. "If I never see this place again, it'll be too soon."

"What should we do about Tamina's entourage?" asked Oz.

I swore. I'd totally forgotten about them.

"Why don't we let Trip and Trap let them out," Charlie said. "After we have a chance to pull down the gate behind the throne room after us. There's no reason they can't live Sideways, where they can't prey on humans. There are enough encroaching fodden for them to eat."

"That's perfect," I said. "I really didn't want to have to send the Exterminators after them. They're still only children. Well, they look like children. When they're not lunging at people's throats."

"They'll be our secret. And they'll be a good deterrent for anyone else trying to set up shop here."

I met Oz's eyes as Charlie talked, and I felt my cheeks growing red.

"Ye gods," Yulia said, "they're like schoolchildren. C'mon, let's walk ahead and leave the lovebirds alone." She started for the door behind the throne and the others followed, Rachel giving us an indulgent smile.

Oz took my hand, his finger stroking my thumb.

"You must be exhausted," he said.

"I've felt better," I admitted. "But I'm okay. I'm human."

"You are." Another gentle stroke across my palm, making me shiver.

"You're not my Master anymore," I told him.

"I most certainly am not."

I tugged on his hand, pulling him to a stop. Then I pulled him to me, and raised my face to his.

The kiss he gave me was gentle as a butterfly's wing, just a brush across my lips. Then another, and another, and then he went in for a real kiss, his lips parting mine and his tongue tasting, gently. I sighed, leaning into him.

His hands moved from my back to my waist to my butt, cupping it gently and pulling me even closer. I wound my own arms around his neck, my fingers in his hair, my mouth opening wider against his...

When we came apart a few minutes later, we were both panting, our eyes dilated with lust and my knees, at least, trembling.

"Take me home," I told my former Master. "And make love to me."

He dipped his lips down for another kiss, but pulled away before it could get too intense.

"Your wish is my command," he said, with a wink.

"And then I want you to show me this list you made, of things to do once I'm human."

He grinned. "We'll have already crossed off my number one priority by then."

I laughed, slinging an arm around him as we started walking toward the door.

"What's number two?"

"Repeat number one a few dozen times. And then get you a Social Security number. I don't suppose Purgatory offers health insurance or a 401(k)?"

I groaned, made a joke about sticking with number one on the list for at least a few days before moving to other numbers, but I stopped him when we got to the little door that led to Tamina's Bridge Sideways.

I didn't say anything, just held Oz's hand as we surveyed the chaos of the throne room. Ash was everywhere, and Tamina and Dmitri lay crumpled in a corner. We should probably bury them, but I really couldn't be bothered. And I never wanted to return here, if I could help it.

Finally my eyes settled on the dark shape of Kouros huddled on the floor. He had, despite himself, saved me from what probably would have been a short, abusive marriage ending in my own death either at the hands of my husband or in childbirth. He'd also given me a thousand years on this earth and powers I'd never dreamed of. But he'd betrayed me, and taken away my humanity for a while, until I'd been able to reclaim it for myself.

He'd been something in my life, and now he was lifeless on the ground. His body growing cold...

His body.

Fuck.

His body.

"Oz, *run*," I shouted, just as Kouros raised himself on shaking limbs. An oozing trail of bright red fire still leaked from his slashed stomach, but he had enough juice in him to point a finger at me.

"I curse you, Lyla," he said, in the ancient language of the jinn. "With my dying breath I curse you. May you be a jinni until my revenge is enacted, my death for your life, the curse of my last blood."

Then he lifted a dribble of his Fire to his lips, power surging out of him in a blast that reverberated through the room, catching both Oz and me and hurling us through the door and through the gate that waited just behind it.

I felt a curious numbness as we tumbled Sideways over the Bridge, landing with a thud on a cold tile floor.

Oz came tumbling after me, face-first, and he probably would have broken his nose again if I hadn't caught him.

With a thick rope of black Fire.

We stared at each other, him floating above me, held up by my magic.

"Here we are again," I joked, weakly. "Curses."

Then I set him down and started crying.

Chapter Thirty-Two

On the third day, Yulia had had enough.

"You stink," she said, using her wisps to pick me up by my armpits and set me on my feet. I tried to crawl back into my bed but she wouldn't let me.

"Shower. Now," was all she said, as her wisps carried me in front of her toward our bathroom. I struggled weakly, but didn't have the will to fight her.

She used another wisp to run the shower, waiting till it was warm enough before shoving me in. Then she soaped me down, humming a Russian lullaby as her wisps lathered me and pushed me around under the water until I was mostly clean.

Towels appeared, held on more wisps, and I wrapped one around my hair. The other one I pulled around my body; then I moved back toward my bedroom.

"Nope," Yulia said, her wisps steering me to the kitchen. "You're getting something to eat, and you're putting on clothes, and we're going over to Charlie's. We have things to discuss."

I sat, disconsolately, in a kitchen chair as Yulia presented me with a ham sandwich. I ate it mechanically, drinking glass after glass of orange juice, which she placed in front of me.

When I was done, I looked at my bedroom with yearning, but she was having none of it.

"Clothes," she said, pointing at the pile she'd set down on the far end of the table. I dropped my towel and struggled into the underwear and sports bra, Yulia's wisps helping me with the yoga pants and T-shirt.

"That's good enough," she said, steering me to the door.

We walked across the moonlit lawn to Charlie's, the November air cold and crisp. I could smell a far-off hint of leaves burning and the scent of winter on the air.

It just made me feel even more hopeless.

Rachel was waiting to open the door as we walked up, pulling me into a crushing, sequined embrace.

"Baby girl," she whispered, before pulling away to look at my face. "Is it so bad?"

I nodded, tears forming in my eyes. She shook her head, tutting.

"I know you hurtin', but you look . . . well, you look scraggly as hell. But we'll sort you out, won't we?"

Then she put an arm around me, and Yulia put a wisp around my shoulder, and we walked into the living room.

Charlie was there, looking resplendent in a padded dressing gown he wore over an ascot and fine linen trousers. Oz was there, too. He looked sad, and handsome, and my heart broke about fifteen times before I sat down next to him—not touching—on the love seat next to Charlie's favorite chair. Yulia and Rachel took the sofa across from Charlie.

Bertha and Trey had the club that night, our second string of dancers performing with Trip and Trap, so we could finally have the talk I hadn't been able to, before now.

"So you're a jinni again," Charlie said. I gave him a "duh" look, but then my eyes teared up.

Oz's hand crept toward my knee hesitantly, as if he were afraid to touch me. Finally he let it rest on the couch with just his pinky touching my thigh. I stared down at it, the tears leaking down my face.

"That's enough," Charlie said, not unkindly. "You've been wallowing for days. I know you needed it, and the gods know I've done my fair share of wallowing in my day. But the time for self-indulgence is over. We have to figure out what to do."

"There's nothing to be done," I said. "Kouros cursed me with his dying breath. You know how strong a death curse is. This could last forever."

"And it might last a week. Or a month. Or seven hundred and seventy-seven years," Charlie said, steepling his hands in front of him. "But in the meantime, you're alive and kicking, Lyla. That's more than can be said for Tamina and Dmitri."

"We never buried them," I said. "We should go back."

"Already done," said Yulia. "Bertha, Charlie, and I went back to release the kids. But before we did that we buried the bodies. And we took down the portal in the throne room."

"Good," I said, but I sounded as listless as I felt. Nothing was good, not anymore.

"So now we have to discuss what's to be done with you." I looked up at Charlie, feeling a flush rise in my cheeks.

"What do you mean?"

"You've been outed, Lyla," he said, gently. "No one knew you could use the Node here, because you'd never been Bound when you lived in Pittsburgh. But word of your ability is already spreading."

"How?" I asked, confusion and sadness making me sound like a child. "No one saw me use the Node except you guys, the jinn who died, Tamina and her minions who are all dead or trapped Sideways, and Kouros."

Oz's pinky strayed closer to me, finally closing around my knee. "Loretta," he said, his voice quiet. "She got away."

I sat back, stunned. In all the chaos of the fight Sideways I'd forgotten about Loretta.

"Of course she did," I said, feeling a tremendous darkness invade my soul. "The worst ones always do."

"I'm sorry," said Oz, his sad eyes letting me know he knew that wasn't enough.

"I'm just a jinni; who cares about me?" I tried, but my voice held no conviction. I knew the truth.

"You're not just a jinni," Charlie said. "You're a jinni that can use Pittsburgh's Node."

I ducked my head and felt, blindly, for Oz's hand. His closed over mine in a warm, comforting embrace I knew I didn't deserve.

"You know what this means, Lyla," Charlie said. I nodded, snuffling.

"Well, I don't!" Rachel said, sounding defiant. "So Lyla is powerful. So what? That just means she can fight off any of those boujie Magi trying to claim her. She can use the Node and send 'em straight to hell, Kmart, or whatever. Right, Lyla?" When I didn't answer she kept going. "And if she can't take care of them, we can. We can keep her safe, can't we, Charlie?"

"I wish it were that simple," I said, my voice sounding rusty. "But it's not. I'm not strong, not unless I'm Bound. And I'm vulnerable to any powerful Magi's Call. You won't be around to save me if I'm Called to Turkey, or Saudi Arabia, or back to Persia, then Bound and taken back to Pittsburgh, or whatever."

"Shit," Rachel said, a defiant declaration. But when she saw the look in my eyes, she said it again, this time sounding sad.

"I know," I said. "But thank you for being willing to help me."

"We're still going to help you, stupid girl," Yulia said, her voice harsh and thick with unshed tears. "I will investigate this curse. Death curses are strong, but they can be broken... maybe."

"And I will use my Sight," Charlie said. "As will Rachel. Sometimes she can See what I miss."

Then my friends all looked at Oz. They'd already discussed with him what he needed to do, I realized.

"And I'll Bind you again, if you won't hate me for it," said Oz, pronouncing the words like he was juggling acid on his tongue.

My hand gripped his, painfully tight. "You hate being my Master," I said, acknowledging everything that meant about who he was, as a person.

"I do," he said. "But I'd hate it even more if something happened to you."

I risked looking at him. I hadn't done more than sneak a peek or two for fear I'd start bawling again. If lifting my curse had been my goal, my sundae, Oz had become the cherry on top that symbolized everything I felt I'd earned for my years spent as a jinni.

Now he represented everything I'd lost.

His lovely silver eyes Flared gently when they met mine, his Magi recognizing my jinni. Oz, the man inside those Magi eyes, looked scared and defeated, but also determined. And hopeful.

"We may never be able to fix this," I said. "You may have to keep me Bound until you die."

"No," he said, with no hesitation. "That's not going to happen. We *will* fix this."

"You can't be sure," I insisted, but he stopped my mouth with a kiss. It was quick, stolen, but it shut me up and filled me with a terrible desire for him, all the more painful because I knew his feelings on the subject of sex when Bound.

"I *can* be sure. We will free you, and for good. None of us will rest till it's done, least of all me."

And for the first time since I'd been re-cursed I felt something other than dread. A spark of hope sprang inside my breast, kindled by the look in his eye and nurtured by the set of his jaw, and the steady, firm way he held my hand.

Then I looked at each of my friends in turn. They were so strong, so brave. They'd come back for me and saved my life. Granted, I'd saved all of theirs a time or two over the years, but that's because we were friends, and we saved each other.

We saved each other.

I was crying again, but this time for an entirely different reason. "Do you really think we can do this?" I asked.

Charlie shrugged. "Maybe. Your last curse was done by the book. Knowing what we know now, I bet Kouros nudged your father to arrange the marriage in the first place, hoping you would approach him. He had time to prepare. But this time he improvised. And while death curses are powerful, they're also brittle. Plus..." His voice trailed off. "There may be other factors," he said, finally, his gaze turning inward in his own particularly creepy way of ending a conversation about a particular subject.

"Then let's do it," I said. "Oz, please Bind me. I trust you."

My soon-to-be Master stood, taking my hands in his. "I swear to keep you safe. And as soon as we know how to lift your curse, I'll free you again."

"I know," I said, lifting a hand to his jaw and letting it rest there. Then he spoke the words, his eyes Flaring, and I felt my jinni swell with power and my soul unite with his again in that terrible subservience under which we both chafed.

When it was done, he rested his forehead down against mine, his expression one of regret and love, and my heart broke a few thousand times more.

Like Humpty-Dumpty, I didn't know if it would ever be whole again.

"So is he moving in?" Yulia asked to break the somber mood, pointing a finger at my Master. She tried to mimic her old animosity, but it was gone. Even she liked Oz by now.

"No," Oz said, sounding as regretful as I felt. "But I will need somewhere to stay. I can go back to that hotel I was staying at…"

"Nonsense," Charlie said, waving his hand as if that were out of the question. "You will stay here. You'll need access to my libraries. *All* of my libraries."

My eyes widened. A secret but ferocious hoarder of knowledge, Charlie had quite a few libraries stashed Sideways, and he rarely let people peruse them without his close observation.

"Libraries?" I asked.

Oz nodded, his lips curving in a sweet smile. "I'm an academic. I research. Instead of ways to make refugee camps safer, now I'll be researching death curses. Did you know Charlie rescued the Library of Alexandria?" Oz said sotto voce, just to me. "He's got it stashed partially in a bathroom closet."

"So you'll stay in the big house?" I clarified, not giving a hoot about the library.

"Yes," he said, keeping his voice pitched just for me. "If we were at your place, I couldn't trust myself. I still have that list…"

"And we haven't even gotten to number one."

His hand squeezed mine again.

"But we will," he said. "As God is my witness, we will get to number one. A lot. Maybe a few times a day, for at least the first month or two."

I couldn't help but laugh, then pulled him down for a kiss. He pulled back way too quickly, but it still felt amazing.

"Maybe this isn't so bad," I told my friends. "Or, even if it is that bad, maybe it's not so bad because of you guys. I don't know how to thank you. You saved me about a dozen times over the past few weeks."

"It's because we're such angelic, wonderful beings," Rachel said, standing up before hoisting her boobs with both hands. "Now let's have some champagne..."

A few hours and a few bottles of champagne later, I was still drifting on my little inlet of hope. Yeah, things looked bad, but I had my friends, I had a Master I was more than a little crazy about, and I had myself.

Including my inner jinni, whom I had gotten used to after all those years, and would have missed, if I was honest.

And I kept up that hope even when Charlie took me aside and told me the truth. That when they'd gone to bury Tamina and Dmitri and let the kids out, there'd been no little pile of ash where Kouros's remains should have been.

"What does that mean?" I asked. He shrugged.

"It could mean everything or nothing. A gust of wind probably hit that corner of the room. But I wanted you to know."

I didn't know what to do with that information, so I simply said, "He made a death curse. Which means he's dead. End of story."

Charlie didn't argue.

By midnight everyone had gone home, leaving Oz and me alone on Charlie's porch. I built up a warm little fire on the table in front of us. It burned only at the top half, away from any furniture, leaving us warm and toasty without destroying anything.

Oz put his arm around me, and I snuggled close.

"We really are going to get through this. I'll find a way to free you; I promise."

I kissed him gently, lingeringly. My own form of promise.

"I know you will. And in the meantime..." I stroked a hand down his chest, which he caught before I hit gold.

"In the meantime I'm still your Master," he said, his voice full of regret.

I let my head fall on his chest, not pushing it. For now.

He stroked my hair and we watched the stars, and I felt such hope, at that moment, that all would be well.

Despite the fact that Loretta, my erstwhile friend turned traitorous, power-hungry turncoat, had walked away scot-free.

And despite the fact that I would soon be a target for every power-hungry Magi.

And despite the fact that the jinni race, which seemed to enjoy trying to kill me, once again knew where I lived.

And despite the fact that I hadn't been able to safely, and finally, dispose of Kouros's ashes.

The Princess Bride told us life isn't fair, and William Goldman was right. But damn if it couldn't be pretty darn beautiful.

Especially in the dancing shadows of my jinni's dark Fire.

Acknowledgments

Books are not written in a vacuum, and I have so many people to thank. First of all, thank you to all the good folks at Orbit Books. You are beautiful human beans who do wonderful things, and I know this book was a particular slog. Thanks to all of my wonderful, supportive colleagues and students at Seton Hill, who are always an inspiration. Special thanks have to go to Philip Palmer, Rachael Herron, and Mario Acevedo, who told me how to fix this thing when I was convinced it was Humpty Dumpty. Huge love to my own family, as well as to Mark Henry, Liliana Hart, Jaye Wells, Molly and Judy Harper, and Heather Osborne, my writer family. And huge thanks to my Pittsburgh Tribe and to Shon Kelley, for all of their support.

extras

orbit

meet the author

Robert Trudeau

NICOLE PEELER writes urban fantasy and is an associate professor at Seton Hill University, where she co-directs their MFA in Writing Popular Fiction. Having recently finished her award-winning Jane True series, she is looking forward to the publication of *Jinn and Juice*, the first book in a series about a cursed jinni living in Pittsburgh. Nicole also lives in Pittsburgh, although she's neither cursed nor a jinni.

introducing

If you enjoyed
JINN AND JUICE
look out for

TEMPEST RISING

Book One of the Jane True series

by Nicole Peeler

Living in small-town Rockabill, Maine, Jane True always knew she didn't quite fit in with so-called normal society. During her nightly clandestine swim in the freezing winter ocean, a grisly find leads Jane to startling revelations about her heritage: she is only half-human.

Now, Jane must enter a world filled with supernatural creatures alternatively terrifying, beautiful, and deadly—all of which perfectly describe her new "friend," Ryu, a gorgeous and powerful vampire.

It is a world where nothing can be taken for granted: a dog can heal with a lick; spirits bag your groceries; and whatever you do, never, ever rub the genie's lamp.

Chapter One

I eyeballed the freezer, trying to decide what to cook for dinner that night. Such a decision was no mean feat, since a visiting stranger might assume that Martha Stewart not only lived with us but was preparing for the apocalypse. Frozen lasagnas, casseroles, pot pies, and the like filled our icebox nearly to the brim. Finally deciding on fish chowder, I took out some haddock and mussels. After a brief, internal struggle, I grabbed some salmon to make extra soup to—you guessed it—freeze. Yeah, the stockpiling was more than a little OCD, but it made me feel better. It also meant that when I actually had something to do for the entire evening, I could leave my dad by himself without feeling too guilty about it.

My dad wasn't an invalid—not exactly. But he had a bad heart and needed help taking care of things, especially with my mother gone. So I took up the slack, which I was happy to do. It's not like I had much else on my plate, what with being the village pariah and all.

It's amazing how being a pariah gives you ample amounts of free time.

After putting in the laundry and cleaning the downstairs bathroom, I went upstairs to take a shower. I would have loved to walk around all day with the sea salt on my skin, but not even in Rockabill was Eau de Brine an acceptable perfume. Like many twentysomethings, I'd woken up early that day to go exercise. Unlike most twenty-somethings, however, my morning exercise took the form of an hour-or-so-long swim in the freezing ocean. And in one of America's deadliest whirlpools. Which is why I am so careful to keep the swimming on the DL. It might be a great cardio workout, but it probably would get me burned at the stake. This is New England, after all.

As I got dressed in my work clothes—khaki chinos and a long-sleeved pink polo-style shirt with Read It and Weep embroidered in navy blue over the breast pocket—I heard my father emerge from his bedroom and clomp down the stairs. His job in the morning was to make the coffee, so I took a moment to apply a little mascara, blush, and some lip gloss, before brushing out my damp black hair. I kept it cut in a much longer—and admittedly more unkempt—version of Cleopatra's style because I liked to hide my dark eyes under my long bangs. Most recently, my nemesis, Stuart Gray, had referred to them as "demon eyes." They're not as Marilyn Manson as that, thank you very much, but even I had to admit to difficulty determining where my pupil ended and my iris began.

I went back downstairs to join my dad in the kitchen, and I felt that pang in my heart that I get sometimes when I'm struck by how he's changed. He'd been a fisherman, but he'd had to retire about ten years ago, on disability, when his heart condition worsened. Once a handsome, confident, and brawny man whose presence filled any space he entered, his long illness and my mother's disappearance had diminished him in every possible way. He looked so small and gray in his faded old bathrobe, his hands trembling from the anti-arrhythmics he takes for his screwed-up heart, that it took every ounce of self-control I had not to make him sit down and rest. Even if his body didn't agree, he still felt himself to be the man he had been, and I knew I already walked a thin line between caring for him and treading on his dignity. So I put on my widest smile and bustled into the kitchen, as if we were a father and daughter in some sitcom set in the 1950s.

"Good morning, Daddy!" I beamed.

"Morning, honey. Want some coffee?" He asked me that question every morning, even though the answer had been yes since I was fifteen.

"Sure, thanks. Did you sleep all right?"

"Oh, yes. And you? How was your morning?" My dad never asked me directly about the swimming. It's a question that lay under the auspices of the "don't ask, don't tell" policy that ruled our household. For example, he didn't ask me about my swimming, I didn't ask him about my mother. He didn't ask me about Jason, I didn't ask him about my mother. He didn't ask me whether or not I was happy in Rockabill, I didn't ask him about my mother...

"Oh, I slept fine, Dad. Thanks." Of course I hadn't, really, as I only needed about four hours of sleep a night. But that's another thing we never talked about.

He asked me about my plans for the day, while I made us a breakfast of scrambled eggs on whole wheat toast. I told him that I'd be working till six, then I'd go to the grocery store on the way home. So, as usual for a Monday, I'd take the car to work. We performed pretty much the exact same routine every week, but it was nice of him to act like it was possible I might have new and exciting plans. On Mondays, I didn't have to worry about him eating lunch, as Trevor McKinley picked him up to go play a few hours of cheeky lunchtime poker with George Varga, Louis Finch, and Joe Covelli. They're all natives of Rockabill and friends since childhood, except for Joe, who moved here to Maine about twenty years ago to open up our local garage. That's how things were around Rockabill. For the winter, when the tourists were mostly absent, the town was populated by natives who grew up together and were more intimately acquainted with each other's dirty laundry than their own hampers. Some people enjoyed that intimacy. But when you were more usually the object of the whispers than the subject, intimacy had a tendency to feel like persecution.

We ate while we shared our local paper, *The Light House News*. But because the paper mostly functioned as a vehicle for advertising things to tourists, and the tourists were gone for the season, the pickings were scarce. Yet we went through the motions anyway. For all of our sins, no one could say that the True family wasn't good at going through the motions. After breakfast, I doled out my father's copious pills and set them next to his orange juice. He flashed me his charming smile, which was the only thing left unchanged after the ravages to his health and his heart.

"Thank you, Jane," he said. And I knew he meant it, despite the fact that I'd set his pills down next to his orange juice every single morning for the past twelve years.

I gulped down a knot in my throat, since I knew that no small share of his worry and grief was due to me, and kissed him on the cheek. Then I bustled around clearing away breakfast, and bustled around getting my stuff together, and bustled out the door to get to work. In my experience, bustling is always a great way to keep from crying.

Tracy Gregory, the owner of Read It and Weep, was already hard at work when I walked in the front door. The Gregorys were an old fishing family from Rockabill, and Tracy was their prodigal daughter. She had left to work in Los Angeles, where she had apparently been a successful movie stylist. I say apparently because she never told us the names of any of the movies she'd worked on. She'd only moved back to Rockabill about five years ago to open Read It and Weep, which was our local bookstore, café, and all-around tourist trap. Since tourism replaced fishing as our major industry, Rockabill can just about support an all-year-round enterprise like Read It and Weep. But other things, like the nicer restaurant—rather unfortunately named The Pig Out Bar and Grill—close for the winter.

"Hey, girl," she said, gruffly, as I locked the door behind me. We didn't open for another half hour.

"Hey, Tracy. Grizelda back?"

Grizelda was Tracy's girlfriend, and they'd caused quite a stir when they first appeared in Rockabill together. Not only were they lesbians, but they were as fabulously lesbionic as the inhabitants of a tiny village in Maine could ever imagine. Tracy carried herself like a rugby player, and dressed like one, too. But she had an easygoing charisma that got her through the initial gender panic triggered by her reentry into Rockabill society.

And if Tracy made heads turn, Grizelda practically made them spin *Exorcist* style. Grizelda was not Grizelda's real name. Nor was Dusty Nethers, the name she used when she'd been a porn star. As Dusty Nethers, Grizelda had been fiery haired and as boobilicious as a *Baywatch* beauty. But in her current incarnation, as Grizelda Montague, she sported a sort of Gothic-hipster look—albeit one that was still very boobilicious. A few times a year Grizelda disappeared for weeks or a month, and upon her return home she and Tracy would complete some big project they'd been discussing, like redecorating the store or adding a sunroom onto their little house. Lord knows what she got up to on her profit-venture vacations. But whatever it was, it didn't affect her relationship with Tracy. The pair were as close as any husband and wife in Rockabill, if not closer, and seeing how much they loved each other drove home to me my own loneliness.

"Yeah, Grizzie's back. She'll be here soon. She has something for you...something scandalous, knowing my lady love."

I grinned. "Awesome. I love her gifts."

Because of Grizzie, I had a drawer full of naughty underwear, sex toys, and dirty books. Grizzie gave such presents for *every* occasion; it didn't matter if it was your high school graduation, your fiftieth wedding anniversary, or your baby's baptism. This particular predilection meant she was a prominent figure on wedding shower guest lists from Rockabill to Eastport, but made her dangerous for children's parties. Most parents didn't appreciate an "every day of the week" pack of thongs for their eleven-year-old daughter. Once she'd given me a gift certificate for a "Hollywood" bikini wax and I had to Google the term. What I discovered made me way too scared to use it, so it sat in my "dirty drawer," as I called it, as a talking point. Not that anyone ever went into my dirty drawer with me, but I talked to myself a lot, and it certainly provided amusing fodder for my own conversations.

It was also rather handy—no pun intended—to have access to one's own personal sex shop during long periods of enforced abstinence...such as the last eight years of my life.

"And," Tracy responded with a rueful shake of her head, "her gifts love you. Often quite literally."

"That's all right, somebody has to," I answered back, horrified at the bitter inflection that had crept into my voice.

But Tracy, bless her, just stroked a gentle hand over my hair that turned into a tiny one-armed hug, saying nothing.

"Hands off my woman!" crowed a hard-edged voice from the front door. Grizelda!

"Oh, sorry," I apologized, backing away from Tracy.

"I meant for Tracy to get off *you*," Grizzie said, swooping toward me to pick me up in a bodily hug, my own well-endowed chest clashing with her enormous fake bosoms. I hated being short at times like these. Even though I loved all five feet and eleven inches of Grizzie, and had more than my fair share of affection for her ta-ta-riddled hugs, I loathed being manhandled.

She set me down and grasped my hands in hers, backing away to look me over appreciatively while holding my fingers at arm's length. "Mmm, mmm," she said, shaking her head. "Girl, I could sop you up with a biscuit."

I laughed, as Tracy rolled her eyes.

"Quit sexually harassing the staff, Grizzly Bear," was her only comment.

"I'll get back to sexually harassing you in a minute, passion flower, but right now I want to appreciate our Jane." Grizelda winked at me with her florid violet eyes—she wore colored lenses—and I couldn't help but giggle like a schoolgirl.

"I've brought you a little something," she said, her voice sly.

I clapped my hands in excitement and hopped up and down in a little happy dance.

I really did love Grizzie's gifts, even if they challenged the tenuous grasp of human anatomy imparted to me by Mrs. Renault in her high school biology class.

"Happy belated birthday!" she cried as she handed me a beautifully wrapped package she pulled from her enormous handbag. I admired the shiny black paper and the sumptuous red velvet ribbon tied up into a decadent bow—Grizzie did everything with style—before tearing into it with glee. After slitting open the tape holding the box closed with my thumbnail, I was soon holding in my hands the most beautiful red satin nightgown I'd ever seen. It was a deep, bloody, blue-based red, the perfect red for my skin tone. And it was, of course, the perfect length, with a slit up the side that would rise almost to my hip. Grizzie had this magic ability to always buy people clothes that fit. The top was generously cut for its small dress size, the bodice gathered into a sort of clamshell-like tailoring that I knew would cup my boobs like those hands in that famous Janet Jackson picture. The straps were slightly thicker, to give support, and crossed over the *very* low-cut back. It was absolutely gorgeous—very adult and sophisticated—and I couldn't stop stroking the deliciously watery satin.

"Grizzie," I breathed. "It's gorgeous...but too much! This must have cost a fortune."

"You are worth a fortune, little Jane. Besides, I figured you might need something nice...since Mark's 'special deliveries' should have culminated in a date by now."

Grizzie's words trailed off as my face fell and Tracy, behind her, made a noise like Xena, Warrior Princess, charging into battle.

Before Tracy could launch into just how many ways she wanted to eviscerate our new letter carrier, I said, very calmly, "I won't be going on any dates with Mark."

"What happened?" Grizzie asked, as Tracy made another grunting declaration of war behind us.

"Well..." I started, but where should I begin? Mark was new to Rockabill, a widowed employee of the U.S. Postal Service, who had recently moved to our little corner of Maine with his two young daughters. He'd kept forgetting to deliver letters and packages, necessitating second, and sometimes third, trips to our bookstore, daily. I'd thought he was sweet, but rather dumb, until Tracy had pointed out that he only forgot stuff when I was working.

So we'd flirted and flirted and flirted over the course of a month. Until, just a few days ago, he'd asked me out. I was thrilled. He was cute; he was *new*; he'd lost someone he was close to, as well. And he "obviously" didn't judge me on my past.

You know what they say about assuming…

"We had a date set up, but he cancelled. I guess he asked me out before he knew about…everything. Then someone must have told him. He's got kids, you know."

"So?" Grizzie growled, her smoky voice already furious.

"So, he said that he didn't think I'd be a good influence. On his girls."

"That's fucking ridiculous," Grizzie snarled, just as Tracy made a series of inarticulate chittering noises behind us. She was normally the sedate, equable half of her and Grizzie's partnership, but Tracy had nearly blown a gasket when I'd called her crying after Mark bailed on me. I think she would have torn off his head, but then we wouldn't have gotten our inventory anymore.

I lowered my head and shrugged. Grizzie moved forward, having realized that Tracy already had the anger market cornered.

"I'm sorry, honey," she said, wrapping her long arms around me. "That's…such a shame."

And it was a shame. My friends wanted me to move on, my dad wanted me to move on. Hell, except for that tiny sliver of me that was still frozen in guilt, *I* wanted to move on. But the rest of Rockabill, it seems, didn't agree.

Grizzie brushed the bangs back from my eyes, and when she saw tears glittering she intervened, Grizelda-style. Dipping me like a tango dancer, she growled sexily, "Baby, I'm gonna butter yo' bread..." before burying her face in my exposed belly and giving me a resounding zerbert.

That did just the trick. I was laughing again, thanking my stars for about the zillionth time that they had brought Grizzie and Tracy back to Rockabill because I didn't know what I would have done without them. I gave Tracy her own hug for the present, and then took it to the back room with my stuff. I opened the box to give the red satin one last parting caress, and then closed it with a contented sigh.

It would look absolutely gorgeous in my dirty drawer.

We only had a few things to do to get the store ready for opening, which left much time for chitchat. About a half hour of intense gossip later, we had pretty much exhausted "what happened when you were gone" as a subject of conversation and had started in on plans for the coming week, when the little bell above the door tinkled. My heart sank when I saw it was Linda Allen, self-selected female delegate for my own personal persecution squad. She wasn't quite as bad as Stuart Gray, who hated me even more than Linda did, but she did her best to keep up with him.

Speaking of the rest of Rockabill, I thought, as Linda headed toward romance.

She didn't bother to speak to me, of course. She just gave me one of her loaded looks that she could fire off like a World War II gunship. The looks always said the same things. They spoke of the fact that I was the girl whose crazy mother had shown up in the center of town out of nowhere, *naked*, in the middle of a storm. The fact that she'd *stolen* one of the most eligible Rockabill bachelors and *ruined him for life*. The fact that she'd given birth to a baby *without being married*. The fact that I insisted on being *that child* and upping the ante by being *just as weird as my mother*. That was only the tip of the vituperative iceberg that Linda hauled into my presence whenever she had the chance.

Unfortunately, Linda read nearly as compulsively as I did, so I saw her at least twice a month when she'd come in for a new stack of romance novels. She liked a very particular kind of plot: the sort where the pirate kidnaps some virgin damsel, rapes her into loving him, and then dispatches lots of seamen while she polishes his cutlass. Or where the Highland clan leader kidnaps some virginal English Rose, rapes her into loving him, and then kills entire armies of Sassenachs while she stuffs his haggis. Or where the Native American warrior kidnaps a virginal white settler, rapes her into loving him, and then kills a bunch of colonists while she whets his tomahawk. I hated to get Freudian on Linda, but her reading patterns suggested some interesting insights into why she was such a complete bitch.

Tracy had received a phone call while Linda was picking out her books, and Grizelda was sitting on a stool far behind the counter in a way that clearly said "I'm not actually working, thanks." But Linda pointedly ignored the fact that I was free to help her, choosing, instead, to stand in front of Tracy. Tracy gave that little eye gesture where she looked at Linda, then looked at me, as if to say, "She can help you," but Linda insisted on being oblivious to my presence. Tracy sighed and cut her telephone conversation short. I knew that Tracy would love to tell Linda to stick her attitude where the sun don't shine, but Read It and Weep couldn't afford to lose a customer who was as good at buying books as she was at being a snarky snake face. So Tracy rang up Linda's purchases and bagged them for her as politely as one can without actually being friendly and handed the bag over to Linda.

Who, right on cue, gave me her parting shot, the look I knew was coming but was never quite able to deflect.

The look that said, *There's the freak who killed her own boyfriend.*

She was wrong, of course. I hadn't actually killed Jason. I was just the reason he was dead.

introducing

**If you enjoyed
JINN AND JUICE
look out for**

HOUSE OF THE RISING SUN

Book One of the Crescent City series

by Kristen Painter

*Every vampire has heard rumors of the mythical place where their
kind can daywalk. But what no vampire knows is that this City
of Eternal Night actually exists.*

And its name is New Orleans.

*For centuries the fae have protected the city from vampire infesta-
tion. But when the bloodsuckers return, the fragile peace in New
Orleans begins to crumble.*

*Carefree playboy Augustine, and Harlow, a woman searching for
answers about her absent father, are dragged into the war. The
fate of the city rests on them—and their fae blood that can no
longer be denied.*

Book One in the brand-new, action-packed urban fantasy Crescent City series, from award-winning House of Comarré author Kristen Painter!

Chapter One

Procrastination assassinates opportunity.
—Elektos Codex, 4.1.1

New Orleans, 2068

Augustine trailed his fingers over the silky shoulder of one of his mocha-skinned bedmates. He dare not wake her, or her sister sleeping on the other side of him, or he feared he'd never get home in time for lunch with his dear Olivia. He felt a twinge of guilt that he'd spent his first night back in New Orleans in the company of "strange" women, as Olivia would call them, but only a twinge. A man had needs, after all.

The woman sighed contentedly at his touch, causing him to do the same. Last night had been just the right amount of fun to welcome him home. He eased onto his back and folded his arms behind his head, a satisfied smile firmly in place. The Santiago sisters from Mobile, Alabama, had earned their sleep.

Outside the Hotel Monteleone, the city was just waking up.

Delivery trucks rumbled through the Quarter's narrow streets, shopkeepers washed their sidewalks clean of last night's revelries and the bitter scent of chicory coffee filled the air with a seductive, smoky darkness. Day or night, there was no mistaking the magic of New Orleans. And damn, he'd missed it.

His smile widened. He wasn't much for traveling and that's all he'd done these past few months. Things had gotten hot after he'd given his estranged brother's *human* friend entrance to the fae plane. Ditching town was the only way to keep the Elektos off his back. The damn fae high council had never liked him much. Violating such a sacred rule as allowing a mortal access to the fae plane had shot him to the top of their blacklist.

Smile fading, he sighed. If two and a half months away wasn't enough, then he'd have to figure something else out. He didn't like being away from Livie for so long. He could imagine the size of her smile when he strolled in this afternoon. She'd been more of a mother to him than his own had, not a feat that required much effort, but Olivia had saved him from the streets. From himself.

There wasn't much he wouldn't do for her.

With that thought, he extricated himself from the bedcovers and his sleeping partners and began the hunt for his clothing. When he'd dressed, he stood before the vanity mirror and finger-combed his hair around his recently grown-out horns. They followed the curve of his skull, starting near his forehead, then arching around to end with sharp points near his cheekbones. He preferred them ground down, but growing them out had helped him blend with the rest of the fae population. Most fae also added ornate silver bands and capped the tips in filigree, but he wasn't into that.

His jeans, black T-shirt and motorcycle boots weren't much

to look at, but the horns were all it took for most mortal women to go positively weak. Standard fae-wear typically included a lot of magically enhanced leather, which was perfect for a city like NOLA, where being a little theatrical was almost expected, but you had to have plastic for spendy gear like that.

Satisfied, he walked back to the women who'd been his unsuspecting welcome-home party and stood quietly at the side of the bed.

Pressing his fingertips together, he worked the magic that ran in his veins, power born of the melding of his smokesinger and shadeux fae bloodlines, power that had blossomed when he'd finally opened himself up to it. Power he'd learned to use through trial and error and the help of a good friend.

He smiled. It would be great to see Dulcinea again, too.

Slowly, he drew his fingers apart and threads of smoke spun out between them. The strands twisted and curled between his fingers until the nebulous creation took the shape of a rose.

Gentle heat built in the bones of his hands and arms, a pleasurable sensation that gave him great satisfaction.

The form solidified further, then Augustine flicked one wrist to break the connection. With that free hand, he grasped the stem. The moment he touched it, the stem went green and royal purple filled the flower's petals. He lifted it to his nose, inhaling its heady perfume. Fae magic never ceased to amaze him. He tucked the flower behind his ear and quickly spun another, then laid the blooms on the sisters' pillows.

Pleased with his work, he picked up his bag, pulled a black compact from the pocket of his jeans and flipped it open to reveal a mirror. The mirror was nothing special, just a piece of silver-backed glass, but that was all any fae needed to travel from one place to another.

"Thanks for a wonderful evening, ladies," he whispered.

Focusing on his reflection, he imagined himself back at Livie's. The familiar swirl of vertigo tugged at him as the magic drew him through.

A second later, when he glanced away from his reflection, he was home.

⚜

Harlow Goodwin held paper documents so rarely that if the stark white, unrecycled stock in her hands were anything else than the death knell to her freedom, she'd be caressing it with her bare fingers, willing to risk any residual emotions left from the person who'd last touched it—it wasn't like she could read objects the way she could people or computers, but every once in a while, if the thing had been touched by someone else recently, something leaked through. In this case, she kept her gloves on. This wasn't any old paper; this was the judgment that was about to bring an abrupt and miserable end to life as she knew it.

They couldn't even have the decency to wait to deliver it until after she'd had her morning coffee. For once, she wished it had been another of her mother's missives pleading with her to come for a visit.

She read the sum again. Eight hundred fifty thousand dollars. Eight five zero zero zero zero. She'd heard it in court when the judge had pronounced her sentence, but seeing it in black-and-white, in letters that couldn't be backspaced over and deleted, made the hollowness inside her gape that much wider.

How in the hell was she going to pay off eight hundred and fifty freaking thousand dollars? Might as well have been a million. Or a hundred million. She couldn't pay it, even if she wanted to. That queasy feeling came over her again, like she might hurl the ramen noodles she'd choked down for dinner. Moments like this, not having a father cut through her more sharply than ever. She knew that if her mother had allowed him into her life, he'd be here, taking care of her. He'd know what to do, how to handle it. That's what fathers did, wasn't it?

At least that's what Harlow's father did in her fantasies. And fantasies were all she had, because Olivia Goodwin hadn't only kept that secret from the paparazzi; she'd also kept it from her daughter.

Oh, Harlow had tried to find him. She'd searched every possibility she could think of, traced her mother's path during the month of her conception, but her mother had been on tour for a movie premiere. Thirty-eight cities in twelve different countries. The number of men she could have come in contact with was staggering.

Harlow's father, whoever he was, remained a mystery.

Heart aching with the kind of loss she'd come to think of as normal, she tossed the papers onto her desk, collapsed onto her unmade bed and dropped her head into her hands. The five-monitor computer station on her desk hummed softly, a sound she generally considered soothing, but today it only served to remind her of how royally she'd been duped. Damn it.

The client who'd hired her to test his new security system and retrieve a set of files had actually given her false information. She'd ended up hacking into what she'd belatedly guessed was his rival's company and accessing their top-secret formula for a new drug protocol. Shady SOB.

She shuddered, thinking what her punishment might have been if she'd actually delivered that drug formula into her client's hands, but a sixth sense had told her to get out right after she'd accessed the file. Something in her head had tripped her internal alarms, something she'd be forever grateful for if only it had gone off sooner. She'd ditched the info and hurriedly erased her presence. Almost. Obviously not enough to prevent herself from being caught.

Times like this she cursed the "gift" she'd been born with. Well, the first one, the ability to feel people's emotions through touch, that one she always cursed. And really it was more than emotion. She saw images, heard sounds, even picked up scents from people. Which all added up to an intense overload—sometimes pleasurable but too often painful—that she preferred not to deal with. The second gift was the way she seemed to be able to read computers. She didn't know how else to describe it, but they responded to her like she could speak binary code without even trying. Finding her way into a motherboard took no more effort than opening a door. That gift had given her a career. A slightly questionable one at times. But a job was a job. Except when it brought her clients like this last one.

A client who was now in the wind, the twenty large she'd charged him not even a down payment on her fine. She should have known something was up when he'd paid in cash, his courier a shifty-eyed sort who was probably as much fae as he was something else. She shuddered. That cash, tucked away in a backpack under the bed, was the only thing the court hadn't been able to seize. Everything else was frozen solid until she paid the fine or did her time.

She flopped back on the bed and folded her arms over her eyes. She was about as screwed as a person could get.

Her eyes closed but it didn't stop her brain from filling her head with the one name she was doing her best not to think about.

The one person capable of helping her. The one person who'd been the greatest source of conflict in her life.

Olivia Goodwin.

Her mother.

Harlow hadn't *really* spoken to her mother in years. Not since their last big fight and Olivia's umpteenth refusal to share any information about her biological father. For Harlow, it was difficult to say what hurt worse—not knowing who her father was or her mother not understanding the gaping hole inside Harlow where her father was missing and yet her mother somehow thinking she could still make things okay between them.

The cycle usually started with Olivia barraging Harlow with pleas to move to New Orleans. Harlow ignored them until she finally believed things might be different this time and countered with a request of her own. Her father's name. Because that's all she needed. A name. With her computer skills, there was no question she'd be able to find him after that. But without a name...every clue she'd followed had led to a dead end. But that small request was all it took to shut Olivia down and destroy Harlow's hope. The next few months would pass without them talking at all.

Then Olivia would contact her again.

Harlow *had* made one attempt at reconciliation, but that had dissolved just like the rest of them. After that, their communication became very one-sided. Emails and calls and letters from her mother went unanswered except for an occasional response to let Olivia know she was still alive and still *not* interested in living in New Orleans.

She loved her mother. But the hurt Olivia had caused her was deep.

If her mother was going to help now, the money would come

with strings attached. Namely Harlow agreeing to drop the topic of her father.

The thought widened the hole in her heart a little more. If she agreed to never ask about him again, she'd have to live with the same unbearable sense of not knowing she'd carried all her life. And if she didn't agree, her mother probably wouldn't give her the money, which meant Harlow was going to jail. A life lesson, her mother would call it.

A deep sigh fluttered the hair trapped between her cheeks and her forearms. Was she really going to do this? The drive from Boston to New Orleans would take a minimum of twenty-four hours, but flying meant being trapped in a closed space with strangers. It also meant putting herself on the CCU's radar, and until her fine was paid, she wasn't supposed to leave the state. At least she had a car. Her little hybrid might be a beater, but it would get her to Louisiana and there'd be no one in the car but her.

Another sigh and she pulled her arms away from her face to stare at the ceiling. If her mother refused her the money, which was a very real possibility, Harlow would be in jail in a month's time. Her security gone, her freedom gone, forced to live in a cell with another person.

She sat up abruptly. Would they let her keep her gloves in prison? What if her cell mate…touched her? That kind of looming threat made her want to do something rebellious. The kind of thing she'd only done once before at a Comic Con where her costume had given her a sense of anonymity and some protection from skin-to-skin contact.

She wanted one night of basic, bone-deep pleasure of her choosing. One night of the kind of fun that didn't include sitting in front of her monitors, leveling up one of her Realm of Zauron characters to major proportions. Not that that kind of fun wasn't epic. It was basically her life. But she needed something more, the kind of memory that would carry her through her incarceration.

One night of *careful* physical contact with another living, breathing *male* being.

The thought alone was enough to raise goose bumps on her skin. She'd do it the same way she had at Comic Con. A couple of good, stiff drinks and the alcohol would dull her senses and make being around so many people bearable. With a good buzz, she could stand being touched. Maybe even find it enjoyable, if things went well. Which was the point.

She was going to New Orleans. The city was practically built on senseless fun and cheap booze, right? If there was ever a place to have one last night of debauchery before heading to the big house, New Orleans seemed custom made for it.

On her Life Management Device, the one she could no longer afford and that would soon be turned off, she checked the weather. Unseasonably warm in New Orleans. Leaving behind the snowpocalypse of Boston wouldn't be such a hardship, but she wasn't about to ditch her long sleeves just for a little sunshine. On the rare occasions she had to leave her apartment, she liked as much skin covered as possible.

She jumped off the bed, grabbed her rolling bag and packed. Just the necessities—travel laptop with holoscreen and gaming headset, some clothes, toiletries and the cash. Not like she'd be gone long. She changed into her favorite Star Alliance T-shirt, set her security cameras, locked down her main computer and servers and grabbed her purse. She took a deep breath and one last look at her apartment. It was only for a few days. She could do this.

A few minutes later she was in the car, a jumbo energy drink in the cup holder and the nav on her LMD directing her toward Louisiana.

⚜

Augustine tucked away his traveling mirror and inhaled the comforting scent of home. The weeks of rarely staying in one spot for longer than a few nights had worn thin. He'd tried a stint in Austin, Texas, another fae Haven city, but a week there and he'd begun to feel eyes on him. Being back in New Orleans was pure happiness. This was the only ground he'd ever considered home, and this house, the estate of retired movie star Olivia Goodwin, was the only place that had ever *felt* like home.

Protecting Olivia and this place was why he'd run to begin with, but she knew he hadn't been the cause of the trouble. Not really. That landed squarely on the shoulders of his estranged half brother, Mortalis. They shared a father but that was about it. They'd never seen eye to eye on anything. Mortalis disapproved of Augustine's life in more ways than he could count and took every opportunity, rare as they were, to make that known.

Despite that, Augustine had helped one of Mortalis's very pretty, very persuasive female friends gain access to the fae plane, specifically the Claustrum, the max-security prison where the fae kept the worst of their kind. Livie had agreed it had been the right thing to do, but she hadn't really understood the consequences.

The sounds of female voices reached his ears. Olivia and Lally, her companion and housekeeper, were out on the back porch enjoying the unseasonably warm weather. He set his bag down and moved softly from the hall and into the kitchen. Their voices were louder now, filtering in through the screen door along with the afternoon breeze. Ice clinked in glasses and the scent of mint and bourbon followed.

He smiled. Livie loved herself a julep on the porch. He leaned in close to the screen, but left the door closed. "Miss me so much you have to drink away your sorrows, huh?"

Both women jumped in their rockers, clutching at their hearts and slopping bourbon and soda over the rims of their glasses.

Olivia shook her cane at him, her shock widening into an unstoppable grin. "Augustine Robelais, how dare you sneak up on two old women like that." She threw her head back and laughed. "Oh, Augie, you're home. Praise our lady Elizabeth Taylor. Get out here and let me hug your neck."

He pushed through the screen door and scooped Livie into his arms. She squeezed him hard, her form somehow frailer than he remembered. He whispered into her silver-white bob, "I missed you more than I have words for."

"And I, you, *cher*." Her hand cupped the back of his head as she kissed his cheek. "I am so glad you're home." She released him, her amber eyes glittering with tears.

He turned to Lally and caught her in a hug as she stood. "I'm sure you didn't miss cleaning up after me, huh?"

Lally clung to him, her voice catching when she finally spoke. "Silly child." She patted his back as she let him go and sat down. "I had so much free time, I read half Miss Olivia's library." She laughed. "I'm still not used to seeing you with your horns grown out, but I'm happy to have you back, no matter what you look like."

He leaned against the porch railing. The warmth of their

love was almost palpable, soothing the ache in his heart from being away. "I appreciate that. I'll be grinding the horns off soon enough."

A wash of concern took away Livie's smile. "Everything all right then? Didn't have any trouble, did you? No run-ins with any Elektos?"

"Not a bit." He couldn't stop smiling. Even the air smelled better. "How about you?"

She snorted softly. "Nothing I couldn't handle."

Which meant they'd been here. That knocked the smile off his face. Anger fueled a fire in his belly, but for her sake he just nodded. Obviously she didn't want to talk about it right now. Or maybe just not around Lally, but there wasn't much Olivia kept from her.

"You home to stay, Mr. Augustine?" Lally looked hopeful.

"Yes." He sighed and tipped his head back, inhaling the earthy, heady scent of the Garden District. Tiny green tips were beginning to show on the trees. In a few weeks, spring would overtake the place. "I hope I never have to run again." He would, though, if it meant keeping these two women safe.

"Good." Lally smiled. "We had enough of you bein' gone."

"That we did." Livie sipped her mint julep, then held it up to him. "You want a drink, darling?"

"No, I'm good. All I really want is to sleep in my own bed."

She took another sip before setting the drink down. "Well, I'll be. You mean you're not heading into the Quarter to see what young thing you might woo into your arms for the night?"

He laughed. Olivia didn't need to know he'd already been there. "I thought I'd take one night off. Besides, tomorrow night is *Nokturnos*. I'll do plenty of wooing then."

"Is that tomorrow? With you gone, I guess it slipped my mind." She looked at Lally. "Did you realize it was the new moon?"

371

"I knew that much, but I can't be bothered with the rest." Lally waved her hand. "All that mask wearing and kissing strangers and carrying on like fools. Humans do enough of that during Mardi Gras."

Augustine raised a brow. "We don't carry on like—well, okay, a little bit like fools, but it's the fae New Year. There's got to be some celebration. Plus the fae need their own party before the tourists invade for carnival and the town isn't ours anymore. This is a big one, too. Since the covenant's been broken and humans know we exist, it's the first *Nokturnos* we can celebrate publicly." He shook his finger at Olivia. "You've got a good bit of haerbinger blood in your system, Ms. Goodwin. You should be celebrating, too."

She waved him off. "Please, *cher*. I've had enough celebrating in my days."

"My lands," Lally exclaimed with a smirk. "You sure came back from your sojourn with a lot of sass, didn't you, Mr. Augustine? Hmph."

He laughed.

"I missed this, I surely did." Lally tipped her head up toward Augustine. "So you'll be kissing a stranger tomorrow evening? Guess that's not much different than most of your evenings." She laughed, clearly tickled with herself.

"And I'm the one full of sass?" But he grinned. "Hey, you want me to have good luck for the New Year, don't you?" A yawn caught him off guard. Before he'd returned home, sleep had eluded him the last few nights, replaced by nightmares so real, they'd driven him to return home. Probably earlier than was prudent, but enough was enough.

Livie immediately looked concerned. "You really are tired, aren't you, *cher*?"

He hadn't slept much last night, either, but he wasn't about to tell them that. He scratched the base of one horn. "You know how it is when you're not in your own bed. It's just not the same."

Lally nodded. "I hear that. You going to make it till supper, Mr. Augustine, or should I put up a plate for you?"

"Depends on what you're fixing."

"Nothing special. Just a little RB-and-R and some hot sausage."

"Nothing special." He snorted. "You know I love red beans and rice. Especially yours. Yes to supper, but first I should probably run down to Jackson Square and see if Dulcinea is around. Let her know I'm back." He'd stayed clear of the Quarter's main areas last night, too, keeping as low a profile as he could without becoming completely invisible to the pretty tourist girls he so enjoyed.

Lally stood. "I'll just go take another sausage out of the freezer."

After she left, Livie gave him a sly smile. "I'm sure Dulcinea's missed you."

He rolled his eyes. "You know it's not like that between us."

"Mm-hmm. I know what you two get up to." She swirled the liquid in her glass. "I know you're both adults and consenting and all that."

He knew what Olivia was hinting at, but the past was the past. "We're just friends."

"Friends with benefits, that's what they used to call it in my day." She lifted her glass to her lips as Lally came back out.

"Y'all still talking about Miss Dulcinea?"

"Yes, why?" Augustine answered.

Lally settled into her chair and pointed toward the back corner of the yard. "She was out here one night. Just sitting in the gazebo past the pool there. I gave her a little wave, but she didn't wave back. Didn't see her again after that, but the next night, a stray cat showed up. Sleek gray thing with darker stripes and these two different-colored eyes that just looked right through a person's soul."

Augustine looked at Livie the same time she looked at him and in unison, they both said, "Dulcinea."

She was one of the oddest fae he knew, not just personality-wise, but because even she didn't know her bloodlines other than that they included fae and varcolai, or shifter. The strange stew of her lineage had given her some rare powers, including the ability to take on random animal forms. In othernatural terms, she was a remnant, a label applied to anyone with mixed othernatural heritage. But in the neighborhood, most called her a changeling.

Lally sat back, resting her arms across her plump stomach. "I figured that was her."

He nodded. "Thanks for letting me know."

She lifted one hand to shake a finger at him. "You definitely should go see that girl. She's pining for you."

Augustine laughed. "Dulce pines for no one. Except maybe this city." It was nice to know she'd kept an eye on Olivia and Lally while he'd been gone. He hadn't asked her to do that and was a little surprised she had, but then maybe he wasn't. Nothing Dulcinea did could really be considered shocking.